dedicated to C—*for teaching me how to love, without even trying. Your strength and individualism are remarkable to behold and are a true inspiration. Oh, and 477,800, to the moon and back!*

a note from the author

Dear Readers,

I'm thrilled to introduce myself and dive into the evolving conversation around content and trigger warnings. I'm a bit of a seasoned soul, having grown up devouring my mother's 1980s historical romance novels by authors like Johanna Lindsey and Jude Deveraux. Picture me as a young reader, tucked under the covers with a flashlight, lost in those sweet, happily-ever-after tales, convinced they held the blueprint for true love. Oh, the blissful naivety of youth! Back then, trigger warnings weren't a thing— though, in hindsight, some of those books could've used them. Not that it would've stopped me!

As my tastes matured, I gravitated toward spicier, darker contemporary authors like Sylvia Day* and J.R. Ward, whose books now line my shelves. When I began writing my own novels, I wanted to blend the nostalgic charm of 1980s historical romance with the bold intensity of modern dark romance. I often wonder what Johanna Lindsey might have crafted after reading something like the *Crossfire Series*. The result is my *At Night* series, a dark*ish* historical romance collection that's close to my heart.

When asked to categorize my novels, I wrestled with the question before landing on "dark*ish*." I know it's not an official term, but it feels right. My stories aren't light and fluffy, but this first book, *Awaken at Night*, starts as a slow burn—perhaps not as dark as some expect from the genre. Rest assured, hold onto your garters, because the series will dive deeper into the shadows as we journey forward together!

That said, I'm committed to being mindful of readers with specific triggers. I want to ensure you know what to expect from *Awaken at Night* and the broader *At Night* series, so you can approach the story with confidence and comfort.

---

* I just attended a discussion where Sylvia Day was a panelist, and I fangirled all over her, especially after she said she'd pre-order my book. I literally cried. She might never read this, but if she does...sorry about that, and thank you so much for all the inspiration!

a dark*ish* historical romance

awaken
at night

HARLOW BRÍGH

ISBN 979-8-9919917-2-8 (Paperback)

ISBN 979-8-9919917-0-4 (eBook)

ISBN 979-8-9919917-1-1 (Audiobook)

Any reference to historical events, real people, and real places, are used fictitiously. Other names, characters, and places are products of the author's imagination.

Cover art and design by Muhammad Waqas

First print edition 2025

HA! Harvick Anderson Publishing

ha-publishing.com

To that end, please be aware of the following:

Bondage

Domination

Spanking, flagellation, other forms of impact play...

Contrapolar Stimulation

Orgies

References to hot homosexual sex

Attempted SA

Sadism

Kidnapping

Violence

And...some characters will die...

Hopefully I have not turned you away, and better yet, perhaps I have piqued your curiosity. If so, please continue, and enjoy!

Love, Harlow

Wealth was no guarantee...

Birth was no guarantee...

Beauty, talent, achievement, distinction—none of these meant anything unless qualified by that elusive term: ton.

—Ellen Moers

prologue

1805

"Hell, and damnation!"

Emerson Haven ripped off a hair ribbon and threw it to the ground, grinding it under her heel.

"Bloody, ridiculous nonsense!"

Emerson was livid. At nearly eleven, she was being forced to become a Lady.

A real Lady. With a family name stretching back generations, who dressed in expensive dresses, was expected to be accomplished and well-spoken, and who naturally elicited regard. Whether Emerson wished for such distinctions...or not.

Local villagers were now making way, doffing their hats, curtsying as she passed, scolding their children for making faces. Mind you, these were the very same villagers who, only last month, would snicker in mirth when they saw her.

"Is this not a load of cut-off bollocks?" Emerson asked no one in particular, stomping off to the small pond near her family's manor.

As an earl's daughter, Emerson supposed she was always a Lady. However, she had always done exactly as she pleased, oblivious to the concerns of ladies, and no one had ever bothered her with such nonsense.

Emerson's mother died tragically while giving birth to her, and her father subsequently buried his grief in the drink. That left Emerson with Kit, her older brother. He was barely nine when she was born, but he became her comfort, her only source of love, her protector.

When Emerson's cries cut through the mournful silence of the manor house, rousing Lord Haven from his drunken stupor and maddening him, Kit moved her to a secluded cottage near the edge of Havenfield. Other than a few members of the household staff, who quietly helped keep her alive, Kit raised his sister the only way a little boy could. With little knowledge of little girls.

There was no one to balk when Emerson began following Kit everywhere as soon as she could crawl. Or when she took to wearing his outgrown clothing once she could dress herself. Nor did anyone question her penchant for building tree forts and bringing home every wounded animal in the parish, rather than learning to sew, draw, or play the piano forte.

When Kit turned thirteen, he went off to Eton for his schooling, leaving Emerson alone for much of the year. Kit arranged for the head groom's wife to watch after her, yet she was remarkably independent for a child of five. When she was not rambling by herself, she would muck stalls in the barn or pick apples in autumn. She went into the manor house only to grab food or extra coal for her fire. As the years went by, her language and deportment grew decidedly shocking and unladylike.

None of that ever mattered to Kit. From the moment he laid eyes on her, he loved her unconditionally, and he found her unusual behavior endlessly amusing. Especially when she would spit and swear or get into fights with village boys. He spent the limited time he was at home from school teaching her things like fencing, riding astride without a saddle, and shooting a pistol.

Everyone else thought her odd, but they were simply too afraid of the drunken Earl of Haven to bring attention to the deficiencies in her upbringing or character. As she grew older, and people saw her wearing her boyish clothes, covered in dirt and twigs, the entire parish accepted it as her normal behavior. Entertaining and worthy of gossip, certainly, but ordinary.

"That was, until *he* came!" Emerson shouted, recalling the reason she was in her current 'ladylike' predicament.

It was four months ago, during the winter holidays. Lord Lathen de Clare, the future Duke of Windemere, came to Havenfield as a guest of her brother. He was riding the most beautiful dappled-grey stallion Emerson had ever seen. She spied them from afar, riding west toward her, while she was climbing the large elm tree near the main road.

Her brother was his usual self. An average-sized gentleman with black, curling hair cut short. Dressed in a well-tailored blue greatcoat, with buff breeches tucked into tall, polished boots. Emerson always thought him the most handsome and brilliant man there ever was, and it never occurred to her to question this belief.

However, riding next to de Clare, her brother looked almost small and dull by comparison. The lord was tall, broad-shouldered, and leanly muscular, and the low winter sun highlighted his rakish, wind-disheveled hair, making the dark waves glow as if someone had painted them with burnished bronze. Despite his simple black greatcoat, breeches, and boots, he stood out from Kit because the lack of fussiness did nothing to detract from his commanding presence.

Emerson had gasped, as a vision of a Greek god rode toward her, steam rising from his powerful steed. Ares's brutal strength filled her mind.

Or Prometheus, bringing that first spark of fire, illuminating the world with its radiant glow. She had giggled at her whimsical thought, the sound echoing softly in the crisp, winter air, before she recklessly dropped to the ground, landing lightly on her feet as they passed beneath.

Her impetuousness caused the spirited grey stallion to rear. Its nostrils flared, eyes rolled wildly, and a massive shod hoof narrowly missed her head. With a muttered oath, the young lord fought to keep his seat, his hands struggling against the reins.

To say he was angry was an understatement. Lord de Clare, initially mistaking Emerson for a village boy, had leapt from his horse while scolding her thoughtlessness.

"You little fool! You could have been killed!" he bellowed, his face contorted with panic. His powerful fist had seized her collar as he shook her.

Twice!

Hard enough that Emerson's teeth had chattered together, momentarily stunning her, and her brown knit cap fell off her head. Long braids, thick and black as raven wings, tumbled down her back at the same moment Kit shouted.

"Bloody hell, de Clare! You are throttling my little sister!"

Struck dumb, Lord de Clare had released Emerson so fast she tumbled to the cold, hard ground, landing with a jarring thud, scraping her palms on unforgiving stones. For a long moment, she sat there, arms and legs splayed, feeling chagrined. Until, with an awkward sigh, she wiped the dust from her hands and shook her head to clear it.

After overcoming his disbelief, Lord de Clare resumed chiding her for acting so imprudently. Yet his tone had softened, and Emerson, still sitting on the ground, blinked up at him with surprise in her lavender eyes. She remembered feeling shocked at seeing such a large, handsome man up close. Especially as his own amber eyes were busy blazing at her with concern.

For the first time, Emerson felt embarrassed by the grime on her face, and she wished she were wearing something besides Kit's hand-me-downs. A flush spread across her cheeks, and one hand instinctively brushed errant hair from her forehead, while the other searched blindly for her woolen cap, with the vain hope that yanking it back on might help her disappear.

The fleeting thoughts had barely registered before Emerson dismissed them. Her jaw snapped shut, eyes narrowing in irritation. Havenfield was her home. Who was he to manhandle and yell at her? If Kit approved of her behavior, it should not have concerned this man.

Fortunately, her brother jumped down from his horse, helped her up, brushing dirt from her legs until a small cloud formed around them. Then he smiled indulgently, tapped her nose, and sent her on her way, ending the confrontation. Emerson recalled grinning back at him as she walked toward the wood, though she spared one last glance at the handsome lord, sticking her tongue out defiantly, right before she disappeared into the brush.

As if the entire episode had not been uncomfortable enough, later that evening, Kit had insisted Emerson eat supper with them in the rarely used dining room of the main house. Emerson agreed, but only because her father was already too far into his cups to join them, and she wished to spend as much time as possible with her brother.

De Clare had sat in a chair across from her, taking in every detail of her person, disdain on his face. The lord watched her eat with her fingers, licking the sauce off each one, and drinking her weak cider with large, noisy gulps. He squinted when she used the sleeve of her sweater to wipe her dripping chin. He winced when she belched, not even bothering to cover her mouth.

A blush, hot and prickling, soon crept across Emerson's cheeks, as unfamiliar self-consciousness washed over her once again. She found herself using her napkin to clean her face. Then she searched through the row of forks by her plate, attempting to copy the one her brother used for each course. But she kept making mistakes, and her exasperated sighs were soon mingling with her knife scraping on her plate and her fork as it fell, clattering on the parquet floor.

Lord de Clare's disapproval was clear, and Emerson's frustration soon blossomed into outright anger. She first glared back at him with irritation. When that had not fazed him, she shrugged her shoulders and ignored him altogether.

As soon as possible, Emerson snagged two hard rolls and a few slices of cold meat and attempted to sneak away. When she left, she overheard de Clare admonishing her brother.

"Really, Kit, you are doing her a tremendous disservice. She is a positive hoyden..." His words lingered in the air, a strange mix of concern and accusation. Emerson pressed her back against the wall with a frown etched on her face. Then she shrugged again.

Why should I care what such a stiff, pompous, snoutband thinks? A smirk had danced across her lips as she slipped outside, taking a deep, cleansing breath. The frigid night air had stung her lungs, but Emerson relished the freedom, grateful to leave de Clare's watchful eyes behind. She even slept in the barn's hayloft that night, in case anyone thought of looking for her in her cottage.

"The horses were far better company anyway, even with the smell of shit. Hell, they probably smell better than he does!"

Thankfully, de Clare only stayed one night. At dawn, Emerson pushed open the hay doors and watched him ride away. Before the main road, right next to the elm tree, he pulled his horse to a stop, turned in his saddle, and gave a single wave back to her.

He knew I was there the whole time.

Emerson's heart had hammered in her chest, but she stood her ground, her gaze unwavering. He flicked his reins, the rising sun catching the hidden copper in his dark hair, until the light cresting the hill eclipsed his silhouette, nearly blinding her.

When he finally disappeared, she had let out a shaky sigh. She stayed at the hay door for some time, long after he left, a strange melancholy settling over her. It was as if the lord had taken some kind of possibility with him.

Bollocks! Emerson shook her head, trying to forget she had ever met Lord de Clare. After all, Kit stayed with her, and she still savored every moment.

*And I refuse to let a condescending blighter ruin even
the memory of our time together!*

However, Emerson had to acknowledge de
Clare's parting shot. Prior to leaving, he cornered her
father before he guzzled his first drink, berating him
for Emerson's poor upbringing. Her father, though
withdrawn from society, evidently respected the
Windemere name enough to listen. A governess was
soon hired, suggesting de Clare's words made an
impression.

Emerson learned of the development before Kit
left. Her father sobered up enough to put his foot
down, calling her to his rooms and insisting she must
listen to everything the woman said. Kit,
unfortunately, agreed with him. Emerson might have
been able to out-wait her father. It was only a matter
of time before he would have been too drunk to
remember Emerson was even around, let alone there
was a woman she was supposed to give heed. But the
day he returned to Oxford, Kit extracted a promise
from her. With serious, loving eyes, betraying a flicker
of guilt, he pleaded for her to obey the new governess.
Emerson reluctantly agreed.

Mrs. Jaymeson arrived at Havenfield almost
two months after Kit left. She moved into the empty
guest wing, away from the earl's rooms, immediately
insisting Emerson join her. Though Emerson tried to
argue, it was nearly impossible to tell Mrs. Jaymeson
no. She was simply too likeable. She had a bright
crooked smile, a round cherubic face, and greying-
red uncontrollable hair that she always tried,
unsuccessfully, to keep stuffed under a shockingly
white cap.

She was also endlessly patient and
unavoidable, always seeming to know where to find
her, no matter where Emerson hid. And no matter
what language Emerson used, Mrs. Jaymeson never

got angry or disappointed. Instead, she would smile serenely and repeat what Emerson said, using the words of a lady.

The worst part was she came with trunks packed tightly with new dresses, shoes, hot irons, and ribbons. Lacy, stiff things, smelling of dried flowers and cedar chests. They made Emerson itch just looking at them. There were also endless lessons in manners and etiquette, dancing and music, and even how to write a proper letter.

Which is utter rubbish. I only ever write Kit. He certainly does not care how I do it!

It was not all bad, she supposed. Each night, Mrs. Jaymeson would brush out her dark curls before the fire, the rhythmic swish of the brush comforting. She also insisted Emerson bathe regularly, scrubbing her ears and toes, and had her sleeping on a feather mattress with soft, clean sheets. And she understood Emerson was not one for being indoors all day, encouraging her to get fresh air often.

Which was what Emerson was doing now, after a particularly boring lesson she already forgot. It was a hot, early summer day, the air still as she finally reached the pond, sitting on the small dock. Only Mrs. Jaymeson's unwavering patience, and her oath to Kit, kept Emerson listening to the buzzing of insects and the slow trickle of water, instead of going swimming. She longed to remove her new lace dress and jump in, wearing only her new chemise and long pantalettes.

Or even go starkers in nothing at all! The scandalous thought made her grin.

She decided it was simply not worth the gentle reproof Mrs. Jaymeson would inevitably give her. Or worse, her forgiveness as she helped Emerson into yet another new dress. She settled for unlacing her stiff brown walking boots and peeling off her white knit hose to swirl her feet through the lazy water.

Two iridescent dragonflies darted through the reeds, skimming the water at the shoreline. She envied their freedom, and her mind drifted from her fancy new clothes and how the villagers were treating her, to the latest letter from her brother.

Kit should be home any day now. Hopefully, he will not bring a certain arrogant young lord with him!

Things could return to how they used to be. When they would ride over the entirety of Havenfield, going hunting and fishing, fighting their pretend duels, and sleeping outside, under the star-filled sky next to a crackling fire. Happy memories filled her mind, a smile playing on her lips as her toes made eddies. She kicked one foot, scattering diamond-like droplets over the surface before they landed, forming dozens of delicate ripples. Each one grew until they finally disappeared, leaving a glassy surface behind, calming Emerson's mind.

With Kit here, I suppose keeping Mrs. Jaymeson around would not be terrible, she told herself begrudgingly. *Not that I want her here...* Though she realized the feather bed was not bad. *Neither are the baths with sweet smelling soap.*

From a distance, the rhythmic thunder of galloping hooves shook Emerson from her musing.

"Kit!"

She scrambled to her feet, accidentally knocking one of her boots into the pond with a resounding *'plop.'* Emerson gasped, mesmerized as she watched it drift toward the bottom, bringing up bubbles, before it vanished.

"Damn, and bother," she swore softly, realizing she was going to be in trouble, even after making such an effort to be good. With a snort, she shrugged one shoulder in a very unladylike manner, glancing around to make certain no one was watching.

"Oops," she added with a cheery laugh, "in for a penny, in for a pound." Then she kicked the other boot, watching it disappear. Her itchy hose followed for good measure, though they only floated on top, which was not nearly as satisfying.

Oh, well, it will have to do!

Emerson felt light, the afternoon sun drying her legs as she grabbed her ruffled skirts high, running barefoot down the well-trodden dirt path toward the stables. As she rounded the entrance, she stopped short, hearing the deep timbre of Lord de Clare's voice drifting out of the large double doors.

"...absolutely imperative Lord Haven and his daughter not learn what *really* happened."

"Then what shall we sae was the cause?" came a rolling burr Emerson did not recognize. She slowly peeked around the corner to see who else had come to Havenfield with Kit and de Clare. There was the tall, dark form of the lord and another, even larger, blonde gentleman. The pair stood with their backs to the entrance, oblivious to Emerson. Surprise washed over her as she compared the two men. The other man's sheer bulk was daunting, a stark contrast to de Clare's already impressive form.

"We shall merely explain he fell from his horse," de Clare answered the other man softly. "At least there would be no scandal."

Emerson's nose wrinkled, her brow furrowed in concentration, straining to hear their hushed conversation. Suddenly, she imagined de Clare's stinging words if he were to catch her hiding by the door, eavesdropping. She backed away slowly, around to the pasture side of the barn. From there, she crouched, no longer minding at all if her dress got dirty, crawling toward a stall with the upper half of the door open. The pungent smell of horse and damp hay filled her nostrils, but she could hear the men more clearly from this vantage. Yet her brother's voice was still absent.

"Should we get a maid tae clean him up first?" the stranger asked.

"Yes, leave the body here, and I will summon the housekeeper. Or better yet, the governess is someone I trust. She will know how to proceed..." Lord de Clare answered, his voice trailing off as he moved away.

Emerson's mind was racing, and an icy shiver crawled up the back of her neck. *I must have misheard them. Why would Kit come home to Havenfield with a body? Where is he anyway? Lord de Clare has no bloody reason to be here without him.*

The men left the barn, their riding boots crunching on the wide graveled path toward the manor house. Emerson quietly opened the bottom door of the stall, slipping inside. An old brown field mare occupied it, snorting loudly at Emerson, as if questioning why a small girl was crawling around in her rushes. Emerson stood, briefly patted the mare's neck to apologize for the intrusion, before going into the center breezeway of the barn, taking extra care to avoid stepping in any horse mess with her bare feet.

Three horses were in the wide center aisle, all showing signs of a long and hurried journey. Two, including Lord de Clare's dappled stallion, were unsaddled. Tim, the head groom's son, was brushing their damp coats near the back doors. The other horse was tied to a post, still wearing a saddle, its weary neck bent. A large bundle, wrapped in a dark woolen blanket, was draped and tied securely across its back. The horse turned toward her, and Emerson recognized her brother's gelding, Chestnut, just as he greeted her with a soft nicker and a quick dip of his head.

Emerson approached with an outstretched hand, as the icy prickles spread from her neck to her entire body, making her feel cold and numb and strangled for breath. She trembled violently, grasping the corner of the blanket, lifting it.

Time slowed down, and the universe lost all color.

There, under the blanket, was the ashen face of her brother, turned awkwardly to one side. Dead, his skin cold to her shaking fingertips. His usually lively dark blue eyes dull and staring blankly into nothingness. Drying blood matted the back of his curly black hair and in rivulets down his neck.

Every horse began to whinny, restlessly prancing in their stalls. In the breezeway, Tim grabbed the reins of the horses he was grooming to prevent them from bolting. Even Chestnut shied away, rolling his eyes, snorting in fright. All this, as a strange, mournful keening surrounded Emerson, filling the barn to the rafters. When a pair of powerful arms pulled her to a hard chest, away from her brother's face, Emerson realized she was the source of the sound.

Lifting her gaze, she saw regret etched into lines around Lord de Clare's pained, dark amber eyes. Suddenly, Emerson *knew* he was responsible. He caused this agony. Her tiny fists connected with his shoulders and ribs. High-pitched screams of her fury punctuated the sound of each impact.

"You killed him! You killed my brother! You lousy, fucking bastard! You poxed arse!" She shouted, striking him over and over, until her hands hurt, her voice becoming hoarse. Not once did de Clare try to stop her. He stood frozen, absorbing her fury.

When she no longer had the energy to fight him, he wrapped his arms around her, sat down on the top step of a mounting block, and rocked her gently while she continued to weep. As her sobs eventually subsided to soft hiccups, she heard de Clare whisper something while he stroked her loose hair, tucking it behind one ear.

"Emerson, I promise you..." he began, his words fading as her numbness drowned out everything else. All she could focus on were the scents of leather, cedarwood, and sea salt filling her nose. It was a smell that would remain etched in her dreams, and she would think of this moment often in the years to come. Emerson had never known such profound and piercing sorrow, and as she drifted into the oblivion of a fitful sleep, she vowed to make Lord Lathen de Clare pay.

Somehow.

chapter one

1813

Lord Lennox de Clare came home a little late. Or perhaps a little early, depending on whom you might ask. As he rode onto St. James's Square, the new gas streetlamps were already flickering out as the lamplighters were using their long poles to tip the switches off.

In the dim twilight of early morning, maids in black and white uniforms swept the steps and beat rugs, the sounds a steady rhythm punctuated by the quick footfalls of young boys in livery as they ran to collect milk and open the coal chutes. A sense of urgency filled the air, as these tasks had to be finished before the gentry woke and might be bothered by them.

Lennox pulled his horse to a stop in front of a sizable limestone four-story house. De Clare House was situated nicely, centered on a large lot to the north end of the square, with wide cobbled streets both to the front and along one side. It had space from nearby houses, with windows and extensive gardens on all sides, a small carriage house and stables at the back, and a lovely view of the park in front.

A young footman in a bright red coat and buff breeches must have been watching for Lennox, as he was there almost instantly. He yawned sleepily, attempting to cover it with a white-gloved hand as his other hand reached for the reins Lennox was holding.

"Good lad." Lennox was jovial as he dismounted and patted him on the shoulder. "Off to bed with you after you get my horse to the stable!"

He passed through the open gate in the wrought iron fence that surrounded the house and hit the front steps two at a time. The oversized walnut door opened as soon as he got to the top, to the stern, impassive face of Giles, the de Clare family butler.

It always amused Lennox that Giles would wait up for everyone in the household to come home, rather than simply assigning a footman to watch the door. The older man's sharp gaze and constancy made Lennox suspect he never slept.

"Welcome home, my lord," Giles greeted him evenly as he held out his hand for Lennox's hat. "I trust you are well?"

"Yes, Giles, quite well, thank you!" Lennox quipped as he breezed past him, through the enormous, two-story marbled entry hall, on his way to the wide staircase that dominated the center of the house as it rose to the fourth floor, winding around a large glass roof lantern which brought in the early morning light to the interior. "But please make sure I am not disturbed for any reason. I plan on sleeping for the next week!"

"Of course, my lord," Giles answered with his usual condescension. "Shall I rouse your valet?"

"No need," Lennox replied over his shoulder as he hit the turn for the west wing of the second-floor stairs, then he chuckled, "I shall do well enough on my own. I have been successfully undressing by myself for several years now."

When he got to his rooms, he left a trail of cufflinks, a cravat, and his jacket on his way through his sitting room to his enormous four-poster bed. After pulling off his riding boots, the half-unbuttoned white lawn shirt and grey flannel breeches stayed on, and he hit the bed face first, snoring softly by the time his head turned on the pillow.

It felt as if he had barely closed his eyes when a loud bang from someone's fist on his door woke him abruptly. Angry at being woken against his express wishes, Lennox grumbled, "Bloody imbeciles," as he yanked his door open, ready to deride whoever was on the other side.

However, it was the one person who Lennox supposed had every right to bang on the door, as it was his house. His Grace, Lathen de Clare, the ninth Duke of Windemere, stood there in the hallway, his brow raised mockingly at his younger brother's disheveled appearance. His fluffy, black mixed-breed dog, found four years ago as a puppy and named Dog, stood with him. Though she seemed a lot happier to see Lennox than Lathen was, if her tail was any indication.

"Busy night, dear brother?" Lathen asked drolly. "I do hope I am not intruding."

"Not at all," Lennox replied with equal sarcasm as he bowed deep at the waist and motioned with a flourishing arm for Lathen to enter. "But to what do I owe such a tremendous honor as an early morning visit from *THE* Duke?"

"Stow it, puppy," Lathen retorted as he swept past Lennox and moved to sit rigidly in one of a pair of wingback chairs that flanked a cold fireplace. Dog followed him, circled twice, then lay protectively at his feet. "I am afraid you will need to make yourself presentable. Our dearest Aunt Lillian will arrive soon. Along with our sister, of course."

"Damn it," Lennox grumbled as he sat, splayed out and slouching, in the other chair. "I thought we had another fortnight before they were to come. The first ball of the season is not for another month!"

"Yes, I believe that was the original plan. However, a runner just arrived to inform me to expect them before luncheon. As that is quite soon, I assumed you would appreciate some time to make yourself respectable."

Lathen, of course, did not need to worry about this, as he always dressed impeccably. This morning, he wore a crisp, white lawn shirt and cravat, and a precise black coat and breeches.

As though he were a vicar, off to church!

In fact, Lennox could not remember ever seeing his brother with anything askew or improper, even when they were children. He watched in amusement as Lathen picked off what must certainly be an imaginary piece of fluff from his breeches with his long, manicured fingers.

"I suppose this means we both need to keep your banker's hours for the whole season?" Lennox asked sullenly. He was not looking forward to having to curtail his usual town amusements. Having lived his whole life as 'a spare,' he had learned to accept the freedom and lack of responsibility. In fact, he welcomed them wholeheartedly.

Goodness knows I never want to be stuffed up like Lathen!

"Not at all, dear boy," Lathen replied, "but you will need to rein it in. Perhaps stay at Nox House, or one of your other clubs, instead of coming home

18

so...umm...late. Of course, Aunt Lillian will require your presence at dinner, balls, and parties, whenever she deems it necessary. Better you than me, though."

Lennox groaned in frustration, his obvious annoyance making Lathen smirk.

"I have plans for this weekend, and it would be rude if I were to cancel so late."

"Then do not, but I would not make any more *'plans.'* At least not until we know what invitations Aunt Lillian accepts." Lathen gave Lennox one last look of disapproval before he got up and walked out with Dog, closing the door and leaving much quieter than he entered. Lennox let out a weary sigh of resignation, then a low moan escaped his lips as he stood and stretched his tired limbs and rang for his valet and a hot bath.

He also made a mental note to send a message to his mistress. To let her know he would not be attending her party that evening. Though he knew he would pay for it later, as she was sure to be vexed with him, and she loved a good pout. She was a relatively new mistress to him but had already shown a tendency towards a quick temper and did not like to be kept waiting. Hoping to appease her, he decided to send a bauble along with his note.

Something sparkly and expensive ought to do the trick. After all, she does that one thing with her mouth so well. It almost makes me forget her sulks.

Of course, having the de Clare ladies in London for the rest of the season meant he would need to limit his visits to his mistress as well. Lathen was right. He was going to be coerced into escorting them around town, especially since his brother loathed to do so. Lennox decided he would cross that bridge when he had to.

Hmmm, maybe I should stock up on fancy trinkets, just to save myself some effort later.

19

After shaving and making himself presentable, Lennox made his way down the stairs to find a controlled sort of chaos. Nearly all the household servants were rushing back and forth over the polished marble flooring, while the housekeeper and Giles gave them directions. They were obviously preparing the house for the arrival of Aunt Lillian and Leighton, his younger sister.

After all, a household with ladies requires far more attention than it does for only two bachelor lords, Lennox mused.

To avoid the pandemonium, he made his way to the breakfast room orangery. He had to squint a little at the brightness let in by the glass ceiling, overlarge southeastern windows, and an open set of French doors that let out into a small side garden. Someone had thoughtfully laid out a light repast on a cart. He took some strong black tea and toasted bread with strawberry preserves, and he sat down with a heavy sigh.

Shortly after he began his meal, the household's bustling energy shifted abruptly. He knew, without looking, that his aunt's coach must have just been spotted, so he shoved the last bite of toast into his mouth and rose to his feet as he tossed back the last of his tea, wincing when it scalded his throat. Then he went into the morning parlor that the ladies usually preferred, just as Lathen was coming in with Dog from a different entrance. He gave a slight nod to acknowledge his brother and took a deep breath to steady himself.

The season, it seems, is ready to begin.

chapter two

Giles came into the morning parlor first and announced, "The Lady Lillian de Clare and the Lady Leighton de Clare, Your Grace, my lord."

Aunt Lillian walked past him with a kind smile and ramrod posture, pulling off her traveling gloves. Leighton came bounding in after her like a breath of fresh, wild wind, with her dark auburn curls flowing behind her. She threw herself into Lathen's arms, nearly knocking him over and making him grunt as he caught her.

Dog danced around their feet, whining in barely suppressed excitement. Leighton was her favorite person besides Lathen, and she had not seen her since last autumn.

"Thank you, Giles," Aunt Lillian dismissed, as he backed out and closed the door softly. "Leighton, really, must you?" she admonished gently, with a good-natured chuckle.

Lathen twirled his young sister in his arms, her light blue muslin dress twisting around them both as she laughed, and he exclaimed, "Good lord, kitten! When did you grow so much?"

At nearly seventeen, Leighton was taller than was usually fashionable. Though her brothers were taller, and with the amber eyes all three siblings bore, and the willowy grace she naturally exuded, she had an exotic beauty.

"Oh, posh, my dear brother! I stopped growing months ago. You simply missed it whilst you neglected us in the country. You need to visit us more. We missed you at Christmas!" Leighton tsked at him as she turned and jumped into her other brother's arms with a squeal, while Dog chased her happily.

"Lennie!"

"Lettie, my sweet girl," Lennox returned her tight embrace and kissed her with an exaggerated smack on the cheek, "I have missed you, darling."

As he released her, he stepped over to his aunt and, despite her feeble protests, pulled her into his arms for a big hug and an even louder kiss.

"Hello, Auntie!"

Aunt Lillian grumbled but returned his embrace with a cheerful smile. She had never married, but she always accepted her spinsterhood with no hint of unhappiness. Instead, she had thrown her life into loving her brother's children as her own. Especially Leighton, whose own mother had died when she was only two years old.

When released, Lillian turned to Lathen and bowed her head gently, murmuring, "Your Grace." Though she cared for him just as much, she knew her nephew was uncomfortable with expressions of affection from nearly everyone but his sister. This was mostly due to his having been raised by a revolving

22

army of nannies and strict tutors his grandfather hired throughout his childhood.

"My dear, Lady de Clare," Lathen responded with a formal bow at his waist, "I hope your journey was not overly difficult? I know it rained quite a bit this past week. The roads from Windemere must have been disastrous."

Leighton, bent over scratching Dog's ears, stood, scoffed, and pulled Lathen toward a plush settee to sit beside her.

"Oh bother, let us not have boring talk of the weather or journeys!" she exclaimed. "I wish to hear about our plans for riding through the park and sneaking me into Vauxhall to see the jugglers and the fireworks and the wild cats!"

Lennox and Aunt Lillian sat on the settee opposite, chuckling at Leighton's infectious charm, as well as the look of horror on Lathen's face at the thought of reining in his sister for the entire season. Leighton was too young for most balls and parties, leaving her ample time to cause trouble while everyone else was busy.

"Oh kitten, try not to give me a heart attack with any of your escapades, please. I am still recovering from the evening ride you and Lady Haven took part in two years ago!" Lathen responded with as much sternness as he could muster. It still upset him to think of what had happened. Or rather, what could have happened if someone had seen the girls and spread gossip.

Two young girls, still in short dresses, alone at night without a proper chaperone. The ton *would have feasted for weeks. Or worse, what if they had encountered brigands and been hurt?* The very idea still brought a chill to his mind.

That day started simply enough. His sister and Emerson had come down from the country with Aunt

Lillian for several weeks to be fitted for new dresses. At fifteen and sixteen, both girls were full of life and energy, and used to a level of freedom the country offered. Lathen never knew who suggested a midnight ride through Hyde Park, though he strongly suspected it was Emerson, since she always seemed determined to do everything in her power to irritate him.

"Oh posh," Leighton snorted and waved her hand. "Do not remind me, brother. I am still incredibly upset with you for your response. My goodness, we brought three armed groomsmen with us." She used her fingers to emphasize her point. "We were completely safe. It was certainly unnecessary for you to send Em away as punishment!"

Aunt Lillian cleared her throat, prompting Lennox to change the subject, and Lathen stayed silent, despite his disagreement. Truthfully, he had wanted to do much more to Emerson than simply send her off to finishing school. He clearly remembered the urge to throw her over his knee and spank her. His justification, after years of her escalating rule-breaking, was her nerve to include his sister in such a potentially scandalous prank.

Later, he acknowledged, if only to himself, there was more to it. At sixteen, Emerson's appearance had changed since he last saw her at Windemere's winter holidays. Suddenly the rail-thin little girl had a delicate woman's body. Fluid grace had replaced her awkward angles and movements. Her bosom, still slight, had the swells of firm breasts accented by her new lightly boned stays. And the oversized lavender eyes, once dominating her small face, now seemed to fit with her rosy cheeks and perfectly arched black brows. Those eyes had not only haunted him for their peculiar color, but because he always remembered them filled with tears, staring accusingly at him. In the ensuing years, they were often melancholy, but when angry, they deepened and flashed with an inner light.

It was not as though she was his usual type. Her body, formed from a lifetime spent outdoors, was not soft and plumply rounded like most of his mistresses and lovers. Nor was she quiet and demure, like ladies of the *ton*. Yet something about her suddenly bothered him. Even now, the memory of her standing proudly, with her hands fisted at her sides, while she glared up at him, made him feel frustrated. Probably because she represented a temptation he had been unwilling to acknowledge, a lure that still made him feel guilty.

She is Kit's little sister, for Christ's sake. I am supposed to be her protector. Even if she were the most beautiful woman in the world, I am not supposed to notice.

His family began discussing the upcoming season with good-natured excitement, and he allowed his mind to wander further, to nearly eight years ago. To the day he had lost his best friend, Lord Christopher Haven. The pain still felt fresh, just as if it had been his own brother, instead of Emerson's. He could still vividly remember the heart-wrenching sound of Emerson's grief when she discovered her brother was dead, her fragile body shaking in his arms, her ineffectual fists striking him through tears and rage.

He remembered accepting her pain and anger, hoping to lessen them somehow. Of course, there were also those eyes. The hollow look of misery in them had disturbed him deeply, and he worried at the time he would never have another memory to replace it.

But fate had other plans for us.

The following year, Lathen's own father passed to the grave, making him the new Duke of Windemere. Not two months later, Emerson's father died as well, leaving her all alone.

It was soon discovered Lord Haven was not as thoughtless as one might have supposed. Before he died, he changed his will to reflect Kit's death and to ensure the care of his neglected daughter.

Luckily, the Havenfield estate was not entailed, and Emerson inherited everything. The manor, the land, and a rather enormous fortune of ten thousand pounds a year. Even the title, Earl of Haven, was given to her through a special remainder her father had sought from King George. This was astonishing, as it was exceedingly rare for a woman to inherit. Though the title would pass to her first male child, or it would return to the crown if she did not marry and produce an heir by her twenty-fifth birthday.

More shocking, Lord Haven named His Grace, the Duke of Windemere, as Emerson's guardian, with control over her finances, property, and person. Until she married someone whom he approved of. At barely twenty-one, Lathen was suddenly responsible for his duchy, a rascal of a brother barely out of Eton, and two young girls. As well as handling Emerson's estate.

Likely, Emerson's father had meant for Lathen's own father to have the responsibility of caring for her, since, at one time, the two of them had also been friends. Regardless, Lathen always took his obligation to Emerson just as seriously as he did with his own sister and brother. This duty made noticing her maturing beauty more confounding, likely fueling his remorse.

"Lathen?"

Aunt Lillian was looking expectantly at him, and Leighton elbowed him sharply in his side, causing him to wince and making Dog chuff and wag her tail. His aunt must have asked a question he had missed during his reverie.

"Pardon me, my dear lady." He motioned for her to continue.

"I was wondering if you had heard from Lady Haven concerning her arrival to London. Leighton and I came to town early, hoping to meet her and make it to the dressmakers before the mad rush in the next fortnight. I sent her a letter over a week ago, but her response has not yet caught up with us. I hope you remember we have the responsibility of not only getting her prepared for the upcoming season, but Miss Atwood as well," Aunt Lillian waved her arms wide before she went on, "It is going to be a lot of work."

Lathen kept his voice passive as he replied he had not heard from Lady Haven.

Nor am I likely to, he thought wistfully as his hand grasped the arm of the settee.

Emerson never included him in her correspondence. If not for Mrs. Jaymeson, whom Lathen had continued to employ as her governess all these years, he would likely not know any of Emerson's activities since he sent her to school.

As for Miss Atwood, she was the only child of the de Clare family barrister and had been the paid companion of Lady Haven for the last two years as well. Lathen had chosen her because Miss Atwood seemed sensible, intelligent, and modest, hoping her character would influence Emerson. At least, those were the reasons he gave when asked. Though he also secretly hoped Miss Atwood might be a good friend to Lady Haven, something he knew she lacked growing up.

So, Lathen made an offer to Mr. Atwood, to send his daughter to school with Emerson, and see her properly introduced into society, as a reward for all his many years of loyal service to the de Clare family. Mr. Atwood had quickly agreed.

It seemed like a good idea at the time. Now, years later, Lathen could admit he was not looking forward to having his home and life disturbed by the inevitable turmoil of not one, but two ladies debuting in London society.

Many things could go wrong with Lady Haven's antics and her potential to become a titillating subject for gossips. He would simply have to keep a close eye on her until he could marry her off.

Hopefully, with as little inconvenience for me or my household as possible.

chapter three

"How much further do you suppose?" Hazel Atwood's enthusiasm was barely contained. Her cheeks flushed pink with health, her sapphire eyes sparkled, and her golden hair escaped her braided twists, framing her lovely face.

With an indulgent chuckle, Emerson reached over to pat her friend's hand, leaning to glance out of the coach window.

"Do not worry, Hazel, it should not be much longer," she assured her confidently. She saw the countryside give way to smaller, closer homes, the coach slowing with city traffic as they entered London's outskirts.

Hazel tapped her feet in response, clearly delighted.

Emerson smiled back, but despite her friend's infectious joy, she was nervous. Her thoughts were consumed by the approaching season and its long to-do list. She was not concerned by ballgowns or parties, however. Instead, she worried about the gentlemen she would meet, and what came after.

Emerson was determined to marry. As soon as possible. She believed it was the only way to get out from under the control of His Grace, the duke. Otherwise, she would not have bent to the expectations foisted upon her for eight years because of him. She was no longer fighting it, though, and was instead embracing her role as a young debutante coming out for her first season of husband hunting.

Fortunately, she now knew how to comport herself in London society, after her two years at Bromwell Seminary for Young Ladies, as well as from Mrs. Jaymeson's continued guidance. She understood the correct way to dress, to dance, to eat and drink, even how and when it was appropriate to laugh.

Which, unfortunately, is almost never! God forbid the gobermouching arses of the ton *ever let someone experience happiness.* The thought made her smile wryly as she realized she had also learned to stop swearing. *Except for in my mind, of course.*

Yet, having her freedom would make all her efforts worthwhile. She could finally manage her own future and fortune and would no longer be forced to endure the duke's company, or live in his homes, for any longer than necessary.

Obviously, finding a husband who would accept her unique personal demands was essential. Hazel had already helped her write documents outlining her requirements to live as she desired. Her wants were fairly simple. She wished to finally move back to Havenfield, and to have control over the estate's finances. Being away from her home for so long felt like part of her soul was missing, a void constantly shadowing her mind. Havenfield was also Kit's burial place, and she yearned to be near him again, to feel his presence. Whether her future husband wanted to join her was of no consequence. She could afford to be very generous with his allowance, and he could live in London if he wished. Or abroad.

Honestly, once he has given me a child, or two, I would not mind if my future husband left and never returned. Emerson smiled to herself, thinking of teaching a little boy and girl all the things her brother had once taught her. She longed to witness their excitement the first time they went riding or shooting or fought with sticks. *It will almost be like having Kit again.*

In her mind, she saw her children, and they looked just like her brother—with hair the color of coal, dark blue eyes, and a cheerful, lopsided smile.

Of course, my true goal is slightly more complex. Emerson desperately wished to learn the truth about her brother's fate. *If I must spend all my money hiring investigators or bribing everyone who ever knew him, I will.* Had anyone been watching her, they might have marveled at the determined glint suddenly in her eyes.

From the opposite seat, Mrs. Jaymeson murmured, and Emerson glanced over. Her governess had her arms crossed under her generous bosom and she was snoring softly, with her head lilting to one side, to the rhythm of the coach.

At the sight, Emerson's mind left her brother, and a soft smile came to her face. She never would have presumed how dear Mrs. Jaymeson would become to her when they first met all those years ago. She supposed her feelings were like a child's unconditional love and dependence on their mother. Though, never having experienced such, Emerson was not sure and often wondered if her relationship with her own children would be similar.

Adding to her confusion, the recent discovery of Mrs. Jaymeson's maternal role in His Grace's life. Long before she had come to Havenfield, Mrs. Jaymeson was once a nanny for the de Clare family. Emerson heard the story one evening, last winter, when Mrs. Jaymeson was ill with a fever. It made Emerson realize how much she still did not know about Lathen de Clare.

'Oh, my darling poppet! I wish for a better relationship between you and His Grace. He is such a sweet boy who just wants love. But his damned grandfather would let no one show him even the smallest bit of kindness or affection. Or else he took them away. That happened to me. I showed the boy love. Nothing more than a simple hug after he had fallen and hurt himself. But the old Duke saw me, and he gave me the sack that same night. With no notice, mind you! I did not see the poor boy again until after his grandfather was gone. When he came looking for me, His Grace was nearly a grown man. He came because of you, of course. He told me there was a little girl who needed me. Even now, I can still see the wonderful child in him, and I see how he tries so hard to do right by you.'

Recalling Mrs. Jaymeson, earnest, her eyes filled with memory, prompted Emerson to reflect on the duke's choice of governess, after their first meeting when she was still a child. She wondered why he had even bothered. Back then, she was certainly not his responsibility. It was one thing to push her father and brother into hiring a governess in the first place, but to search out a specific person, like Mrs. Jaymeson, felt personal.

Did he sense a kinship between us, feeling I also needed love? Or did he just know I could not resist trying to please someone as wonderful as Mrs. Jaymeson?

Now, Emerson had Hazel, too. A true and beloved friend whom she sometimes thought of as the other half of herself. Not because they were the same, but because they were so different, in the best ways. Where Emerson was often quick to temper, Hazel was patient, and when Emerson would usually jump headfirst into something without thinking, Hazel was often her voice of reason. Emerson also helped Hazel. She encouraged her to go outdoors and taught her how to climb trees and to swim. Even if she had to pull her friend's nose from a book to do so.

Because of Hazel, the last two years were not as burdensome as they could have been. In fact, they were amazing. Though loath to admit it, especially to His Grace, she had grown from her experiences with Hazel and did not mind being a lady beyond her title. Somehow, it felt right.

Emerson understood the duke was also responsible for bringing Hazel into her life. She felt a deep sense of gratitude. Even if she still resented how high-handed he was, forcing her to do everything as he wished.

Like shipping me off to school without even asking if I wanted to go!

Emerson recalled the last time she saw the duke, two years ago. Admittedly, the childish lark of riding in the park with his sister had been her idea. It had taken a lot of convincing to get Leighton to go with her, though Emerson had refused to tell him so, and, to Leighton's credit, she had not tattled.

De Clare had stood in front of the desk in his study, lecturing them both without raising his deep voice, his brows lowered in disappointment. It did not take Leighton long before she burst into tears and began apologizing profusely. She was always a sweet girl and never wanted to upset her brother. Emerson, on the other hand, refused to ask his forgiveness.

"What, exactly, do you plan to do about it, Your Grace?" she stood proudly and glared back at him, her small hands fisted by her sides, "It is not as if you are our father, and we should have as much right to do as we please, as any gentleman!"

She vividly recalled Leighton's shocked intake of breath at her audacity and the duke's anger briefly crossing his face. He was a man who never seemed to lose control, no matter how much she had pushed him over the years. Emerson flushed, feeling an almost perverse sense of pleasure at seeing his stiff façade crack, even if it was just for a moment.

Before he responded to her, de Clare sent his sister to her room. Emerson remembered lifting her chin even higher and bracing herself, waiting for him to yell, as he had the day they first met. Instead, he walked up to her, stopping close enough for her to swear she felt the heat of his frustration radiating off him, and stared down at her intensely. She recalled having to tip her head back so she could keep looking at him and seeing his eyes flash again and a small tic at the corner of his mouth as he clenched his jaw. She straightened her back and tried to match his anger, but unexpectedly, swirling in the depths of his amber eyes, she glimpsed something she did not recognize.

Whatever it was, her lower belly clenched strangely, and warmth spread from her chest and through her body, making her face flush and her lips part as it suddenly felt hard to breathe.

For his part, de Clare pulled back abruptly, looking confused as he searched her face, like he sought an answer to an unasked question.

"Emerson, I have only ever wanted what is best for you. To honor my best friend after everything happened," he told her cryptically. Then he dismissed her without saying another word about her midnight ride. They had never again spoken face to face.

He still wrote her a letter each month, commending her on how well she was doing in school. She never wrote him back, as she knew Mrs. Jaymeson was already doing so. Sometimes guilt gnawed at her for this, since it was a bit childish, but she usually pushed it away, reasoning if His Grace wanted to converse with her, he could send for her.

The night she last saw the duke was one Emerson had revisited often, trying to understand why she felt so peculiar staring at him. Also, because the next day His Grace sent her off to school like she was a naughty child, and she had not been back to London since. Nor had she returned to Windemere, the duke's country seat, where she had been living in the years after her father's death.

She assumed His Grace no longer wished for her to influence his sister or was simply tired of dealing with her. His letters never explained his reasoning either way, and Emerson tried not to think about it much, as it always seemed to cause a hollow, yet vaguely familiar ache in her chest.

'I promise you, Emerson...'

"A penny for your thoughts?" Hazel always seemed to know when she was lost in them.

"To be truthful, I am worried," Emerson admitted. "I am not sure how I am going to be received. As you well know, the Duke of Windemere and I did not part on the best of terms."

"Oh, bother. Truly, I do not believe you have anything to worry about, Em. His Grace has been nothing but kind and thoughtful to us these last two years. I know you have always been cross with him because he was made your guardian. It was a difficult thing, losing your family, after all. You must admit he has always taken great care to ensure you have everything you need. Plus, you had to be ward to someone. It could have been so much worse!"

Hazel was such a lovely and positive person. She could never understand why Emerson felt such ire towards the duke, having only ever seen how they lived comfortably in apartments he secured for them near the school, with Mrs. Jaymeson, of course. There were also the new dresses they received every season, servants to meet their needs, and trips to the seaside during their school breaks.

Emerson never told Hazel of the day she learned of her brother's death. Or how she once blamed de Clare, though she never understood what happened. Her feelings had softened as she grew older, often revisiting everything she saw and heard that day. She recognized His Grace had also suffered from losing Kit. Not as much as she, but in his own way, it broke him.

'I promise you, Emerson, if there was anything I could have done, I would have. I tried. Kit fell, and I arrived too late to help him. He was already gone. I am so sorry. I would give everything I have in this world to make this different. But I

36

am going to do all I can to protect you. I swear this. On Kit's soul, I swear.'

Those were the words de Clare had whispered above her head while he rocked her to sleep in the barn. They still haunted her and often made her wonder how hard it must have been for him to bring her brother home to her, and how patient he was to stand there and take it while she screamed and hit him like a mad person.

However, even though the blame had tempered with time and maturity, Emerson was more determined than ever to learn the truth. The whole truth. She never lost the suspicion there was more the duke had not told her. There was still the overheard conversation between him and the tall blonde gentleman, after all.

It was something he thought would ruin me if anyone were to discover the truth, something he does not wish me to know. And it is why I must wait, until after I am no longer subject to His Grace's whims, to learn what I can.

Hazel was right about one thing, though. Emerson's life could have been much worse. With no close relations, she could have been sent to live with someone truly awful, without friends or companions. So, Emerson knew she needed to shake off her reservations for the time being and make the best of her circumstances, until she could improve them herself, through a good marriage.

"Well, I cannot find fault in his choice of companions for me!" Emerson finally responded with a grin and a quick hug around Hazel's shoulders. "Nor can I be upset at his generosity towards you. I could not fathom trying to do what we are about to do, if I had to go through it all alone."

Hazel grasped her hand, squeezing it tightly in return, and squealed with delight, her feet still tapping with involuntary excitement. "Yes! I never dreamed I would have a sister, but I have now, with you. Who could have imagined I would have a season such as we are about to experience? I thought I was going to marry a gentleman farmer, or a vicar, or maybe a barrister, like my father."

For that reason, Emerson promised herself she would hold her tongue and behave toward the duke. Despite any compulsion she felt to vex him, she refused to ruin anything for Hazel. It would be awful if de Clare decided she was too much of a bother and sent them both back to the country. Or worse, he could take Hazel away from her for good.

To accomplish this, she had come up with a plan to avoid His Grace as much as possible. A difficulty for sure, as she was staying in his London home for the season.

But it is not impossible. It is a big house, and London is a big city.

"All I ask, Hazel, is that you help me keep busy and not fall on my face in front of the entire *ton*! I need to find a husband as soon as possible."
Hazel rolled her eyes and scoffed with unladylike exaggeration.

"Do not be ridiculous," she retorted. "We shall marry for love, and I will accept nothing less for either of us. You, of all people, deserve to find a gentleman, a lord, who is going to be a wonderful husband and father."

Before Emerson could respond, the coach turned a corner, and shouts from the groomsmen and driver alerted her they had arrived at St. James's Square.

Mrs. Jaymeson awoke with a start, snorting loudly, as if she was interrupted mid-snore. "Oh, my

38

poppets, we are here!" she exclaimed as she reached up to straighten her white cap over her head, trying to stuff several errant tufts of hair back into place.

Hazel and Mrs. Jaymeson chattered together as the coach turned the last corner. Neither of them felt the same apprehension Emerson was experiencing as they got closer. They pulled to a stop outside of de Clare House, and a footman opened the door, allowing a stream of light to fall across Emerson's face. There was no more time left to worry.

chapter four

It was an unseasonably warm winter afternoon, nearly a week since the de Clare ladies had arrived in London. In his study, Lathen was busy with several account books, laid open on his desk, reconciling the family's various holdings. Dog whined, lifted her head, and tilted her ears as if she heard something.

Four days ago, a letter came from Mrs. Jaymeson, requesting a coach to London. They were expecting Emerson and Miss Atwood, and he assumed they had finally arrived.

"Are they here, Dog?" he asked as he leaned over and patted her soft black head. "Well, I supposed the house is about to get exciting, as there will be many new hands to pet you!" He grinned as she snorted, and her long tail wagged, thumping loudly when it hit the floor.

Lathen rose from his brown leather chair and crossed from his study through the center hall to the morning parlor. Dog followed, her paws making tiny clicks on the marble floor. Aunt Lillian and Leighton were already there. Lillian sat on her favorite settee, while his sister bounced near a large window, excitedly waving to someone outside.

"My lady." He bowed his head respectfully to his aunt. She nodded back, though she continued the embroidery in her hands. From an overheard conversation the night before, he knew she was making items for Lady Haven's and Miss Atwood's trousseaus. It was a kind gesture, as neither girl had a mother to help them with such things.

The sound of footsteps approaching made him tense with his back to the door. Lathen could not see the door open, but he heard Giles announce, "Lady Haven and Miss Atwood, Your Grace and my ladies."

Lathen turned slowly, not sure what to expect after the last two years, when he and Emerson parted so suddenly. He immediately focused on her. Dog saw her and rushed to push Emerson's hand with her nose. He watched as Emerson bent to scratch Dog's ears before she straightened.

She looked much the same, though slightly taller and more mature in her long dress, her hair pinned up in a simple twist. She was still slim and walked with the lissome grace he had noticed two years ago.

Interestingly, she appeared to be just as wary as he felt. Her eyes met his briefly before shifting away, her posture stiff as she turned toward his aunt to acknowledge her.

His sister pushed past him before anyone else could greet one another.

"Em!" Leighton exclaimed, gathered the shorter woman in her arms for a tight hug, nearly lifting Emerson's feet from the ground. Dog's tail wagged even faster as she chuffed happily around their feet. "I have missed you terribly. But, as I am rotten at writing letters, I shall not be upset with you for not corresponding with me enough!"

Emerson pulled back and grinned, revealing slight dimples in her cheeks Lathen had never noticed.

I suppose I have not seen her smile like this, Lathen thought to himself. It made him sad to think this was true. *She should smile every moment of every day.*

"I have missed you as well, Leighton, but hopefully we shall never again part for such a length of time to make either of our poor writing habits matter!" Emerson laughed as she gestured to Hazel. "I trust you remember Miss Atwood?" she asked as she turned to her companion. "I know she has visited Windemere with her father several times."

"Of course," Leighton replied warmly, flushing as she recalled her aunt's lessons in manners. "Welcome to de Clare House, Miss Atwood."

Hazel bowed her head, and with only a slightly wavering voice to betray her nervousness, she responded, "Your Grace, Lady de Clare, Lady de Clare." She turned to each, giving three formal, if wobbly, curtsies.

Lathen gave a cursory nod back but kept watching Emerson's face intently. She still would not look at him, despite Miss Atwood's obvious acknowledgement.

"As Leighton explained, welcome, my dears." Lillian put her needlework down and rose to greet them. "I am delighted that you are both here at last. We have much to do to get ready, and I have sent a note to the modiste to make an appointment for tomorrow morning. We should still have plenty of time to get the first ballgowns and day dresses ready before your debut next month."

"That sounds perfect, Lady de Clare," Emerson returned brightly, "Miss Atwood and I are very much looking forward to it."

Emerson's effortless chat with his aunt frustrated Lathen, as she ignored him, fully aware of his presence.

It is deliberate! The girl is purposely avoiding me! He could not believe it.

Having never experienced anything like this before, Lathen was not sure what to do. Though he knew it was churlish, maybe even infantile, he felt the urge to demand her attention. To stamp his foot or shout, perhaps. More than anything, he just wanted to see her lavender eyes looking up at him again.

With little thought about how it would appear to anyone else, Lathen finally gave into his compulsions. He took several steps to stand right in front of Emerson. And waited. The conversations in the room drifted off awkwardly, and from behind him, he heard Leighton gasp. Even Dog stopped wagging her tail and looked doubtfully up at him.

"Your Grace?" The question in Emerson's tone was clear. Yet despite his presence, her eyes remained fixed on the ground, a silent refusal further infuriating him.

"Welcome back to London, Lady Haven. I wish to speak with you in my study. At once!" he snapped, turning on his heel to leave, confident she would follow.

chapter five

Lathen strode into his study, crossed to the window behind his desk, and again turned his back to the door. He heard Emerson enter moments later, and from the light taps on the floor, he knew Dog had followed her.

"Please, close the door."

He had used the sentence before, often reprimanding Emerson or his siblings in this room or his Windemere study. Yet for the first time, he realized he was not sure it was a good idea to have Emerson shut behind a door with him.

Alone.

He heard the door latch before he could delve into the thought too deeply, and he turned to face her. His frustration was a deafening roar in his head, every moment her gaze refused to meet his, adding to the noise.

"Come here," he practically growled as he rounded his desk, his tone brooking no argument.

Emerson closed the distance, staring at the beautifully patterned Aubusson carpet under her satin slippers. Lathen could feel his heart beating faster with every step she took, before she stopped at an arm's length from him. Her lips pressed together as she still denied him her gaze.

Please. I just need to see her eyes. I am uncertain why, but I need them. His fingers flexed involuntarily while he waited in vain. *Damn her, why is she doing this? To me!*

"Lady Haven," he began brusquely, impatience and pettiness driving him to add, "I hope you are ready to behave while in London. At least better than the disobedient child you usually mimic."

Emerson gasped loudly, and Lathen knew he had broken the rules of decorum by speaking to her in such an ungentlemanly way, but he simply did not care. He said it only to make her raise her eyes to his.

It worked!

Triumph surged through Lathen as Emerson lifted her chin in a familiar stubborn tilt he had missed. Her lovely eyes deepened, nearly violet as they sparkled with anger.

Emerson recovered quickly, though, and her long black lashes fluttered to a close over her eyes, deliberately denying him again. She then lowered her gaze to the carpet once more and took a deep breath to calm herself before answering.

"Yes, Your Grace, I believe I am prepared for everything. The education I received was more than adequate, I assure you," she said stiffly, betraying her upset. "But if you will excuse me, the trip was tiring, and I believe I shall go to my rooms and rest until dinner." She then turned, without waiting for a response or a by your leave from him.

Without thinking, Lathen grabbed Emerson's arm and pulled her back, so quickly she cried out in surprise and lost her footing. He caught her, pulling her close while leaning over her. Their faces were within inches of each other, closer than they had ever been before, and there was no escape for either of their gazes.

Emerson was holding her breath, and she released it in a rush, raising her hands to his shoulders, her fingers trembling against his soft coat. She lifted her face closer, as though asking for a kiss, her brow creased with confusion.

Lathen knew what she wanted, even if she did not. Their gazes locked as he lowered his mouth. Their breath mingled, and he could smell the delicate scent of orange blossoms and feel the tips of her hardened breasts pressed into his chest. Emerson's eyes fluttered to a close as he watched.

A sudden, intense heat flushed through him as his manhood stiffened, pressing uncomfortably against his breeches. His hands tightened around Emerson's shoulders in reflex, as the urge to press her even closer was almost inexorable.

Just as he lowered his lips toward Emerson's, a mere hairsbreadth away, Dog made a low whine. Emerson's eyes snapped open, her gaze shifting from dreamy, unfocused longing to bewildered confusion. As though unsure of what she was experiencing or where she was.

She has absolutely no idea. The girl is not even trying to entice me, and here I am, moments away from laying her down on this carpet and taking her! After all, the door is closed...

Lathen knew he had lost control and shook his head to clear it from the unwitting temptation. He quickly righted Emerson, holding her arm while she steadied herself. Then he stepped back, taking his own cleansing breath and trying to relax his tight muscles by rolling his shoulders.

"I think it best you return to the other ladies," he said with as much evenness as he could muster. "Thank you for your time, Lady Haven."

Lathen then turned in dismissal, deliberately ignoring the questions on Emerson's face, needing to distract himself from the ache of his arousal. He wished he could explain what happened, but he did not fully understand it himself.

"What the hell was that?" he muttered in frustration to Dog after Emerson rushed from the room, closing the door firmly behind her. With a questioning tilt of her head and soft whimper, Dog seemed as baffled by his behavior as he was.

He sat at his desk with a groan, his stiff manhood pressing against his trousers, wondering why he acted like such an ass. Usually, he had a very moderate temperament. His upbringing taught him to control his feelings, treatment of others, workload, and relationships with women. He acknowledged to himself he needed control now. It was as much a part of him as breathing.

But with Emerson, it has always been a struggle. That part is not new.

When she was younger, she was the only one who dared to question or disobey him. Now, she seemed to have moved past it, and though it made no sense, her change bothered him. Obviously, he was right before. It was time to marry her off so she would be someone else's problem. It was also clear he needed to head to his club to relieve his frustrations.

Before I do something I will truly regret.

Dog came over, nudging her head into his lap, her large, dark eyes gazing up at him with understanding.

"You are a good dog," Lathen gently scratched her ears and let out a heavy sigh. "At least one of us knew it was a terrible idea."

chapter six

Rather than returning to the parlor, where her distress would be obvious, Emerson went upstairs to the third-floor rooms she would be sharing with Hazel. She closed the door to their sitting room with a deliberate quiet, betraying her inner turmoil. With a heavy sigh, she leaned back, her knuckles turning white as her fingers curled into fists, digging into her palms until they ached.

What the hell was that all about? she wondered.

The duke's behavior was puzzling. Sure, when she was younger, she often pranked and bothered him, but it had never been like this—an unprovoked confrontation from him.

The look on his face! It was not anger, not fear, but something else. Some emotion changed his eyes, until they resembled the dark hue of Mrs. Jaymeson's medicinal brandy. Rich, liquid gold with warm swirls of light. Déjà vu hit Emerson, and she struggled to recall when she last saw that look. Then it hit her. *It was the night, two years ago, before he sent me away.*

More confusing to Emerson was her own reaction to Lathen touching her, and the way he had pulled her close. The lingering heat left her skin damp and strangely tingly, a sensation both unsettling and oddly pleasant. She felt wet in other places as well. It made little sense.

A forceful push from behind sent the door swinging open, making Emerson jump back to avoid being pinned against the wall. Hazel burst through, her blue eyes wide with concern.

"Are you all right, Em?" She came over and grasped Emerson's clammy hands, searching her face. "I kept waiting for you to return. Oh! The look on His Grace's face. He seemed angry with you, for absolutely no reason. I do not understand."

"Neither do I, but hopefully you can now see why I am determined to avoid him. Perhaps I will get lucky and find someone to marry at the presentation ball. I just need your help to find the right man!"

Hazel nodded. Her wide, unblinking eyes showed awareness of something more Emerson withheld. Yet she did not press.

Not for the first time, Emerson was grateful to have someone to whom she could reveal nearly all her secrets. However, she could not tell Hazel what happened in the study. Not yet. Not until she better understood de Clare's actions and her own reaction.

Instead, Emerson walked over to the dressing mirror and touched her face with trembling fingers. She looked at herself critically, wishing, not for the first time, she was different. She would love to look more like Hazel. Her friend's plump bosom, rounded hips, and beautiful flaxen hair always made Emerson slightly envious.

"Do you suppose I am attractive enough to catch a husband?" she asked softly, "Preferably one not too old or too hard to look at. Or to be...with."

If it had been anyone else, besides Hazel, they might have thought Emerson was searching for a compliment. But Hazel knew her friend was still uncomfortable with being feminine, and she often wished she could spend her days riding through Havenfield in a pair of breeches. She also knew Emerson was terrified of what would one day happen in the marriage bed.

Hazel gently placed her hands on Emerson's shoulders, met her eyes in the mirror, and replied, "You are stunning, my dear. I promise you will have so many suitors your biggest difficulty will be deciding whom you love most!"

"Oh Hazel, I am not sure I know how to love." Emerson sighed and turned around. "I think I will be happy merely to find someone I can trust, and who will sign my marriage agreement."

And someone who will let me be myself, instead of trying to change me into some puppet of the ton, she added in her head.

"Love is not as complicated as you seem to think, Em," Hazel murmured, "and although I cannot describe it exactly, I can assure you, you will know it when it happens. I once read 'love looks not with the eyes, but with the mind.' So, I suppose your mind will know, even if you do not! Besides, tomorrow is just the first day for us to ensure you are ready for the season. We have time, and no matter what, I am here to make sure you find someone worthy of you."

Emerson supposed she was right. After all, Hazel had read every book she could find and was far wiser about the world than she was.

Certainly, she must know more about love, as I know nothing at all about it!

The girls embraced tightly. As they pulled apart, a quick knock at the door distracted them. It was Mrs. Jaymeson coming to help unpack their trunks, already brought up by footmen.

"There you are, poppets," she called out cheerfully. She quickly got to work, and with the girls' help, everything was soon put to rights.

The evening passed quickly, a relief after their long journey. The three of them were exhausted from their travels and requested a light supper for the small sitting room between the girls' bedrooms. That way, they did not have to dress to join the family in the main dining room. For her part, Emerson was grateful not to have to face Lathen again that night.

Later, after changing into her nightdress, Emerson fell asleep, her dreams filled with snifters of warm brandy and scents of leather, cedar, and seaside winds.

chapter seven

Mercier's was the most fashionable dress shop in London. To get an appointment with Madame Delphine Mercier herself, rather than an assistant, meant you were somebody in society. Even the *nouveau riche* could not see Madame Delphine, you must be a member of the *ton*. Of course, neither Emerson nor Hazel understood the significance of being fitted at Mercier's that morning. They were merely excited to get their first gowns, dresses, pelisses, and warm cloaks.

Madame Delphine was a compact, tidy woman with silver-streaked black hair worn in a severe bun at her nape. At first glance, her modest, high-necked slate gown seemed simple, but closer inspection revealed its extraordinary simplicity. Hand-stitched and intricately embroidered, it fit the older woman perfectly. It was one example of the precision and craftsmanship Madame Delphine prided herself on.

This attention to detail was evident in every garment she made. Her quick motions wasted nothing as she measured, cut, and pinned the fabric to the girls while they both stood before her in their undergarments. She rattled off numbers and fabrics in a mix of French and heavily accented English to her assistant. Sometimes even to the fabric itself, which she spoke to as if it were alive.

Emerson and Hazel might have felt uncomfortable being handled so, except Madame Delphine seemed detached and uninterested in them as people. She treated them like living mannequins, and thankfully, they could see the humor in the situation. They traded amused glances, both finding it hard to contain their laughter.

It seemed ridiculous to be standing there silently, while Madame Delphine held up various silks, velvets, and muslins, then tsk or mutter to the fabric in earnest conversation. She spoke just as much with her hands as she did her voice. Even Lady de Clare and Leighton, sitting across from them in comfortable chairs, struggled to hide their grins behind delicate cups of tea.

"You shall *revenez*," she paused and held up two fingers to them, "return in *deux jours* for your first dresses *s'assurer* they are fitted to *parfaitement!*" With a flourish, she kissed her fingertips, emphasizing her words.

"Of course, Madame Delphine," Lady de Clare responded deferentially, surprising Emerson. "We will come first thing."

Several hours into the fitting, the assistant took Hazel to pick out ribbons and trims, while Lady de Clare and Leighton left to search for fabrics. Emerson found herself alone in the large back dressing room. Standing on a platform in a partially pinned dress pattern, Emerson closed her eyes, rolling her tired shoulders, when the curtain slid aside. She assumed it was Madame Delphine returning with the extra pins she had gone after.

Emerson yawned and lifted her eyes. To her surprise, she saw a woman she did not recognize, walking tentatively into the room. The woman was beautiful but had a strained expression, making her pale green eyes mournful and causing lines around her pursed lips. Near her left temple, a small white scar faded into her hairline.

"Lady Haven?" the woman asked so faintly Emerson was not sure she had spoken.

"Yes?" Emerson replied curiously. After her initial wonder at the pretty stranger, Emerson noticed other details of her appearance. Her dress, though lovely muslin print, had a dropped waist nearly a decade out of season and threadbare wrists. Her straight chestnut hair was pinned up, but it was askew, as though she had done it herself, without the benefit of a mirror.

Before she could learn more or ask the woman's purpose, Madame Delphine returned. At first, the older woman looked shocked as she stared at Emerson and the stranger, but she quickly recovered and began shooing the woman out with a barrage of irritated French, waving her arms. She was speaking too fast for Emerson to catch anything but the words *"incroyable"* and *"dames entretenues."*

A kept woman? Emerson wondered what Madame Delphine meant.

"Do you know who she was?" Emerson asked after the woman left in a rush. She had the distinct impression that the dressmaker had recognized the stranger.

"Not one you need to worry about, *mademoiselle*," Madame Delphine answered firmly, glancing over her shoulder and crossing herself with a muttered prayer. As if she was worried the other woman might return.

Hazel soon rejoined them, along with both the de Clare ladies, and Madame Delphine and her assistant got back to finishing the last pins for their patterns. Emerson completely forgot about the strange woman, as well as Madame Delphine's unusual reaction to her. There were simply too many other things happening.

After, when the girls were redressed in their day dresses and pelisses, the four of them walked out of the *modiste* into the noisy bustle of Oxford Street. The girls were excited, chatting animatedly about which fabrics were their favorites, while Aunt Lillian looked on with affection.

An elaborate carriage pulled to a stop in front of them. Not until a footman jumped from the back and opened the door did they notice. Two fashionably dressed ladies stepped down to the sidewalk. A younger and an elder, they looked too similar with dark blonde hair, brown eyes, pursed lips, and noses slightly too long for their faces to be anything but mother and daughter.

As Emerson watched, the cheerful smile left Lady de Clare's face, and a mask of propriety slipped in to replace it.

"Lady Willoughby," Lady de Clare nodded briefly and spoke in a deliberately civil tone.

"Lady de Clare," the older of the two women replied with equal stiffness, and she barely tilted her head in return. Her eyes narrowed as she turned to stare at Emerson, Hazel, and Leighton in turn.

"Girls, may I introduce Lady Willoughby and her daughter, Miss Millicent Willoughby," Lady de Clare gestured to the pair before turning back, "and this is Lady Emerson Haven, the ward of His Grace, and Miss Hazel Atwood, whom we are sponsoring this season. Of course, you know my niece, Lady Leighton de Clare."

The mother gave a brief nod, while the daughter eyed Emerson and Hazel, responding with an unconvincing smile. "It is lovely to meet you both. Of course, I am thrilled to see you again, Lady de Clare," she added as she took a step toward Leighton, her smile broadening noticeably. She was interrupted before she could do more than greet Leighton with a proper curtsy.

"Well, I am terribly sorry, but we must be off. We have more appointments to get to today. You know how it is. I am sure." Lady de Clare, noticing their carriage had arrived, gently guided Leighton toward it, ignoring Millicent Willoughby's consternation. Settled inside as the carriage joined London's slow traffic, Lady de Clare looked serious, explaining who the Willoughby ladies were.

"The Lord Willoughby is the fourth Viscount of Salford. I came out with Lady Willoughby. Before she became a lady, she was the daughter of a wealthy textile factory owner from the north. Her family made their money from some rather unsavory practices, I believe. Something involving how they get their cotton and wool, and how they treat their poor workers.

"Her daughter is coming out this season with you. If she is anything like her mother, a thoroughly sour and malicious creature, I would advise you all to be on your guard. They also have a son who is to inherit the title, but not necessarily the wealth. However, it is unlikely any of you will meet him as a suitor."

All three girls exchanged quick, nervous glances before responding in unison.

"Yes, ma'am."

They were entering a new world unfamiliar to at least Emerson and Hazel. However, being at finishing school had prepared them to be careful around some people. More than once, they had dealt with girls who cared more about gossiping about others than learning how to be a proper lady, or how to be a good friend.

The carriage rolled over the cobbles, and after visiting London's fashionable shops, the four ladies returned to St. James's Square, trailed by footmen carrying piles of parcels.

"Well, well, well," came a voice from the second-floor landing as Emerson walked through the front door to the wide hall, "did you leave any bobs and bits for the rest of the poor ladies of the *ton*?"

Emerson looked up, a wide grin spreading across her face, and she saw Lennox leaning over the railing.

"Hello, my lord! It is so lovely to see you again. Where have you been?"

Lennox came flying down the stairs, jumping when he hit the last few steps, and pulled Emerson into a tight hug.

"I have been up to a house party for the week," he answered cheerfully, then as he turned and noticed Hazel standing slightly behind Emerson and his sister, he added, "though had I known just how charming the company was here, I would never have gone. I thought we were expecting you in a few days."

"Well, your aunt asked me to arrive earlier so we could do our shopping and fittings. I came with my beloved friend. May I present Miss Hazel Atwood? I do not believe you two have met. Though I suppose you know her father, Mr. Atwood."

Lennox walked up to Hazel, a charming smile on his face, and reached out for her hand. He kept his eyes on hers while he bent and dropped a light kiss on the back of her knuckles. Emerson noted, with some shock, his lips touched Hazel, not just the air above her hand.

"The pleasure is all mine, Miss Atwood."

"Lord de Clare," Hazel responded with a quick curtsy and a blush rising becomingly to her cheeks.

Emerson looked back and forth between the two of them with a quizzical expression on her face. Then to Leighton, also witnessing and amused by the situation. Yet they held their tongues, and Lady de Clare distracted them when she came inside with the last footman, handing her gloves to Giles, who was holding the door open for her.

"Lennox, my dear boy, you have returned," she sounded surprised upon seeing him. "I thought you would not be back until after the weekend."

Lennox bent to give a quick kiss to both of his aunt's cheeks.

"Yes, well, I found it quite tiresome in the country. Far too much shooting and not nearly enough dancing. And, of course, I missed your beautiful face, Auntie."

"Ah, such impudence! Fortunately, it is always livelier with you here, so one does not mind overmuch!" She smiled indulgently at her nephew and moved away to climb the stairs. Leighton giggled, gave her brother a quick hug, and followed her.

"Will we see you at dinner?" Emerson asked, raising her skirts to climb the stairs.

"Yes, I believe you shall," he responded with his eyes still on Hazel.

Emerson and Hazel went to their shared sitting room, exhausted from the long day, but also giggling over the exchange with Lennox. It gave Emerson an idea she kept to herself. She knew Lennox, for all his charm, would never be a good match for herself. Her deep, familiar affection for him was brotherly, but he might suit her friend.

Everyone knows Lennox is a bit of a rake, but perhaps a suitable woman like Hazel could reform him! Emerson smiled, then let the thought drift away. There was simply too much to do to worry over matchmaking.

chapter eight

The last weeks had been chaotic and wearying. Filled with *modiste* appointments, millinery appointments, shoe appointments, trousseau appointments, and so many more. The sole purpose of each new day was to prepare the girls for their first season. A new lady's maid was hired to help, and now, the night had finally arrived.

It was the evening of Queen Charlotte's Birthday Ball. The girls were ready to debut alongside the upper echelon of society. The *ton*. Fortunately, Lady de Clare and Mrs. Jaymeson, with painstaking attention to detail, planned every aspect of their appearance. From their jeweled hairpins down to their satin slippers, they were bathed, powdered, and dressed to perfection.

Though Emerson knew she was ready, she felt out of place. All the clothes were too fine and new, especially the style and cut of her dress at her bosom.

It had never been so exposed, and she kept tugging the fine white silk with her kid gloved hands.

"Please stop!" Lady de Clare hissed under her breath as she approached from behind, watching Emerson in the mirror. "Every other young lady will be dressed exactly the same, I assure you!"

This was an argument they already had many times over the last weeks. Ever since the first of the finished ballgowns began arriving from the *modiste*.

Emerson supposed Lady de Clare, with her privileged upbringing and extensive social circle, undoubtedly knew more about such things than she did. She stopped pulling at her gown and did her best to sit still as the maid finished the last adjustments to her hair, firmly pinning three white feathers so they would last the night.

Instead, she touched the single freshwater Baroque pearl at her neck. It hung on a long white satin ribbon tied with a bow at her nape. Shimmering purple in the candlelight, she admired its simplistic, twisted beauty.

The necklace was a gift from His Grace. It arrived the day before in a red leather box. She assumed it was merely a polite gesture, but she felt excited by her first gift from a man.

Even if it is from him.

"I believe all is done, m'lady," the maid said softly, with a slight northern accent. Her hands were shaking as she stepped back to assess her work, before reaching forward to place one last pin.

"Thank you very much, Alice," Emerson replied gratefully. She could admit the twists and curls on her head looked splendid. Much better than anything she or even Mrs. Jaymeson had ever managed, though she would never tell her governess so.

As it was, Mrs. Jaymeson sat in the corner, handkerchief clutched tightly, watching with watery eyes and a grin as Emerson prepared.

"Well, do you suppose I will pass muster?" Emerson asked her.

"Oh, my poppet," she sighed, her happy tears barely held back, "I simply cannot explain how much I enjoy seeing you all grown. But I must admit, I miss the little girl I chased from the stables. You were, by far, my feistiest charge, and you have always kept me on my toes!"

Emerson laughed at the memories Mrs. Jaymeson evoked and was grateful when she felt some of the tension leave her shoulders.

I really have come a long way.

Hazel came in from the adjoining sitting room, with a huge smile on her face. Her own ballgown was nearly the same as Emerson's. Though Emerson noticed Hazel filled out the *décolletage* more. Around her neck was a single pearl as well, also a gift from His Grace. Though Hazel's was a delicate pink and matched the tiny tea roses embroidered at the bottom of her outer skirt. Whereas Emerson's paired well with the small sprigs of lavender stitched on hers.

How did he know which colors would match? Emerson wondered, as she again touched the iridescent pearl in the mirror. *They are too perfect to be a coincidence.*

"Em! You look beautiful!" Hazel's excitement broke Emerson from her musing.

"Oh, my goodness. You as well!" Emerson squealed breathlessly back as she turned and stood to embrace her.

"All right, girls. Do not muss your hair! Let us go, for we must not be late, especially tonight!" Lady de Clare rushed them out the door and to the stairs. She stopped to check their trains, ensuring proper pinning, before Mrs. Jaymeson's final wave of good luck as they descended.

At the bottom, Lennox and Leighton were waiting in the large entry hall. Behind them, in the shadows, Giles was standing with another footman, and in their arms were several long cloaks.

Lennox was dressed immaculately in a black satin coat with midnight blue threading shimmering in the candlelight and a crisp white lawn shirt with an elaborately tied cravat. He was to escort the ladies to the ball. If he was upset by this, he was at least hiding it well.

Leighton, on the other hand, had a petulant expression on her face. She was still too young and would not have her own coming out until next season. It felt arbitrary, and she desperately wished she could go with them, but Lathen and her aunt had both firmly said no. Emerson knew it was difficult to be the one left behind and gave her friend a reassuring smile.

"Ladies," Lennox bowed deeply, took a dark grey cape Giles was handing to him, and placed it over his aunt's shoulders. He then moved to help Emerson, but as his hand reached for her cloak, Lathen walked into the hall with Dog. Everyone turned, looking expectantly at him.

"Allow me," Lathen said brusquely and held out his hand, making a large silver ring on his finger glint off the bright light from the huge chandelier overhead. Emerson focused on it, noting its onyx stone with a silver inlay resembling a quarter-moon. Most signet rings were ornate and gaudy, but this one was simple in its elegance. Looking up, Emerson saw Lathen's eyes fixated on the pearl choker at her throat. Then, his gaze lowered, and he seemed to notice how low-cut Emerson's empire gown was. He jerked his eyes up to meet hers, a flicker of something unreadable in their amber depths, then looked over to his aunt with skepticism.

A flush burned Emerson's cheeks, and she raised her gloved hand once more to cover her exposed bosom.

"No, do not," Lathen told her quietly, and draped the velvet lavender cloak over her shoulders, brushing the soft skin above her collarbone with his fingertips. Emerson inhaled as shivers followed his touch.

It was surprising. In recent weeks, Emerson had followed the plan she made when she first came to de Clare House. With how busy she was, it was easy to avoid the duke. Except for family meals, and in passing, she had not seen him at all. It was almost as if he was trying to keep from her as well. Yet he was here now, touching her, standing so close she felt his body's heat, sparking more excitement than she had felt all day. All month.

"Are you coming, Your Grace?" Hazel inquired innocently as Lennox placed her own pink cloak. Emerson flushed at the idea.

"No, I do not believe I am," Lathen replied, still staring at Emerson. "But you all have a wonderful evening. You look lovely," he added quietly to Emerson alone. Then he turned without another word and climbed the stairs. Dog licked Emerson's hand and wagged her tail, before she bounded after him.

Emerson watched him go, willing him to turn, her skin tingling from his touch and Hazel's question. She kept looking at the stairs, even after he disappeared, and disappointment washed over her, leaving her cold as the excitement faded.

It makes no sense. I certainly do not want him around me. So why should I be discontented by him not attending the ball?

Lennox cleared his throat, forcing her gaze back to the group.

"Shall we?" He asked with a raised brow and a knowing look.

Emerson's ears went red with embarrassment. "Of course, my lord."

Everyone, except Leighton, exited through the front door, which Giles held open, before settling into the waiting carriage at the curb. They did not have far to go. St. James's Palace was a mere half mile down Pall Mall, but their driver struggled to exit the square amid the lined-up carriages and coaches.

"Now do you see why it was so important for us to leave when we did?" Lady de Clare sighed as she saw how slowly they were moving.

The evening was crisp and scented with snowdrops and freshness, as it had rained earlier in the day. The girls were quiet, eyes wide, as they rode the short distance, while Lennox and Lillian chatted, explaining what to expect that evening. Emerson knew they were trying to help, but it was only making her more uneasy. Hazel's apprehensive look showed she was faring no better.

Finally arriving at St. James's Palace, their footman let them out, and they made their way to a large gate near the palace entrance. An older man in green livery held out his white gloved hand for the invitation Lady de Clare carried. Without it, none of them could have entered.

After removing their cloaks in the entry hall and handing them to an attendant, they passed through enormous doors and waited in an outer drawing room with the entire *ton*. Anticipation was palpable. Every time someone new walked in, the room buzzed with whispers and loud, pointed gossip about the newcomer.

"...she is the daughter of a baron. Three thousand a year, I hear..."

With curiosity, Emerson watched as the girl in question walked by, her head held high with self-assurance. Then the gossips moved on.

"...her mother is sickly and has not had a son. The estate is entailed, so she and her three sisters will need to marry well, or else..."

The new girl blushed as she shyly made her way through the room.

"...but they have no connections or money..."

"...the father once shot a man in a duel..."

"...her brother married an American heiress to fill the coffers. Hard to do with the war and all..."

"...I highly doubt she will marry this season. She has no money and has a very ill-favored look about her..."

With each new debutante, the *ton's* merciless nature became clearer. The air grew thick with judgement and rampant chatter. It made Emerson shudder to think about what they said when she entered.

Does everyone know my father was a drunkard? Or how I did not wear dresses until nearly eleven, and was forced? Do they know how desperate I am to marry? Does anyone know what happened to Kit?

The arrival of Lord and Lady Willoughby, and their daughter, only served to increase Emerson's anxiety. Millicent Willoughby wore a white silk dress with an extravagant floating organza overlay, tiny seed pearls sewn along the edges in an intricate fleur-de-lis pattern. More gleaming pearls hung like teardrops from an enormous diamond collar necklace. Still more strands were woven through her hair and on the pins holding her three feathers in place.

The woman behind Emerson spoke unrestrainedly to her friend, her words a steady stream Emerson could not avoid hearing over the room's hum.

"The Miss Willoughby...her mother married up. Far up. They are as rich as Croesus. Well, the grandfather is anyway. But I hear the family longs for a much higher title for her."

"Well, they have enough money to buy the title, I suppose. But it will not be quite enough to hide her nose!" her friend whispered loudly back to her.

"Yes, but I think they will have to buy a wife for her brother as well. It is what I hear anyway..."

Emerson wondered what they meant but got distracted as a delicately beautiful girl entered along with an elderly companion, and the two women moved on to discussing them.

"She is the granddaughter of the last *Marquis d'Orléans. Émigrés*, you know. They had to flee during the terror, when she was just an infant. The grandmother smuggled her out of Paris in an apple cart with whatever jewels she could hide in her swaddling. Her parents were one of the first to lose their heads. The grandfather died months later of consumption while he was still in the Bastille."

"Yes," her friend agreed excitedly, "but I hear they are virtually paupers now. Her and her grandmother are living on nothing but British kindness and air. And is she not a little old to come out? Twenty, I believe."

"Maybe, but she is exceedingly handsome, and still has the family name and history, I suppose. Even if the money and the property are gone. Good breeding will always be worth more than gold, you know..."

Like everyone else, Emerson turned her head to look at the French girl as she moved past. The gossiping woman was right. She was exquisite. Her blonde hair, so light it was nearly translucent, and silvery blue eyes, so clear they shone across the room. Her gown, though cut in a similar fashion to everyone else, was quite plain, with no embroidery or overlay. A simple French twist held her hair back, with no jeweled pins or embellishment, only the three feathers all debutantes wore. However, where the plainness might have detracted from someone else, Emerson felt it fit her etherealness better. The girl needed nothing to make herself stand out, and her age seemed to give her a steadiness many of the younger girls lacked. Emerson might have envied such beauty and confidence, but the poor girl's heartbreaking tale moved her to wish her well.

Even my life has been easy, in comparison.

The gossiping ended abruptly, the sudden silence punctuated only by the rustling of fabric and shuffling of hundreds of feet. The time had come for each family to enter, one at a time, and be presented to the Queen. When it was their turn, Lady de Clare gave their names to the Assembly Master, who announced their arrival in the next, much larger parlor.

"The Lord de Clare, Earl of Bridewater, and Lady Lillian de Clare, present to Your Majesty: Lady Emerson Haven and Miss Hazel Atwood."

Emerson felt exposed as every head turned, the whispering murmurs growing louder as people craned their necks from the back for a better view.

They had been prepared for what to expect, but it still felt unreal. A hush fell as the two nervous girls advanced, their eyes fixed on the Queen and her entourage, before they dropped their gazes and bent into flawless, well-practiced curtsies. So low the three feathers in their hair brushed the smooth stone floor. They stayed down until the Queen waved for them to rise.

"My, my, my. You are both quite spectacular," the Queen declared as the girls kept their heads bowed respectfully. "Come closer so I can see you better!"

Without hesitation, they went forward several steps. Emerson's ears echoed with the Queen's words, muffled and distant, like she was listening through a thick seashell, making it hard to focus. Luckily it was Lady de Clare to whom the Queen addressed her questions.

"So, this is the daughter of the late Earl of Haven, eh?" the Queen murmured as she leaned forward and peered at Emerson, her keen gaze taking in every detail. "Or perhaps I should call her Lord Haven, since my husband afforded her the right."

Lady de Clare smiled graciously, and she responded loudly. Either for the Queen's benefit, or so everyone else in the room could hear. "Yes, Your Majesty. Lady Haven carries the title of Earl of Haven," prompting gasps quickly silenced by the Queen's glance. "She has been the ward of my nephew, His Grace, the Duke of Windemere, for the last seven years," Lady de Clare continued.

As they talked a bit more back and forth, Emerson took the opportunity to peek up at the Queen. She wore a voluminous rose-colored gown, which, on anyone else, might be considered slightly out of fashion. Rubies and diamonds adorned her throat and tiara, her white-streaked hair piled high and well-powdered. Behind her to one side was a rather large and extravagantly decorated birthday cake.

Nothing else could penetrate Emerson's mind. Luckily, Lennox was there to grasp her elbow gently and help her walk away when the Queen had finished with them, waving condescendingly for them to leave.

The rest of the presentations went on for some time, but they continued into the main ballroom. A blur of introductions to those claiming acquaintance with Lady de Clare, Lennox, or His Grace overwhelmed them, nearly every gentleman requesting their dance cards.

After more than an hour, Queen Charlotte was done with all the presentations. The ballroom quivered with anticipation as she entered and seated herself on the dais, her ladies-in-waiting following her like leaves swirling around her feet. Musicians began tuning their instruments, creating a vibrant, almost chaotic soundscape, signaling the dancing would soon begin.

Emerson and Hazel opened their dance cards, finding both filled with unfamiliar gentlemen's names. Not even Lennox was there. Emerson slowly ran a finger down her list, one page at a time, trying to count all the unfamiliar names.

"How are we to dance the whole evening with strangers?" Emerson asked Lady de Clare with an astonished whisper.

"An empty card would be the first sign of an unsuccessful season," Lady de Clare explained patiently. "But do not worry, my dears. There will be breaks for refreshments, the cutting of the cake, and such. You will simply make do. Just remember to always smile and never, ever, show weakness to the *ton*."

Lennox, who was standing behind them, glanced down at Emerson's card as well.

"I am simply devastated," he moaned dramatically, while placing a hand over his heart, "I

70

tried to get your first dance and just missed out. But alas, I shall endure. I will get the first dance one day."

Emerson turned and smiled at him gratefully. He was teasing, of course, as was his nature, but his silly grin helped to calm her.

The master of ceremonies slammed a golden staff onto the dais, bellowing the dancing was about to begin. Two gentlemen, identified by their dance cards as Lord Oliver Bellamy and Mr. Rutherford Brown, approached Emerson and Hazel for the first dance. The gentlemen bowed, awkwardly reintroduced themselves, and put out their elbows to lead them to the dance floor.

Once they got to the center of the room, they lined up with the other couples and everyone bowed and curtsied dutifully to the Queen before facing their partners and doing the same. Emerson suddenly felt grateful for her school's rigorous dance training, as many eyes held onto their every move.

It feels like we are at the theater, and we are actors on the stage!

As the lively music started, Emerson found solace in the intricate footwork and graceful movements of the quadrille. It was a welcome distraction from all the people who were watching her and the stranger in front of her.

Come together and touch hands. Turn while glancing softly at your partner. Step back and forth, meet in the middle. Hold your train out of the way so you do not trip. The mundane thoughts helped her nerves.

Lord Bellamy was a nice enough partner. He danced as if he was not exactly comfortable doing so but learned how because it was expected of him. He smiled uneasily and tried to engage her in conversation as they met hands once more.

"It is a wonderful evening for a ball, is it not, Lady Haven?"

"Oh, yes, lovely indeed," Emerson responded. It felt forced on both their parts. Which made sense when she thought of it.

I do not know him from Adam, yet I am supposed to dance and smile as though it is the most natural thing.

Emerson looked over to see Hazel struggling with a similar problem. Hazel's cheeks flushed, a nervous smile on her lips, as her partner stuttered, trying to fill the uncomfortable void with conversation.

Poor Mr. Brown. Hazel's charming beauty must have flummoxed him! He is practically tongue tied.

It was even worse when they switched partners and the man in question had to turn with her instead. His stutter seemed to grow to a point where he was nearly apoplectic. He flushed bright red, as though angry with himself, worsening his stutter.

Emerson felt bad for him, and she smiled kindly and tried talking to him instead.

"It is a very wonderful orchestra. I do not believe I have ever heard such beautiful music. Of course, I have been mostly in the country, so I have not had many opportunities..." She continued chattering about nonsense, filling the silence so he did not have to do so.

Mr. Brown realized what she was doing, and he gave her a grateful look before they switched back to their original partners. He had calmed enough to speak more clearly. She overheard him compliment Hazel's dancing, expressing eagerness to see her during the season, and requesting to call on her the next day.

When the dance was over, the gentlemen led them back to Lady de Clare's side. Soon after, two

72

new partners came to replace them. The evening wore on much the same, with one dance after the other. Emerson soon lost count, only remembering the names of two of her other partners.

One, Sir Walters, was an older gentleman with greying bushy side-whiskers and a generous smile revealing several missing teeth. He amazed her with stories from his time in the army, fighting the Mysore in India, and the French in Portugal. He had a good sense of humor and made their conversation flow easily. Unfortunately, though he was looking for a wife to settle down with in his later years, Emerson could not envision herself marrying someone his age.

He is older than my father would be, for goodness' sake. It would be a wonder if he could even produce children!

The other, Lord Virgil Farnsworth, a viscount and adequate dancer, also asked to call on her the next day. They danced the first waltz of the evening, a new dance requiring partners to stand close, facing one another, without lining up or switching. This was the first time Emerson had danced the waltz with a man. At school, they learned with their other classmates. Usually it was Hazel, or their dance teacher, who she would take turns following or leading.

So, to have a man's hand at her waist was unusual. However, Lord Farnsworth was not much taller or larger than her, and he did his best to make her feel comfortable. His conversation was mostly about nature and books, and he had a genuine smile.

"Do you get out riding often, Lady Haven?"

"When I am in the country, I go every day, but we do try to ride through Hyde whenever we have the time."

"I was in Hyde today," he looked excited, "I saw a remarkable butterfly just off the Row. I tried to catch it, but I just missed."

Emerson listened as Farnsworth continued to tell her about his nature collection, but her mind wandered. *His Grace said I looked lovely...*

"Lady Haven?" The music was drifting off and Lord Farnsworth was standing before her, watching her curiously.

Emerson ducked her head and flushed, realizing the dance was over and she had not noticed. Farnsworth took pity on her and smiled kindly while he held out his elbow. Just before he left her, he bowed and kissed the air over her hand.

"Do not fret, Lady Haven. I know I tend to drone a bit, but your company was worth every moment." Then he left, before she could answer or reassure him. She made a note to apologize to him if he still came calling the next day, just as another gentleman came to claim the next dance.

chapter nine

Emerson was with yet another partner, whom she had already forgotten, her feet numb and her cheeks sore from smiling, when the murmurs in the ballroom suddenly changed. It began like a slow wave rising from one end of the ballroom and crested in the other. It was not long before she heard what had caused the commotion.

Someone dancing behind her loudly whispered, "Oh, my, it is His Grace, the Duke of Windemere!"

Emerson almost missed a step but instead straightened her back, refusing to look around and see if it was true or not.

When the dance was finally over, and they returned to Lady de Clare, Emerson saw the gossip was correct. The duke stood behind his aunt in a precisely tailored black jacket, watching Emerson approach with a hooded expression, his amber eyes serious.

"Your Grace," her last partner bowed deeply and greeted him with deference. Lathen barely spared the poor man a glance and a brief nod, before returning his gaze to Emerson. The man walked away without another word to her, not even to ask if he could call.

Which is probably for the best, as I still cannot remember his name, or even what he looks like, Emerson mused as she stared back at Lathen.

"I believe the next dance is mine," Lathen announced, striding around his aunt's table toward her.

Emerson was momentarily shocked, but she recovered quickly, looked down at her card, and responded pertly, "No, I do not believe so, Your Grace. Not unless you are Mr. Richards."

The gentleman in question arrived at that moment, looking remarkably uncomfortable. He bowed to the duke, stammered an unintelligible excuse, and fled, nearly knocking over a table and another man. Emerson stood there bemused.

Alone, with His Grace.

"As I said, the next dance is mine," Lathen whispered in her ear, taking her hand and pulling her toward the dance floor. Emerson had no choice but to go along, or to make a scene in front of everyone. Obviously, the second was not an option.

What is he doing here? It makes no sense. Emerson's mind raced, and the tingling sensation returned to her skin. *According to him, I look lovely...*

As another waltz began, Lathen pulled Emerson close, closer than usual, and swept her expertly into the dance. She glanced up and saw he was looking at her with the barest hint of a smirk.

"You should not look so smug, Your Grace. You frightened away poor Mr. Richards," Emerson admonished him.

76

"Ah, but can you imagine having to dance with him? Your poor toes," Lathen stated wryly as he spun her around. "I mean, did you see him trip over his own feet whilst trying to get away?"

Emerson had to admit she had, but she kept it to herself. It was hard to hold a conversation while being held so close to him. She was afraid if she continued to look at him, she would feel the same spreading heat she had when he held her in his study. As it was, she was doing her best to ignore a quickening flutter in her lower belly.

She kept her head turned and her gaze went to his large hand enveloping her much smaller one. The one he with his crest ring. His grip left her with an impression of strength and warmth, sending shivers down her arm. His other hand barely grazed her waist, yet it was searing her skin through the thin silk of her gown. All the unfamiliar sensations made it hard to breathe.

Does he know? The very thought mortified her and brought heat to her cheeks. *Why is he here?*

Despite her confusion, she mused how effortlessly they moved together. Even with her struggles to endure his touch, the music was a gentle hum between them. Lathen was a wonderful dancer, leading her with ease. His fluidity let her melt with the movements instead of having to concentrate on each step.

Though she had been dancing all evening, this was the first time it did not feel like a chore. Even with the two gentlemen she enjoyed dancing with, she had to focus on their words to respond appropriately. Now, she was getting lost in the dance. As though her body was following every movement of his without thinking, like they were part of the music.

Is it because of him? This ease, this comfort? This feeling of being alive?

"You are an excellent dancer," Lathen broke the silence and her thoughts. "I suppose they taught you at school?"

"Why are you so surprised?" Emerson winced at her defensive tone.

"I am not surprised," Lathen answered gently, then added, "I am merely grateful to not get my own toes trod upon, I suppose. This whole dance could have been disastrous."

A flash of temper hit her, and Emerson gasped at the assumptions he must have had. But when she looked up to retort, Lathen was smiling. It was only a slight grin, with one corner of his mouth turned up, but it was there.

He is teasing me! She realized. *Odd. I did not know he had it in him. Why is he here?*

She tried to scowl, but it was impossible to keep her outrage alive when he was being lighthearted for a change.

Well, it is a game two can play!

"If anything, I am surprised you know how to waltz, Your Grace. It is such a new dance, after all, and you are quite old."

Lathen's eyes widened as though he was not used to anyone teasing him.

"Am I really so old?" he asked.

"Yes, Your Grace, you are positively ancient," Emerson mischievous grin revealed her dimples. She was enjoying herself. Not just because of the dance but simply being with Lathen, having a friendly conversation between equals. It was a refreshing change, even if it was only temporary. She assumed the duke would be back to his usual stuffy self once their dance was over.

Where is this change coming from? Emerson wondered. *And why is he here? With me?*

At some point, she noticed most of the crowd staring. Including the Queen who was, even now, leaning forward in her large chair and peering at them thoughtfully while whispering to one of the ladies standing next to her. As if she, too, was curious about them, and wondering why the Duke of Windemere had come to the ball.

Why is he here? The question reverberated in her mind once more, still unanswered.

She was grateful when their dance was over, and Lathen let go of her to leave the dance floor. Grateful, but strangely bereft at the same time. Especially when the hand lightly leading her dropped from her back as they approached his aunt's table.

Lady de Clare was not alone. While they danced, a large group of older ladies joined her, all with daughters in tow. The first to push their way forward were none other than Lady Willoughby and her daughter.

"Your Grace, how delightful to see you again," Lady Willoughby simpered. "May I present my daughter, Miss Millicent Willoughby." Both curtsied deeply, bowing their necks towards the floor. Millicent batted her eyes demurely as she rose, in a way Emerson knew she could not emulate, even if she tried.

"Ladies," Lathen nodded back tersely, "it is lovely to see you. All of you." He politely bowed to all the other women who were elbowing their way to get closer to him. It was amusing to watch, and Emerson had to raise her gloved hand to cover her grin as she moved to avoid being crushed by the other ladies.

"If you will excuse me, I came to check on my ward," Lathen said, grabbing Emerson's hand before she moved too far, pulling her before him like a shield. "Now I am afraid I must leave, as I have an appointment elsewhere." He let Emerson's hand fall and departed just as quickly as he had come, leaving behind nearly a dozen disappointed mothers, and their daughters.

Without another word, Millicent Willoughby gave Emerson an icy glare and walked away with her mother. The other ladies departed slowly, gossiping about the duke's handsomeness, bemoaning the lack of introduction. Or even a dance!

Hazel came up from behind and squealed softly to Emerson as she grabbed her arm.

"Oh my gosh, Em!" she whispered. "You danced with His Grace. In front of everybody. Every man here is going to see how desirable you are and will want to dance with you too! It shall not be long at all before you get so many offers of marriage you will need to hide from some of them!"

Emerson blushed, her mind still going in circles, trying to understand why His Grace had come at all. He had seen them off at the house and told Hazel he was not coming to the ball. *And then to change his mind, all for one dance?* He explained it was a matter of duty, but that made no sense. *His brother and aunt are both here, and we are at St. James's Palace, perfectly safe. So, why?*

The ball continued long into the early morning. Hours later, returning home tired with sore feet, Lady de Clare explained the night's triumph. "We should expect a deluge of callers," she warned the yawning girls before shooing them off to their rooms.

In bed, Emerson tried recalling the gentlemen she met, hoping her mind noticed something her eyes missed, as Hazel predicted. It was to no avail. All she could see was Lathen...his body moving smoothly as he danced...his teasing smile...his powerful hands as he held her.

Why had he come?

'*You look lovely,*' she heard as she drifted off.

If someone asked her the next day, she would have sworn the duke whispered those words into her ear while she slept.

chapter ten

Emerson was suddenly alert, her eyes wide, heart fluttering. Her room was dark and hushed, and she was not sure what woke her. Then a loud growl from her empty stomach broke the silence. She had been told not to eat at the ball except for one bite of the Queen's birthday cake, and she was too nervous to do so beforehand. She lay still for a few moments before deciding to sneak downstairs to find a snack from the kitchens. With a grin, she realized she had not visited the kitchens at de Clare House since childhood, when she and Leighton pilfered tea cakes while Giles was not watching. She figured it was late enough to get away with it again.

Not bothering to grab a robe, Emerson tiptoed across the sitting room, opened the door while she bit her lip, and went into the hall leading to the stairwell. When she reached the third-floor landing, she looked over the railing and waited, wondering if Giles was in his usual spot by the grand entry. It would not stop her from getting food, but she knew Giles would rouse a maid, and she was excited to do it herself. Silence greeted her, and she decided it was worth the risk. She padded down the steps as quickly and quietly as she could.

At the bottom of the stairs, she heard something. She froze, a tiny gasp escaping her lips. Indistinct murmurs were drifting down the hallway from her right, where the library and the duke's study were. Her stomach growled, reminding her the kitchens were to the left, toward the dining room, down another set of steps.

Curiosity got the best of her, and she inched to the right instead, her feet padding quietly on the cool marble floor. When she neared the end of the hallway, she saw the study door slightly ajar, a sliver of light cutting through the darkness. Emerson could not help herself. She leaned forward, one eye closed, to peek through the crack. A roaring fire illuminated a figure pacing restlessly back and forth.

"Damn it!" a low voice growled from inside, followed quickly by the sound of breaking glass.

Emerson straightened and took a step away from the door. Her intuition, sharp and insistent, urged her to turn around and return to the safety of her own room, to not even bother with the kitchens. But fearing the duke was hurt, she slowly pushed open the door instead.

"Your Grace," she walked in tentatively, "are you alright?"

"What are you doing here, Emerson? Go back to bed. Now." The duke responded with his usual brusque tone, the one he used when he expected to be obeyed without question.

He stood near the window, looking odd and disheveled. His hair was no longer brushed back, and he had waves falling over his forehead, obscuring his eyes. Missing his coat and cravat, his lawn shirt open at the neck and sleeves rolled, he revealed a tanned throat, forearms, and a glimpse of hair across his chest. Also, he called her Emerson, instead of Lady Haven. Something he never did, at least not since she was a child.

"I was worried you injured yourself," she responded, ignoring his instruction, continuing to move toward him in her bare feet.

"Stop!" he bellowed as he strode purposefully to her. "I broke a glass."

Gently, he slipped an arm under her knees and another behind her back, cradling her toward a large ottoman by the fireplace.

"Stay there," he commanded.

He then went to a small, ornate drink cart tucked away in the dimly lit corner of the room. Emerson watched, mesmerized, as he poured golden liquid from a crystal decanter into two tulip-shaped glasses, bringing one to her.

"Here. Drink this," he told her gruffly as he held it out.

Bewildered and speechless, Emerson took the glass with trembling fingers, and sipped from it hesitantly, noting the liquid was the same color as his eyes. The flavor was surprisingly good, and a comforting warmth spread through her empty belly with each swallow, taking her hunger with it.

"What is this?" She lifted the glass, turning it into the light from the fire.

"It is a cream sherry. From Spain," he explained softly. "What do you think?"

"I believe I like it." Emerson grinned, feeling grown up for perhaps the first time since she had come to London for the season, instead of just a child pretending to dress up. Then she remembered why she had come into the room at all.

"Are you okay, Your Grace?" she asked him again, her voice soft and compassionate.

"Yes, I am well. And you? How was the rest of your evening? It seemed, when I saw you at the ball, it was quite a success. *You* were quite the success."

"Your aunt assured us it all went very well. The presentation to the Queen, and the ball. Though I will never understand everything. I mean, I had no time to enjoy any of the evening. It was just so...much. So much gossip. So many dances. So many gentlemen. I can barely remember any of their names or faces," Emerson explained wistfully. Then she looked up and realized it was not entirely true. She remembered everything about her dance with him. The feeling of his hand on hers. The look in his eyes. The sound of his voice. Everything.

"Can I ask you a question, Your Grace?"

"Yes, if you will do me a favor," he responded as he sat down on the couch opposite her, his knees nearly brushing hers, giving her his full attention.

"Of course," she replied in earnest. She enjoyed having him speak to her like an equal once again.

"When we are alone, call me Lathen," he said in a low voice, while leaning forward so he was gazing straight into her eyes. "Please."

The last word came out sounding almost desperate, and Emerson was shocked. She quickly regained her composure, though, nodding slowly in acceptance.

"Lathen," she tried it out, his name sounding nearly foreign on her tongue, "why did you come tonight?"

"I came because I needed to see you dancing in your ballgown," he explained, still focused on her lovely lavender eyes.

"My ballgown?"

"Yes. You looked so beautiful in the hall before you left. Grown, and ready to be out in the world. As though everything you deserve was about to finally happen. Truly, I just wanted to see you dancing at your first ball."

After another pause, and another sip, she asked again, still not understanding.

"But why?"

Lathen could not explain. Even now, with the fire caressing her skin, he could not tell her why.

She looks enchanting. Magical. Like the night goddess Nyx*, bathing in an inferno.*

He did not know why he felt so compelled to see her at the debutante ball. He usually avoided them like the plague. They were always full of simpering *ingénues* and their overreaching mothers. All of whom would love nothing more than to catch a duke. Having no desire to marry and interests far from naive misses, he never attended.

After helping Emerson with her cloak, her image in the elegant, revealing gown lingered vividly, yet he intended to change and head to his club to forget her. At least there, he knew he would find someone whose interests aligned with his own. Someone experienced, unlikely to try entrapping him.

So, why, for no other reason than my surprise at seeing Emerson looking so exquisite and womanlike in her new gown, did I suddenly feel an overwhelming compulsion to go?

Realizing Lathen was not answering, Emerson turned and her nearly empty glass clinked as she put it down on a small tray, and she moved to get up. In doing so, the fire backlit her delicate white nightgown, and Lathen saw the swell of her small flawless breasts, their pert nipples pressed upward against the gauzy fabric. His mouth went dry.

My god, you are perfect, he thought to himself, *I wish I could taste you.*

"Pardon me?" Emerson turned back, her eyes wide with shock.

Lathen realized he must have spoken aloud. *It must be the drink,* he mused. He had been drinking heavily since leaving the ball. Something he was not usually inclined to do. Driven by spirits, and his unguarded desire, he repeated himself.

"I want to taste you."

Emerson did not know how to respond, but the feeling from before was suddenly back, the burning in her belly. Made even more acute by the glass of sherry. As she watched Lathen rise from his seat to stand before her, it became a giant flame.

Lathen grasped her arms and pulled her up until she was standing on the ottoman. His height put her face nearly level with his, close enough to see gold flecks in his eyes and smell sweet sherry on his breath. Lathen lifted his hands and touched her cheeks gently, before running his fingers through her unbound hair, almost roughly at her scalp, pulling her head back. Emerson's gaze became expectant, and her lips parted with wordless invitation.

With a nearly closed mouth, Lathen leaned down and touched his lips to hers, the pressure gentle yet insistent. As if he did not trust himself to do more.

Emerson was not sure what to do, but when Lathen pulled back, a surge of frustration came over her and she clutched at his arms, desperate to keep him close. The kiss was pleasant. His taste was sherry, and his lips were powerful and soft in equal measure.

It was not enough. She wanted more.

"Please...Lathen...will you teach me?"

Lathen inhaled sharply and closed his eyes at her request.

"You do not know what you are asking. You are playing with a fire that could burn you, *Nyx*," he growled. His hands flexed, as though fighting the urge to pull her close.

"Please," she begged, "I need to know." Her damn curiosity was shouting in her head and drowning any fear. She barely registered he had called her the Greek goddess of night. All she knew was her body, languid from her first drink, desperately ached to feel him dance against her again, and she found herself mesmerized by his mouth. She bit her bottom lip from the want.

Lathen's emotions crossed his face. A battle waging. Finally, he closed his eyes and sighed in resignation. When he opened them, their fire burned hotter than the hearth behind Emerson.

"Close your eyes," he whispered roughly, "and do not open them, no matter what."

Emerson did as she was told, waiting impatiently for him to kiss her again, but he did not do so right away. The crackling fire and Lathen's movements filled the room, overwhelming her senses. She heard him move their glasses back to his desk, then he crossed to close the door to the study. Locking it. She felt her pulse quicken as he neared again.

He surprised her with a tender kiss to her neck, and her loud gasp filled the room.

"Shh. Remember, keep your eyes closed," he told her again.

Then he slowly kissed his way to her ear and bit it. Hard enough to be almost painful, but not quite. She felt the bite echoing softly in her lower abdomen. It made no sense to her. His kisses moved lightly along her chin, to the other side of her neck, and up to her other ear. This time he pulled her lobe into his mouth and suckled on it gently. It sent shivers down her spine and made her arch toward him for more, her hands finding his shoulders to steady herself. It never occurred to her there was more to kissing than lips touching one another.

He pulled away, and Emerson felt his mouth's absence acutely, nearly opening her eyes to beg him to continue. She bit her lip instead, soon discovering she did not need to worry.

"Good girl. I am going to kiss you now. A proper kiss. I am going to put my tongue in your mouth," he warned her with a growl as his hand grasped her chin and he ran his thumb over her bottom lip, soothing it. "Do you understand me?"

"Yes," she breathed in a ragged voice she almost did not recognize as her own.

Lathen touched his lips to hers, softly this time, gently sucking on her bottom lip and then her top. Then he lightly traced each lip with his tongue, patiently urging her to open for him, making an approving groan when she did. Without another warning, he entered her mouth.

The flame inside her exploded in a searing blaze of pleasure, and she moaned, a low, provocative sound of awakening. Without hesitation, she wrapped her arms around Lathen's neck, tangling her fingers in his hair and drawing him close, eliciting an answering groan from him.

Emerson's quick response amazed Lathen. Her open enthusiasm and lack of artifice were incredibly attractive. He did not have to guess if she was acting for the benefit of his title, or for what he could give her. There was nothing between them except a single kiss.

She was also a quick learner. Her tongue was soon matching his, curling around, massaging. Their movements became synchronous, reminding him of the perfect harmony they experienced when they waltzed at the ball. Every time he did something new, she would respond eagerly, following his lead.

A rush of heat curled down his spine and his manhood swelled. He was suddenly desperate to feel closer to Emerson and he raised her nightgown slightly to lift her by her bottom and wrap her lithe legs around him. He sank back down on the plush couch and pulled her core tight against his hardness.

The unfamiliar sensation caused Emerson to cry out in a mixture of surprise and ecstasy. Her eyes fluttered open in amazement.

"Close your eyes again," he told her firmly. She obeyed immediately.

Lathen continued, and she followed. The fire spread relentlessly, a pleasurable heat licking at his body. Needing more of her, he moved his hands to caress her perfect breasts.

Emerson arched, pressing into his palms. As though it was not enough for her, she released his hair to cover his hands, pushing them closer. Lathen chuckled and gripped her wrists. Once again, her eyes snapped open.

"Do not make me tie you up, *Nyx*," he said roughly, and moved her hands back to his shoulders. Emerson blinked slowly, Lathen's words hanging heavy in the air between them. Then he used his thumbs and fingers to pinch her nipples through the soft material of her nightgown.

A dark, visceral moan tore out of her mouth, and she threw her head back, her eyes wide, but unseeing, her spine bending in reflex. Her hips jerked forward involuntarily, making her center rub against his hard bulge.

A searing electric current coursed through him, overriding his conscious thought. Her hips thrust again, seeking the same friction. And again. And yet again. Each time, something inside him was getting tight, twisting his vitals.

Coming to his senses, he dug his fingers into her hips, stilling them. Pushing her back. Leaving himself aching.

"Emerson, you need to stop!" he explained, his voice strained and ragged, in pain. "You are about to cross over to a place you are not supposed to go. Not yet."

Emerson's eyes widened in confusion as her world came back into focus. It was clear she did not understand what he was stopping, but her face flushed bright red as she lifted to her knees and attempted to climb off his lap. Lathen, mindful of the glass, stood, wrapped his arms around her back and bottom, and carried her to the door.

Out in the quiet, dark hallway, he lowered her slowly, the friction between their bodies feeling like a betrayal to their unmet desire. He brought his hand up to her face, the pads of his fingers brushing lightly against her skin as his thumb stroked her cheek, and he tucked a strand of hair behind her ear.

"I am so sorry, Emerson. I never should have allowed that to happen," his face was stern. "Run to your room. Now!" He added forcefully, not even worrying if someone else might hear him.

Emerson gasped at his sharp tone and rushed off, her bare feet slapping the marble tiles, echoing in the empty hall and stairwell.

Lathen stood in the hallway, watching her run away, determined to wait until he heard her door close before he moved to follow her up the stairs. He hoped the finality of her door slamming shut would prevent him from rushing up the stairs and taking her to his bed instead of her own. It was how he saw the look of yearning she gave over her shoulder as she got to the second-floor landing. A shaft of moonlight from the high sky lantern above touched her skin, giving it a radiant, luminous quality.

As he was still in the shadows, he was certain she could not see him. Which was good because he had never had to fight so hard to stay in one place before. He trembled, beads of sweat forming on his already overheated skin from the effort.

The way she moves, so guileless and unaware, she does not know how tempting she is. Lathen held his breath as she stood there in her innocent white nightgown, the dark curls of her hair cascading down her back to her shapely buttocks, her delicate features highlighted in the moonglow. He desperately hoped she would continue up the stairs. Or come back down to him. He could not decide which was truer. *She really is a night goddess, tempting me with her power over my darkness.*

What he had said was honest, though. She was not for him to take, no matter how tempting she might be. His lifestyle was incompatible with a naive young girl, especially one needing his protection. She deserved to be happily married and to have a family of her own. To live safely in the country the way he knew she preferred.

It is my duty to ensure all of that happens.

Only after Emerson vanished from view for several minutes did Lathen feel safe to follow. With a deep sigh, he rolled his shoulders, easing the tension from his muscles, and slowly ascended the stairs to his rooms on the second floor.

A sound behind him made him freeze as his hand reached for the door.

"Your Grace?"

chapter eleven

Lathen turned.

Wrapped tightly in her dressing gown, his Aunt Lillian was waiting in the darkened hallway. A heavy sigh escaped Lathen as he relaxed, but he was not sure if he was grateful it was her, or disappointed it was not Emerson.

"Yes, Aunt, what can I do for you?" he asked simply, too tired to wonder why she was there.

"May I speak with you? In your sitting room."

Lathen's brow rose. It was not exactly a time for conversation. It was nearly three in the morning, after all. However, the earnest look on his aunt's face showed she had something important to discuss. With a slight shrug, he opened his door and waved her inside.

His valet had left several candles burning, so Lathen easily led her into his rooms. Dog was inside, lying on a cushion by the low-burning fire. She lifted her sleepy head, looking curiously at them, as Lathen gestured to a pair of simple Sheraton chairs by a large window overlooking the moonlit square.

After they sat, Lillian looked evenly at Lathen and took a deep breath, before beginning.

"You know Lady Haven is a very acceptable girl, and your family would absolutely approve of such a union." It was a statement, not a question. When Lathen tried to interrupt, Lillian raised her hand to stop him.

"Please," she continued, "I know you are going to say you are not interested, but I would like you to listen. Emerson Haven is an excellent match. With her breeding and fortune, she will make a good wife for someone. So, if you want her, take her. Make her your Duchess of Windemere. Let her give you several children to carry on our family name. She is practically family already. Her father and yours were very close, almost as close as you were to her brother. However, Your Grace, if you do not want everything I just described, I must insist you leave her be."

Her words, especially their finality, shocked Lathen into silence. That rarely happened to him. He also wondered why she felt the need to tell him this now. It was not as if she could know what just happened between himself and Emerson in his study.

Is all this simply because I danced with her? He understood the *ton* might overstate his actions, but he did not expect this from his aunt.

Anger stirred at the idea of anyone, even his aunt, daring to tell him to avoid Emerson, but having just had the same thought, he kept silent. He closed his eyes for a moment, calming down, trying desperately not to think of how sweet Emerson's kisses were. Opening his eyes, he saw his aunt waiting patiently for his reaction.

"I understand," he finally responded. It was already late, and he was not inclined to explain his struggles with his aunt. He also could not tell her to mind her own business, without revealing how her words affected him.

"Very good," Lillian answered matter-of-factly as she rose from the chair with a simple elegance only decades of practice could give. "I shall leave you to your rest, then."

Once she left, Lathen went to his bed. He lay there for a long time, unable to sleep, despite his exhaustion. His mind kept replaying what happened in his study. The softness of Emerson's lips and her fervent, yet guileless touches. He was not used to enjoying inexperienced women. Numerous women of his acquaintance knew exactly what he wanted, without needing his instruction.

Surely that is preferable. I really must make it to the club as soon as possible.

As he drifted off to sleep, lavender eyes burned into his mind, and soft, erotic gasps lingered in his ears like a haunting melody.

'Please...Lathen...will you teach me?'

chapter twelve

The sun was high when a chambermaid came to open the heavy curtains and rouse Emerson. It had taken her nearly an hour to fall back to sleep after what happened downstairs in Lathen's study. Now, in the bright light of day, it seemed extraordinary, making her wonder if it might have all been a dream.

Perhaps it did not happen? She thought to herself as she lay in her bed, deciding if she even wanted to get up. *Maybe it was not me, but* Nyx, *an actual goddess who went down the stairs and kissed Lathen. Someone else must have begged him to teach her. That must be it!*

With her eyes still closed, Emerson lifted her fingertips to her lips. They were tender to the touch and, as her hand drifted downward, she found her breasts ached as well. She missed having Lathen's strong hands to soothe them, to tease them.

I suppose it must have happened! Her mind went over it all. From the moment she walked into his study, to when she caught him, standing in the shadows, watching her walk away.

"Mornin' Em!" Hazel came in from their joined sitting room, pulling Emerson from her daze. Her cheerful tone, typical of her morning nature, secretly irritated Emerson. Her day dress and perfectly pinned hair proved she had been awake for some time.

Emerson, in contrast, groaned loudly and rolled over, pulling a feather pillow over her head. Besides being tired, she felt bewildered. Her sole goal at the beginning of the season had been to get married as fast as possible. Mostly to get away from Lathen. After last night, she did not know what she wanted. She could barely even remember the ball. Instead, Lathen filled her mind. Worse, Hazel, her usual confidante for everything, was here, yet Emerson felt compelled to keep last night secret. She hated keeping secrets from her.

Perhaps I should tell her? Maybe she will have some idea how I can proceed. The more she considered it, the more she worried Hazel would be too shocked. However, a deep whisper in her mind argued for her to keep what happened to herself, as though sharing it would take the mystery away.

Or worse, prevent it from happening again.

"Come on, sleepy head," Hazel practically sang as she jumped onto the bed and pulled the pillow from Emerson's grasp. "You must get up. Lady de Clare says we should expect callers soon!"

Hazel was right. Emerson knew she needed to get dressed and meet with her suitors. Last night, walking back to her room, she realized Lathen was dangerous. She could not foresee what Lathen described as 'a place' she was 'not supposed to go,' but she knew she had neared something ruinous.

Mystery or not, I must stay away.

After Alice pinned up Emerson's hair and helped her into a modest light blue day dress deepening her eyes, she joined Hazel in the orangery. Inside, Lathen and Lennox were sitting in the sunlight, finishing a late breakfast. They stood as the girls entered.

"Well, you ladies were smashing last night!" Lennox exclaimed, "Absolutely the two prettiest ladies at the ball."

"Thank you, my lord," Hazel murmured and went to the table. Lennox held out a chair for her.

Emerson blushed, looking under her lashes at Lathen, trying to gauge his feelings. He seemed to be back to his usual stiff self, his face impassive, as though nothing of note had happened last night. He also did not seem to want to be around her. As she approached, he placed his napkin on the table and excused himself from the room without looking in her direction. An uncomfortable silence filled the air when he left. Lennox cleared his throat, but then he moved to pull out a chair for Emerson as well.

Just as plates were brought out for them, bells chimed at the front door, and they heard a commotion coming from the entry hall. Soon, Lady de Clare and Mrs. Jaymeson rushed in, both looking flustered.

"Oh, my word," Lady de Clare gasped, wringing her hands anxiously, which was remarkable, as she was normally quite calm. "I knew you girls would have callers, but I was not expecting this! I believe every eligible man in London has shown up at our door!"

"Yes, poppets, you must eat something and then come quickly to the drawing room," Mrs. Jaymeson added.

Curious, the girls jumped from their chairs and went to the doorway, taking turns peeking around the corner.

Astonishingly, so many gentlemen filled the drawing room there were not enough chairs or sofas to seat them all. They watched Giles opening the doors to the smaller morning room, across the wide hall, to accommodate everyone.

"What shall we do?" Emerson whispered to Lady de Clare.

"Well, we will all go in and sit. Your job is to be modest and lovely, while I will endeavor to whittle out the unsuitable gentleman. Starting tomorrow, Giles will know who he should admit, and who shall be turned away. That will make it easier in the future." Lady de Clare squared her shoulders to leave, then turned with a bright smile, appearing younger than her years. "Truly, I have never seen this, but I should have known, given your beauty, you girls would be in high demand."

Emerson was embarrassed. The idea of all those male eyes upon her was unsettling, even though it was obvious Lady de Clare was thrilled the girls were so popular.

Yet, the afternoon did not pass as Emerson had imagined. She thought it would be filled with men fawning all over them. Talking of their beauty and accomplishments, swearing their devotion. Instead, most of the gentlemen seemed to only be interested in chatting amongst themselves and one upping each other. They paid little consideration to her or Hazel. The only exceptions to this were Mr. Brown, Sir Walters, and Lord Farnsworth.

Mr. Brown sat quietly near Hazel. Occasionally, Emerson would catch him looking at her friend with a besotted expression, but he did not speak to her, nor to anyone else. Emerson supposed, due to his stutter, he could be forgiven for his silence.

Sitting across the room, in one corner, was Sir Walters. His arms crossed and his eyes closed and, based on the noises occasionally coming from him, he seemed busy napping, rather than courting. He had come in with an attendant who held his arm to help him to his seat, and Emerson was once again struck by his age.

There was also Lord Farnsworth, who came with a small book of poetry by Robert Burns. Handing it to Emerson, he softly explained it was his favorite. Though not fond of poetry, Emerson was flattered that he shared it with her. It was more romantic than the other gentlemen. She had hoped to give him an apology for her distraction when they danced the night before, but unfortunately, he did not stay long. He explained he needed to gather flower samples, then rushed off, straightening his spectacles.

After that, it was mostly nonsense. Just when Emerson thought she would scream at another boast about racehorses or estates, a tingle grazed her nape.

Lifting her head slowly, she saw Lathen standing in the dim shadows of the hallway outside of the drawing room. He was hidden, just like last night, and when she glanced back, his intense gaze burned into her, making her heart race. He was far enough away so no one else in the room could see him. His expression was inscrutable, but her stomach fluttered as memories once again came rushing back to her.

His kisses. She again raised her hand to her mouth, her fingertips barely grazing her bottom lip.

It made no sense to her. Even in a room filled with other gentlemen, Emerson could only see Lathen. She longed to go to him, to feel his lips on hers once more. Instead, she dropped her hand and forced her attention to the two gentlemen sitting on the settee across from her and did her best to ignore Lathen.

When she looked up again, he was gone. She felt the loss as an ache somewhere in her chest. She tried to rub the soreness away, but it did not help.

'I am going to kiss you now. A proper kiss.' The memory of those words, and the thrill of her first, real kiss, would forever remain with Emerson, regardless of whom she married. She supposed it might be all she could ever take from last night.

chapter thirteen

The next three weeks were a blur of parties, teas, balls, nights at Almack's, rides in Hyde Park, the theater, afternoon callers... Frankly, Emerson was becoming disenchanted by her first season. Also, she was upset because she had not talked alone with Lathen again.

It felt like he was deliberately evading her, even more than before. He secluded himself in his study when her callers arrived, and before Emerson left for evening engagements, he vanished into the city. As though he did not wish to see her once she dressed in her finery. He only returned home after everyone was asleep.

One night, hoping to catch a glimpse of him, she tiptoed to the second floor landing to wait for him to come home. He did not return until after the clock struck two, going straight to his rooms. As he passed below, a faint scent of bergamot and honey drifted upward. She inhaled, but he must have heard her.

His head snapped around, eyes narrowing when he noticed her. Yet, he did not say a word. Not even to admonish her for being up so late. Instead, he turned back, entered his sitting room, and shut the door firmly, even taking a moment to lock it behind himself.

Yes, he does not care to see me!

She felt hurt at the idea and frustration nearly overwhelmed her. Which was ironic since she once had the same goal of avoiding him. Now she desperately waited for the times she could see him, even if it was only as he passed by the drawing room or at dinner with the entire family.

Well, truthfully, I would like more! Emerson could admit she missed him. His embrace. His kisses. Nearly every night, she lay in her bed thinking of 'the place' Lathen stopped her from going to. Her imagination would take her somewhere new before the darkness of sleep would overtake her, the mystery remaining unsolved.

Besides Lathen pointedly ignoring her, she was upset because at least four gentlemen had formally requested her hand in marriage. As her guardian, Lathen's approval was required, but he refused them all outright, and none had returned to de Clare House. The last one actually cried when Giles held the door open for him to leave.

It was getting to be a bit of an *on dit* within the *ton* about how harsh the duke was during his refusals! Now the crush of gentlemen, who used to call each day, was thinning out. Some moved on to try their hand elsewhere, while others had already become engaged. Emerson was worried she needed to hurry. She had to make a choice and inform the duke before he said no to yet another suitor.

Or the ton *might leave me behind and shelve me! That would be the worst thing to happen.* Though

Emerson's mind knew she was being silly to panic so early, the prospect of being labeled an old maid was a fear of every young debutante.

"Can I get you a fresh cup of tea, Lady Haven?" Lord Virgil Farnsworth asked, interrupting her musing. Besides Sir Walters, who was even now asleep in his favorite chair, Lord Farnsworth was one of the few gentlemen who still came almost daily. Sometimes it was just a quick stop to say hello, but he was at least dependable, even though Emerson was certain he had yet to ask Lathen for her hand.

Though he was always kind, she admitted she felt no attachment to him. She kept waiting for something to happen, but her mind was certainly not occupied by thoughts of him, and she felt no fever under her skin when he was near. Not like she did with...

No! She mentally shook herself. *I must not think of him!*

Lord Farnsworth was such a cheerful fellow, as though nothing ever bothered him. And he was a consummate gentleman. He always secured his name on her dance card and never called without a single flower, a book to borrow, or a pencil sketch of something seen in the park that morning.

She realized Lord Farnsworth could very well be the type of man who would agree to her marriage terms. Therefore, despite her lack of feeling, she kept him on her list of possibles and did her best to treat him kindly, even if she felt a little guilty about it.

"Yes, please, my lord. I would be grateful," she handed him her cup. When he returned, instead of sitting across from her again, he took the seat right next to her on the small settee, close enough for his leg to lightly brush against hers.

Under his breath, his voice shaking, he spoke fervently.

"Lady Haven, I hope you do not find me too forward. I wish to tell you how beautiful you are. How much I admire you. I often find you in my thoughts and affections!" He put down the cup of tea and reached over, gently taking her hand in both of his.

Emerson was slightly shocked though impressed by his temerity of declaring himself in the crowded drawing room, with other suitors watching curiously. Not to mention Hazel and Lady de Clare. Even Mrs. Jaymeson was there, sitting in one corner, knitting absently while she kept an eye on everyone.

Emerson stared back at him with a critical eye. He was a slightly built man, with narrow shoulders and hips, and stood only a little taller than herself. He kept his thinning blonde hair neat and in place with Macassar oil. His eyes were nice enough, though perhaps a little dull, and always slightly hidden behind a pair of smudged spectacles. They were watery hazel, with darker brown flecks she had never noticed before. His small, closely trimmed mustache made her wonder if it would tickle if he kissed her.

Perhaps I could ask? Not now, of course. But maybe it would help me stop thinking of Lathen's kisses? Maybe all kisses are like his and I just need to experience another to get over him.

Before Emerson could respond to Lord Farnsworth, a hush fell over the drawing room, pulling her from her reflection. She looked up to find Lathen had entered, almost as if she had conjured him with thoughts of his kisses.

Or perhaps it was the idea of kissing someone else! She thought offhandedly as her heart slammed in her chest.

He stood just inside the open double doors, sunlight catching his eyes as he glared down to where Lord Farnsworth was still clasping her hand. She tried to pull back but found Farnsworth was holding tight. As if to prove he was brave and unbothered by Lathen's entrance, Lord Farnsworth patted her hand softly and placed it on her lap. Then he rose, fixed his spectacles, and bowed deeply to Lathen.

"Your Grace," he said mildly, yet with a slightly tremulous voice betraying his discomfort, "I wish to thank you for bringing your ward to London. The season would not have been so spectacular if not for her presence. She is quite special."

Lathen nodded curtly.

"Lord Farnsworth, I had not realized you were one of Lady Haven's suitors. I suppose I should have paid more attention," he said dryly. Then, without even looking at Emerson, he added dismissively, "If you will excuse us, I need to speak with Lady Haven about a private matter." Then he left, expecting she would follow.

With a flush of embarrassment, Emerson rose and made her apologies to everyone in the drawing room, especially Lord Farnsworth, and she rushed after Lathen.

Leaving, she saw Hazel and Mr. Brown, seated nearby as usual, watching curiously, but she had no explanation, even if time allowed. She was just as confused.

After weeks of ignoring me, what could Lathen want so urgently? It really is quite rude of him.

Usually, Lathen waited behind his desk for her. This time, he was standing next to the door, and he grabbed her arm to pull her into the study, shutting the door firmly to keep her shriek of indignation from escaping.

"What are you doing, Your Grace?" she exclaimed, trying to pull her arm from his grasp.

Lathen was not about to let her go. He seized her other arm instead and pulled her close, speaking between clenched teeth.

"What am I doing? What about you, Lady Haven? Do you let every man touch your person so familiarly?"

Emerson stopped struggling and her eyes rounded in shock.

That is what this is about? She was dumbfounded.

She thought Lord Farnsworth's handholding and declaration were innocent, sweet even. She barely noticed it, other than it was an opportunity for her to inspect Lord Farnsworth up close. It certainly had not moved her, and she had no feelings of guilt for her part.

"He only held my hand!" she responded with a hiss. "Surely there was no impropriety in his doing so! You, of all people, are a hypocrite! This is ridiculous." Emerson glared up at him before challenging him, her hands on her hips, "So, why have you interrupted my time with my callers?"

In the back of his mind, Lathen knew Emerson was right, but he felt irrationally frustrated. More specifically, passing the drawing room and seeing Lord Farnsworth touch her, he felt an unfamiliar flash of emotion. It took every ounce of willpower he possessed to not immediately enter, pull Emerson away from the other man, and throw her over his shoulder as he carried her from the room.

It was not merely any man touching her. It was also because he knew Lord Farnsworth well. They had attended Eton, and later Oxford, together. Though Farnsworth was never really in his circle of friends. Always small and sickly, he never played sports or rode horses with other boys. Later, when all the boys started going to pubs and discovering barmaids, he never went along then either. Instead, he spent much of his time in the woods, finding specimens, or in his room drawing. In secret, and sometimes to his face, most of the boys had called him 'creepy crawly Virgil.' Though he never participated in such folly, Lathen had always believed there was some truth to the name.

If I am not good enough for Emerson, he thought of the darkness he carried within, and the secrets he kept to guard Emerson's reputation, *then Farnsworth definitely is not! He is small and weak, and he certainly could not protect her the way she needs.*

Lathen knew he could explain about Farnsworth without looking like a jealous lout. He settled for giving her an order instead.

"Lady Haven, I forbid you to speak with Lord Farnsworth again! Henceforth, he will not be permitted into de Clare House! Is that understood?"

Emerson narrowed her lavender eyes and lifted her chin in the stubborn tilt he recognized. It gave him a thrill to see it again. He had missed her spirit.

"Your Grace!" she began heatedly, his title practically an epithet on her tongue. "I shall not cut Lord Farnsworth from my list of suitors. You have already chased off every eligible man who has asked for my hand. I know you are my guardian, but this does not give you the right to stop me from choosing my husband!"

"I have every right to keep you from making a terrible choice! Your own father made me your guardian. It is my duty!"

"Then I would challenge you to give me one good reason why Lord Farnsworth would not suit!" Emerson shot back.

Lathen looked at Emerson. Her heaving bosom and small countenance, which should have retreated from his anger, showed a strength of character he had never seen in another woman. She was magnificent to behold, but her question sat heavily in the silence between them.

Even if Farnsworth is not good enough for her, why have I kept her from accepting the men who already asked?

The other suitors were mostly after her money, but he could have handled that. He could have arranged an allowance for them, leaving the bulk of her estate secured. Many successful marriages were built on much less. If they could see to her safety, including from her own persistent independence, they might just suit. So, why did he turn them all away?

Because you are mine! Lathen's mind shouted, even as his conscience tried to deny it.

With this, he pulled her even closer. He waited a mere breath away from her lips. It was just enough time and space for Emerson to protest if she wished, believing he still had the strength to leave her if she did, before he covered her mouth with a heated kiss.

Emerson was far from objecting. The warmth in her belly went from a low simmer to a roaring fire the moment his lips touched hers. She stood on her tiptoes to reach him better, and Lathen let go of her arms to grasp her bottom and pull her off her feet. Up to him. Once again, she felt the firmness behind his breeches pressed against her belly, and she wanted to feel it at her center again. As if he could hear her thoughts, Lathen lifted her skirts and picked her up by her thighs, wrapping them around his waist.

He must have carried her over from the door, but Emerson, lost in his kisses, did not notice. Suddenly, she realized her bottom was on his large wooden desk, just as he was shoving papers off and lowering her back to it.

Lathen broke their kiss but kept his face close, letting her see the fire in his amber eyes and feel his lips move over hers as he spoke, "We really should not do this, but I must touch you, *Nyx*. I cannot help myself."

To avoid breaking the spell, Emerson held her breath and did not answer him. His words and conflicted eyes showed his struggle. She did not wish for him to come to his senses once again and stop them before they even began.

Instead, Emerson lifted her mouth and kissed him the way he had taught her. She bit his lower lip and then sucked on it gently, making him moan. When her tongue entered his mouth, sliding against his, Lathen lost whatever control he was holding onto and kissed her back with equal measure.

At some point, Emerson felt Lathen's powerful hands at her ankles, lifting her feet up on the desk and then gently smoothing her silk hose up her legs, dragging the hem of her skirts up as well. Lathen pulled back from the kiss and inhaled sharply, seeing the intricate ribboned tops of her hose and delicate white bloomers Madame Delphine had assured were the latest French undergarments.

As if dazed, Lathen stared, brushing with trembling fingers the fragile lace lying softly at her core. Emerson gasped, and her hips rose to meet his hand. A voice in her head was screaming at her, telling her she was doing something forbidden. Her body ignored the voice, shoving it into a room, and locking it away. The yearning she felt was much, much louder.

"Touch me again," she insisted boldly.

His eyes darkened at her demand, but did as she asked, bending down to kiss her roughly. Then, without warning, he grasped her delicate bloomers in one fist and pulled. The soft material tore apart like tissue paper in his hand, leaving Emerson exposed. She gasped, eyes widening, but it was nothing compared to him touching her bare skin.

Lathen stared down at her. He got to see the wonderment on her face when he took one finger and gently slid it down her soft downy curls and over her tight, hidden bud, where Emerson felt her entire world centered at that moment.

Lathen moved his finger in tiny circles, sliding over the bundle of nerves, making her moan and arch her hips in a plea for more. Her head turned from side to side, lacking any control. Lathen grasped her chin and entered her mouth once more, just as he took his wet middle finger and entered her body. His tongue and finger mimicked each other. Slowly, in and out. Giving Emerson time to learn how to match her hips to his rhythm.

She gasped into his mouth, moaning incoherently, grabbing the edges of the desk to keep herself grounded.

She could feel colors.

They were all around her, reminding her of a swirling dancer with scarves she had once seen at the theater. The fire in her belly burned at her core like molten liquid metal. Except she could feel an aching vise developing even deeper. Tightening further, every time he entered her. She felt lost, but she knew there was more, an elusive mystery waiting for her. She wanted it more than anything.

"Lathen," she gasped, pulling back from his kiss, all propriety forgotten. "I need..." she drifted off and a frustrated sigh escaped her as she realized she could not articulate what she wanted.

"Shh, I know, *Nyx.*"

Lathen leaned back and caught his first glimpse of Emerson's womanhood. She was beautiful and pink. Like a delicate seashell nestled in dark curls, glistening with her desire.

His knees weakened, mouth dry with a thirst older than time. He had intended to make her come softly while stroking his fingers over her. He wanted to give her something she would remember, even after they parted. Something safe. Now, after seeing her, he needed to taste her. To have her desire in his mouth. He knew it might be too much, possibly shocking her into stopping him. Again, he told himself he could do so if she asked. He had to take the chance.

Lathen pushed Emerson's ankles further apart and pulled her bottom closer to the edge. He then dropped to his knees and, before she could protest, latched onto her clit and sucked on it gently. Emerson arched her back and moaned loudly. Lathen stopped abruptly as he suddenly remembered the house was full of people.

Including all of Emerson's suitors. *Including Lord Farnsworth.*

The very thought annoyed him. Out of equal parts irritation and a need for secrecy, Lathen yanked off his cravat and stood. He did not slow at Emerson's questions, nor her feeble attempt to stop him, and he tied it around her mouth.

"Now, you be a good girl and stay quiet," he told her sternly. "Understand?"

Emerson nodded, wide-eyed, in agreement.

Satisfied, Lathen took two fingers and rubbed them down her folds again, and slid them inside her slowly, stretching her.

Even though she was drenched, Lathen could feel how tight she was. His cock jumped at the thought, weeping behind his breeches. He shook his head to clear it, knowing he still could not take her.

But I can taste her! I may die from starvation if I do not!

He once again bent down and, while keeping his fingers inside her, used the tip of his tongue to tease her, lightly circling her clit. He used his other hand on her belly, exposing her tiny nub even more.

Despite her promise to keep quiet, Emerson began to whimper as her hips arched to meet his mouth. Lathen could only hope no one would hear her, because he could not stop. His fingers curved, twisting as they entered her.

Lathen knew when Emerson was going to come. Her hips lost their languid rhythm, and she had unknowingly grasped his hair with her hands, pulling him closer. But watching her fall apart was like nothing he had ever experienced. He could still feel the spasms tightening around his fingers as he continued to rub her clit with the flat of his tongue, hoping to bring her down gently. There would be no such relief for him. It was out of the question, but he knew he needed to get Emerson out of his study before he broke and did something they would both regret.

Emerson's eyes were closed, and her chest was rising and falling with ragged breaths as she floated back, becoming whole once more.

"Emerson," Lathen whispered tenderly, as he pulled his fingers out of her and stood, wiping his lips on his handkerchief. "You need to get up and go back to the drawing room before you are missed, and someone is sent to fetch you."

Emerson's eyes fluttered open, and after a moment, refocused on his face. As he watched, her body went from soft and pliant, to stiff and flushed with embarrassment. She sat up quickly, shoving her skirts down to cover herself.

Lathen leaned forward to untie his cravat, but Emerson smacked his hands away and did it herself. Luckily, it was not tight, so there was barely a mark. Still, Lathen had to restrain himself from soothing a thumb over her cheek.

After jumping down from the desk and smoothing her skirts, Emerson practically ran to the door. Once there, she paused, keeping her back to him.

"Your Grace?" she asked with formal stiffness.

"Yes, Emerson?" His sigh was heavy with disappointment at her return to protocol.

"Have I been compromised?" A choked sob threatened to break through her words, and Lathen suspected she was on the verge of tears.

"No," he was firm, "you have not."

He supposed it was open to interpretation, withholding how close he came to unbuttoning his breeches and slamming into her. How close he still was.

Without another word, Emerson opened the door and slipped away silently. Other than her citrus scent and her sweet, earthy taste lingering on his tongue, it was as if nothing had ever happened.

Then Lathen turned and saw the state of his desk. *There is my evidence, I suppose,* he thought offhandedly as he walked over to pick up the important papers he had thrown to the floor. Near one leg of the desk, he saw a bit of white material sticking out from underneath. He bent down and retrieved it. It was Emerson's lacy undergarment he had torn in his haste. He knew he should probably throw them out. He brought them to his nose and inhaled instead. She had a delicate, feminine scent and, even if he never tasted her again, he would never forget it. He put the underwear in one of his desk drawers, inside a strongbox, and locked it.

A silly memento to keep, but mine nevertheless!

chapter fourteen

Kissing Lathen in the dark of night, when everyone was asleep, was one thing. She could pretend it was a night goddess, after all.

But what Lathen just did to me was...

Well, Emerson was not sure what it was. It was certainly nothing she had ever heard about or been expecting. It was mysterious and marvelous, and yet she instinctively understood it was something she was not supposed to have experienced, even if the realization came too late.

Afterwards, she did not go back to the drawing room. Her scattered thoughts could not handle being around people, especially all those gentlemen who presumably believed she was someone they could see themselves marrying.

Am I still? Or will everyone know what I have done? Can it be seen on my face?

Worried, she sent a message of illness with apologies and crept upstairs to her room. A quarter of an hour later, Hazel found her lying face down on the bed, the room still, except for Emerson's soft tears.

"Em?" she approached warily.

Emerson did not know what to say. She usually shared everything with Hazel, but she had been keeping her exchanges with Lathen a secret. Now she worried this, what she had let Lathen do, crossed a line.

If I was worried about a kiss shocking her, surely this would dismay her. But even as her mind argued for her to remain silent, Emerson realized she had no choice. *I must tell her! I do not know what to do anymore! I need help.*

"Oh, Hazel," she sobbed, her voice muffled by her pillow, "I have done something wrong. I think, maybe, I have been ruined!"

Taking a deep breath to gather her thoughts, Hazel responded to Emerson in her typical, blunt way.

"Em, do not be ridiculous. All he did was hold your hand. Surely His Grace did not get too upset over something so innocent. I mean, it was forward of Lord Farnsworth, but it certainly was not your fault."

Emerson looked up at her friend, baffled for a moment, before she realized her meaning.

"Oh, that." She waved the incident with Lord Farnsworth off with her hand. It had already left her mind. "I am not referring to him."

"Then, what?"

It came out in a rush. The entire story. She told Hazel of the first time she had been close to Lathen two years ago. She spoke of the heat she had felt deep inside. She talked of the first day they returned to London and of the night of the debutante ball. Then finally, she revealed what had just happened in the study.

Everything.

Emerson kept a close watch on Hazel's face to see her reactions. Certainly, there was something. Hazel's eyes, which showed her usual care and concern, gradually widened. Her hand, which started over Emerson's at the beginning of her tale, drew back slowly, ending up over her mouth to cover her gasp just as the story ended.

Then, a long silence.

Say something! Emerson's mind screamed at the quiet. Until finally, she could take no more!

"You think I am a horrible bit of baggage!" she cried and went to rebury her face in the bed.

"Oh, my gosh, Em, no!" Hazel replied quickly and tried to pull her friend back up. "Though, I am a bit shocked." Then she paused thoughtfully. "I never would have guessed His Grace had it in him. He just seems so stuffy and proper."

What?

"I do not understand," Emerson replied, as she sat up again. She would have asked more, but Hazel jumped off the bed.

"Stay right there. I have something to show you." Hazel tossed over her shoulder as she left toward her own room. She returned with a thin book in her hand.

Emerson knew Hazel read a lot, more than a lot, yet she failed to see how a book was going to help her current predicament. She was about to question her again, but once more Hazel cut her off.

"I know you have always been a bit sheltered. We both lacked mothers to tell us the way of the world, especially about men. However, I had one advantage. I had a father who let me read everything in his library." She held up the book and shook it like it was something important. "I suspect this book was one from his youth, long forgotten. I found it covered in dust, hidden behind a boring book of maps. I think, perhaps, it is going to be helpful to you. It certainly helped me understand more about what is possible between men and women than I once did." She handed it to Emerson and sat back down next to her.

Emerson had to admit, the pull of her curiosity was so strong, it was eclipsing her worry. She looked at the cloth cover, old and frayed at the edges, and whispered the title to herself.

"'L'Escole des Filles ou la Philosophie des dames' or The School of Venus or The Ladies Delight, Reduced into Rules of Practice."

She looked over at Hazel, the unspoken question obvious in her eyes.

"Trust me," Hazel responded with confidence, and she raised her hand to rub small circles on Emerson's back. "Just read it. I am going to tell Lady de Clare and Mrs. Jaymeson that you are indisposed and cannot go out this evening to the theater. You take your time. We will talk more when I get home tonight!"

Then she left.

chapter fifteen

Emerson read all afternoon.

She paused briefly when someone brought supper and tea to her sitting room, building a fire and lighting candles. Then she reread parts of the book.

And again.

And then again.

She blushed often, admitting a heat swirled in her belly, similar to Lathen's touch. Not as strong, but still...down there. The book was about a young woman named Katy and how she learned to be a good lover.

Wow, am I like Katy? Katy knew nothing about lovemaking. And there is so much to learn!

She was sitting by the small fire in her bedroom, with the book lying face down, forgotten in her lap, when Hazel returned. Deep in thought, she did not realize she was no longer alone.

"Well?" Hazel nudged her lightly with her hip and Emerson looked up with solemn eyes. Eyes with new understanding hidden in their depths.

"I never knew," she whispered with awe.

"I know." Hazel was gentle as she sat in the chair next to her. "I think we are not supposed to know, because well-brought-up, *proper*" she emphasized the word and rolled her eyes, "young ladies are deliberately kept ignorant of such things. At least the current wisdom says so. However, I have always believed that knowledge is important. If we are to marry, it is best we know what to expect! It will help us know how to please our husbands."

"Hazel, if all of *that* is for marriage, then what I have done with His Grace must certainly be wrong!"

"Bother!" Hazel said with a rather unladylike snort. "I have read enough to know nothing you have done has ruined you. Certainly, what the duke has done *to* you is not exactly proper. *He* should definitely know better! But he obviously has feelings for you. Em, he wants you! Honestly, I am surprised we never considered the possibility."

"The possibility of what?"

"Well, of your marriage to His Grace, of course!"

Emerson's eyes widened, her shock obvious to Hazel.

If Lathen wants me, why does he keep sending me away? And why does he never finish what he started? She now understood there was more. *A final act!* She said so to Hazel.

Hazel contemplated this before giving a shrug with one shoulder.

"I do not know. I mean, you would obviously be a suitable wife for him. You have the right birth, and property, and a large fortune. You bring a title for your first son, though the Duke of Windemere needs none of this, of course. You also have excellent character, and you are beautiful! The list goes on, Em."

"He says nothing of having any affection for me." Emerson whispered.

"Perhaps, given your history, he is unsure of your feelings toward him? How many times have you told me about how you have deliberately provoked him? I mean, it is possible I am overly romanticizing everything, but I am certain he is engaging with you because he wants you! Maybe you just need to nudge him in the right direction. Let him know you are open to the possibility. After all, something must bind you together after all this time." Hazel's excitement grew with her conclusions.

Emerson rolled her eyes. "Yes, we are bound because he was Kit's best friend, and now he is my guardian."

"Oh, Em, please," Hazel sighed, grabbing Emerson's hands and looking into her eyes. "I know this is hard to accept, but it must be more. Being someone's guardian means you are obliged to see to their welfare. Food. Shelter. Clothing. Eventually, ensuring they are married off. That is all. His Grace has done so much more. He treated you as family. He cared for you gently, and at his own expense. He has always made sure you had everything you needed, including me! There must be a reason. I am telling you. Perhaps at first it was an obligation to Kit, but something changed two years ago when he sent you away. I really believe he wants to be with you."

Emerson was not as certain, and questions swirled in her mind. *If Lathen wants to marry me, why is he letting me receive suitors at his home? Why must I attend every ball and party, looking for a husband? Why has he spent most of the season avoiding me?*

It was a long evening. The girls talked until the sun was lighting the eastern sky, outside their rooms. With the dawn, a tiny kernel of hope blossomed in Emerson's heart. She started to believe Hazel could be right. In the end, they came up with a plan.

"So," Hazel yawned sleepily, "we both agree?"

"Yes, I will go to His Grace tomorrow, or rather later today, and ask him to clarify our relationship. He either needs to stop touching me," Emerson paused, because the thought of never again feeling what she felt with Lathen made her long for him even more, "or he needs to agree to marry me."

"Yes! It is for the best, Em. I am sure it will work!" With that, Hazel stood, gave Emerson a hug, said goodnight, and headed back to her own room.

After she left, Emerson's fragile optimism waned and soon became a hollow pit in her belly. She knew she deserved to have everything. A husband, children, a comfortable home. Happiness. She hoped Hazel was right and Lathen would give them to her, but if not, if she had to walk away, she worried happiness might not be possible with another man.

What is it about him? She wondered. *I am constantly surrounded by gentlemen, and yet none have made me feel anything even close.*

chapter sixteen

After staying up all night, Emerson slept more than she expected. Luckily, no one questioned or disturbed her because everyone assumed she was ill. When she finally rose and Alice helped her dress, it was already early evening, and the house was quiet. Hazel had gone out to a small party with Lady de Clare, and Mrs. Jaymeson was off visiting a friend.

It is perhaps for the best. If I were to run into any of them, I might lose my nerve. Although uneasy, Emerson was resolved. She knew she must talk with Lathen.

She went down the stairs slowly, trying to avoid anyone else, and crossed the empty hall. Reaching the hallway leading to Lathen's study, she heard voices from the other side of the house, coming toward her. She certainly did not wish to be seen next to Lathen's study. Without knocking, she jumped inside quickly and shut the door behind her. Immediately, she realized Lathen was not in the room and, as the voices came closer, he was the one approaching.

And he is not alone!

Without considering her situation's absurdity, Emerson rushed to the large wooden desk, the only cover, and hid underneath. She tried not to think of when she was last in Lathen's study and was on top of the very same desk.

Yanking her skirts aside and pulling the chair toward her, she heard the door open. Lathen entered, his deep voice, instantly recognizable, making her stomach flutter. His brother and another man were with him. So worried about being caught, she took a moment to recognize the other voice's Scottish burr.

It is the man from the barn! It had been many years, but the day Kit died was one forever etched in her memory. She had often wondered who the other man was.

"I am tellin' ye Lathen, it is her!" The mystery man insisted, clearly agitated.

"I believe you. I just cannot believe she would be so imbecilic! She must have known I would find out she is in London." Lathen was colder than she had ever heard him.

"Do we know where she is staying?" Lennox asked.

"No, but she likely has some old scourge to pay her way. She never lacked the ability to manipulate others to her course." Lathen replied, his voice tight.

The three men spoke back and forth. There was a discussion of acquaintances in Spain, and how long since they were heard from. Then talk of the Napoleonic War, and its impact on travel. Emerson did her best to follow the conversation, but most of it went over her head. She was also anxious every time Lathen approached, for he was pacing in his fury, getting closer and closer to where she was hiding.

Suddenly, just as Emerson was certain she was going to be exposed, the door to the study flew open and hit something behind it, making a rattling noise.

"Lord Warwicke!" Leighton exclaimed as she burst through the doorway.

She obviously knows him! Emerson thought, then gasped quietly as Dog, who must have come in with Leighton, stuck her wet nose under the desk. *Oh, dear lord, please go away!* She tried to shoo her away gently.

"Och, hello m'lass," the man responded with a loud chuckle and a grunt, as Leighton must have thrown herself at him for a hug. "Yae've grown! Pretty soon the gentlemen'll come hollerin' in droves!"

Luckily, Dog was more curious about the others, and after giving one last sniff, she left with her tail wagging, and Emerson sagged in relief.

"Please, do not remind me!" Lathen sounded pained. "I already have enough of that in this household."

"Do not be daft," Leighton laughed with a musical lilt, "I already know who I shall marry, so there is no need for a coming out. Nor for any suitors to come to de Clare House and bother poor Lathen!"

All three men chuckled, their fondness for Leighton clear.

"Well, kitten, I suppose it is something I can look forward to," Lathen told her indulgently, "though I should chastise you for barging into my study without knocking. So, please, take your leave, and take Dog for a walk in the garden, if you do not mind."

Leighton pouted and moved closer to the newcomer.

"But Lathen, we have not seen Lord Warwicke in forever. It has been over a year."

"Yes, I know, and I am sure he will make time for a more thorough visit before he must leave again. For now, we have things we need to attend to. So, off with you. Please." Lathen was firm, yet gentle, as he led her to the hallway. He shut the door behind her, despite her protests, and locked it.

"Och, Lathen, when did the lass get sae big?" Lord Warwicke asked after she was gone. "The last I saw of her, she was still in short dresses!"

"Trust me, I am not exactly excited at the prospect of her growing up. If I had my way, I would lock her up in the country and let her become a spinster. Unfortunately, Aunt Lillian assures me this is not an option."

The men laughed again, before going back to the discussion they were having before Leighton interrupted them. Emerson still did not understand why they were all so upset, especially Lathen, but she soon jerked to attention when she heard Lord Warwicke say her name.

"Is Lady Haven still unaware of Marien?"

Who is Marien? She wondered.

"Yes, we got the chit out of the country the same day, before anyone found out," Lathen replied before shouting, "so, what the fuck is she doing back?"

Overwhelmed by Lathen's fury, Emerson shivered and pulled her knees closer to her chest. No matter how angry she had ever made him, intentionally or not, she had never heard him so enraged. It scared her.

"Well, I told Madam Irina tae keep the doxy there," Lord Warwicke explained, "so we can go noo', if you wish, and take care of 'er."

"That is good. Let us go and fetch her. I swear, though, I gave the woman one chance after what happened to Kit. One chance, and she broke our agreement. I will not be so kind a second time, and I will be damned if I let her ruin Lady Haven's reputation now!"

At the mention of Kit, Emerson had to cover her mouth with both of her hands to keep her gasp from escaping. She had so many questions running in her head as she heard the men depart, and she could only think of one way to find answers.

chapter seventeen

This is foolish!

Emerson realized it right away. Every time she had been impulsive or adventurous before, like riding through the park, she always had someone else with her. But this, driving around in the evening, alone in a closed hack, with no escort. If anyone were to recognize her, it could be disastrous.

There was no help for it, however. It seemed providential a hired hack was dropping someone off on the square, allowing her to follow Lathen's carriage. She simply had to know where Lathen, Lennox, and the mysterious Lord Warwicke were going.

And who is this woman Marien who made Lathen so angry and apparently knew Kit? Why were they so worried I might learn of her?

Perhaps it would lead nowhere, but she felt she could finally uncover something about her brother's death. If not, certainly she might learn something about Kit's life when he was away from her.

She had not gone very far when the small hack she was riding in pulled to a stop. From above, she heard the driver call to her.

"Miss, they stopped and got out o'er on the next block. Ya want me to pull up there?"

Emerson peered out of the open window. They had stopped on a street she did not recognize. The houses were smaller and less fashionable than those on St. James's Square, yet the neighborhood remained respectable, with lamplighters flipping switches to dispel early evening shadows.

She poked her head out of the window and saw the de Clare carriage driving away. "Yes, please," she told him, and they pulled forward, coming to a stop in front of a well-kept stone house, with a glossy black painted front door.

Inside her mind, an argument was going on. Part of her shouted she should stay inside the hired hack and return immediately to the protection of de Clare House. She could always talk to Lathen when he got home. There was always the chance he would put her off, as he had in the past, but it was the safest option. Yet another part urged discovering who was in the house and why Lathen sought to confront them.

Yes, who is Marien?

The latter won out just as the driver opened the door.

Emerson paid the man from her small hidden reticule and rushed up the walkway before she lost her nerve. When she reached the porch, she hesitated for a moment to steady her racing heart, and she noticed the house had a discreet metal plaque next to the door. It read *Nox House.*

There was no cord for a chime, so she grasped the metal knocker instead. It was shaped like a simple silver circle. However, closer examination revealed an intricate etching of the moon on the metal. She knocked quickly and stepped back to wait.

Almost immediately, the door opened, and a smartly dressed older woman stood inside, looking out at her curiously.

"Yes, may I help you?" Her strong accent was unfamiliar to Emerson.

"Good evening," Emerson smiled primly and tried to sound cheerful and confident, "I am here to join His Grace and Lord de Clare. Oh, and Lord Warwicke." It was a bluff, but Emerson hoped the woman, as a servant, would not be bold enough to question her.

Leaning forward, the woman glanced out the doorway. Then to the left and right, down the street. Then she raised her brow and narrowed her eyes.

"You are by yourself, m'lady?"

Later, Emerson realized the question should have raised alarm, prompting her to retreat to the street. However, she merely confirmed she came alone. The woman nodded her head in one stiff motion.

"Come in then," she said firmly. "Follow me, please," she continued and closed the door quickly.

Emerson saw a narrow, sparsely decorated entry with well-polished grey marble floors before they went up a set of wide stairs to the next floor, then down another empty hallway with several doors on each side. Candles and mirrors lined the windowless hall, and their footsteps echoed on the uncarpeted floor, creating an eerie atmosphere. The woman stopped in front of the last door on the right and opened it, motioning for Emerson to enter.

132

Emerson walked in. Quickly, she realized it was a small, dark bedroom, and no one was inside. She spun around as the door slammed shut behind her, and she gasped as she heard the key turn in the lock. She knew it was likely futile, but she rushed to the door to turn the knob and to pound on the door anyway. It was solid, and after a few minutes of hitting it, her hand ached, so she stopped. She took stock of the room instead.

It was odd. An incredibly tall, solid four-poster bed dominated the narrow space on the far wall. But it was covered in black tufted leather, instead of linens. The walls were painted black as well, making the already tight space feel even more intimate.

Along one sidewall, an enormous gilded mirror spanned floor to ceiling. In front of it, there were two unusual iron rings. They were bolted and hung, about two meters apart, from the ceiling, by long, thick chains.

Strange!

She had to admit it made her curious. She walked over to them, and standing on her tiptoes, she brushed her fingers across the bottom of one, and watched it swing, creaking quietly above her head.

There was also a small window behind the bed. Emerson ran over and saw it overlooked the cobbled street. She tried to open it, but it refused to budge, so she let the heavy drapes fall back in place. If it was not for the abundance of candles glowing around the room, and the fire crackling low in the black marble fireplace, reflected in the large mirror, the room would have been almost oppressive.

In front of the fire, the only other furniture in the room was a long, narrow wooden bench, perhaps six feet wide, with no back on it. Since Emerson's choices for sitting were either the strange leather bed, or the bench, she took a seat at one end of the bench, facing the door.

She waited.

As the minutes ticked by, Emerson felt herself alternate between anger and anxiousness. She could not stay still, so she kept getting up and walking to the window, to the door, and back to the bench. During one of these trips, she saw Lennox and Lord Warwicke rushing a small, cloaked figure to the de Clare carriage. Frustrated, she nearly banged on the glass and screamed at them to stop, but she decided it was better not to let them know she was there.

Obviously, I have the right house, and Lathen must still be here!

Instead, she stomped back angrily to the bench to wait once more. Then up again to the window. To the door. To the bench. Making the triangular trip, over and over again.

When the door finally opened, and Lathen slowly entered, all thoughts of finding out what feelings he may have for her had fled. Emerson was ready to throw one of the heavy brass candlesticks at his head instead.

"It is about damn time!" She hissed furiously as she stood, her hands fisted by her sides.

Lathen did not respond. In the silence left by her outburst, he turned and closed the door softly. Then, to Emerson's shock, he locked it again and put the key in his pocket. He walked toward the bed's end and sat, facing Emerson. The seconds filled the void between them, but still Lathen just looked at her, stone faced.

"What are you doing here, Emerson?" His voice was strained when he finally spoke, though a twitch in his jaw hinted at his true feelings.

"I followed you," she answered honestly. She kept the overheard conversation from earlier to herself.

"Alone?"

Emerson had learned her lesson about answering the question. She lifted her chin stubbornly and chose not to respond. Instead, she sat down, crossed her arms, and watched Lathen. He no longer looked calm. It seemed the idea of her coming to this place by herself made him furious.

"You do not know what your curiosity has gotten you into this time, Emerson," he whispered roughly, and he rose to his feet to tower over her.

"Get up. Now!" he demanded.

Emerson's stomach flipped. Something about the tone of his voice had changed. It was deeper...darker...even more commanding than usual. It compelled her to obey. She rose on shaky legs and tilted her head to look up at him. He bent down so his face was closer to hers.

"I think it is time you learned a lesson about misbehaving, Emerson." His soft voice did not fit the severity of his comment.

Emerson did not know how to respond. She held her breath, waiting for something to happen. Seconds went by, but it might have been hours.

"Now, take off your clothes. You will not be needing them here."

chapter eighteen

Emerson's breath came out in a rush.

She was not expecting *that!* Unsure of what to do, Emerson took a small step backward. Then another. Until the back of her legs hit the wooden bench. Her eyes were darting from side to side, looking for an escape.

"There is nowhere to go," Lathen reminded her. He did not bother to stop her, because he was right. Instead, he watched her like a graceful predator with his captured prey, confident his meal was going nowhere.

Emerson racked her brain for a response. She felt trapped, yet her mind kept going over passages from Hazel's borrowed book. Images of using one's hands and mouth to please a lover kept flashing through her mind. The now familiar heat swirled in her lower belly. Somehow, her panic seemed to heighten the sensation.

Is this it? She wondered. *Will I discover the final mystery of lovemaking tonight?*

"Emerson," Lathen broke her from her thoughts. He said nothing else, just her name and a rising of his brow to show his growing impatience.

I want to know.

With no thought to consequences, Emerson unbuttoned her short spencer with shaking hands. She removed it carefully and placed it on the bench. Next was her dress. She tried to reach behind her to get the small buttons on her back, but she suddenly realized why it was necessary for her maid to help her.

"Turn around," Lathen told her roughly. She did so quickly and shivered as she felt his warm, strong fingers brush against her spine, making quick work of the tiny buttons. He wasted no movements and soon the dress fell off her shoulders and Emerson watched it pool on the ground by her feet. Next, Lathen untied her stays and the ribbons holding her underskirts in place. They joined her dress on the ground.

"Now, go stand over there," Lathen pointed to the end of the leather bed.

Emerson obeyed.

She tried hard not to feel self-conscious about wearing nothing but her thin lacy undergarments and her silk hose with their small pink ribbons tied around her thighs, all of which were made of materials so gossamer they were nearly transparent. Emerson was focused on what was meant to come next and did not wonder when she saw Lathen pick up all her clothing, walk over to the door, unlock it, and unceremoniously toss the whole bundle outside! He bent to the floor for a carved wooden box, brought it back, and relocked the door.

"Lathen?" she questioned warily.

"Hush," he silenced her, "I think it is time you and I got one thing straight, Emerson." He placed the box down on the bench. Then he continued with the same dark tone that quivered in her belly, "You have always seemed to enjoy challenging me, and in the past, I have allowed it. Mainly because I did not want to break your spirit or curious nature. I still do not. However, when it comes to making you safe, I will let no one hurt you. No one. Including you. You have gone too far this time, and it is my responsibility to make certain it never happens again."

Emerson was hypnotized by Lathen's voice, and the anticipation of what might happen. At first, she did not grasp his words or notice, as he sat on the high bed beside her, the predator had returned. She only saw him as compelling. When it finally registered, it was too late. Lathen pulled her between his strong thighs, trapping her.

Even though he was sitting down, she was eye to eye with him. Close. It reminded Emerson of when he first kissed her.

I want to kiss him again!

Emerson leaned forward, her eyes fluttering closed, and her lips parted gently in expectation. Just as her lips were about to meet his, Lathen grabbed her chin. Her lavender eyes snapped open with doubt.

"Oh *Nyx*, you are such a magical temptress." Lathen rubbed his thumb across her lower lip. "I would adore getting lost in your kisses, but I would be remiss if I did not finish what needs to be done. Right now, we need to finish your lesson. After, if you still want me to, I promise I will kiss you. Everywhere. I will touch you. Everywhere. Until you see the stars and beg me to stop because your skin is oversensitive from my kisses."

Emerson's pulse leapt at his words and the thought of him touching her. But also...the lesson.

What kind of lesson can he mean?

Lathen did not make her wait long.

"I am going to spank you, Emerson." He said this so evenly Emerson thought she misheard him. She tried to pull back, but his muscular thighs tightened around her hips, and his hands encircled her wrists like steel shackles.

"There is no fighting this one. You will feel it. Tonight, there will be pink marks only you will see in your mirror. They will soon fade, but hopefully the memory will stay with you and will help you to understand how important your safety is to me."

Lathen pulled her down to the side of the bed. He kept her thighs trapped between his, let go of her wrists, and pushed one large hand on her lower back to keep her in place. Emerson shrieked, and she used all her strength to push herself up and wiggle free, her breath quickening from the effort.

It was useless. Lathen ignored her pleas and easily kept her still with only his hand.

Then he waited.

Nothing happened, and after more than a minute, Emerson stilled and relaxed, and her breath slowed. Rather than striking her, she realized Lathen was using his spare hand to gently trace the edges of her soft bloomers around her bottom.

"Are these from Madame Delphine?" he asked, his voice husky. Too mortified to answer, Emerson squeezed her eyes shut and nodded.

"I really must send her a thank you note and ask her to make you more." He said this matter-of-factly before he grasped the delicate material and, once again, tore them from her!

Lathen cut short Emerson's shout of outrage as he swung down and smacked her bottom. Just once. The crack hit the black walls of the room like thunder.

No one had ever struck Emerson before. Certainly, it smarted, but she found the anticipation and the sound were far worse than the pain.

However, Lathen had more planned than a simple spanking. He stood abruptly, bringing her up with him. He easily recaptured both her wrists in one of his large hands as he leaned over and opened the wooden box. From inside, he pulled out two matching leather cylinders, about four inches wide and rigid. Each had a strap with a buckle and a metal ring attached on the outside. Inside they were lined with what looked to be soft white sheepskin.

Emerson stood there, unmoving and watching with wide eyes, while Lathen took her left wrist and slipped it through one of the cuffs, tightening it and securing the buckle. He did the same to her other wrist. Neither felt uncomfortable. So, she just continued to watch him curiously, flexing her wrists, until he reached back into the box and pulled out a looped bundle of thin rope.

That was when Emerson balked. She lifted her hands in front of herself to ward him off as he came closer. It was useless. Her strength was no match for his. He quickly took one end of the rope and tied it through the ring on the left cuff, even as she tried to push his shoulder away from her. Then he used the rope to tug her over to the mirror on the wall, positioning her so she was facing it. He took the other end of the rope and, reaching above, wove it through both iron rings hanging from the ceiling. It caused her left arm to lift above her head. All the while, Emerson struck him with her free hand, calling him every foul name, forgetting she should not swear as a lady.

Lathen ignored her, like she was a mere mosquito buzzing around. Finally, he grabbed her other hand, attaching the rope's end to the cuff's ring, tightening and testing it before tying the last knot. Then he stepped behind her to admire his handiwork.

Emerson was astonished. She felt no physical discomfort, but the rope lifted her arms above and outward, the mirror making her near-nakedness in chemise and hose unavoidable. Especially when Lathen came close behind her and used his foot to spread her legs apart, making her body a giant X.

She had never seen herself so exposed. Her mind was telling her she should look away, but she could not help but stare at the dark curls at the juncture of her thighs. Even now her core was aching with need.

For him.

She wanted him to touch her.

"Please," she whispered thickly to him. She barely recognized her own voice.

"Please, what?" Lathen bent down and breathed back in her ear, so close his lips were their own delicate caress, making her shiver.

"Let me go Lathen. I promise I will never go out unescorted again!"

"Oh *Nyx*, I am not sure I believe you, but I can promise you, after tonight, you will never do it again. Or, at the very least, you will understand the consequences."

While Emerson watched in the mirror, Lathen stepped over to the box again and pulled out a black leather riding crop.

chapter nineteen

Lathen walked back slowly, pulling the crop through his fist and then flicking it onto his palm. As if he was testing the feel. Then he stopped behind her and drew the soft fronds down her spine. She arched at the sensation, gooseflesh lifting on her arms, the tips of her breasts tingling. With exaggerated slowness, he came around her front and let the crop tease up one arm and under the sensitive hollow of her collarbone and down to her left breast. Her taut nipple tightened even more and thrust out through her thin chemise.

Emerson could not look away. Her entire world focused on the path of the crop. With a small flick of his wrist, Lathen let it come down on her nipple and she gasped. It was not painful, but her breast hardened even more!

"Oh *Nyx*, you like that." Lathen smirked. It was not a question.

Emerson did not respond, but her cheeks warmed, and she wondered if it was wrong. Even so, she was grateful when he continued and drew the tip of the crop over to her other breast and used it to draw tiny circles around the tip. Her nipple rose to meet the caress. Especially when Lathen bent down and pulled it into his warm mouth, leaving behind a damp see-through mark on her chemise, revealing the rosy peak.

Lathen kept his gaze on Emerson's eyes as he lowered his arm and the crop drew a line down the center of her chest and abdomen, making her whimper. Her abdomen clenched reflexively, and her lower back arched outward.

She remained fixated on Lathen's path as though it had the answers she needed. *He is not going to do what I think he is. Is he?*

Before she could say a word to stop him, Lathen circled the tip of the crop through her downy curls and then drew it downward between the crease of her womanhood.

Emerson's head dropped, and she watched with wide eyes as the crop came back up and over her hipbone and around to her backside. Lathen moved around her again, to where she had to lift her head and watch him in the mirror. She saw him lift his arm.

When the riding crop came down, it was quick. Emerson heard it whistle in the silence before it struck her bottom. She hissed through her teeth. Slowly, Lathen let his arm rise again while he locked eyes in the mirror. When it came down again, it was so fast she did not see it before hearing the 'thwack.' Again, it stung, but she believed she could handle it, and she made a quick decision to grab the ropes, bite her bottom lip, and not give Lathen the satisfaction of seeing her upset.

He seemed to know what she was doing. With a determined set to his features, he lifted his arm, over and over, only to come back down. Each time, the crop landed in a slightly different place. Igniting her entire bottom with tiny licks of fiery pain.

Emerson was soon pleading with him to stop. Promising him anything. ANYTHING! If he would just stop!

Lathen kept going. All the while he was whispering dark promises to her, about how she deserved to be punished. Describing how pink and beautiful her ass was getting. Explaining how he wished she could see what he was seeing. Telling her how he wanted to kiss the skin there. Lick her. Stroke her.

What? Her mind screamed, and her knees went weak, her hands still grasping the ropes to help her stand.

When he finally stopped, Emerson thought her bottom was on fire. Strangely, it was like the heat she felt in her belly when Lathen touched her. Between her legs, she felt a wet rush as her core clenched at the thought. She was so confused.

She stood there, the unshed tears shimmering in her lavender eyes, staring into the mirror at Lathen. She realized he was stroking the area he had just spanked with the riding crop, as if proud of his work. Her entire backside was slightly numb, so she did not mind overmuch.

As she watched, Lathen dropped the crop, its sound loud in the silence, his hand moving around her hip toward her core. Without hesitation he entered her roughly with two fingers.

The universe exploded!

What the fuck?

Emerson moaned incoherently, and her head fell back onto Lathen's shoulder. She let go of the ropes and her legs buckled as she came violently. The cuffs pulling at her wrists and Lathen's fingers inside her were the only things keeping her from falling.

"Good girl," Lathen said in a ragged voice as he continued to plunge his fingers into her, while his other arm wrapped around her waist tightly to keep her in place against his chest. Close enough for her to feel his hard member against her lower back. Even as the haze of her orgasm was still upon her, she knew she wanted more.

Emerson remembered the world would come back together, but unlike last time, the cords in her body were re-tightening before it could. Especially when Lathen dropped the hand from her belly and used his fingers to draw circles about the swollen bundle of nerves above her core. He knew exactly how to touch her to make her desperate again.

Sweat dampened Emerson's temples as her skin became overheated, her legs shaking from the effort to keep herself upright. She desperately wanted to touch Lathen the same way he was touching her, and she tried to turn around, but the rope at her bound wrists kept her arms stretched out and firmly in place, and her shoulders ached from the effort.

"Lathen," she whimpered, "please!"

"Tell me, *Nyx*. Tell me what you want."

Emerson's need battled her embarrassment, but she thought back to a particular part of the Venus book, just as Lathen entered her deeply, making her moan. Her desire won, and she used the phrase that started everything.

"I want to taste you."

chapter twenty

Lathen froze. In the mirror, he stared into Emerson's eyes, his face tense, his cheeks hollow from his deep breathing, as though he was wrestling with himself. Finally, he slowly withdrew from her core, making her ache as her moisture welled down her thighs. He made quick work unbuckling both cuffs, rather than bothering with untying the rope.

From her vantage, Emerson could see the pronounced bulge behind his breeches, pressing the material outward. From reading Hazel's book, she knew what she would find there. She even knew why his member was hard and erect, and some names she could call it. How she could touch it and, hopefully, how to make him as mindless as he made her.

This new knowledge probably should have made her nervous, but Emerson's curiosity and yearning made her desperate for experience. She wanted to touch him with her hands and her mouth, not just read about it. Most importantly, she wanted to experience the final mystery.

After releasing her, Lathen walked to the bed and sat down expectantly, waiting to see what she would do. Emerson took a deep breath to steady her nerves, and she followed him, absently shaking out her arms. Once she was standing before him, she knew she was ready.

I want this. Badly.

She reached for his shirt. Her fingers trembled with excitement as she worked her way from the top button to the bottom, pulling the tails out of his breeches and pushing it off his shoulders. Lathen leaned forward and lifted his hips to help, but otherwise, he just watched.

Emerson stood back to take in all she had revealed.

Oh...

My...

God...

He is simply beautiful!

She was speechless. He really was a Greek god. He was covered in bronze skin, as if he made a habit of swimming in the summer without clothes. The flickering candlelight made dancing shadows from his ropelike muscles as they flexed with every slight movement and breath he took. He had a dusting of burnt umber hair across his wide chest, narrowing as it went lower.

And even lower.

She followed the trail with her eyes first, then with her fingers, making his stomach muscles jump, until it disappeared in a thin line below his breeches. The breeches had silver buttons up both hips, and Emerson used both hands to undo them.

Lathen continued to watch her intently, his face flushed and glowing eyes hooded, but he did not stop her or offer her any help. She started with one side, and then the other, and then pulled the front flap forward.

She gasped.

Oh...

Emerson had read about it. She had even traced her fingers over a sketch in the book. Yet nothing could have prepared her for the sight of Lathen's manhood springing forward upon release.

It was enormous. Like a thick root of a tree with a wide crest near the top. Below, a heavy sack, covered in the same dark umber hair, gave off the very essence of virility.

How the hell is that *supposed to fit inside of me?*

Emerson's eyes flew to Lathen's face. His expression was inscrutable, but she felt a challenge emanating from him.

She was not about to back down now. She squared her shoulders, took a deep breath to steady herself, and slowly reached forward with trembling fingers, grasping his member with one hand. It was velvety soft, but hot and hard under the skin at the same time. She remembered the book said to move her hand, so she tightened her grip and pulled slowly. Up and then back down.

"Fuck!" Lathen hissed loudly through clenched teeth and let his head fall back. His hips flexed, making the muscles on his thighs jump.

Emerson felt powerful. She lifted her other hand, placing it below the other, and used both to draw over his skin, from the base to the tip. Over and over, until she noticed a small droplet of moisture weeping from the tip. It rolled slowly down the wide crest.

Emerson instinctively leaned forward and used her tongue. First to taste the salt of him, then to swirl around the blunt tip, before opening her mouth to fit as much of him inside as she could. She glanced up to his face and saw as Lathen, the man who was always in control, fell apart.

My hands. My mouth. I did that! Her mind was practically dancing with joy at the thought of having such power over him.

Just as she began to feel smug, Lathen came forward and buried his hands deeply into her hair, making several of her hairpins fall to the floor, pulling her head back far enough to see her face clearly.

"*Nyx,*" he growled through clenched teeth, "relax your throat. I am going to fuck your mouth!"

Emerson was speechless, her eyes wide. The book had not prepared her for that, but his words painted a vivid picture! She could see what he wanted, and the vision made her insides flip, and her skin felt feverish.

Lathen started off slowly. Gently. Testing her limits and seeing how much of his enormous member she could take in her mouth before her eyes watered as she stared up at him, and where she would choke. He watched for where she lost all control and looked panicked at not being able to breathe.

All her limits.

Once he understood them, he went faster, grasping her hair to position her mouth exactly how he wanted it.

Emerson knew she was no longer in control, and her hands moved from his manhood to brace herself on his muscled thighs. Yet it did not matter. Losing control allowed her to relax, and to learn. She figured out how to open her throat as he asked, to let him inside even deeper, to breathe through her nose at the right times and let her tongue rub along the base each time he withdrew.

Again and again, Lathen thrust into her mouth and pulled almost all the way out. Emerson dug her nails into his upper thighs and stared up at him with her wide lavender eyes. Suddenly, his tempo increased, and he pushed in one last time. He growled and every muscle in his body tightened, and Emerson felt the warmth of his seed spill down the back of her throat. She swallowed on instinct, tears running down her face, feeling a surge of excitement and satisfaction.

"Good girl." Lathen spoke with reverence, his breath still heavy, sweat dotting his brow. He pulled out as he released her hair and smoothed it back. Then he gently wiped away her tears with his thumbs and traced her wet, reddened lips.

Abruptly, he tugged her up to kiss her roughly before he threw her onto the tufted leather of the bed. He then bent down to remove her light chemise, leaving Emerson in nothing but her silk hose with their delicate pink ribbons.

Feeling slightly embarrassed, Emerson moved to cover her breasts with her hands and pressed her knees together, tilting them to one side. Meanwhile, Lathen bent to remove his boots and breeches, but when he turned and saw her, he tsked and brushed her hands away.

"It is too late to be shy now, *Nyx*. You just had my cock in your mouth!"

Emerson's cheeks flamed at his words and the vision he painted. He was right, of course. Her modesty was trivial when he was standing before her, completely naked. And she could not stop staring. His body was completely different from hers. Where her belly was flat and soft, his had rows of visible ridges of muscle. Two deep grooves led from his narrow hips to his manhood, unlike the gentle flare of her hips and soft dimples above her bottom. He was hard and lean everywhere she was soft and curved. He also bore scars where her skin remained untouched, a small, perfectly round burn mark on his lower abdomen near his hip, etched with a faint crescent shape like a waning moon. Another, a thin, jagged line, cut across his upper arm, a faded trace of some long-ago injury. She longed to touch them, to trace them, soothing and memorizing their faint outlines, but he stepped closer, drawing her gaze to his face.

"Besides, you have nothing to hide, *Nyx*. Your bosom is simply beautiful. I have never seen breasts so perfectly formed," he added tenderly before raising a hand and spanking her left buttock, making her shout in surprise as her already tender bottom tightened in reflex.

"Now, spread your legs for me. I want to see if your cunt is as stunning as I remember!" Lathen made this into a command. The tenderness vanished, his voice resuming the dark, authoritative tone her body craved.

Emerson blushed even more at his words, but without hesitation, she did as he told, letting her knees fall to the sides. In doing so, she saw his manhood was still hard, jutting forward like it was reaching out for her.

This is it! He is going to make love to me. Finally!

"Yes," he whispered in near worship. "You are so gorgeous. You have nothing to hide from me." He reached to touch her downy curls. "Here." He leaned up to cup her firm breasts. "And here!"

Lathen crawled up to the bed like a prowling animal and laid down, gliding his large body against hers. The friction and weight made her moan, and she felt his manhood lying heavily against her core as he bent forward on his elbows to kiss her again.

It was all so intense. The yearning, the want, the need. The unique sensation of warm skin against skin. Lathen kissed her deeply, his tongue dancing with hers. Her legs spread wide to accommodate his hips and his member was lying against her lower belly, close to where she wanted it most.

Driven by pure physical desire, Emerson grasped Lathen's lower back and lifted her hips at the same time. She was incredibly wet, and his arousal was hard as stone. That was all it took to nudge him in the right direction. Emerson gasped as Lathen barely entered her, his immense girth stretching her virgin entrance, burning deliciously.

Emerson's hands moved lower, digging her nails into Lathen's backside, trying to pull him even deeper. Suddenly, he came to his senses, straining away from her, scrambling until he was up on his knees.

"Emerson, no!" Lathen shouted as he grasped her arms, and arched forward to hold them tightly by her head, as he strained to keep his lower body away from her.

An uneasy silence, broken only by their heavy breathing, filled the space between them. Lathen closed his eyes, as if he was in pain, and he hung his neck, pressing his forehead to hers. His hair, normally perfect, was wild and formed a curtain around his face.

"No," he repeated, but gentler, "we cannot, *Nyx*."

Emerson was confused. He had touched her in every way but one.

Why does he not want to make love to me? She knew instinctively it would be amazing. *So, why?*

Before she could ask, Lathen lowered himself, pulling away from her core, and latched his lips onto one of her hard, aching nipples. At this, all her worries left her. She felt there was a string Lathen was pulling directly from her breast, down to her lower belly. He suckled hard. Then bit it sharply, making Emerson shout, before using the flat of his tongue to soothe the pain. He made his way to the other breast and gave it the same treatment. He then sat back on his knees, and while watching Emerson's face, used his forefingers and thumbs to pinch and twist her nipples.

"You like that, *Nyx*?"

Emerson, her back bent like an archer's bow, was too caught up in sensation to answer with more than a garbled moan.

Lathen pinched them even harder, making her cry out. It was painful, yes, but it nearly made her come again.

"I asked you a question!" Lathen commanded roughly.

"Yes!" Emerson opened her eyes and shouted back to him loudly. "I love it!"

"Good girl."

Lathen released her nipples, and the blood came rushing back, making her gasp. Emerson was trying to adjust to the unfamiliar sensation when he shifted down and grabbed both of her legs and threw them over his shoulders. His mouth went directly to her clit, and he sucked hard, his cheeks hollowing.

Emerson's second orgasm crashed over her. It was like a horse at a fast gallop. There was no way to stop it or get out of the way, even if she had wanted to. There was also no way to come down from it gently this time. It just kept going until Lathen slipped two fingers deep inside her, curling them so he stroked the inside wall of her womanhood. She came for the third time.

Emerson screamed as the colors rushed around her. The world went dark.

chapter twenty-one

Emerson floated back to consciousness as someone gently caressed her naked back. Gooseflesh rose on her arms, and a shiver ran down her back. No one had ever touched her so before, but she enjoyed it, her lips curving into a lazy smile as her eyes fluttered open. The room was darker, as though most of the candles had been blown out.

"Are you okay?" Lathen asked gently from behind her. She rolled onto her back and saw a concerned look on his face.

"Yes," she smiled shyly, and she finished rolling over to her other side so she could face him. Then she glanced down and frowned. Lathen was fully dressed, and he looked as if nothing untoward had happened. He was his usual in-control self. Even his hair was brushed back in place.

That is too bad, Emerson thought wryly. She would forever carry the memory of him losing control, if only for a moment. *He can never take that away from me.*

But there was still one question she wanted an answer to.

Well, several, but I shall start with the one before I lose my nerve.

"Lathen? Why will you not make love to me?"

Lathen lifted his brow in surprise before his control slipped back like a set of wooden shutters. He did not answer right away, and Emerson at first thought he would not tell her. She started to turn away, but he stopped her with a hand on her shoulder.

"Emerson, you must understand. We cannot do that. I am extraordinarily grateful for every chance I have had to pleasure you. Honestly, you are a temptation I have never experienced before, and God knows I have done everything in my power to keep my distance. Do you understand why?"

Emerson thought about it for several moments before the answer dawned on her. The realization hurt more than she wanted to admit.

"It is because you have no desire to marry me," she answered him stiffly. She did her best to keep her composure, blinking back tears threatening to spill.

"Emerson, listen, please. I have no wish to marry anyone. It is not you. It is me. *I* am the broken one. *I* could never be a proper husband to you. There are reasons for this. I cannot explain it to you, but there are circumstances I cannot change, things begun before your birth."

Emerson now realized she and Hazel had been naïve. Especially when they concluded Lathen must want her. In their minds, they thought wanting her meant he wanted to marry her.

I am so foolish! He had no intention of marrying me. Ever!

Emerson was again embarrassed by her nakedness, especially since Lathen was so put together. She covered her breasts with one arm and tried to roll over to the edge of the bed to look for her clothing, forgetting everything but her chemise and torn bloomers were outside the locked door.

"I need my clothes, Your Grace," she said in a wavering voice, still desperately trying to keep from crying from her frustration and disappointment.

"Emerson," he tried one more time to reason with her, "I really want you to understand. You deserve better than me, and I owe it to Kit to make certain you marry well!"

Emerson lost what little control she had left. She whipped around and pushed his chest with both hands, her nakedness forgotten in her flash of anger.

"Do *not* talk to me of my brother!" she was shrill, practically screaming. Still feeling hurt, his mention of Kit made her emotions boil over into fury. "You do not want me. You keep saying I must understand. Well, I understand, I am not stupid. I promise I will not push myself onto you again, Your Grace!"

Lathen sighed heavily, but he did not try to reason with her anymore. Instead, he got up and went to the door, pulled out the key and unlocked it, and retrieved her clothing. He took the time to gently fold everything on the bench before he left her alone so she could dress.

As she was tying her underskirts, she could hear him speaking to someone in the hallway, but when she went over to press her ear to the door, she could not identify who it was or what he was saying to them. Exasperated, she yanked her chemise and dress over her head, hearing a tearing in her haste. She went toward the bed, searched under it for her destroyed underwear, but was frustrated when she

156

could not find them. With an annoyed sigh, she sat on the bench to wait.

I will be damned to hell before I use that bed again! She glared at the offending piece of furniture, as well as the cuffs still hanging from the chains and rope. Both were stark reminders of her reckless behavior, and Lathen's lack of feelings for her.

When Lathen finally came back, he had a dark hooded cloak with him. Emerson stood, and tried to take it from him, but he put his hands on her shoulders and spun her around, despite her protests.

"Hold still," he said abruptly as he tightened her stays and buttoned up her dress.

Despite her irritation at his highhandedness, Emerson did as he asked, but only because it would be unseemly to return to de Clare House in her current state of undress. She was reminded of her missing underwear, and almost asked him about them, but decided she was too embarrassed and kept silent. When he was done, he grasped her shoulders and turned her back around and rudely shoved the cloak in her hands.

"Here, put that on and make sure the hood stays up. It is imperative that no one sees you leaving here. Hopefully, no one saw you enter." His brows lowered and his tone was serious.

Emerson had questions, but the look on Lathen's face told her it was not a good time to ask them. So, she kept silent as he gripped her arm and led her out into the hall and down the stairs. The same woman who greeted Emerson and locked her in the room waited by the front door, opening it as they approached. Emerson still refused to speak, but she glared at the woman, trying to at least show her how angry she was.

"Master," the woman said to Lathen, her heavy accent making it sound exotic, and she bowed low, nearly to the ground, as they walked past. Emerson found it odd, but Lathen ignored the servant's farewell, pulling her quickly toward the waiting de Clare carriage, returned at some point.

Lathen did not even slow so the footman could jump down and open the carriage door before he got there himself, yanked it open, and hurriedly lifted Emerson inside and quickly followed her. As Lathen shut the door, the carriage sped off, pushing Emerson against the seat.

At his unusual behavior, Emerson's curiosity finally bubbled out.

"Why are you so concerned about someone seeing me there? What is that place? Why did she call you master instead of Your Grace?"

Lathen ignored her, but she could see the muscles in his jaw working, revealing her questions had provoked him.

Emerson did not care. She felt an urge to poke at his armor, even more than she did as a child. Then, it was a game. Now she wanted to show him she would no longer bend to his control. After a few moments of thought, she asked him another.

"Who is Marien?"

Lathen whipped his head around so fast it shocked her, and she gasped, leaning away.

"Where did you hear that name?" he asked tightly.

But two could be stubborn. She lifted her chin as he glared at her, waiting for her to answer. Emerson could tell she had struck a nerve, and she inwardly cheered.

Let us see how he likes to wait for answers.

Eventually, she shrugged and turned away. If he was going to continue to keep secrets, so could she. Irritated, Lathen leaned forward and grasped her chin, forcing her to look back at him.

"Emerson, I am only going to tell you this once. Marien does not concern you. Nor does Nox House. You are never to go there again! As far as you and me, you made your promise, and I will give you mine. I will keep my distance from you as well. You will be well married and safely away from me. As soon as possible."

This time, Lathen did not expect a response. He dropped his hand and turned to look back out the window, saying nothing else to her the rest of the way home.

When they returned to de Clare House, Lathen jumped down and walked to the front door without looking back, leaving the footman to help Emerson. She was shocked by his deliberate lack of manners, until she understood he meant his words. He was going to keep his distance. She felt a pang in her chest, because despite her angry words, and Lathen's rejection, she still wanted him.

Badly.

chapter twenty-two

"Wow!"

...

"Just, wow!"

...

Hazel was rarely speechless. If Emerson was not so embarrassed and discouraged, then she might have laughed at seeing her friend so flustered. Hazel was even blushing and was using her hand to fan herself.

It was early the next morning. Hazel had rushed in as soon as she woke, still in her nightclothes, and jumped into Emerson's bed, making several feathers float in the air. She was eager to find out what happened, and why Emerson had come home so late. Emerson had just finished telling her everything. Thankfully, her friend had listened to the entire story, with no judgement.

Questions...well, there were a lot of those. Hazel seemed to know when Emerson was holding back. Emerson answered all questions, her face reddening from embarrassment, but now, relieved, she was grateful. She was tired of trying to figure everything out on her own, and clearly, she did not understand Lathen.

Emerson enjoyed being with him intimately, of that she was certain. Even now, she craved him. Yet Lathen wanted her only for secret caresses, perhaps not even for those anymore.

He said he will not touch me again. A heavy sigh escaped her.

Also, he had been truthful about one thing. She would never forget what happened last night. Including her punishment. Even now her bottom felt tender with each movement she made, and last night, as she dressed for bed, she had gently trailed her fingers over the light pink marks in her mirror. Both were tokens from Lathen. While she probably should have some resentment, each minor ache made her remember how ready she had been for him when he was done with the riding crop. How quickly she reached her climax.

Perhaps there is something wrong with me. Why else would I want him so much after everything? She chewed on her bottom lip in worry.

"I am all astonishment!" Hazel interrupted her dark thoughts. "I just do not understand why His Grace does not want to marry you, Em! I had thought he was more honorable. I truly did. And for him to strike you? It is incomprehensible!"

"Yes, I am puzzled too, but it is not as though I can change anything. His Grace was quite adamant," Emerson explained, though she did not comment on the punishment. She was not ready to admit it was not as bad as Hazel seemed to think. When she thought of everything after Lathen released her, she was not bothered. Many of the mysteries of lovemaking had been, at least in part, revealed to her.

He had made love to her mouth and her breasts. She had tasted his essence, just as he had hers.

But where do I go from here? Now I know he does not want me for anything. Did he find me lacking? Her mind flashed over everything she said and did last night. It was a continuous loop, a vicious cycle she could not escape. *Maybe I was too forward. Perhaps his usual partners are more experienced than I am.*

"Mayhap," she began as the doubt overwhelmed her, "I should leave London. Or at least de Clare House. I could ask to go abroad, or back to the country?"

"Em, no!" Hazel sounded indignant. "You cannot. This is your one chance to marry well, to a proper English gentleman. I think, instead of running away, it is time you dig in your heels and fight for what you deserve. I will help you. We shall find you someone even the duke cannot turn away, and no matter what happens, we will keep you from being alone with His Grace again!"

Emerson's head dropped in defeat, and tears burning her eyes since last night slipped down her cheeks. She was grateful for Hazel's confidence and friendship, and her offer to help her fight, but she remained unconvinced.

If I fight, how can I hope to win? Lathen is simply too powerful. Even if I could, what does winning even look like? Marrying someone else, but always wondering about Lathen? Even now, I ache for him in ways beyond just my sore backside.

Also, Emerson believed it was unnecessary for her to avoid him, even though she said she would not bother him again. After all, he told her he would not seek her out. Lathen was nothing if not a man of his word.

I thought he cared, but he obviously does not. Feeling dejected, Emerson wanted to pull the heavy drapes and fall into a dreamless sleep. In fact, Emerson would have liked to stay in her room for the rest of the day. If anyone asked, she could say it was to recover from her recent illness, though the real reason would be to give her the time to mend her wounds. Not on her bottom, but rather her heart.

Unfortunately, the ladies of the house were all committed to a tea at Lady de Clare's oldest friend's home, and there was no persuading her to let any of the girls beg off. The nagging questions about Lathen, and the dull ache in her heart, would have to wait. At least until tomorrow.

chapter twenty-three

The de Clare carriage pulled up to Farrington Hall, a large estate with extensive grounds near Kensington Palace in London. Lady de Clare, Leighton, Emerson, and Hazel were all dressed in lovely muslin-print afternoon dresses, with short spencers to ward off the cool drizzle of the day.

The ladies walked in the door and joined a crush of fashionably dressed, wealthy women, all sitting or strolling around two sizable adjoining drawing rooms. They were mingling and chatting in smaller groups, drinking tea from dainty porcelain cups, and eating miniature sandwiches from trays being walked around by unassuming servants.

"I am going to find Lady Sutcliff and give her a quick chat," Lady de Clare said cheerfully before she wandered off, leaving the three young girls to find a place to sit in the crowded rooms.

Lady Ophelia Sutcliff was a tiny woman with wavy, shoulder-length ash blond hair, kept loose, unusual for a society woman. At first glance, she looked extremely delicate, as though a hard wind might blow her down. Upon closer inspection, one noticed her sparkling blue eyes, a generous smile, and a profound strength of character. Lady de Clare and Lady Sutcliff had known one another since childhood and remained steadfast friends for over forty-five years.

Lady Sutcliff was also a cousin of King George, and the granddaughter of a former king. She had been born too far down in the line of succession for anyone to worry about but was close enough to the crown to be influential within the *ton*. She was a widow with an enormous fortune from her two deceased husbands, and though she never had children of her own, she spent much of her spare time on charitable causes and hosting balls and parties.

Every year, when the season was near the halfway point, she threw this tea party, only inviting a select group of ladies. Ladies who had passed muster and were general favorites. Getting an invitation was essential, almost as important as getting a voucher to Almack's. If you did not get one, everyone assumed there was something wrong with you or your family. On the ride over, Lady de Clare explained all of this.

Mindful of this, Emerson observed the other ladies wandering the drawing rooms. Near one corner, she recognized the French waif from the debutante ball, rumored by gossips to be the granddaughter of a marquis lost during the troubles. Although the girl attended most events they did, Emerson knew only her name, Lady Sabine Rousseau, and her frail grandmother, who spoke little English, always accompanied her.

A proper introduction had not yet happened, though Emerson could admit she was still curious to know her. She was so quiet and shy, and incredibly beautiful, with a graceful, almost effortless elegance easily admired. Emerson doubted they would remedy the oversight today, as Lady Rousseau and her grandmother sat with a group including Miss Millicent Willoughby and her mother.

In recent weeks, the Willoughby ladies attended nearly every ball and party Emerson and Hazel did, their sharp tongues and love of gossip apparent. Even more than most members of the *ton*, which was saying something. Luckily, Emerson and Hazel had listened to Lady de Clare's sage advice and avoided them as much as possible. It was quite easy since Millicent Willoughby had not tried to get to know them either.

In fact, ever since Lathen had danced with Emerson at the Queen's birthday ball, the Willoughby ladies, and their closest friends, seemed to enjoy snubbing them at every opportunity. It was never obvious. Mostly, they childishly walked away whenever Emerson came into a room. It was not ideal, but at least they had not done to Emerson, or Hazel, what they had done to some other ladies.

Several pretty girls debuting with them suffered diminished prospects due to unseemly rumors. Usually whispers of inappropriate behavior or gossip of being alone with a man, without a chaperone. As a result, almost all had been whisked from town or married off rather quickly, to men they might not have considered otherwise. No proof was offered against the poor girls, but it never seemed to matter. Their seasons were over.

Certainly, nothing they were accused of was even close to what I have actually done. The thought made Emerson shiver as she worried over Lathen's words from last night. *'It is imperative that no one sees you leaving here. Hopefully, no one saw you enter.'*

No one could prove the Willoughbys started the rumors, but Lady de Clare suggested they had. She also assured them the *ton* would never dare to try such a thing with any of her girls, because the Duke of Windemere, and their family's powerful friends, would protect them. Though she reiterated the need to use caution around them, just to be safe.

They had not been at the tea long before Emerson saw Millicent Willoughby approaching with a practiced smile. She came over alone, without her mother or any of her friends. It was unusual to see her without her armor.

"Lady de Clare, Lady Haven, Miss Atwood," she said with exaggerated politeness and a small nod of her head, lacking warmth in her eyes or tone, "it is so wonderful to see all of you."

The three girls stood, responding in kind as Millicent approached Leighton and sat on the chair's edge beside her. Curious, yet cautious, everyone sat as well.

"Lady de Clare, I am especially glad to see you! It has been far too long. You have grown up so much since last summer. How is your family, dear?" Millicent kept the smile overwide on her face and leaned forward, touching Leighton's arm with a false familiarity.

"My family is quite well," Leighton responded graciously before a mischievous glint came to her eyes and she continued, "though, I suppose what you are really wondering is how my brother, the duke, is doing. Am I correct?"

Millicent stiffened and pulled herself upright, but she kept her smile in place. Her face pinched and cheeks went blotchy with the effort, making her nose look even more pointed than usual.

"I am uncertain what you mean m'dear," she responded with the same syrupy tone.

Leighton let her own smile fall, and she simply tilted her head to one side and stared at her knowingly. Silence stretched between them awkwardly.

"Well, if you ladies will excuse me," Millicent finally added tautly, "I shall leave you all to your tea. Perhaps I will call later in the week."

After she rose stiffly, she went back to join her group, and Leighton could not help but let out a soft snort of derision.

"I understand ladies wanting to go after my brother, both for his title and his handsomeness. After all, it is rare to find the two together," she giggled a little, "but usually, most ladies at least try to hide their natures better when they attempt to use me to get close to him."

"I agree. That girl reminds me of a snake winding through the grass, just waiting to strike," Hazel responded quietly.

Emerson nodded with her own agreement, though with some concern. Even now, Millicent, her mother, and their friends shot furious glances in their direction, their heads bent together in a whispering huddle.

It would not do for them to set their sights on us.

The French girl was also looking their way, seemingly uneasy, like she felt uncomfortable about whatever was being said. It made Emerson wonder why she was sitting with the Willoughby ladies at all.

Surely, she and her grandmother must know the Willoughbys are dangerous to be around. She is far too pretty for Millicent Willoughby to not feel threatened, and she has no connections to save her.

Yet Emerson quickly dismissed the whole occurrence, as Lady de Clare and Lady Sutcliff approached them from the other room, and all three girls rose to give a proper curtsy.

"Lady Sutcliff," they murmured respectfully in unison.

"Oh, such beauty and youth," Lady Sutcliff clasped her hands gleefully to her slight chest. "It is brilliant to be in the company of those on the cusp of everything wonderful in life!"

"I agree," Lady de Clare smiled affectionately. They sat down to join the girls, and a servant rushed over to serve them tea from a silver-plated cart.

The conversation was lively. Mostly about past gossip from when Lady Sutcliff and Lady de Clare were young and even turned full circle to involve the current season.

The girls mainly just listened, afraid to interject and have the conversation stop. To them, it was shocking how many scandals the two women knew about. Stories of stolen kisses. Young girls of their acquaintance who ran off to Gretna Green to marry their beaus, without waiting for banns or a special license! At one point, Emerson heard something, making her straighten and listen intently.

"I saw Willoughby's youngest was over here," Lady Sutcliff wrinkled her nose as though she smelled something spoiled. "I will never forget what *she* did to get her beau to marry her all those years ago."

Lady de Clare murmured agreement, but her shifting in her chair showed the topic's discomfort. Before she could change the subject, Lady Sutcliff continued, unaware.

"Of course, now her daughter is out this season and is trying to climb the same ladder as her mother. They want a lofty title and will not be satisfied with less than an earl. It annoys her mother endlessly her daughter is a miss, not a lady." She snickered and added too much sugar to her tea. "It is necessary, I suppose, for I believe her elder brother is a friend of Molly, and I doubt there will be another Lord Willoughby." She looked knowingly as Lillian lifted a lace gloved hand over her mouth to cover a gasp.

Emerson did not understand, but from behind her she heard Hazel gasp softly as well.

"Lady Sutcliff," Leighton interjected after sensing her aunt's discomfort, "can you tell me of your end of season ball? My aunt and brother have finally agreed to let me attend since it is so close to my birthday. I am very excited!"

The conversation was successfully steered away from the current gossip, but Emerson was still feeling anxious. Lady Sutcliff's stories confirmed just how entrenched the *ton* was in everyone's lives, and how sometimes mere hints of impropriety could lead to one's downfall.

It is always for the young lady, never for the gentleman! A flush came to Emerson's face at the thought.

If a single stolen kiss could lead to a lady being compromised, she could only imagine what would happen to her if anyone learned of her involvement with Lathen, or how she had gone alone to Nox House. Likely, even the de Clare family's power could not protect her from ruin if it got out.

Emerson looked over once more to where the Willoughby ladies were sitting. A shiver ran down her back at the venom and whispers still coming from them, and she had to force herself to look away.

Hazel is right, it is time to finish my husband hunt, before it is too late.

chapter twenty-four

While Emerson was getting ready for bed, Mrs. Jaymeson came in to say goodnight. After being at the tea party all afternoon, she had come home and stayed in her room for the rest of the evening, so she had missed seeing her governess at dinner.

"Are you still feeling poorly, my poppet?" Mrs. Jaymeson's voice was gentle as she came up behind Emerson while she was brushing her long hair in front of the mirror. They locked eyes, and it took much of Emerson's strength to not break down and cry again. Unlike with Hazel, whom she could confide in, she knew everything between herself and Lathen would shock her governess too much.

One must keep secrets. No matter how difficult they might be.

Instead, Emerson smiled brightly as Mrs. Jaymeson took the brush from her hand and continued to work through her curls. She closed her eyes, letting the simple moment take her back to the first time Mrs. Jaymeson brushed her hair, when she was still a child. It was comforting after the last few days.

"Oh, Mrs. Jaymeson, I am well," though she sighed heavily and let her shoulders fall. "But I am quite tired after the last couple of months. I never realized how much thought it would take up inside my head. So many gentlemen have come calling, but I am uncertain if I like them, let alone want to marry any."

It was an honest statement, even if it was an incomplete one.

"I know, poppet. Making the right decision for a husband is going to take effort, though you should always be ready in case he finds you first. I remember my Arthur," Mrs. Jaymeson's voice caught for a moment, and she paused her brushing to look up to the ceiling. "He was such a proud man. He asked me to marry him at the first dance I went to when I was barely sixteen! The very night he met me. Can you imagine such a thing?"

Emerson gasped as she watched Mrs. Jaymeson in the mirror.

"Did you say yes?"

"Oh, heavens no! My father would have skinned him alive if he had gone to him then." But she kept smiling softly at the memory and resumed brushing absentmindedly.

"When did he finally ask your father for your hand?"

"Well," she began, then hesitated with pursed lips, as if she was wondering if the story was too much to tell her young charge. Then she shrugged and grinned. "It took another year of him making certain to come to every dance or party I got invited to. He also went to church and sat in the pew behind us every Sunday. My father was quite a devout man, you know." Her grin widened, eyes sparkled, before she finished. "But really, it took him stealing a kiss outside of the town hall, and my father catching us."

Emerson locked eyes with Mrs. Jaymeson in the mirror. She could tell the older woman was nervous revealing this story. To be fair, if this conversation had happened several months earlier, Emerson likely would have been shocked.

Now, she just giggled and asked, "Was it a good kiss at least?"

Mrs. Jaymeson chuckled heartily, stopped brushing Emerson's hair, and sat beside her.

"Why yes, poppet, I believe it was! If nothing else, it helped me to understand he was the right choice for me. I knew then I never wanted to be kissed by anyone else."

Emerson's breath caught. Mrs. Jaymeson's words hung in the air, heavy with unspoken meaning, as if she was hinting at something. She was staring hard at Emerson's face, searching for an answer.

Does she know about what Lathen and I have been doing? But no, that made no sense. Only Hazel knew. *And Lathen, of course. Not that he would tell anyone.*

Yet, it was clear Mrs. Jaymeson was encouraging her to make a choice. As Emerson had already come to the same conclusion, she only smiled back at her.

Perhaps I just need to try a little harder. She thought of several gentlemen who had hinted they would like to go to Lathen and request her hand. She had yet to encourage any of them.

This did not include gentlemen who had gone to Lathen on their own. After much thought about it, Emerson realized she was grateful the duke had thrown those particular gentlemen out on their ears.

Gossip had taught her they were social climbers or looking for a fortune to help pay off debts. Or both.

But I will be damned if I let him know! Especially now.

She knew it was time for her to choose from the remaining gentlemen who still called on her. She would simply pick one and tell Lathen he needed to give his approval.

He said he wanted me to get married to someone else, after all. 'As soon as possible.' Those were the words he used.

Mrs. Jaymeson's hints and Lathen's outright demands for her to marry notwithstanding, she was going to give herself the rest of the month to decide. She had been thinking about it all evening, but her governess gave her a new idea.

Maybe I should at least kiss someone else before I decide. After all, Lathen is the only man to have ever kissed me.

The thought stayed with her after Mrs. Jaymeson left, and she struggled to fall asleep. She kept trying to decide which prospect she felt the slightest attraction toward.

Who can I see myself kissing? Touching? Making love to for the rest of my life? Or at least until I have a child.

None of the gentlemen fit the bill. Of course, there was Lord Farnsworth. She had already thought of kissing him once before. She remembered sitting close to him and really seeing him for the first time. After everything she had experienced with Lathen, the idea of kissing Lord Farnsworth was suddenly unappealing, but she would consider it. She yawned, rolled over one last time, and finally fell asleep.

Lathen came to her in her dreams again.

Lathen, without his shirt, his muscles casting shadows in the firelight.

Lathen, with his hair mussed and his head thrown back in his passion.

Lathen, with his amber eyes flashing, commanding her to open her legs for him... *'It is too late to be shy now,* Nyx.'

chapter twenty-five

"Och, Lathen, ye are nae paying attention," Greyson grumbled.

He was right.

They were playing cards at White's. It was not their favorite club, but it was the most popular with the men of the *ton*, and appearances must be kept. However, Lathen's mind was on other things. His hand kept drifting to his pocket and twisting around the soft white material of Emerson's ruined underwear. He had taken them the other night when she was still sleeping. He did not want to consider why he had kept them in the first place, or why he had not at least put them in the lockbox with the other pair. Instead, he put down another card by rote rather than following suit.

"Sorry, Grey. My thoughts are..." Lathen shrugged one shoulder before continuing heavily, "...elsewhere."

"Shall I make a guess tae where?" Greyson smirked with a wicked glint in his eyes. "Or rather, wae whom?"

"I would much rather you did not."

Lathen was not in the mood to be dragged by his friend, especially not in front of the other gentlemen at the table, who were both studiously staring at their cards, but were obviously listening. To convey this point, he casually tilted his head to them while Greyson watched. They had known each other long enough for Greyson to understand Lathen's aversion to gossip.

After they lost their bets and left the table with their pockets several guineas lighter, there was no way for Lathen to avoid talking. Greyson led him to a quiet corner with two fingers of scotch, folded his tall form into one of the leather overstuffed chairs, and leaned forward expectantly.

"Well," he began quietly, "spill it, my friend. Whatever has gotten yer knickers in such a bluidy twist."

It was not a request.

Lathen considered for a moment, then he sighed in resignation and sat down as well. He knew Greyson was the only person in the world he could talk to about what was going on with Emerson, but there was also a chance his friend would not understand. It was not about compromising a young, innocent girl. Nor about carrying her torn panties in his pocket. Greyson would merely chuckle and ask for details. Greyson believed if a woman deliberately chose to be alone with a man, she chose to be compromised. Except Lathen was messing around with Emerson, their dead friend's little sister.

If the roles were reversed, and someone was meddling with Leighton...? Lathen knew they both would kill any man who dared to so much as look in her direction, let alone someone who had touched her the way Lathen had Emerson. *I suppose I must grasp the nettle and hope it does not sting too much.*

Lathen explained his problem. Quietly, to avoid being overheard in the club. Of course, he omitted salacious details and certainly would not mention lacy undergarments, knowing he would never hear the end of it. When he was done, he leaned back and waited.

Greyson stared for a while before breaking into a wide grin and loud guffaws, turning several men's heads. "Here I have been worried ye have been avoiding the club because yer tadgers gone soft, but ye have been rolling in yer scratcher with Kit's sister!" Greyson added through his laughter, slapping the arm of his chair.

"Shush," Lathen glanced around, glaring to ensure everyone turned away from them. "Grey, keep it down, for Christ's sake. The last thing I need is for someone to overhear. Besides, I have not exactly taken her to bed. The girl is still a virgin, and I have no intention of changing that. Ever."

Greyson sobered, absorbing the information, and set his glass on a nearby table. Then his eyes widened.

"Wait a bluidy moment! Are ye saying yer not going tae marry the lass?"

"Lady Haven is..." Lathen drifted off, looking toward the ceiling as if seeking answers from the heavens. "Well, she is unique. Singular. There is no one quite like her and she deserves someone who can see her rarity and treat it as it should be. To love *her* as she is, rather than trying to change her into more of the same. You know, perhaps better than anyone else, why I could never love her the way she deserves."

"We are nae of us entitled to love," Greyson responded softly, "We can hope fer it. Perhaps give it and pray it is returned. Maybe ye and Lady Haven could—"

"No!" Lathen cut him off abruptly, the finality in his tone obvious. "I cannot, I tell you!" he still added, then pursed his lips and leaned back in the chair as though he was done speaking on the matter.

Greyson frowned and shoved his hand through his hair. Just as Lathen had guessed, he was upset at the idea of Emerson being used by anyone without being protected by marriage. It was the same battle Lathen had been having with himself for the last few months. Truthfully, it had been two years since he first felt tempted by her, but he did not feel like explaining to Greyson. At least he had done the right thing then.

"Ye have tae stay away and get the lass a proper husband, ye ken?" Greyson declared matter-of-factly, still scowling.

"Damn it. Yes, of course I understand. I have done my best to stay away from her. I even thought about leaving and heading for our India property until the girl is married. Unfortunately, with this Marien problem, I must keep close until the chit is dealt with."

They both knew the problem Marien represented. Lathen thought he had taken care of her, as she had been on the continent ever since Kit's death. They wished they could have handled her differently, but decided that night the best way to protect Emerson was to send Marien away. Lathen spent enough money to ensure she would never return.

Yet here she was, in London, again. Lathen wished he knew why, but unfortunately, he did not. The night Emerson followed him to Nox House, he was obviously distracted and could not question Marien. Then somehow, when Lennox and Greyson had taken her away, she had jumped from the carriage and disappeared down an alley, and into the busy London traffic before they could stop her. Lathen had hired men searching for her ever since, to no avail.

The priority was to find and deal with Marien before Lathen could leave town, but there was still the matter of what to do with her once they found her.

Perhaps I should take her to India with me and settle her there with my steward. It would be much harder for her to get back from there than from France. Though the idea of being trapped on a ship for months with Marien disgusted him.

Greyson nodded soberly as though he understood the enormity of the Marien problem. Then he grabbed his glass and took another deep drink.

"Lathen, are ye sure ye cannae keep the lass?" he tried once more. "I mean, after Marien is dealt with, once and fer all, there is nae reason for ye tae not have a wife and some bairns."

Lathen snorted, dismissing Greyson's suggestion as absurd.

"You know I cannot. My needs make it impossible. Nor do I have to do so. After all, I have Lennox to carry on the family legacy and name. He may be irresponsible, and he is certainly taking his time sowing oats, but at least he does not have my problem. When the time comes, I am certain Aunt Lillian will bring him to heel. Or I can always tighten the purse strings."

Greyson stared back, pondering, his face passive. He had his own reasons for not marrying, but Lathen had nothing to prevent him, at least none

Greyson deemed valid. His friend had a dark past, but a kind soul. He deserved to have someone.

From what he heard, Emerson seemed the perfect woman to complement his friend. Lathen had obviously kept the more sordid tales to himself, but it was obvious to Greyson she was not a cold fish like so many of the ladies of the *ton*. She was also not afraid to stand up to him. Perhaps she was the woman who could fulfill his friend's needs and make him happy.

'She is unique. Singular.' Lathen's words came back to him. Greyson had never heard him talk of any of his mistresses in such a way.

He had never met the girl himself, but he had often heard of her spirit and character from Kit when she was still a child. Later, after their friend's death, Lathen regularly mentioned her in letters, sometimes more than Lennox or Leighton. Usually, he wrote about her escapades and how she frustrated him, but hidden in his words, Greyson always believed Lathen was extremely fond of her. All this only confirmed his suspicions.

Greyson decided to let the topic rest for now. It was not worth the argument as Lathen had always been intractable in his beliefs. Pure stubbornness. However, if their best friend's sister could be a proper match for Lathen, it was the best solution. At least in Greyson's opinion.

He liked this idea better the more he thought about it and could not help but wonder if there was a way to help the situation along.

Maybe just a small push. He tilted his glass back and finished the last swallow of his scotch. He was nothing if not a planner, and he felt one forming in his mind. *Perhaps matchmaking is nae my specialty, but I cannae see how it could hurt.*

chapter twenty-six

The season always went on, even if some might wish for it to slow down. Or cease altogether. This evening, nearly two weeks after Lady Sutcliff's tea, the entire de Clare household was full of energy and excitement. It was the night of the Royal Masquerade Ball. Even Leighton was going, though only because Lathen was also attending. After all, one does not decline an invitation with a royal seal, and this invitation had listed them all by name.

The de Clare staff had been rushing about the entire week, making certain each member of the household had a matching domino and cloak, and completing any last-minute errands to ensure everyone's attire and person were perfect. It was a point of pride for everyone, from the lowest parlor maid to Giles, for the de Clare family and their houseguests to present well to the royal family.

Hazel and Emerson spent the entire day getting ready in their rooms. Now they stood in front of a large mirror in astonishment. Alice, their maid, had worked wonders. Artful twists pulled their hair up and trailed in long curls down their backs. Their ballgowns, specially made by Madame Delphine for this event, fit them perfectly. The masks they wore added a bit of mystery and drama to their excited faces.

"Wow," Hazel breathed and smoothed her hands over her middle. She had never looked prettier.

"You are spectacular!" Emerson grinned.

"Me?" Hazel pushed Emerson's shoulder playfully. "Every gentleman will trip over themselves to get in your circle tonight! I will do my best to push the fops out of the way, though."

Emerson blushed. She knew her friend was trying to help. In the last weeks, Hazel had been true to her word. She had stuck to Emerson like stamped wax, going everywhere with her, and keeping track of every man who came near. As Emerson had predicted, Lathen was not one of them, and she was beginning to worry Hazel was spending too much of her time trying to help her, and not enough time with her own suitors.

"Hazel, I appreciate your concern, but perhaps we can both take a break tonight." She gave Hazel a hug to soften her words. "After all, it is a masquerade, and no one will know who we are."

"Oh, fine," Hazel grinned, her rosy cheeks brightening her blue eyes, "but only if you promise to have fun, too."

Emerson put a hand to her heart. "I swear."

"All right then, but I suppose we should get going, or we will be late, and Lady de Clare will come clucking her tongue at us."

"Yes, that would not do!" Emerson tried to look serious, but her face broke into a wide smile.

Hazel squeezed her hand, and they left, gathering their skirts as they descended the steps. Both de Clare brothers were waiting at the bottom. For the first time, Emerson took notice of how outwardly alike they were to one another. With black domino masks and matching coats, and their dark hair similarly styled and swept back, with bronze highlights flashing as they turned, it was quite difficult to distinguish between the two of them. They were the same height, with wide shoulders and narrow waists fitting trim breeches, their polished black boots reflecting chandelier light.

Lennox's eyes lit up as he spotted them, a grin spreading across his face, and Emerson immediately knew which was which, despite their resemblance. She realized Lathen rarely smiled, at least not as she noticed.

Well, that is not exactly true. He smiled at me the first time we danced!

Before she could delve into the thought too deeply, Lennox came forward to grasp both of her hands. His eyes swept downward, taking in her royal purple velvet dress and her matching satin mask and cloak. For the first time, the girls wore bold colors instead of pastels usually signifying their unmarried status.

"Em, you look simply breathtaking," he said and glanced quickly over at Hazel. He seemed fascinated by her sapphire satin gown and mask. It took him a moment before he continued with a softer tone, "You both do."

Emerson again saw the connection between her two friends. In the last months, she had noticed how Lennox gave Hazel many subtle gestures and looks when he thought no one was paying attention. It always ended there. Of course, he continued to go to most of their functions, but he almost always disappeared to play cards and drink with the other gentlemen. Occasionally he would deign to dance with other ladies, but never with Hazel, or Emerson for that matter. He spent the rest of his free time out around town, at his club or at parties with his own friends.

I guess he prefers spending time with men and likely women we have never met. Probably because they are a bunch of rakes and scoundrels, and lightskirts. Just like Lennox. She sighed inwardly. *Oh well, I suppose it was too much to hope he could be reformed.*

"Stow it, puppy," Lathen interrupted Emerson's thoughts, looking sternly at his brother. Then he came forward as well. "But he is correct. You both look incomparable."

Emerson felt her breath catch. All it took was Lathen's deep voice, and she felt the now familiar tightening in her lower belly and wetness pooling between her thighs. She closed her eyes and, instead of darkness, she saw Lathen as he was the last time they had been alone. Naked, with firelight moving over his tanned skin.

She heard Hazel murmur a thank you to both brothers for their compliments, and she shook her head to clear it. When she opened her eyes, Lathen was staring at her knowingly, as though he could read her mind. Emerson's cheeks reddened.

Joyful laughter came from up the stairs, and Emerson tore her eyes away. Leighton and Aunt Lillian were coming down. They both wore beautiful new gowns. Like Emerson and Hazel, Leighton was in a colorful, long dress for this ball. Until now, her dresses had not only been lighter colors but were the shorter dresses of childhood as well. It was obvious she was taking full advantage of her chance to leave them behind for the evening.

She had pinned her long auburn hair halfway up, displaying curls falling past her back. It looked phenomenal when combined with her rich green satin gown and bejeweled venetian mask.

Lathen circled his sister twice and stared down at her sternly. In brooding silence.

"Well, my dear brother," Leighton finally demanded with a teasing tone and a precocious smile, "are you not going to do the gentlemanly thing and compliment us?"

Everyone knew Lathen was having a hard time with the idea of his little sister growing up, but they did their best to hide their laughter at Leighton's pertness. Even Giles, who was waiting near the door, had to look away and clear his throat.

"Well, kitten, you definitely look charming." He glanced at Lillian in her fitted dark grey gown and matching mask. "Of course, Aunt, you do as well." But as he looked back at his sister's low-cut gown, he continued severely, shaking a finger at her. "Remember, you are to stay close and only dance with myself or Lennox. No one else!"

Leighton let out an unladylike snort and rolled her eyes as she answered him.

"Yes, Your Grace, I understand your decree," she gently mocked. Then her face broke into a grin, because nothing was going to dim her enthusiasm. She knew being allowed to go to the ball tonight was a boon, regardless of whether she could dance all night.

After all, she would see many of the same men around next season, without the pressure. Besides, she was serious about already knowing who she wanted for a husband. A few balls would not change her mind. She did not need Lathen to loosen his rules.

"All right, you two," Aunt Lillian tsked affectionately, "let us be off. Or else we will be late!"

After Lathen and Lennox donned their cloaks and everyone checked to ensure their masks were secure, the party exited through the door Giles held open, making their way to the large de Clare coach. With six of them, they were not using the smaller carriage, but it was still a bit of a squeeze. However, everyone's spirits were high. Even Lathen seemed to enjoy everyone else's eagerness, especially Leighton's, and he managed an indulgent smile, even if he was not particularly excited about going to another ball.

The Pall Mall was already slow going. Carriages, barouches, and larger coaches lined up for over a mile, all trying to get to St. James's Palace.

"Bloody hell," Lathen murmured under his breath, "we could have walked there faster."

He was right. It was barely a half mile from St. James's Square. However, it took them nearly three quarters of an hour before their coach stopped and a footman in the King's Livery opened the door.

They alighted at an enormous two-story portico with three giant iron candelabras hanging above, lighting the space like day. Emerson was tilting her head back to take everything in, when suddenly she lost her footing as she stepped down from the coach onto the red carpet below. Lathen was there and he caught her, holding her close in his powerful arms for a moment, long enough for her to feel his warmth and shiver in response.

It was over before it began, and Emerson felt empty when Lathen set her aside once she was steady, especially since he did not appear to be affected in the slightest. It had been so long since he touched her last, even the light marks on her bottom had faded, and she almost missed the reminder they represented.

As Lathen walked away, she felt a sting of loss and was grateful for Lennox's presence. He held out his arms, one to Hazel and one to her, and led them toward the door. Up ahead, Lathen was doing the same with his sister and aunt.

Walking away from me, again.

chapter twenty-seven

Lathen handed their invitation to the chamberlain, and they all walked inside slowly. It was astonishing to Emerson and Hazel. They had been to the palace before, for their debut, of course, but they could hardly remember taking the time to look around.

This time, they took notice of everything. Gigantic crystal chandeliers lit the rooms, revealing a recent renovation, after a fire several years before. New furnishings, art, and carpets glowed. Precious royal portraits and landscapes by famous painters covered the walls. Unusual carvings, statuaries, and silk tapestries from all over the Imperial lands were placed about on pedestals and in nooks.

Those in attendance were all dressed with special care as well. Velvet, silk, and fine wool gowns of every color imaginable spilled out and shimmered across the floor, giving the impression of a broken-open jewel case.

Varied and unique masks adorned everyone. Some had added enormous feathers and sparkling crystals, precious stones, and pearls, all in their attempts to stand out in the crowd, which was ironic when one considered the object of the masque was to remain anonymous.

It was all just so much excess. The sound of the hundreds of voices lifted in excitement in the connected drawing rooms was cacophonous and nearly overwhelming, and the competing perfumes and powders made it hard to breathe. Everyone wearing intricate masks led to a feeling of anticipation and mystery, adding to the thrill of just being at the palace. Anyone could be anyone else, after all!

Lathen led their party through to the large ballroom. It was a warm night, and several sets of glass doors on the far wall were open to a stone terrace lit with tall torches. Along the other walls, gilded mirrors reflected the light from the chandeliers, and there were numerous backless couches and chairs with small tables spread about.

"There," Aunt Lillian pointed to an empty table with several upholstered chairs, "let us sit until the dancing begins."

Lathen nodded and led them over, pulling out chairs for his aunt and sister. When Emerson and Hazel came around, he did the same. But as Emerson sat, she felt his finger brush against her back, and she stiffened.

Surely it was an accident. She forced herself to relax.

Almost immediately, people began walking by, many of them taking the time to greet Lathen and exchange pleasantries with Lady de Clare.

So much for being anonymous. I suppose, even in the masks, the de Clare men are conspicuous.

It was not long before the Queen arrived with her ladies-in-waiting and one of her daughters, Princess Mary. All the chatting fell to murmurs, then to near silence, as they made their way to the dais at the other end of the room. Everyone stood respectfully, then bowed and curtsied as the Queen and the Princess passed.

Queen Charlotte wore an embroidered peacock blue and green gown, carrying a small feathered handheld mask she did not bother to raise. Her hair was pulled back, piled high and powdered, and she wore a tiara of diamonds and emeralds. Dripping from her ears and neck were emeralds, pearls, and diamonds.

The Princess was far more moderate and was wearing a simple gown of dove grey satin and a matching mask with no embellishments except for silver stitching. Having never married, Mary was her mother's constant, well-behaved shadow, and she still considered herself in mourning for her other unmarried baby sister, Princess Amelia. It was a sad, cautionary tale many mothers of the *ton* whispered to their daughters to frighten them into catching a husband. After all, if the Princess could end up an old maid, so could they.

The Queen sat down on a large throne-like chair with a flourish, leaving Mary to sit in a smaller chair positioned slightly behind her. In the last year, since her son had become Prince Regent, it should have been him greeting the peerage from the throne, but no one ever knew which functions he would attend, let alone bother to host.

So, the Queen continued to hold court occasionally, and, like her birthday ball, the annual Masquerade Ball was something she looked forward to all season. It was one of the few times she would leave her own cloistered home in Kew. She did not like to leave the King alone, of course, but some events were a matter of history. Her birthday ball, for instance. Her husband started it long ago, and she kept it going to honor him.

Unlike the debutante ball, however, this night was less formal and livelier. Attendees were not just families looking to marry off their daughters, or men looking for wives. Nor was it for the gossips looking for the next *on dit*. Instead, practically the entire *ton* was there, and then some. It was a poorly kept secret some mistresses even attended alongside wives and daughters. After all, anonymity could titillate even the most sedate of people, even the Queen.

As everyone in the ballroom watched with bated breath, the Queen gestured and murmured something to the Master of Ceremonies. He moved to the edge of the dais, squared his shoulders, and struck his large baton onto the wooden floor, and trumpeted: "Her Royal Majesty, Queen Charlotte, welcomes you all to the Masque Ball. It is her decree for the dancing to commence!"

Cheers met the announcement, and soon couples were making their way to the middle of the ballroom.

Lennox came over to Emerson with a big grin and bowed over her hand dramatically and gave the air above it an exaggerated, smacking kiss, like a cross between a courtly fop and the jester.

"My dearest lady, I once swore to you I would have the first dance, but alas, I have never managed to get my name on your card. Would you do me the extreme honor?"

Emerson blushed and laughed softly at his endearing nature. No matter how upset she was, he could always make her smile.

It really is too bad he is not ready to settle down. I still wish more for him. If only he would grow up and notice dear Hazel, she thought as she took his hand and followed him toward the ballroom floor.

Out of the corner of her eye, she saw a tall blond gentleman approach their group. He bowed and said something to Hazel, making her smile and take his hand. They soon joined them on the dance floor, and Lathen luckily accompanied Leighton, so she could dance the first quadrille as well.

They lined up in two long rows, with gentlemen on one side and ladies on the other. After everyone acknowledged the Queen, the intricate steps began with the music and Emerson smiled when Lennox came up to her and they bowed to one another, turned and circled. Lathen and Leighton were dancing next to them, and when they switched partners, Emerson felt a familiar spark as her hand touched Lathen's when they met in the center.

She tried hard to focus on the steps instead of looking at him, but to her chagrin, she kept catching herself glancing up at his masked face. The intensity of his precise movements and his dark amber gaze were difficult to ignore as they circled one another.

If she was not so distracted, Emerson might have questioned why Leighton was busy staring at a gentleman dancing several feet away. The tall man who had asked Hazel to dance, who was now turning with a lady in a canary yellow dress and a white feathered mask. They switched back to their original partners, and Emerson was glad when Lennox smiled and teased her. It was a welcome distraction.

"You seem quite far off, Lady Haven. I am sorry for being such a terrible bore!" he joked.

"Oh yes, I am practically yawning over here, from having to dance with you, my lord," Emerson replied, doing her best to keep a straight expression.

Clutching his chest, Lennox dramatically stumbled through several steps, a pained expression twisting his face.

"Oh, my dear lady, you have cut me to the quick. I am not sure I can ever recover."

Emerson was unable to resist the temptation to smile. His ridiculous acting made her giggle, showing her dimples.

Lathen stiffened when he heard Emerson's joyful laugh and glanced over as he turned again with his sister. Like he was a blind man who had the briefest moment of sight, he could not help but wish her smile was meant for him alone. During the all too brief moment, while they were dancing, he had felt a nearly overwhelming desire to pull her close and take her from the ballroom, where they could be alone.

As it was, he had been in a state of near arousal ever since he watched Emerson come down the stairs from her rooms. This was made even worse when she fell against him when she left the coach. He even had to force himself to set her down, instead of pushing her away. Or worse, crushing her closer and forgetting they were not alone. The effort of walking away from her had made him tremble.

Of course, taking her anywhere is not an option. No matter how much I might want to. But it is good to see her smile. She deserves to be happy.

Lathen forced his attention back to Leighton. She was not smiling, but her elegant dancing and statuesque beauty made her stand out. His sister was growing up and it was only a matter of time before he was going to have to worry over finding her the right husband as well.

She deserves to be happy, too.

When the dance was over, they all returned to Lady de Clare, including the tall, blonde gentleman, who was with Hazel. Up close, Emerson still did not recognize him. Luckily, Lennox obliged her curiosity.

"Lady Haven, Miss Atwood, may I introduce a dear friend of our family, Lord Warwicke."

Emerson stiffened at the name and hoped she could wipe the shock from her face before anyone noticed.

"He went to school with Lathen." Lennox continued, "but he goes out of town often, as his home is in the Highlands, and we rarely get to see him anymore. So, we are all happy he is back in town with us!"

Lord Warwicke grinned widely, showing a row of even, white teeth, and he gently took Emerson's hand in his enormous one, and bent his tall frame to kiss the air above her knuckles.

"My dear Lady Haven. I have heard much of ye. Fer many a year. I was lucky tae have been able tae count yer brother, Kit, as one of my closest confidants when we were but wee lads."

It took all of Emerson's strength to force a smile. Her cheeks ached from the effort. Seeing the face behind the mysterious Scottish voice shocked her. The room suddenly felt warmer.

Lord Warwicke was incredibly tall and even wider up close. His blonde hair was windswept and naturally wild. Perhaps it was a tad longer than was in fashion, but on him, it worked. His sea-blue eyes sparkled, even with the shadow cast by his black mask, and she could tell he was in high spirits. Overall, he was handsome in a rugged, unconventional way, fitting his accent.

If not for the unsettling memory of the first time she saw him, Emerson believed his charm and handsome features might have captivated her, but she could not help but remember him coming to Havenfield, discussing with Lathen what to do with her brother's body. She remembered he knew about Kit's death, and a desperate urge surged within her to grasp his hand, pull it to her bosom, and beseech him with all her questions from that day.

However, she had more strength than she realized. She kept all her queries to herself, smiling instead, and responded politely.

"Lord W-Warwicke," she began haltingly, "it is such a pleasure to meet another of Kit's friends. I know so little of his time when he was away at school, and I would enjoy learning more."

The music was starting again.

"Well, perhaps ye could honor me with a dance? I could oblige and tell ye some of our less loorid tales." Greyson grinned and held out his hand.

chapter twenty-eight

Emerson could not believe her good fortune. Perhaps she could ask her questions after all. She took Greyson's hand, smiling up at him.

As they passed Lathen, she noticed a deep scowl on his face. He directed his displeasure not toward her, but to his friend.

Perhaps he is worried Lord Warwicke might tell me something he does not wish me to hear? The thought ignited a fire of determination within Emerson. She would use every feminine trick she had ever learned, especially over the course of the season, to persuade Lord Warwicke to give her the information she wanted. *Flirting is certainly not an art I do well, but if ever there was a time for me to try, it is now!*

Greyson had her full attention as he clasped her hand in his much larger one and placed the other at her waist. The orchestra swelled, filling the hall, as he led her through a waltz. His touch felt a little odd to her at first. It was not the discomfort she usually had when dancing the newer waltzes with strange gentlemen, and certainly not the heat she had felt when dancing with Lathen. It was something in between. Pleasant, yet novel.

Of course, there was some physical awkwardness. His imposing height forced her to tilt her head back quite far for her to see his face, making her neck ache. At such an angle, fluttering her lashes and smiling coyly seemed almost ludicrous.

As if sensing her discomfort, Greyson smiled and leaned down to whisper softly to her. "I used tae let Lady Leighton stand on my toes when she was a wee bairn. I suppose it will nae do here." His eyes sparkled with amusement as he lifted the hand from her waist for a moment, gesturing to the royal ballroom.

Emerson's anxiety lifted, and she could not help but laugh out loud at his comment. His irreverent teasing reminded her of her brother. It made sense these two would be friends. Then, she remembered herself. Even though the masque was a less stuffy event, she realized she needed to guard herself more. The *ton* would still gossip for much less than a simple laugh.

"Shame on you, my lord. Now everyone here is going to wonder what we are talking about!"

"Aye. But let 'em gaff. It is good fer their sour complexions." Greyson let his head fall back as he chuckled and reflexively squeezed her waist before leaning back down. "Enough about them. I believe I owe ye some stories of yer brother. Did ye know we all first met when he and His Grace were in a scrap? I had tae hold the eejits back so they would nae get flogged by the headmaster fer fighting their first week at Eton."

"No!" she exclaimed. "I cannot believe it. I mean, I can believe it of my brother, but not of the duke. He is always so..." Emerson searched for a way to explain what she meant, while still being polite.

"Stodgy?" Greyson's eyes twinkled as he suggested without such worry.

"Well, I was going to say proper, I suppose. But yes, we shall go with stodgy," she finished with a grin that showed off her dimples again. "What were they fighting over?"

"Well, if I remember correctly, it was about ye. And Lady de Clare. The younger, of course." Greyson said with some obvious discomfort, as though he was embarrassed to explain further.

"Lord Warwicke," Emerson teased him lightly, "I believe you are blushing." She wanted to know more, but she did not want him to think he was telling stories she should not hear and become tight-lipped.

"Nay, lass," he smiled again, "I just dinnae think it wise tae tell ye exactly what was said. Suffice it tae say another lad made unseemly remarks, and they both took offense."

"Oh," Emerson's brow rose, "then they were not fighting one another?"

"Nae, they both tried tae take on a lad from another house. A couple of years higher, I believe. A big lout with an even bigger mouth."

So, Kit and Lathen first connected from a common incident. I never knew. It made sense, though. She knew both were protective, especially of their sisters. She still wondered what the other boy had said, but it was obvious Lord Warwicke would not explain.

"You all became good friends that day?"

"Aye, and every day after," he told her proudly. "The three of us were inseparable. Of course, yer brother and Lathen bonded over their pride. I suppose they first kept me 'round because I was bigger than most of the boys in year three, and I could knock heads wae the best of 'em. Wae yer' brother's mouth, it definitely helped!"

Emerson laughed again. She could not help it. Greyson's witty comments reminded her of her brother's sharp tongue and sarcastic humor. It was also something she struggled with over the years.

I guess it runs in the family, not knowing when to keep our thoughts to ourselves.

"I do wish I knew more of him during that time," she said with an expectant note. "He was gone much of the year. Except when he came home during the holidays, of course."

"Aye, that was always verra' important tae him. I remember I would usually go back with His Grace to Windemere fer the holidays. It was much closer than going to my *clachan*. Kit was always welcome tae come as well, but he wanted tae go home. Tae ye."

A deep ache resonated in Emerson's heart. As a child, she was resentful of her brother always being away at school, and of the friends he had made. After all, any time he was there, he was not with her. Now she was grateful he had those friends. She could not imagine her life without Hazel.

"You went to Oxford with them as well?" she asked.

"Aye, I did. Though neither yer brother nor I were the students His Grace was. I imagine we did nae have the same expectations forced upon us as Lathen." Greyson lifted his gaze to the ceiling as though he were sifting through memories. "We spent much of our time mad wae it."

Emerson lifted her brow again at his honesty, gratitude nearly overwhelming her.

Perhaps he will continue telling me the truth.

"Lord Warwicke…" she began tentatively before finishing in a rush, "were you there the day Kit died?" She knew he was. Or at least he had helped to bring his body home, but she assumed he was ignorant of what she had witnessed.

Greyson did not respond right away. As the last movement of the waltz was coming to a close, she thought he might not answer her at all. The music ended, and the dancers shuffled away, but Greyson held Emerson for a moment longer before pulling away, a sudden awkwardness filling the space as he cleared his throat and averted his gaze.

"Aye, lass. I was." It was so soft it was nearly lost in the vast ballroom.

chapter twenty-nine

Greyson grabbed Emerson's hand, this time firmly, and led her back to the area where Lady de Clare, Lathen, and Leighton were all still waiting. Hazel and Lennox must have been off dancing as well.

The closer they got, the deeper Lathen's scowl became, etching into his face like a stone carving. Leighton also appeared unhappy, but she at least had the grace to hide it better.

Emerson could not be concerned with them. She feared she had pushed Lord Warwicke too far and he would simply return her and leave. Then he would not have to answer any more of her questions. Fortunately, once they were standing in front of Lathen, he turned to her instead and grinned. He looked totally unbothered.

"Well, that was verra' lovely, Lady Haven," he said cheerfully, though a little overloud. "I wish I could keep on blatherin', as I have so many more wild tales to tell ye! Perhaps I can call at de Clare House this week, and we can reminisce more about that time. What say ye, Your Grace?" he asked Lathen raucously while clapping him on the shoulder for good measure.

"But of course," Lathen answered dryly. His scowl vanished, replaced by an intense gaze making Emerson feel like he could read her thoughts.

For her part, Emerson was busy comparing Lathen and Lord Warwicke. When they were standing right next to one another, it was easy to see their differences. It was not just their coloring or because Lord Warwicke was so tall. It was also their personalities. Lathen's seriousness contrasted sharply with his friend's affable, almost reckless attitude. Even the way they stood was different. Lord Warwicke's limbs were loose, and his hip was cocked to one side, with his hand in one of his pockets. Lathen's back was straight and proud, as though the Queen was standing before him.

Emerson found Lord Warwicke's nonchalant demeanor charming, but a powerful, almost irresistible pull from Lathen kept drawing her gaze back to him. Like a rope connecting her to him, the pull was getting tighter with each breath she took. The feeling was palpable, surprising her no one else could sense it.

Still, she longed for a way to keep Lord Warwicke from leaving them, without raising suspicion. Maybe she could dance with him once more, and hopefully, talk again.

It was Leighton who managed this. She walked up cheerfully and stood next to Lord Warwicke, before laying one of her hands on his arm familiarly.

"Well, Lord Warwicke, the next song is soon to begin, and I am only allowed to dance with my brothers," she grinned cheekily before directing the next to Lathen, "but perhaps my brother will give an exception for you?" Lathen nodded his approval, but kept his gaze trained on Emerson.

"Ah, lass," Lord Warwicke bowed to her and held his hand out in a flourish, "I would be honored." Then he added in a teasing tone, "Though I suppose yae will nae longer be needing tae stand on my toes like ye have done fer many a year?"

Leighton gave a low husky laugh, a bit out of character, and took his hand. As he led her away, she lowered her voice so only he could hear her.

"I assure you, my lord, I am grown and can now stand on my own."

Emerson knew it was unlikely she could avoid dancing with Lathen entirely, but as the first notes of another waltz began, reminding her of the only time they had ever danced together, she silently wished he would not ask her now.

No such luck, dammit.

Lathen did not even bother to ask. Instead, he gripped her hand and pulled her to the dance floor, joining with all the other couples seamlessly.

It was both difficult and simple to dance with him. Difficult because he once again held her a hair's breadth too close. It was not inappropriate, but close enough to make breathing difficult. Yet it was simple, his expert leading allowing her mind to wander as she followed effortlessly.

"Do you want to tell me what is going on in that head of yours, Emerson?" Lathen leaned down and whispered in her ear.

She knew he was reading her, but she assumed he would keep his thoughts to himself after their last encounter.

"Not really."

I will keep my own thoughts. Thank you very much.

"Not really?" Lathen's golden eyes flashed in irritation. Obviously, he was not onboard with Emerson evading him. He leaned down enough to look her directly in the eye. His irritation charged the air between them, an electric pulse she felt even through her mask.

His annoyance did not bother Emerson. It gave her a small thrill. *At least he is facing some of the maddening frustration I have been experiencing.*

"Your Grace, I appreciate your concern, but I think after our last..." she chose her next words carefully, "...conversation, it is best I figure out my life on my own. Without you." The last was said firmly. She wanted to mean it.

Lathen lifted his brow, as though he was not used to anyone standing up to him. Emerson always enjoyed challenging him, but she usually felt timid when she did. But this was different. She felt empowered.

"Emerson, I know you are upset," he began evenly, "but I thought you understood I still want what is best for you."

"Then why do you turn away every gentleman who asks you for my hand?"

"I told you before. They were not worthy of you."

Emerson turned away thoughtfully. *He never explained to me why none of the men were acceptable. Just that they were not good enough for me.* After learning more about them, she knew she had missed something with each of them, things he saw clearly. That realization gave her an idea.

"Your Grace, perhaps we should take this from a different perspective. Maybe you can give me a list of all the men you know who *are* worthy of marriage, and I will pick one of them? Perhaps Lord Warwicke would suit?"

Lathen did the unthinkable and missed a step. It was minor, and perhaps no one else in the room noticed, but Emerson did. Ironically, she only threw Lord Warwicke in as an afterthought. She was not seriously considering setting her cap for him. She barely knew him.

"Very well," Lathen recovered, his answer succinct. "I will see what I can do."

He scowled again, clearly disliking the idea of Emerson being attracted to Lord Warwicke. She took a bit of perverse pleasure in the knowledge.

What else can I say to bother him?

Emerson smiled smugly but did not keep prodding him. The unexpected hint of jealousy from Lathen, or at least the possibility he was capable of such, was a small, but significant step. It might not work, and perhaps was not the right direction, but she found satisfaction knowing Lathen struggled, too.

chapter thirty

Leighton was enjoying her waltz with Greyson. It was their first dance outside a family party, unlike those when she was a young girl in short dresses with lace flounces, her long hair tied with ribbons. Everyone was right. She had grown quite a bit in the last year, nearly four inches, but for the first time she was grateful for her height, because she now seemed to fit into Greyson's arms perfectly.

Much better than Emerson or Hazel! She thought bitterly, before feeling a bit guilty. It was not as if either girl had done anything wrong. *They do not even know.* She suspected both girls would keep their distance if they realized her claim on Greyson Warwicke. *However silly it might be to anyone else!*

Since she was twelve years old, Leighton knew she wanted to marry Greyson Warwicke. One day, while visiting Lathen, he became her champion, saving her from boys teasing her height and thin frame. They had surrounded her while she was in the village, shouting things like *'fawn legs'* and *'pussy willow.'* Greyson had walked up, cuffed one of the boys on the ear, and threatened to wallop them all if they ever bothered her again.

After they ran off, he sat with her, hugging her as she cried. She was feeling miserable, and tired of being awkward, but Greyson told her not to worry. *'Dinnae fash yerself lass. Those bluidy eejits are going tae kick themselves one day when they realize how pretty ye are.'* Her tears dried, heartache vanished, and she knew he would be her perfect husband. She had even told him, while he was still holding her.

Yet he laughed, tugged on one of my curls, and said he was honored. It was obvious he was only indulging me.

Leighton knew it was not malicious. Greyson thought of her as a child, after all, with a child's feelings and affections, but the memory stuck with her, and it still stung. Now, five years later, she was more than ready for him to see her as a woman.

If only I did not have to wait for another year to really show him.

"Well, lass, I must say ye dance rather well these days," Greyson said good-naturedly.

Leighton simply smiled back. The familiar condescending tone he used, just like her brothers', grated on her nerves and she longed to correct him. Instead, she shrugged in a rather unladylike manner and swallowed her response.

He will see me soon enough!

But he continued.

"And yer hair looks lovely, all done up," he smirked, gently tugging a curl, as he did years ago. "But I have to admit I miss the pigtails, lass."

It really is too much!

Leighton took a deep breath, to cool off her temper, before she smiled serenely and answered him just as the final chords of the waltz drifted off.

"Well, my dear Lord Warwicke, these days I only wear the braids in my bedroom, but you are more than welcome to come and see them for yourself. If you are brave enough."

With that smart retort, Leighton turned on her heel and made her way back to her family, leaving Lord Warwicke behind. It took everything she had to not turn and look back at him. Just as she had returned safely, she could not resist. He was still standing there, looking utterly stunned, with his jaw hanging open. Staring at her. A giggle escaped Leighton's lips.

Hopefully, he will now see I am grown.

She would have taken great pleasure in continuing to flirt with Lord Warwicke for the rest of the evening, but it was not long before she realized he had disappeared from their company entirely. Leighton kept the ache of missing him to herself. Her brothers would never approve.

chapter thirty-one

After Lord Warwicke and Leighton danced, Emerson watched with disappointment when he turned and walked away, instead of coming back.

Well, there go my answers, she thought wryly.

Leighton returned by herself, obviously in high spirits. After her own dance with Lathen, Emerson felt uncomfortable standing next to him, still acutely aware of their conversation, and she wished Hazel was with her. Unfortunately, her friend had not yet come back from her last dance.

"I think I will go search for Miss Atwood," she leaned down and whispered to Lady de Clare, hoping Lathen would not try to accompany her.

"All right, my dear. I believe she is over there." Lillian waved toward a nearby refreshment table. As usual, she was doing her duty and keeping a close eye on everyone.

Emerson smiled gratefully and walked away. Though she felt Lathen's eyes trailing her, he did not follow. She found Hazel drinking a glass of punch and talking with Mr. Brown.

That gentleman certainly is constant. As she approached, Emerson tried to look at him objectively, but she simply could not see him as a proper match for her friend, and she hoped Hazel could see it as well.

She is too special for such a boring man. Everything about him is as his name implies... Brown! Dreary! Dull! He is practically unnoticeable, if not for his stutter. Although, even in his fancy togs and a mask, I can still tell exactly who he is because he is still so boring. I suppose the adage is true: You cannot make a silk purse out of a sow's ear. As soon as her unfortunate thoughts were finished, Emerson felt ashamed. She knew Mr. Brown was a perfectly nice man, and he would likely make a good husband for some lady, she just wished for more for Hazel.

Emerson took a glass of punch from a footman in livery and white gloves and waited. As soon as it was polite, she leaned close and whispered that she needed to go to the ladies' dressing room. It was the easiest way to pull Hazel away.

Inside, Emerson finished first and was busy looking in a large mirror and tucking a few stray wisps of hair back in place when a dark-haired woman in a daringly low-cut and shockingly red velvet dress approached her. She stood behind Emerson, leaning into the same mirror, though others were available.

"I love your gown," she caught Emerson's gaze.

Emerson was about to thank her politely and leave, but the other woman continued.

"Did I see you dancing with His Grace earlier?"

Emerson was used to strange women coming up to her recently. When one was the ward of a wealthy duke, she supposed it was to be expected.

At least I do not get as many offers of false friendship as poor Leighton does.

"I suppose," Emerson answered vaguely. She again patted her hair and continued to watch the woman to see if she recognized her behind her mask. Something about her made Emerson uncomfortable, and even though she still felt the urge to walk away, her curiosity made her stay.

"I used to know His Grace, too. Very well." The stranger continued, softly, so no one could overhear, and she smirked knowingly. Her overfamiliarity was irritating. "Although I knew a friend of his much, much better."

"Oh?" Emerson's continued curiosity made her ignore her annoyance.

"Yes, perhaps you knew of him?" the woman paused, and her eyes bore into Emerson's in the mirror, "Lord Haven?"

Emerson gasped and turned immediately to face the other woman. She reached for her arm and gripped it with both of hers.

"Wait, you knew my brother?"

The woman sneered, and she yanked her arm from Emerson's grasp as if her touch was distasteful.

Emerson's mind was spinning, and her tightly pulled stays were suddenly making it hard to breathe. She could swear the woman was enjoying her distress, her eyes brightening maliciously behind her mask.

"Oh, yes, my *lady*," Emerson's title came out insincere, and the woman laughed again. The sound was distorted and unnatural.

"As I said, I knew him extremely well. We were close for several years. I was there the night he died."

"Wait, what is your name?" It was a desperate question, even to Emerson's ears.

Just as Emerson recognized the woman's green eyes, and the small scar near her hairline, as belonging to the same beautiful woman who had tried talking to her at the dressmakers, she answered.

"Marien."

The room spun, heat pressed in, and the strange woman's face blurred as shadows took over.

chapter thirty-two

Emerson's eyes fluttered open to Hazel patting her on the cheek and an anxious washroom attendant waving a fan over her. She blinked, trying to bring focus to her hazy vision.

"W-what happened?" she stuttered, confused.

"I do not know, darling," Hazel answered worriedly as she took Emerson's hand and squeezed it gently. "I was coming out of the water closet and saw you faint. Perhaps from the heat. It is awfully warm in here tonight."

In a rush, everything came back to Emerson, and she lifted her head to see if the woman who called herself Marien was still there.

She was not.

With gentle hands, the attendant and Hazel carefully helped Emerson to her feet. After regaining her composure, Emerson took Hazel by the elbow and whispered to her about what happened and the strange woman.

"A scarlet red dress?" Hazel asked and looked around, searching the dressing room.

"Yes, like a bright ruby. She had pinned up dark hair. Not as black as mine, though. She has a small scar on her temple and wore a black mask with small red feathers on one side." Her words sounded desperate and hurried as she tried to remember every detail.

"I think I saw her leave." Hazel looked pensive. "But honestly, Em, I do not remember seeing her before. Such a bright red is a daring color to wear. It would be noticeable, even tonight."

"Well, the evening has only just begun, so let us both be on watch for her. Hopefully, we can find her again, and get her to talk," Emerson said, still feeling rattled. She was not prone to fainting, but it was the second time she had done so recently. The last was with Lathen, and she did not want to think about it. This was different. Marien's sinister countenance, unnoticed during their first meeting, now stood out. The memory alone made her head spin again, and she had to grab onto Hazel once more to steady herself.

Emerson wished she could have continued her conversation with Hazel, but their discussion was interrupted by Miss Willoughby and her friends entering the dressing room, chatting noisily. They came to a sudden halt when they realized there were others in the room. Millicent Willoughby had her usual haughty stare as she took in the attendant, who was still hovering and fanning Emerson.

Emerson and Hazel shared a knowing glance. Then, without saying another word, they gathered their skirts and left.

chapter thirty-three

Late into the evening, the ball continued. Drinks were flowing, and the ballroom got ever louder with laughter and good cheer. If their minds had not been focused elsewhere, all three girls would likely have enjoyed themselves. As it was, they all danced nearly every dance. There was no end to young gentlemen congregating near their party to claim their hands. Lathen even relented at one point and let Leighton dance with other gentlemen, mostly because he was tired of her constant requests for him to accompany her.

Yet he still watched her, and Emerson, the whole time. Closely.

Near midnight, Emerson saw Marien again. She was dancing with a gentleman she was sure she knew, though he was doing his best to disguise his voice, quizzing her on who he might be. She was playing along, smiling coyly, when a flash of bright red drew her attention from outside, on the wide stone terrace.

Emerson stumbled back from her dance partner and immediately searched for Hazel. Her friend was only two couples away, and luckily, she had also noticed the woman. She confirmed this by nodding matter-of-factly toward the door, just as Emerson did.

"Good sir," Emerson began to the gentleman who was waiting awkwardly in front of her, "I do hope you will excuse me, but I believe my friend needs me. The heat..." she murmured vaguely and drifted off, barely hearing his stammered protests.

Hazel met her at the open doors to the terrace and hooked her elbow through hers. If anyone were to take notice of them, it would appear as though the two ladies were simply going out for some fresh air.

"Did you see where she went?" Hazel leaned close to whisper.

"Only that she walked to the left."

The only thing in that direction was a set of wide stone steps leading down to the garden. Emerson knew it was not exactly improper for the two of them to go for a short walk together, though it would be much better if they had an escort. Though the physical reminder of Lathen's punishment might have faded, she was very aware of what choice she was making.

Just as he said I would be. Emerson shook her head to clear it.

"I suppose, since it is a masked ball, we can claim it was not us if anyone says we ran off to the palace gardens," Emerson said firmly as they descended and went through a manicured break in the hedgerow.

With a quiet "Yes," Hazel agreed, and together they stepped toward the dense bushes. It was not long before they realized the hedges were not just a border, but an entrance to a maze. The shrubs were tall and thick, and they could not see over to the other side or how deep the labyrinth went.

"Perhaps we should go back and wait until she comes out?" Hazel suggested nervously.

Emerson was not about to let Marien get away again. She had been waiting for years for answers about her brother. Obviously, Lathen would never tell her anything, except Kit fell from his horse. Lord Warwicke did not seem inclined to talk about the subject either. Lathen thought he was protecting her by keeping the knowledge from her, but she was determined not to let him stand in her way this time.

Her decision made, Emerson squared her shoulders and turned to Hazel. "Listen, Hazel. I must go on," there was a slight waver in her voice to betray her own apprehension, "but I would completely understand if you wished to go back." After all, it was not fair to let Hazel get into trouble as well.

"Oh, bother," Hazel scoffed and waved Emerson's words off with her hand, "if you go, I go. It really is simple."

Emerson hugged Hazel tightly and, once again, felt gratitude for having someone she could trust so completely. Together, they grasped their kid-gloved hands and went deeper into the maze, until they came to a split. They stood there for a moment while looking both ways, deciding what to do next.

"You go left, and I will go right," Hazel finally announced confidently. She was always the most logical of the two. "Just make certain to not go too far and pay close attention so you can find your way back!"

Emerson agreed, though she felt her anxiety continuing to build in the pit of her stomach as she walked alone. She swallowed, shoving it down, since it was not something she could worry about at that moment.

Hopefully Lathen will never find out!

She did as Hazel suggested, saying out loud to herself, "right...left...left...right..." so she would not get lost. Before long, she realized she had gone far enough and would be better off going back.

As she turned around, it was apparent the maze was more complicated than she had realized. Nothing looked familiar and she continued forward frantically, the feeling of uncertainty gnawing at her with each step. She stopped at a cross of paths she could not recall passing. Her breath was coming in quick gasps, and she only had one thought on her mind. *Marien must be here somewhere!*

In front of her, she heard a twig snap and heavy footfalls approaching rapidly.

chapter thirty-four

Hazel took deliberate steps. At each cross, she turned right, repeating the entire way back to herself. As she prepared to return, worried about Emerson, she overheard loud whispering around the next corner. Hazel slowed, inching her way closer. She did not dare go around the hedge, but she got to where whoever was talking was just on the other side.

"So, you spoke to her?" The bitter murmur of the man's voice was unfamiliar to her. Yet she was certain the refined London tone belonged to a gentleman.

"Yes, but the stupid chit fainted when I told her my name." The woman must be Marien. Hearing her friend being referred to so crudely, Hazel clenched her fists.

"But how can she know you? I heard that bastard de Clare has kept knowledge of you from her. He keeps her so sheltered, it is impossible for anyone to reach her. This is why I sent you!"

He knows more about Emerson and His Grace than a mere stranger. And he does not care for the duke. But who is he? She tried to get a little closer, wishing she could see through the thick hedge.

"Well, I know nothing about it, but she went pale and dropped to the floor. I can only imagine she knows something. Her tatty blonde friend came out just then, so I could not wait around and tell her to meet me as you asked."

"Well, I suppose it might be time for me to get more involved. I will think of a way for her to get the message, hopefully without de Clare's knowledge. Perhaps the girl knowing of you could be helpful."

"As long as I get what I am owed from the bitch, I care not how we do it!" From her hiding place, Hazel heard the malice in her words, and it frightened her. She shivered and backed away quietly, not wishing to be discovered by them.

Silently, Hazel worked her way back. She was nearly where she left Emerson, when an arm came from behind her, lifting her off the ground, and a hand smothered her cry before it could escape.

Hazel knew what could happen to a young woman out at night alone. Even in a palace garden. She fought fiercely, her heel striking someone's shin, her elbow jabbing a thickly muscled chest.

Her attacker let out a muffled "Oof," before she heard a rough whisper in her ear, "Stop! Miss Atwood, it is me!"

Hazel recognized Lennox's voice instantly, her body sagging in relief as he let her slide down his chest.

When her feet touched the ground, Hazel twisted out of his grasp and, without thinking, smacked Lennox's cheek. His head did not turn, but his eyes widened in shock. Unfortunately, as she was wearing kid gloves, it was not as satisfying as it should have been.

"How dare you scare me, my lord," she accused him with a cross glare. "I thought you were attacking me!"

"Shh," he placed hands on her shoulders to calm her. "I was trying to stop you from going around the corner, and I need you to be quiet. There are people from the masque just on the other side of this hedge, near the main exit. You are not supposed to be here alone. Especially not alone with me." The last was said in a chastising tone, which sounded odd coming out of Lennox's normally irreverent mouth.

He is right. Hazel knew it would not take much to ruin her. She had neither fortune nor a title. If she were compromised, even from an innocent mistake, no one would hesitate to spread the rumor to the *ton.* Not even being sponsored by the de Clare family could protect her.

"Well, I was in there with Emerson. We have never seen such a labyrinth, so we went exploring. Unfortunately, we got confused and separated." It was a small lie, but the story of Marien, and why they were really in the maze, was not her truth to tell. Especially not to His Grace's brother.

"Yes, Lathen saw you two go inside. He is in there, looking for Emerson now. We just need to wait until he finds her, then we can leave together. Hopefully, no one else noticed you leaving." Even in his whisper, he still sounded admonishing.

They lingered quietly, Hazel doing her best to ignore him. She had to admit it bothered her Lennox found her. If it was His Grace, she would not be so irritated. Yes, she would have been anxious if it was the duke. He still scared her a little.

But Lennox is like a naughty child who caught me doing something, and now pretends he is more responsible than I. The idea grated on her nerves, but she tried to let it pass.

Minutes ticked by, and after finding their exit was still blocked, Lennox glanced down with a determined gaze. "I think we should go back inside the labyrinth. We can sneak back into the palace, through another way I know," he quietly explained to Hazel.

"You know of another entrance to the palace?" Hazel asked, amazed as Lennox led her back through the maze. It was obvious he knew exactly where he was going. He was practically running in his haste, not even hesitating when they reached a split or turn.

"Well, yeah," he looked over his shoulder to answer. He smiled sheepishly and explained, "My sister and I used to come here and play when we were children. With Princess Mary. I usually just explored the grounds while the girls played with dolls and such."

Hazel stared at his back in wonder. They really were from different worlds. He played with royalty as a child. She spent her childhood in her father's small study, with her nose in every book she could find. She did not even have someone she considered a friend, beyond her imaginary ones. Not until Emerson, of course. It was unfortunate as she found Lennox to be kind, charming, and exceedingly attractive.

Oh, well, she thought wistfully, *it is not as if he is interested in me. Plus, he is a rake. Any woman he marries will always wonder which bedroom he is in.* She worried she was trying too hard to convince herself.

Unaware of Hazel's thoughts, Lennox quickly led them to a hidden exit in the hedge, out to a vast kitchen garden. From there, he found an open door into an enormous kitchen and pantry.

Inside, several female kitchen servants and a buxom cook chattered away while they worked to put hundreds of small sandwiches and cakes on platters. Silence fell as they looked up with curiosity at the two interlopers.

"Hello, you lovely ladies," Lennox said charmingly, while standing right in front of Hazel, blocking her from their view. He leaned over and took a tiny fruit tart and popped it into his mouth in one bite.

"Oh, yummy," he grasped his stomach and gave an exaggerated groan, "these are simply fantastic. I wish I could steal from the Queen and bring you all home to feed me! Thank you so much for all your hard work, ladies."

Hazel rolled her eyes. All the women simpered under his words and his magnetic smile. Even the cook, who was old enough to be his mother, blushed and batted her eyes at him, and handed him another fresh tart, which he took gratefully.

After he ate the sweet, they left, with Lennox looking around every corner. When they finally entered the ballroom, Lennox immediately joined a gavotte already in progress. He spun Hazel around and grinned down at her, winking.

"Well, I guess we got away with your lark," he puffed his chest with pride. "Though I suppose I should remind you again to take better care," he added with a bit of cheek. Being the irresponsible scoundrel was his normal routine, so trying to sound stern was not exactly his forte. He seemed to remember this, and his eyes sparkled with humor.

"Well, yes, my lord. You are correct, but I did not intend to end up all alone out there. As I already told you, Lady Haven and I were separated by accident." She answered stiffly, still worried for her friend. Now that Lennox had moved from chastising her to teasing her, she found she was even more annoyed and frustrated at having to explain herself again.

What is the use? I could elucidate further, but I cannot understand it for him! She swallowed her retort, realizing Lennox would probably not see the irony in his statements.

Hazel remembered the first time she saw Lennox, when they were children. Even then, he was misbehaving, sneaking around somewhere he was not supposed to be. Though he had not noticed her, and she had told no one what she witnessed, not even Emerson. Admittedly, she had only seen him because she was also where she was not supposed to be, and this was why she had always kept the secret.

He has not changed much since then. Lennox spent much of his free time running off, often where he should not be, and avoiding any kind of responsibility. His aunt was always bemoaning having to chase him down or remind him of his obligations. *So, who does he think he is to tease me or tell me how to behave? He is a casuist, through and through!*

Lennox flashed his roguish grin at her and added an extra couple of spins to the dance, making her giggle. Hazel mentally shrugged, realizing it was pointless to stay angry with him.

"By the way, the ringing in my head has finally stopped. You have quite the left hook, Miss Atwood."

Hazel gasped as he mentioned her striking him. She looked at his face and saw a slight reddening on his tanned cheek. She felt bad for a moment, until she saw his mischievous look.

"Well, my lord, I am certain you have had worse," she told him primly, before adding, "Certainly, you have deserved more, at one time or another." Hazel could not help herself, though she regretted it almost immediately.

Oh. My. Goodness. That was forward.

Lennox barked out laughing. She obviously amused him, and he leaned down to answer her so no one else would overhear.

"Oh, my dear Miss Atwood. I have indeed had worse, though I am not sure if I have ever enjoyed it more."

What is that supposed to mean? Hazel blinked in confusion.

The music ended, saving Hazel from having to answer. She nodded pertly, and they went back to where his aunt and Leighton were sitting. Several older ladies had joined them, including Lady Sutcliff.

She is perhaps one of the biggest gossips in the ton! Hazel mused to herself as she looked around.

"My dears, there you are!" Lady de Clare exclaimed. Hazel did not see Emerson or Lathen anywhere. She hesitated to respond to Lennox's aunt while others could hear, so she did not ask about Emerson.

Lennox leaned over and whispered in his aunt's ear. Hazel could tell by the look on Lady de Clare's face something was wrong. It was the sudden smile giving it away. A bit too wide, and not quite reaching her eyes. To her credit, though, she held it together in front of the other ladies.

Another reason Hazel knew she did not belong. She was about to lose her mind over her missing friend and could not stop herself from wringing her hands and shifting from one slippered foot to the other, while her eyes scanned the dance floor.

As Hazel was doing her best to hide her own panic, a palace footman walked up, with a note for Lady de Clare. She skimmed it and kept the same smile in place as before, but she waved up to Lennox and whispered back to him when he came close. Hazel knew she could not ask what was going on, not in front of Lady Sutcliff or the others, but fortunately Lennox soon came back over and leaned down to whisper reassuringly in her ear.

"All is well, Miss Atwood, so you can stop your fretting. My brother took Lady Haven back to de Clare House. She had a terrible headache. He will send a carriage back for us." Lennox grabbed two glasses of Regent's Punch from a servant walking by with a tray. "Here, drink this," he murmured as he handed one to Hazel.

Hazel took it from him with a grateful nod, and felt her shoulders relax, but only a little. She was glad to know Emerson was no longer alone and lost in the maze, but her brow furrowed with apprehension at the thought of Emerson and the duke alone.

Damn and bother! It was my responsibility to keep them apart.

She also kept that information to herself. Taking a cue from Lady de Clare, Hazel forced a smile as she took a small sip from her glass, the citrus brightening her tongue before the Madeira and brandy burned, trickling down her throat. Lennox watched her, his eyes twinkling as if anticipating a grimace at the strong liquor, but she was not about to give him the satisfaction. Instead, she took another deep swallow and brightened her smile.

Huh. Perhaps I could fit in after all.

chapter thirty-five

Emerson's heart hammered against her ribs, a frantic rhythm she felt in her ears. The crunching of heavy boots on the gravel grew louder. It was definitely not Hazel, as her soft slippers would never make so much noise.

She turned in a full circle, looking for a place to hide until whoever it was passed by, but there was nowhere to conceal herself. There were only rows of well-manicured, dense hedges, with marble benches and statues placed in tiny alcoves every so often. She was standing at a crossroads in the maze, with shadowy paths going in all four directions. Lost and unsure of the approaching person's direction, she worried any path would trap her further in the maze, and she might never find her way out.

So, she stood there, paralyzed with indecision, until it was too late. A tall, dark figure rounded the corner behind her, making her whirl around in fright, realizing they had already seen her.

"Emerson!"

She visibly sagged in relief when she recognized Lathen growling angrily at her. She ran to him.

"What do you think you are doing out here? Can you imagine if someone else found you?"

Lathen was furious. He had thought when Emerson snuck out of the house, and he had punished her, she would have learned her lesson. He trusted she was just stepping outside for some air when he saw her leave the ballroom with Hazel. When he realized they were not returning, he went to the terrace, found it empty, and felt completely shocked and betrayed.

If anyone else discovered her, she would have sent tongues wagging for the whole week. Or worse, if someone hurt her! The very thought made him shake with fury. He grabbed her upper arm and practically dragged her toward the nearest exit.

Now that he was with her, he was less worried about her being seen. Yet, in his chest, the fear over her safety lingered, making him tense and on edge, and he decided it was best they not return to the ballroom. He could not stomach the idea of more dancing and the inconsequential chatter of the *ton*.

"Where are we going?" Emerson demanded as she tried to keep up with his longer strides, practically tripping on her long train when she could not keep hold of it.

Lathen ignored the question. Irritated by his silence, Emerson did not ask him again, and other than a feeble attempt to pull her arm from his grasp, she did not try to stop him. She instinctively understood it was not the time to push, not with the heat of his anger rolling off him like flames from a fire, and not with nearly every member of the *ton*, including the Queen, inside the ballroom, now close enough to hear a French gavotte.

They left the hedges from a different place than Emerson had entered, and Lathen took her inside the palace through a side door leading safely past the ballroom. Although the music continued, she saw only the King's liveried footmen stationed at intervals down a long hallway. They were doing their best to ignore Lathen practically dragging her past them.

He came to a sudden halt at the end of the corridor, causing Emerson to run into his back. Lathen barely noticed, other than to steady her as he pulled her to his side. He turned to a young footman, the man's face paling visibly as the duke spoke directly to him.

"Do you know of Lady de Clare? She is over by the large painting of waterfowl, to the left of the dance floor."

"Y-yes, of course, Your Grace," he stammered and bowed.

Lathen dropped Emerson's arm and took a small leather notebook from the inside pocket of his formal waistcoat and jotted something down with a pencil. He tore off the paper, folded it, and handed it to the nervous young man.

"Please take this to her straight away."

Then, still without looking at Emerson, he grabbed her arm again and kept walking toward the exit and over to the colonnade, where they were originally let out by their coach.

Once there, they were not alone. Other couples were drifting out from the masque and were already waiting for their carriages. Lathen still had to send for theirs. Emerson knew it was probably a bad time to reason with Lathen, but she guessed he would not make a scene. Lightly, she touched his arm with her free hand, her other arm still clasped in his.

"Please, Your Grace," she whispered, "would you let me go? I promise not to run off."

"As if your promises mean anything at all," he snapped, but Emerson could tell he was softening when he relaxed his grip. She supposed it would have to do.

They waited in silence. Emerson was without her cloak, but she did not wish to suggest going back inside for it. Yet as the cool evening air drifted over her skin, she shivered. Lathen noticed, shrugged his own coat off, and draped it over her shoulders. A gasp escaped Emerson, but she accepted it wordlessly. As angry as Lathen was, his consideration surprised her. The warmth of his jacket eased her tension, and as she took a deep breath, the delicious smell of new leather, cedar branches, and fresh sea air surrounded her. She closed her eyes at the memories it evoked.

When the de Clare coach finally arrived, Lathen gently lifted her in as the footman opened the door. Instead of joining her immediately, he went to the front to murmur something to his driver. Then he climbed in and sat across from her. Emerson was feeling relaxed and thought, maybe, Lathen was ready to forgive and forget. As the coach lurched forward, she glanced up and met Lathen's intense gaze.

All is not forgotten. Or forgiven.

chapter thirty-six

Lathen glared back at her. He was still wearing his mask, and the shadows cast from the passing lamps on the Pall Mall made him look sinister. His silence made the noise of the hooves and wheels over the cobbles overloud. It did not take long before Emerson felt the need to fill the void with an apology.

"Your Grace, I am so—"

Lathen raised his hand, cutting her off as he yanked off his mask, threw it across the coach, and continued to glower. Clearly, he was not ready to listen. Emerson sat back and returned his stare, deciding she could wait him out.

After all, the drive back to de Clare House will be quick. His temper matters naught when there is little he can do about it. At least for now.

It soon dawned on Emerson the trip was taking far longer than it should have. She turned and lifted the edge of the curtain, but she did not recognize the houses they were passing by.

"Where are we going?"

Silence was still his only answer, and Emerson felt her own anger rise. Yes, she had done something foolish, but she had a good reason, and he would not even hear her explanation or apology.

"Fine! Do not talk to me then. Just tell the driver to take us back to de Clare House this instant!" She shouted at him as she stripped off her own mask so he could see her frustration. She was tired of his heavy-handed demeanor, refusing to be intimidated.

Still only silence. Though Lathen lifted his brow in a mocking response.

My anger is nothing but a bit of amusement to him! Emerson's face went red and, with no thought beyond the moment, she bared her teeth and flew across the coach with her nails in claws, ready to scratch his eyes out.

She never reached him. Lathen easily grabbed her wrists, turned her, and fell against her, pressing her onto her back against his seat with the weight of his chest.

"Careful, *Nyx*," he smirked down at her, his face so close Emerson swore she felt his lips brushing against hers. He shifted to the side to give himself some distance. "You should sheath those talons before someone gets hurt."

"You, I hope!" Emerson cried through clenched teeth. It made her livid he was calling her by the name he used when they were intimate. She jerked her arms, but his hands were like vices, keeping her in place.

"Really? *You* wish to hurt *me*? How interesting."

"Yes, I want to wipe that smug look off your face!" Emerson continued to struggle against his hold, grunting with the effort, but it was useless. He held her tight until she got tired, her breath coming in heavy draws.

Lathen was stunned. And turned on. Never had a woman been so angry at him. It was a novel, exciting experience, and if he was not so furious with her, he might have taken the time to explore the idea.

However, this was not the time. As her guardian, Lathen knew he needed to deal with Emerson. Again. She was constantly doing things could get herself hurt, not just compromised, but physically hurt. He needed to make her understand, once and for all, it would not be tolerated. If she wanted to go into the maze tonight, all she needed to do was ask, and he would have gone with her.

Or perhaps I would have asked Lennox to go, so she could not tempt me. But it is irrelevant. She went in with only Hazel and somehow got lost. By herself! He felt another surge of fury at the idea and closed his eyes to control himself.

When he opened them, he looked down at Emerson. Her hair, a tangled mess of curls and waves, had fallen in disarray around her shoulders. Her slight bosom was heaving after all her efforts. So much so her low-cut gown could barely contain her taut breasts, and the shadow of her rosy nipples were peeking above the decolletage.

Around her neck was the ribbon choker with the midnight pearl he gave her at the start of the season. He remembered seeing it in the window of a small shop on Bond Street as he walked by, the day after her return to London. It had reminded him of Emerson's confused eyes after he had almost kissed her, and he had felt compelled to go inside and purchase it, perhaps as an apology for his behavior. He had not given it to her then. He held on to it for nearly a month, and even sent a servant to find another, for Miss Atwood, so he could give them both as gifts for their debuts.

With sudden wonder, Lathen realized he must have waited so the necklace would seem less important than it was, because seeing her wear it now pleased him deeply, despite his frustrations. He let go of one of her wrists so he could reach down and touch it.

He immediately regretted it.

Emerson was not done. He missed catching her before she connected her closed fist to his cheek.

"Damn it, you hellcat," he snarled and grasped both her small hands in one of his. He then went behind her neck to untie the bow of the necklace. Emerson struggled even harder, baring her teeth and screeching, once she understood his plan to restrain her with the ribbon, but he was too strong and determined. He swiftly rolled her onto her stomach and secured her wrists at the small of her back. Then he flipped her over again, trapping them under her.

"You bastard!" She spat up at him.

With a dark chuckle, Lathen leaned back in the other seat to admire his handiwork. A lock of his burnished hair had fallen forward, and he took the time to push it back, roughly.

"Emerson, you are just too stubborn and reckless for your own good," his voice was softer as he lifted his hand to trace her face. Now that he had her under control, his anger eased, and he felt immense pleasure at seeing her restrained. He leaned over to kiss her gently.

And barely avoided her trying to bite him!

"Ah, *Nyx*," he chuckled and soothed his thumb over his lower lip, "only you would bite the one who feeds you, and I doubt you would even regret it."

Emerson kept glaring. She was still half sitting, half lying on the coach seat, and her legs were slightly askew. Lathen looked down and saw part of her velvet skirt was twisted and already raised to her knee. He decided to help with what she had started and raised it the rest of the way. To her hip.

"Lathen!" Emerson sounded desperate and resumed her struggles. "We agreed. You do not want to marry me, and I do not want to be with someone unless they wish to marry me."

But Lathen knew her resolve was fading. It was the catch in her breath when he touched her cheek, the way her nipples were already stiffened and begging at the edge of her gown, and most damning of all, as his fingers drifted up her leg, past her loose undergarment, he found the wetness of her desire at the juncture of her thighs.

He lightly skimmed her core with one finger and asked, as her hips were rising for more, "Are you sure, *Nyx*?"

When Emerson did not answer him, Lathen slipped two fingers under her lace underwear, and entered her roughly, making her gasp and arch her back.

"I asked if you really want me to stop. Because I will, if you ask me to."

Despite being lost, Emerson managed to shout an answer.

"No! Please, Lathen, do not stop!"

Leaning down, Lathen kissed her again. This time Emerson returned his kiss with all the passion that had been anger just a few minutes before. She sucked wildly at his tongue and bit his lips, but in a way that made him moan back at her and press even closer. He continued to enter her with his fingers while using his thumb to draw small circles around her bundle of nerves, driving her wild.

Emerson struggled to pull her arms free again, this time so she could touch Lathen. She longed to thread her fingers through his dark hair, to pull him closer and bring him deeper inside her. Yet not being able to touch him also made her feel out of control and heightened the other sensations she was experiencing. The buildup was becoming something familiar to her. The tightening in her lower belly. The colors blurring at the edges of her vision. Then, just as the world was about to explode, Lathen stopped.

It took Emerson a moment to realize his hand was still, and Lathen was no longer kissing her. As her vision cleared, and the precipice seemed like it had moved far off, she looked up at him with confusion.

"What is wrong, *Nyx*?" he asked her with a low growl, but his eyes suggested he knew a secret Emerson did not.

Before she could think about it further, Lathen slowly restarted moving his hand, delving deep inside her. Deliberately, twisting his fingers so they touched some secret place only he knew of. Emerson moaned, curved toward him, and lost herself again. She was so close. Chasing the colors.

And he stopped. Again.

"Lathen!" she cried in frustration, lifting her hips, twisting, desperate to finish.

His free hand touched her face, brushing stray hairs from her dampened brow. He leaned forward to kiss it almost tenderly, before asking her again, "What is wrong, *Nyx*?"

This time, Emerson was clear-headed enough to realize passion was not moving Lathen the same way it was for her. Even though she could see his manhood pressing against his breeches, his eyes showed only icy determination.

"Lathen, why?" she whispered up to him. "Why are you doing this?"

Instead of answering her, Lathen moved his hand again. Emerson desperately fought to remain impassive, as he was. She tried to steady her hips, clenching her thighs to still his hand.

It did not work. Lathen knew just how to touch her, and where. His other hand dropped to the bodice of her dress, and he tugged gently, to lower it below her breasts, just as he leaned forward to take the tip of one inside his mouth. He teased it gently, maddeningly, swirling his tongue around the nipple. Her thighs soon loosened, and her hips again tilted to meet his hand. She was so wet and ready for him that it was almost excruciating.

She screeched, enraged when he once again stopped. Lathen lifted his head and clucked his tongue at her.

"Can you imagine what it feels to have someone promise you something, over and over, only to have them go back on their word?" His voice was light, almost indifferent, but his eyes burned with a blazing amber fire.

When Emerson did not answer him, Lathen took his smallest finger and went even lower, near her bottom. Her eyes flew open.

Surely, he does not mean to touch...there!

When she still did not respond, Lathen leaned down and looked Emerson right in the eye.

"Well, do you?" he asked again as he slowly made small circles around the tender tissue he found. It felt forbidden. Dark. But it also nearly sent her over the edge.

"Ahhhh," she threw her head back, and a garbled scream came out as he stilled his hand yet again. "Please," she begged, sobbing from her need.

"Answer me, Emerson. You are a smart girl. Why do you keep defying me?"

"I do not know!" Emerson finally cried out desperately, needing him to end what he had started. Lathen's hand moved again as sweat trickled down her back. She kicked off one satin slipper while thrashing about.

Then dark, desperate pleas began to come out of her mouth, begging him to take her...to fuck her...hard. To make her come.

Words she never would have known how to use before reading the book and listening to Lathen when they were last together.

Lathen still appeared calm as he stopped once more. Though, if Emerson was not so lost, she would have noticed his whole body was shaking from the effort.

Blind rage consumed Emerson when she drifted back down. She understood he was doing this on purpose. He was not going to let her finish. *This* was her punishment. He would not hurt her, but as far as Emerson could tell, *this* was far worse. Worse than using the riding crop on her backside. Worse than spanking her with his palm.

"Please stop, Lathen. No more!" A sob escaped as she pleaded with him, and tears fell down her cheeks in streams. Her body was on fire, twisted like heated metal. It was astounding to ache so much for something she had not even known enough about to want several months ago. As her body cooled, an empty void crept in.

Lathen stopped the moment she said those words, withdrawing his fingers. She watched through her tears as he calmly fixed her dress and reached behind her to untie her wrists. Her shoulders ached from having laid on them for so long, and she shook them out as she righted herself, looking sorrowfully at Lathen when he sat back across from her.

"How can you be so cruel?" she asked in a small voice as she wiped the tears from her eyes.

"I am cruel?"

"Yes, unbelievably so," Emerson lashed out.

"Well, I suppose you think it now, but let me ask you something," he crossed his arms, "what do you think would happen to you, to your person, if you were caught, alone, by some brute in the city?"

Emerson lowered her hands to her lap slowly. She understood his point, but she was not willing, or ready, to admit she was wrong. Not after what he just did. The coach kept going sedately over the cobbles as Lathen waited for her answer.

"No, you do not know?" he pushed, his voice impatient. Emerson turned her face to the window. "You are a bright woman, Emerson, so I will not insult you by explaining it yet again. Nor will I talk once more of your broken promises. However, I will always uphold my vow to protect you." With that, Lathen knocked on the roof near the driver and the pace of the horses picked up.

It was not long before they arrived back at de Clare House. Lathen must have asked the driver to just circle the square.

When they got out, Lathen told the driver to return to the palace for the rest of the household. He then grasped Emerson's elbow and led her inside and upstairs to her rooms, but he did not say another word to her. When he left, she slammed the door, threw the lock, and stood in the middle of the sitting room, unmoving, for some time. Her entire body felt both rigid and exhausted.

Looking down, she saw the ribbon of her pearl necklace tangled in her hand. Her fist tightened reflexively around it, before she threw it across the room, but the lack of noise when it hit the soft carpet was unsatisfying. In a huff, she pulled off her new gown, tearing several buttons in her haste, and unceremoniously left it in a pile on the floor. Mrs. Jaymeson would be disappointed if she saw it, but Emerson did not care at the moment.

Instead, she ran into her room, collapsed on her bed in her chemise and underskirts, buried her head in a pillow, and cried softly to herself. It was all too much for her to understand, but she was certain of one truth. Her body was still desperately craving Lathen.

chapter thirty-seven

The rise and fall of voices echoed up the stairwell as the rest of the household returned home nearly an hour later. Leighton's cheerfulness and Lennox's playful teasing were easily recognizable to Emerson, even if their words were indistinguishable. Hazel, however, must have rushed up the stairs, because she entered their rooms while everyone else was still chatting below.

"Em," she cracked open the bedroom door and whispered tentatively into the darkness. Emerson had yet to light a candle.

Numb and still confused, Emerson wanted to hide under her covers and vanish. She was not even sure how to tell Hazel what happened, and she thought pretending to be asleep might be the best course. But as Hazel waited, a sob broke free from Emerson and her friend rushed in and crawled onto the bed, wrapping her arms around her.

"Please, my darling, talk to me. What happened after we parted?" Hazel's anxiousness was obvious.

"Oh, Hazel, I am not sure what to say."

"Well, usually it is best to start at the beginning. We can figure it out together."

Emerson was ashamed and filled with regret. The drive home had been replaying in her mind for the last hour as she lay there, weeping silently. Sure, it still made her angry Lathen had punished her again, especially how he did it, but her mortification stemmed from her own behavior, her own words, her desperate pleas for Lathen to finish what he had started. She worried her actions were reminiscent of a common strumpet and her face flushed crimson at the memory, the bitter taste of guilt making her wish to keep what happened a secret forever.

Hazel, with her usual patience, stayed quiet and waited.

And waited.

Until Emerson could no longer help herself and told her everything. Hazel listened intently while tracing soothing lines on Emerson's arm. When she finished, Emerson expected to hear her friend's shock, but her anger surprised her. Hazel jumped from the bed and started pacing, stopping right next to Emerson, glaring, with her arms crossed.

"I simply cannot comprehend how His Grace could do something so horrid, like you are a naughty child who needs *his* correction. I have a mind to go and tell him off! In fact..." Her words unfinished, she wheeled around and made for the door.

Emerson gasped, her eyes wide with alarm, and grabbed at Hazel's skirt, stopping her mid-stride, and almost falling off her bed from the effort.

"No, Hazel, you must not!" The last thing Emerson wanted was for Lathen's anger to fall upon

Hazel. "Please…" she whispered, her sincerity unmistakable despite her trailing voice.

Hazel huffed, blowing a strand of hair from her face, and crossed her arms again. "Fine! But he better watch out, or else." She suddenly stopped, realizing there was not much she could do. "Well, I certainly have no intention of letting him be alone with you again. I am mad I let it happen tonight." She resumed her pacing, her frustration obvious.

Emerson watched, still worried about what her friend must think of her. She stared at her hands and asked in a small voice, "You have said nothing about my behavior tonight."

"You?" she scoffed. "I fail to see how anything you or I did was wrong. It is not as if something happened to us in the maze. We were at the palace, after all. I swear, I am tired of us being treated like we cannot take care of ourselves and need their protection. It seems to me, the only person you need to be wary of is the duke!"

"But Hazel, the things that I said."

"Posh, you said what you felt, what was inside your heart. I have experienced nothing like that, but I certainly hope I will someday, and I would like to think I would be unable to keep quiet, too." A smirk played on Hazel's lips for a moment before her expression turned serious, her eyes narrowing slightly. "Besides, if His Grace had kept his hands to himself, as a true gentleman should, you would never have been in that position. He walks around like a stuffed-up shirt that knows everything and controls everyone, when really, he is the person we need to keep you safe from. I am just so infuriated!" She stamped her foot with such intensity it shocked Emerson.

Is she right? Do I need to stay safe by keeping myself from Lathen? Emerson wondered.

Before, when Hazel suggested as much, she had thought it unnecessary, because she believed Lathen would keep his promise not to touch her again. Emerson remembered the disappointment she had felt at the idea.

Even though he touched me again, neither of us received the pleasure we could have. I suppose, if I am being honest with myself, that is the real reason I am so upset. So, no. I do not want to keep myself safe from him. The realization surprised Emerson.

"Hazel, I appreciate you so much. I really do." She pulled her friend back down for a tight hug. "For tonight, I think I just need to sleep. Hopefully, my head will be much clearer tomorrow."

Hazel returned her hug and stood back up to leave. As she got to the door, she paused, then turned.

"Em, just because we are women does not mean we should be ashamed when we want something. Or someone." With those cryptic words, she left.

Emerson knew Hazel was trying to help, but it did not stop her mind from running wild, going over and over the entire night, wondering what might have been, if only Lathen had heeded her desperate pleas and given her what she wanted.

I wish he had made love to me. I want him more than I have ever wanted anything else.

A sharp pang of guilt pierced through her thoughts as she realized she had completely forgotten about Marien and Lord Warwicke. It felt like she was betraying her brother's memory somehow, but as she explained to Hazel, she hoped her head would be clearer after she slept. She sighed and rolled over.

chapter thirty-eight

After such a busy night, the house was still quiet when Emerson woke, even though it was already late morning. She did not ring for her maid, instead putting on a simple skirt and blouse, ignoring her stays in favor of a light chemise, and made her way down to the orangery. She was sitting at the small breakfast table, with a cup of scalding hot tea warming her hands, staring absently into the garden, when Giles came in, carrying a silver tray. A single folded letter was on top, addressed to her in a scrawling hand she did not recognize.

"This came for you only a moment ago, Lady Haven," Giles said politely as he bent down to let her take the envelope.

"Thank you, Giles," Emerson replied with a wan smile, the best she could manage at the moment. She was still preoccupied with the previous night's events and opened the note with little curiosity. Only after reading the letter twice did she grasp its meaning. She rose swiftly, refolded the paper, and secreted it in her sleeve as she rushed back upstairs to find Hazel.

Inside her dressing room, Hazel was busy getting her hair put up by Alice, leaving Emerson with no choice but to wait. Unable to sit still, she began pacing, her restless energy a palpable object in the otherwise quiet room. For a few minutes, Hazel watched her in the mirror, before she asked the maid to return later.

"Goodness, Em, what has put such a bee in your bonnet?"

As soon as Alice was gone, Emerson pulled the note from her sleeve, practically shoving it into Hazel's hands in her eagerness.

Hazel unfolded the parchment and read it aloud.

"'To Lady H. I beg of you to make time today for a ride along Rotten Row. Take the north path at 12 o'clock and make haste to the Serpentine. I have information of great importance you should know.'"

Hazel turned the note over twice, searching for clues.

"It does not say who it is from. Who sent it?" she asked.

"I am not sure," Emerson answered in a whisper, "and I do not wish to ask Giles who delivered it, and let him know anything about the note."

Her reasoning was simple. If Giles knew what was in the letter, he would likely tell Lathen.

"I feel strongly it is from Marien, and Lathen does not want me to know anything about her. If he found out about the letter, he would never allow me to meet with her today."

As she considered the implications, Hazel chewed her lip thoughtfully.

"Perhaps you are right, but I must tell you something I learned last night as well."

In all the excitement from the masque, and what came after, Hazel went to bed without telling Emerson about the clandestine conversation she had overheard between the strange man and the woman she suspected was Marien. Emerson listened intently as Hazel explained, her hands clenching her skirt.

"Who do you think the man was?"

"I am uncertain," Hazel answered. "It was too hard to hear them as they were practically whispering, and I did not dare to catch a peek for fear of being discovered. I am almost positive it was a gentleman, however, and whoever he is, I believe we should use caution regarding them both. They were not talking of nice things."

"Absolutely, I agree." Emerson racked her brain, wondering how Marien and this strange man could know so much about her when she knew nothing of them.

"I think you are right, though. Marien knows something about your brother," Hazel continued as she put her hands on Emerson's shoulders and looked into her eyes. Then she added gravely, "But Em, she is not someone you can trust. She wants something from you and is not above wishing you ill."

Emerson nodded. A shiver ran down her spine as she remembered the malice coming from Marien when they met last night in the ladies' room, and she decided Hazel was right. She would need to be cautious.

They came up with a plan. They would go to the park this morning, as the note requested, but instead of taking a driver and the open barouche, they would go on horseback and take a single groomsman. That way, Hazel could distract him. Hopefully long enough for Emerson to continue up the north path just before noon. She would only be several lengths ahead of them. Close enough to shout if she needed help, but hopefully private enough to speak with Marien by the lake without being overheard.

They rang the bell, and in a rush, both girls changed into practical riding habits, and Alice, sensing their urgency, hastily pinned up their curls beneath wide-brimmed bonnets. When they were ready, they headed down the stairs, as it was already nearly ten.

"Oh, my! How wonderful!" A shout came from the landing above. Looking up, they saw Leighton rushing down the stairs toward them. She was also in her habit.

"You are going riding?" she asked brightly as she pulled on her brown leather gloves.

Emerson and Hazel exchanged a swift glance. Their plan would work much better if Emerson only had the one groom to shake loose, but neither could think of a reason for Leighton to not come along. At least not one that would not raise suspicions or hurt her feelings.

Hazel recovered first and smiled broadly, before answering, "Yes, to Rotten Row."

"Oh, how providential!" Leighton was happy. "I was to go there with my good friend Miss Trammel, but I only just received word she is feeling under the weather. I was hoping to tempt you both to join me instead. The morning is just perfect for a ride!"

As they left de Clare House, Emerson realized Leighton was right. While they waited for their horses to be brought around from the stables, the sun shone brightly overhead, and a light breeze scented with summer caressed her face. If not for her worries, she would have revelled in the gorgeous day, and riding through the park with her friends.

Nearly everyone in London appeared to be enjoying the park as well. Rotten Row, the wide lane through Hyde Park, was a crush. Open-topped barouches carrying ladies with parasols fought for space with gentlemen and ladies riding on horseback. All were vying for the best places to see and be seen.

Emerson was restless because they were going so slowly, and began to shift in her sidesaddle, feeling the rhythmic sway of her mare beneath her. She still had plenty of time to make the rendezvous, but she was unsure how to get free from both Leighton and the groomsman. As ideas swirled in her mind, Leighton's excited murmur startled her.

A familiar figure appeared ahead of them, causing Leighton's face to break into a wide, delighted grin. She flicked her reins to get her mare to canter, rushing to catch them.

"Lord Warwicke," she called out cheerfully and raised her hand in greeting.

Startled, Lord Warwicke turned his horse around. When he saw Leighton, he visibly flinched, and a frown creased his brow.

"Lady de Clare," he forced a smile, "how *braw* tae sae ye. Is His Grace with ye?" He looked over her head to scan the crowded lane. Instead, he saw Emerson and Hazel walking their mares towards them, and he nodded politely in their direction.

"My brother?" The idea made Leighton snort. "That would mean he pulled his nose out of one of his ledgers before tea. Very unlikely, I assure you."

Leighton glanced behind Greyson and noticed he was not alone. She tilted her head to get a better view of the pretty woman with him.

"Oh, hello there." She lifted her hand and smiled widely. "I do not believe we have met."

A hint of uncertainty crossed Lord Warwicke's face as he turned. He inhaled deeply, then turned back and began introductions as Hazel and Emerson pulled to a stop alongside Leighton.

"Lady de Clare, Lady Haven, Miss Atwood. May I present Mrs. Nichols?"

The woman in question came forward and inclined her head to each girl and murmured a low greeting, but her deep blush revealed she was uncomfortable.

"Well, we must be off." Lord Warwicke pulled his reins abruptly, but Leighton interrupted him again.

"It is lovely to make your acquaintance, Mrs. Nichols. Would you like to take the air with us?" she asked cheerfully.

Emerson and Hazel exchanged glances. Lord Warwicke and Mrs. Nichols's desire to leave was obvious. Leighton, however, did not seem to notice.

At that moment, the chapel bells around the city began to chime. Emerson knew it was time for her to head up the north path. She slowly backed her horse up, while Hazel shifted forward to cut her from the view of the others.

When she was far enough away, she turned and clicked her tongue to get her mare to go a little faster. It was not ideal, as she would now be too far from her friends if she needed to shout for them, but she reasoned there were many other people in the park and she would be safe.

Well, safe enough. Emerson fought back thoughts of Lathen and what he would say about what she was doing. *Not to mention what he might do.*

Ahead of her, Emerson saw the opening in the landscaping where Serpentine Lake was. There were dozens of people strolling and riding about, but she recognized none of them. She pulled to one side of the path and slid down her horse and then tangled her reins in a low bush to make sure it stayed while she walked toward the lake.

Emerson's unease grew as the minutes ticked by and no one approached. She was just returning to her mare, wondering how she was going to climb into her saddle without looking like an ungraceful ninny, when someone called from the other side of the path.

"Lady Haven!"

She turned quickly and let out a sigh of relief. From a shadowed thicket, Marien stood, waving to her.

Emerson walked over and stopped several feet away. From that distance, it was obvious in the daylight Marien was as pretty as Emerson had first assumed, but also older than she realized. Perhaps ten years older than Emerson.

"I am here as you requested. What is it you needed to tell me?" Emerson was brief and direct, as she knew they had limited time. Hazel could only keep everyone away for so long.

"Yes. Will you walk with me?" Marien motioned behind her, away from the path, toward the gloomy wood. Emerson had a moment of indecision. It felt wrong, but she needed to talk with Marien. It might be the only way to learn about Kit. With a curt nod, she pushed past the brush, yanking her skirt when it got caught, and followed the older woman deeper into the trees.

They continued until they were far enough away from the north path only a faint murmur of voices reached Emerson, and the figures of others walking by the lake were mere blurs in the distance. Emerson's nape began to prickle, and she felt something was wrong. She stopped, looking around, and though she did not see anyone besides Marien, she remained where she was and called ahead.

"Please, you have mentioned twice now you knew my brother. I must know how."

Marien turned with her lips pressed into a tight smile.

"Oh, yes. I knew Kit. He was my fiancé."

chapter thirty-nine

Gasping, Emerson swayed and clutched at a low-hanging branch to steady herself.

Is this possible? How could I not know something like this about Kit? She had thought she knew him better than anyone else in the world.

"I do not understand!" she finally exclaimed, "my brother never told me he was engaged. He made no mention of you in any of the hundreds of letters he wrote me, or when he came home. And he was so young when he died, barely twenty. Hardly an age for a man to look for a wife." Emerson's mind was spinning.

"We met when he attended Oxford. My father was a dean there," Marien explained. "We were young, but we fell in love. If anyone had found out, they would have sent me away, so we met secretly and told no one. He promised we would marry as soon as he finished his studies."

Emerson listened intently. There seemed to be some truth in Marien's voice, even if her words felt preposterous.

Why would Kit not tell me? Perhaps, he was waiting...

She was about to ask more questions when Marien continued, "Kit was finally ready to go home and tell his father, to tell you, and arrange our wedding, but his friends took him away from me the evening before he was to leave, and I never saw him again. He died that night."

Emerson wrapped her arms tightly around herself, as she worked to breathe. Nothing Marien was saying made sense.

If his friends went away with him, how could they have found him, as Lathen has always told me?

"Do you mean His Grace, the D-duke of Windemere? And Lord Warwicke?" her voice caught as she asked.

"Yes, of course. Those three were always together. His Grace, in particular, wished to get Kit away. He never approved of Kit marrying a commoner like me, but your brother did not care what his friends thought. He was not so pompous. He loved me." Again, Marien sounded so sure, especially when she spoke of Kit's love. Emerson felt a frost creeping over her, draining all the warmth and color from the beautiful day.

Has Lathen been lying to me this whole time? Was he with Kit when he died?

Emerson took several steps forward, grasped Marien's arm, and asked earnestly, "Wait! How did Kit die? Did he fall from his horse?"

Marien's green eyes flashed, and a chilling, bitter laugh escaped her lips.

"Is that what *he* told you?" She snorted in disbelief. "His Grace is lying to you. Do you not see?

He was part of it all. It is because of him your brother is dead!" Her voice was nearing a shout when she finished.

Emerson barely noticed. In horror, she dropped the other woman's arm and took a step back. Then another. Her head was shaking back and forth. *No, no, no!* The denial roared in her mind, as if she could make everything the woman was saying go away. Overwhelmed by pain, none of her many questions escaped her lips.

Except one.

"How did Kit die?" She asked again, barely above a whisper.

chapter forty

A furious shout came from behind Emerson, and a huge stallion came crashing through the brush.

"Lady Haven!"

Emerson turned and saw Lord Warwicke jumping off his horse and striding toward them before he even pulled to a complete stop.

Marien gasped and spun around to run deeper into the wood. Lord Warwicke crossed the distance with his long legs, seizing her upper arm before she could get far.

"Grey!" she hissed, and twisted her body. "Let me go!"

"Haud yer wheesht!" he shouted, giving her a rough shake, "and dinnae call me that! Only mae friends call me that, and yer nae friend."

Lord Warwicke then ignored the other woman and turned to address Emerson again. In his anger, his brogue thickened, and she struggled to understand him.

"Lady Haven, ye need tae go back tae yer cuddie noo'. The others are waiting fer ye tae return tae de Clare Hoose."

Just as Emerson was going to argue, Hazel interrupted, grabbing her hand, pulling her away.

"Come on, Em, we must go. Now." She spoke under her breath, but her voice was firm.

Emerson glanced behind her. Leighton had also dismounted and was watching them curiously. There was no way to keep this meeting a secret now, and Emerson realized Lord Warwicke would not let her speak to Marien.

With a heavy sigh, Emerson's shoulders fell, and she let Hazel lead her back to Leighton. The groomsman was also there, holding all their horses and, one by one, he helped lift the ladies back into their sidesaddles.

Angry, unshed tears filled Emerson's eyes, threatening to spill over. More than ever, a torrent of questions overwhelmed her mind, but she would not find any answers in Hyde Park. Not now.

While everyone else patiently awaited Lord Warwicke to come back and join them, Emerson snapped her reins and cantered away. She did not give a damn if anyone followed or who might see her riding home without an escort.

chapter forty-one

There was a moment of indecision, but eventually Hazel, and then Leighton, turned and followed Emerson. Greyson watched them go, his gaze lingering long after they disappeared. He took several deep breaths before he dared speak to Marien.

As it was, he had to loosen his grip on her arm, because the temptation to snap the thin bone was too strong. This surprised him, as he was usually very slow to anger and had never even struck a woman, for any reason.

But if any woman deserves it, it is Marien. These thoughts were not helping him calm down, so Greyson tilted his head back, letting the dappled sunlight through the leaves fall on his face, and tried to remember why it was so important to handle her in the right way.

Emerson. And Kit. And Lathen. This is all for them. My anger is irrelevant. Greyson turned back and glanced down at Marien.

"What are ye doing here, Marien?" he kept his voice even, only a slight tick near the corner of his mouth revealing his anger. "Ye know ye should never have come back tae England, and ye certainly never should have contacted Lady Haven. It was the deal ye made."

"The deal be damned," Marien sneered. "There are things I am owed. You all thought to foist me off with mere pennies and a hovel in the middle of nowhere!"

"Owed! Hell slap it intae ye, woman!" Greyson could not help but shout back at her. "Yer lucky tae nae be strung up by yer scrawny neck, ye harlot!"

Marien's lip curled in contempt. She was once a bonnie lass who could make any man look her way. Greyson remembered as much, but her twisted face and wild eyes made the scar on her temple turn white, and any resemblance to that girl was faint at best.

Her clatty character does nae help, he thought offhandedly.

"I ask ye again. What do ye want from Lady Haven?" His tone was calm, though after several moments passed without an answer, he emphasized his words with a slight shake, making Marien stiffen.

"The chit owes me," she whined. "She has everything that should have been mine!"

It took Greyson a moment to understand. Emerson had inherited Havenfield and all its wealth. All of which would have been Kit's if he was alive. In Marien's warped mind, she should have married Kit and had access to everything. There were so many reasons this was absurd, but Greyson knew it was not the time, nor the place, to reason with such a madwoman.

I need tae get her somewhere where she cannae do anymore harm, Greyson thought to himself. After a moment, he knew exactly where to take her. *Although this time I will make sure she does nae get away.*

"Come on," he was terse. Instead of bothering to answer any of her outrageous claims, he dragged her back toward the path, ignoring her straining and loud protests.

Genevieve Nichols was still waiting for him on her horse. She was a rather patient woman, but her raised brow revealed her disbelief at the turn the day had taken.

"Dinnae sae a word," he warned. "My apologies, but I need tae take care of something. It would be best if ye returned home, lass. I will be by later."

Genevieve was straightforward, modest, and uncomplicated, and she knew better than to question him. It was one of the main reasons why Greyson enjoyed her company when it suited him. Without another word, she nodded and pulled her reins.

"Your mistress?" Marien smirked knowingly.

"Cease yer blather," was the only answer he gave as he lifted her up onto his horse, mounting behind her. It was not far to Nox House, and luckily Marien was no longer trying to make a scene. Instead, she seemed like she was thinking. Calculating. Greyson could not help but notice as she turned, looking up at him.

A strange look came to her face. At first, Greyson did not realize what it was, especially since he was trying to stare over her head while she was sitting sidesaddle, and he was astride. Then Marien leaned back, lifted an ungloved hand to his chest, and slipped her fingers through a gap in the buttons to graze the warm, bare skin under his shirt.

"You know, Grey, we could always have some fun. If you need a mistress, I remember a time when we were friends. There are things I could show you. Things I have learned while I was away..." She said this breathily, while she fluttered her lashes. Greyson supposed Marien was trying to look sensual, but the very idea of being intimate with her made his skin crawl.

He grabbed her hand firmly, with a forced gentleness, and placed it back on her lap. It took all his willpower not to dump her to the ground.

The bampot dinnae even ken how much I detest her!

Greyson barely kept from grimacing and instead looked ahead stoically. The black door of the Nox House entrance was just ahead, so he only had to hold his tongue for a few more minutes, just long enough to get Marien inside and behind a locked door. Then she would be Madam Irina's problem until Lathen could be told she had been found.

chapter forty-two

When she returned to de Clare House, Emerson was more than half the block ahead of everyone else, so she slid down from her mare without waiting for the groomsman to help. It was not very graceful, but she did not care. She looped her reins over the iron fence, grasped her skirts and ran up the front steps and through the front door just being opened by Giles as she reached it.

She halted in the middle of the entry hall, breathing heavily, as she had a moment of indecision. Part of her wanted to confront Lathen right then. Her impulse was to run to his study and yell at him until he heard her. But another part of her wanted to go to her room and cry until her heart stopped hurting. Perhaps then she could think clearly.

The choice was taken away from her as she looked up to see Lathen coming down the stairs with Dog. He watched her standing in the hall and could tell she was distraught. He stopped in front of her, searching her face, and lifted a hand to brush an errant wisp of hair back behind her ear, leaving it there to cup her cheek.

It was a touching gesture she would have usually enjoyed. At any other time, Emerson would have felt a skip in her heartbeat and a flush of warmth in her body, but now she only felt a coil of anger as it tightened around her heart.

"Emerson, what is wrong?" he tilted his head and asked her gently.

Before Emerson could answer, Giles opened the door again to admit Leighton and Hazel. Lathen immediately let his hand drop and took a step back. He also lost his tender look, and his normal indifference returned.

God forbid anyone knows he wants to touch me. Or worse, he might have feelings! Emerson wanted to cry out and had to tighten her own hands into fists to keep herself still.

It was the last straw. She was tired of all the secrets. Not just about her brother.

All of it.

The touches, the kisses, the not being good enough for Lathen to make love to, let alone to marry, but just good enough for him to caress her behind closed doors and in darkened carriages. If it was all in secret, of course.

"We need to talk, Your Grace. Right this instant!" She practically shouted, before poking Lathen in the chest and rushing away, down the hallway, toward his study. Emerson did not care if she was ordering around a duke, or if anyone overheard her.

When she reached Lathen's study, she shoved open the heavy oak door with such force it banged against a high cabinet along the wall behind it. The crash made a gold framed miniature fall face up to the carpet.

Through the haze of her anger, Emerson saw it was a painting of a beautiful strawberry-haired woman with eyes the color of shiny new guineas. She had seen the woman before, in a large portrait in the sitting room at Windemere. She realized they must both be paintings of Lathen's mother. The eyes were the same as his, though her hair was much brighter, a shade Emerson had only seen glimmers of whenever Lathen was standing in the sunlight.

Emerson realized she had no such object to remember her own mother, and a wave of sadness hit her. She felt a touch of remorse over her behavior and sensed the coil in her chest loosen. Just a little. She was about to pick the miniature up off the floor, when Lathen came in behind her, shut the door quietly, and bent to collect it himself. He took a moment to put the miniature back in its rightful place, then turned to watch her warily.

"Emerson," Lathen spoke as if he were addressing a spooked horse. "I know you are upset about last evening. It was a hard lesson, but I do not regret it. I will always do everything in my power to make sure you are safe."

Emerson's mind went blank. It took her a moment before she realized Lathen thought she was mad about what had happened in the coach, about him touching her and not letting her find her completion.

The bastard has no idea! None! If only it were that simple.

All the anger that had gone to a simmer when the portrait fell came rushing back, slamming into her, twisting in her gut. She wanted to scream again. She wanted to run over and hit Lathen, the way she had the day Kit died. This time, however, she was certain she could actually hurt him, at least a little.

He deserves it. He let me care for him. I was prepared to ignore him until I could marry, but he taught me things I should never have known until marriage, and all the while, he was lying to me! Somewhere in the back of her mind, Emerson knew she was confusing the two issues, but she was so furious, she did not care.

Luckily, what came out of her mouth was deadly calm.

"I met with Marien today. At the park. She told me everything."

The trepidation and concern left Lathen's face, and the shutters behind his eyes closed completely. Only his usual mask remained as he walked over and sat in the stuffed leather chair behind his desk. He leaned forward, put his elbows on top, and formed a tent with his fingers, making his silver ring sparkle in the sunlight coming through the window behind him. He waited patiently for her to continue.

Tension and silence stretched the distance between them, until Emerson could not take it anymore and finally broke.

"I know you were there when Kit died. I know you are to blame." Emerson surprised herself by saying this calmly as well. A glacial shell seemed to surround her, imprisoning the turbulent storm of her anger within. She still desperately wanted to scream and fight, but it was a wild animal in a locked cage.

Lathen lifted his brow, and he finally responded.

"You know this?" His voice sounded incredulous. "Because some woman, a virtual stranger, told you a story, and you believe her?"

Emerson lost her surface composure. Her rage made her crack and the angry tears she had been holding finally burst forth.

"She said she was there that day. Kit's last day! Kit was in love with her. They were going to be married. He could have had a life and children and happiness. He could be at home, in Havenfield, with me. But you did not want that, did you?" By the end, she was screaming. She could not keep herself contained anymore. Tears streamed down her face and onto her chest and she did not bother to brush them away.

When she was done, her chest heaved with sobs, and Lathen continued to watch her dispassionately from behind his desk.

Say something, damn you!

The clock on the mantle ticked loudly as the seconds went by, and Emerson felt the anger slowly draining from her and again, the hollow grasp on her heart crept back to replace it.

Since the season started, she had been so consumed with Lathen she had stopped feeling the emptiness her brother's death had left behind. Or at least stopped aching so much from it. Now, it was back, and worse, the tentative feelings of attachment she had been having toward Lathen felt like a sad echo in an overlarge cavern. They were still there, but she could no longer find where they were coming from.

Emerson's tears waned, and her head dropped in defeat.

He will not tell me anything more than he ever has. His secrets are always going to remain like a wall between us.

With sorrow, Emerson turned and started for the door. As she reached for it, she heard Lathen get up from his chair and rush across the room to stand right behind her. He put his hand on the door to keep her from opening it and he was so close she could smell his unique cedarwood and leather scent and feel his heat radiating toward her icy skin.

It would have been easier if Emerson could cut off her feelings, but as it was, a flicker of desire still sparked in her lower belly. She felt a yearning, a wish things could be different.

"Emerson," his voice was rough. "Do you truly believe what she said? That I could have harmed Kit or lied to you all these years?"

Emerson stiffened. She did not know what to think anymore. Part of her desperately wanted to lean back into Lathen's warmth. It would be so easy to let him melt the ice in her chest, but first, she needed him to tell her what really happened. She needed to know the whole truth at last, because while she did not know what happened, she believed Lathen was still lying to her about something. Or at least withholding some truth.

Instead of answering him, Emerson grabbed the handle with both hands and forced open the door, making Lathen's hand drop past her face to his side. After stepping over Dog, who was lying patiently outside of the study door, she left without looking back.

chapter forty-three

Watching her brother walk away, Leighton's eyes widened in shock. No one talked to Lathen that way. Ever. Never ever.

He is the Duke of Windemere, after all.

Leighton turned to Hazel and noticed she was taken aback as well, but there was something else besides astonishment. Her face was flushed, and her eyes were narrowed in irritation.

She looks like she wishes she could throttle my brother. Clearly, she knows something I do not.

Leighton found it frustrating she had obviously missed something, as she prided herself on knowing more about the world than her brothers and aunt could ever imagine. It was not difficult, as everyone thought she was still a child, and often talked in front of her, of things they believed she would never understand.

So, what is going on between Emerson and Lathen? What did I overlook? Her mind had no answers, so she decided to ask Hazel.

"Well, Miss Atwood, it would seem you and I should talk."

Hazel turned to Leighton with a raised brow. She tried to compose her face into innocence, but Leighton was not falling for it.

"Come on," Leighton coaxed, putting her arm through Hazel's, pulling her toward the morning parlor. Once inside, she shut both sets of doors before turning back to Hazel, her arms crossed.

"Alright, spill your tale."

A cascade of emotions flickered across Hazel's face, each one vivid and fleeting. Worry knitted her brows together. Frustration followed, tightening her jaw. Yet it quickly gave way to determination, her gaze sharpening and her lips pressing into a resolute line. Leighton stood by, observing the silent procession of feelings with curiosity, waiting patiently for Hazel to answer her.

"Lady de Clare—"

Leighton cut her off immediately with an unladylike snort and a roll of her eyes.

"Please," she said with an exaggerated sigh, "I think we can move past that, do you not? You really must call me Leighton, and, if it is quite all right with you, I shall call you Hazel."

"Very well, Leighton," Hazel grinned and began again, "I hope you do not think me terribly rude, but I am afraid I cannot reveal any confidences to you."

Leighton looked taken aback for a moment before she walked over to a chair, sat down, and turned to Hazel with a thoughtful expression.

"Yes, of course. I would never wish you to do so." Then she gave Hazel a mischievous smile. "But I suppose, if I correctly guessed what was going on, and you only nodded, you would be telling no one's tales. Would you?"

No one could easily lead Hazel astray, and she knew exactly what Leighton was hoping to accomplish. However, since they were both witnesses to today's drama, both in the park and the hall, she could not blame the girl for being curious. Like Leighton, she was tenacious and did not readily let things go. A simple explanation would not deter her. Neither would a fib.

"No, I suppose it would be fine," she answered cautiously, and she sat across from Leighton and waited for her to continue.

Leighton grinned and looked up at the ceiling, pondering.

"Well, my brother went to the Queen's birthday ball. I know he danced with Em. It was all my friends could talk about for days, because it is something he never does." She leaned her left elbow on the arm of the chair and used her fingers to tap her chin while she thought.

Hazel kept silent and still, trying not to reveal anything on her face.

"There is considerable gossip about Lathen turning down every offer of marriage for Em. A man left here in tears because he was so harsh to him, and he was very mad at Lord Farnsworth for touching her hand one day. Oh, and they left the masque early last night. Together!" she continued, her excitement building as she believed she was on to something.

Hazel still did not comment.

"If you add the moment in the hall just now, one might conclude Lathen is secretly in love with Emerson! But perhaps she is only just learning about it?" Leighton pursed her lips and looked bemused, as though she was doing a puzzle, and there was still a missing piece. "Though, why would she be so upset about Lathen's feelings? It is such a joyous thing, after all. It would make her my sister!" She finished with a wide grin.

Hazel could not help but offer a return smile at Leighton's enthusiasm. Her deductions were so innocent, but Hazel could see how she had reached them.

After all, Emerson and I came to similar conclusions, and we had the benefit of much more information than Leighton does.

After a moment, Leighton lost her smile and became pensive again.

"Wait!" she resumed, "who was that woman Em met in the park and what did she say to her? And why was Lord Warwicke so furious when he found them? I have known him since I was a child, and I have never seen him look so upset. Then Em left, and came home, and was angry with Lathen."

Hazel was at a loss for words. It surprised her Leighton was able to make the connection between the two different situations so quickly, but she answered as honestly as she could.

"Well, I do not know what the woman said to Emerson to upset her. Nor do I know why Lord Warwicke was angry at seeing them talking. I suppose, considering the timing, it could be why Emerson was upset and rather firm with His Grace."

"Oh, posh," Leighton scoffed and rolled her eyes again. "I would rather you said nothing than talk around the truth."

"No, really, I do not know what they talked about!"

"But you know who the woman is." She said this firmly. It was not a question.

"Yes, I believe I might know who she is," Hazel hesitated to say the name, "but in all honesty, I have never met her."

Would it be revealing too much? She still did not want to share Emerson's truth, but the determined look on Leighton's face told her she would not let this go, and she was incredibly close to figuring it out on her own. *Besides, maybe Leighton knows something we do not. If nothing else, she knows her brother, and how best to deal with him. Certainly, better than we do.*

With a heavy sigh, Hazel decided she was going to let Leighton in on their secret, but only as far as Marien was concerned. She would not reveal anything about the intimacies between Lathen and Emerson.

"The woman's name is Marien. Have you ever heard of her?"

Before Leighton could answer, the door furthest from them was shut with force. They had been so involved in their conversation they had not heard it open. It was not a slam, but definitely someone closing it in a hurry.

The girls gasped and turned at the sound. Lennox stood there, holding a small plate of sandwiches, staring at Hazel, looking more than a little annoyed.

"Miss Atwood. Do you want to tell me how you know of Marien? And why you are discussing her with my little sister?"

chapter forty-four

Lennox's cross tone differed dramatically from his usual lighthearted one. It made his words even more remarkable.

Hazel froze. She did not know what to do. This was not at all what she had planned, not that she had a plan. Even the thought of telling Leighton had made her uneasy, but this really was too much.

I might as well write a bloody pamphlet and post it on the front door! Em is going to be so disappointed with me!

Leighton spared Hazel for a moment by walking to stand before her brother, breaking his furious glare.

"Lennox! How dare you intrude on our private conversation? Then to try and intimidate poor Miss Atwood with your tough attitude." Leighton raised her finger and kept poking her brother in his chest, punctuating nearly every word.

Confounded, Lennox lifted his brow and took a step back.

"Now Lettie," he tried to charm her.

"Do not 'now Lettie' me!"

"Okay, I am sorry," he raised his hands, putting the plate of sandwiches between them, as though to ward off an angry animal, "but I am simply trying to figure out what is going on. That woman is not someone either of you should concern yourselves with."

"Well, now we are concerned, so perhaps you would be so kind as to enlighten us as to who she is," Leighton cajoled and then pulled Lennox by his sleeve towards the circle of chairs where Hazel was still sitting. "But first, you really must apologize for being such a tyrant to Miss Atwood. It was rather ungentlemanly of you," she added firmly, used to getting her way with Lennox.

Lennox flushed, but he bowed deeply and searched Hazel's face before murmuring softly, "My deepest regrets, Miss Atwood. Hearing you mention that woman shocked me, and I lost my composure. It is no excuse, of course, but I hope you can forgive me."

Hazel felt a flutter in her lower abdomen when she looked back at the earnest expression in his eyes. It astonished her because today was the first time she had witnessed Lennox being completely serious. First, she saw it in his anger, and now, in his remorse. It was a striking difference from his usual carefree demeanor. Even when he admonished her last night at the ball, he did so mockingly.

Hazel simply nodded, unable to answer. For now, she pinned her hopes on Leighton's ability to get information from her brother, hopefully without having to reveal anything to Lennox at all.

"Well, there you are, dear brother. You are forgiven. Now, if you would be so kind, please spill your tale," Leighton coaxed sweetly, before grabbing one of the sandwiches off his plate, taking an unladylike bite, and motioning for him to sit down with them.

Hazel had to cover her smile. Having also been subjected to Leighton's persuasion, she was just now realizing how good the girl was at it.

Lennox looked uncomfortable, but he eventually shrugged and conceded. It was almost as if he understood his sister's determination and figured it was not worth the fight.

"Well, Marien was a woman Lathen, Lord Warwicke, and Lord Haven knew while they were at Oxford. She was the daughter of a man who worked there."

"Is she a gentlewoman?" Leighton interjected.

"Well, sort of, I suppose," Lennox thought for a moment. "Her father is an educated man. Obviously. I think he was the third son of a gentleman, but he had no title or family wealth. Her household, a rather large one with six daughters, was all living in a small cottage on the university grounds. I do not believe there was much money to be had. Certainly not enough for the girls to have any kind of dowry. So, Marien had very few prospects."

"Then how did she come to know three lords? Surely, she did not run in their circle." Hazel could not stop herself from asking. She knew well how strange her own circumstances were, and how lucky she was to keep company with Emerson and the de Clare family, and everything else it entailed. It sounded like Marien's status was even below her own, so it was not likely she would have met them socially.

Lennox looked chagrined and shifted in his chair while looking toward the door. For an escape. The answer was clearly something he wished to avoid.

Leighton leaned forward and smacked her brother on his arm.

"Come now. Do not be such a puritan brother. It is not like we know nothing of the world." This was said smugly. Leighton was tired of everyone patronizing her.

Lennox cleared his throat, and his face went bright red. He still did not reply, but his nonanswer was, in its own way, a confirmation.

Was Marien Kit's mistress? Hazel asked herself. *Is that how she knew him? But why all the secrecy and elaborate schemes to meet with Emerson?*

Leighton came to a similar conclusion. She looked flustered and sat back in her chair before finally asking, "Was she a doxy?"

Lennox, taken aback, snorted in nervous laughter.

"I do not even want to know how you have heard of that!" But he relaxed in his chair, and he continued with his story. "Well, from what I have heard, she used to sneak into the local pub, through a back door. She first tried to be friendly with Lathen and Grey, but after they turned down her favors, she focused on Kit. He liked her, I suppose. I guess she was a pretty and vivacious gel once, but she had thoughts above herself. When it was time for them to leave Oxford for good, and go home, Kit tried to break it off. She took it quite badly. And..."

Lennox's mouth snapped shut, and a shutter fell over his face. He shook his head as if to clear his mind.

"Anyway, that is all I can say about Marien, but perhaps now you will be so kind as to tell me how you know of her." He finished and turned back to Hazel.

He was not angry like before, but he looked determined. Hazel did not know how she was going to avoid telling them what she knew.

From the entry hall, they heard the bell ring at the front door, saving her from having to answer. Giles opened it almost immediately and, even through the closed door of the morning room, there was no mistaking the deep brogue of Lord Warwicke asking to see Lathen.

Lennox and Leighton jumped from their chairs. It was almost comical to watch them rushing to be the first one to reach the door leading to the hall. Leighton ended up elbowing her brother rudely in his midsection, making him expel his breath dramatically, and was the one to yank it open and call out a greeting.

"Lord Warwicke!" she exclaimed brightly while waving him toward her. "Please, will you not join us?"

Greyson glanced down the hall toward Lathen's study before turning back to Leighton. He was agitated and sweaty, as if he had been running.

He had just left his package at Nox House and galloped his horse dangerously fast through the cobbled London streets to get to de Clare House. Now he just wanted to let Lathen know everything about what happened in Hyde, and where he stashed Marien.

"Hello again, lass." He bowed to Leighton and sent a curt nod to Lennox, who was standing right behind her. Then he turned back toward the study, throwing over his shoulder, "I hate tae be a crabbit, but I really must sae His Grace at once."

"Wait!" Leighton shouted rather indelicately, "he is busy at the moment, I believe."

Greyson halted and turned.

"Is Lady Haven in with him?"

"Yes, I believe so."

Greyson sighed, realizing he needed to wait, and his long legs quickly ate up the distance as he joined them in the morning room. He noticed Hazel as he entered and bowed to her as well.

"Miss Atwood."

"Lord Warwicke," she began to rise from her chair before he motioned for her to stay.

Greyson paced to the window, then back, his impatience threatening to overwhelm the room.

"Grey," Lennox went over to him, "is there something I can help you with?"

Greyson shifted his gaze back to the two ladies in the room before returning to Lennox and replying quietly to him.

"I really need tae talk wae Lathen." He lowered his voice even more, "I have the jade he hae been looking fer."

Leighton was not about to be excluded, especially after working so hard to uncover everything thus far. She walked over to them and interrupted casually, "Do you mean Marien?"

Greyson was not easily shocked. He merely looked down at Leighton impassively, and then back at Lennox with a raised brow.

"Do not look at me," Lennox put his hands up defensively, "I am not sure how they learned of her." He was not about to explain how he had told them even more of Marien's story than they had already known.

"Well, lass," Greyson directed a resolute stare to Leighton, "I dinnae believe this is any of yer' concern."

A moue formed on Leighton's face, but Greyson just shook his head with resolve. He was also not one to easily fall for feminine wiles, certainly not from Leighton, whose youth and inexperience rendered her attempts almost artless.

"Nae, lass, I am serious. Now if yae ladies will excuse me, I need tae speak with His Grace. I cannae wait any longer."

Greyson left the room. Lennox followed him with an uncomfortable look over his shoulder as he left.

Hazel was uncertain whether Lennox was more upset about the women being dismissed so abruptly by Lord Warwicke or having shared too much of his own knowledge with them. But she took a moment to put everything she had learned from him, with all she and Emerson already knew.

So, Marien was Kit's mistress, but he tried to end their affair, and somehow, she still feels entitled to something. From Emerson, of all people. Marien also has a friend helping her who does not care for His Grace or Lord Warwicke. Who is he, besides being a gentleman? And what do the two of them hope to gain by reaching out to Emerson in secret?

Hazel tried to think logically, but there were still too many gaps in the picture for her to see it. She needed to get Emerson alone and find out what she had learned from Marien today, and to share with her all Lennox had let slip. Then they might unravel the mystery.

I can only hope Emerson understands the part I played today, however unintentionally.

chapter forty-five

Greyson reached Lathen's study and pounded on the door with the side of his fist.

"Yes," Lathen's rough response was muffled, "enter."

Greyson went inside and Lennox followed, firmly shutting the door behind him. Lathen was sitting at his desk with his head in his hands. His fingers were pulling at his hair. Dog was sitting at his feet, looking concerned, and she barely glanced at the newcomers.

"Lady Haven is nae here then?" Greyson approached cautiously. He had never seen his friend look so affected, except for the day their friend Kit died.

"No," Lathen was terse, and he sat up, fixing his wild hair, but behind his eyes, there was a touch of sorrow. "She was already here and left..." his voice trailed off.

"Did she tell ye I found her and Marien together? Deep in the north wood of Hyde."

Lathen glanced up, looking confused at this new information.

"You found them?"

"Aye, I happened tae be in the park, and met with yer sister, Lady Haven, and Miss Atwood. The next thing I knew, Lady Haven was gone. I looked up all the paths until I found 'er cuddie tied off. She was off in the wood, walking with that clatty bitch."

Lathen's eyes brightened, and he leaned forward eagerly, and slapped both hands on his desk, the sound a crack that made Dog flinch.

"Were you able to grab her?"

"Och, dinnae be so daft, mon. Of course I got hold of her. I had tae send Lady Haven home, ye ken? But yae, I tossed the tart onto my cuddie and took her tae Madam Irina's."

Lathen stood so fast he knocked over his fountain pen, which rolled onto the floor, but he paid it no mind. The melancholy had left his face and a fierceness bordering on maniacal had replaced it. Dog let out a short yip and danced at his feet as he stormed around the desk.

"This is unbelievable, Grey!" Lathen slapped his friend's shoulder. He smiled as well, but it came out as more of a grimace. "Here I have had runners looking in every rathole in London, and you find Marien because she searched out Lady Haven. Did she say why?"

"Nae, not really. She tried to play jezebel for a minute. Then she was blatherin' aboot Lady Haven owin' her."

"What? How can that bitch think Emerson owes her anything?" Lathen's fury was obvious. "Well, we shall see Marien gets everything she is owed!"

Standing back, Lennox watched them quietly, bewildered. Lathen had never been overly emotional about anything or anyone. Even after their mother's death, when Lathen told him about it, his brother remained stoic, and that was when they were both children. Now, although Lennox knew Lathen must do something about Marien, for the first time he worried about what might happen at Nox House.

He is acting like a madman!

"Let's go now, before she slips out of my grasp again!" Lathen exclaimed as he pulled his greatcoat from a hook, buttoning it as he strode toward the door.

As he walked past, Lennox grabbed his arm, bringing him to a halt. Lathen turned with a glare and snapped through gritted teeth.

"What?"

Even Dog stilled and dropped her ears from the ferocity coming off Lathen.

"Lathen, wait. I do not think you should go when you are this upset. Marien is safe at Nox House. She is not going anywhere. We can wait, at least for a bit," Lennox tried to sound reasonable, hoping to calm his brother down.

"I damn well am going now. That slattern deserves my anger and everything that comes with it!" He yanked his arm from Lennox's grasp and walked out.

Lennox turned to Greyson for help, but their friend just shrugged and followed Lathen. With a sigh, Lennox left as well. Hopefully, his concerns were unfounded. After all, neither his brother, nor Greyson, had ever been anything but fair to every woman they met.

They even treated Marien well after Kit died, despite her deserving more than what she got.

chapter forty-six

Hazel watched Lennox until he disappeared down the hall to Lathen's study. Exhausted after the conversation with Leighton and Lennox, as well as the worry over what was going on with Emerson and His Grace, she wanted to disappear.

"I believe I will go up to my room and rest. I am getting a headache after today," she said softly to Leighton.

Leighton had watched Lord Warwicke and her brother leave as well, but now she turned to Hazel and put a hand on her shoulder to comfort her.

"Of course. But first, Hazel, I really must apologize."

"To me?" Surprise registered on Hazel's face.

"Yes, I feel bad for pushing you. I honestly felt it was for the best. To get it all out. I did not intend to cause you any discomfort, but I can see I did. Though, if I am honest, I think there is more to this story than either of us knows, but I promise I will not again ask you to reveal something you do not wish to share."

Hazel was thankful Leighton was not pressing her anymore, though she was also grateful to have her as another confidante. Maybe, with her help, they might be able to finally figure everything out. After all, it was clear Leighton was good at getting people to talk. Hazel leaned forward and gave her a quick hug.

"Do not worry yourself. Like you, I think, perhaps, it is a good thing there are not so many secrets. Maybe things will settle and our friend and your brother, can find their happiness, whatever it looks like."

"Wait," Leighton gasped, "are you saying there is something between them?"

Hazel chuckled and put her finger to Leighton's mouth.

"Shh. Another time. Okay?"

Leighton lifted one shoulder and had the good grace to look chagrined, even if she was not.

"Well, I had to try!" She grinned mischievously.

"I know." Hazel replied, still smiling. "You would not be you if you did not try!" Then she lifted her skirts and climbed the stairs.

When she got to their rooms, Hazel found everything in disarray. It looked like everything Emerson owned had exploded all over the sitting room, as well as Emerson's bed and chairs. Her friend was rushing back and forth, throwing things into a large travel chest she had pulled from the closet.

"Em," Hazel approached warily, "what are you doing?"

Emerson turned, and Hazel could see tracks of tears streaming down her face. She gasped and raised her hand to reach for her friend, as if she could stem the flow.

"Oh, no, Em!" she rushed forward instead, and enveloped Emerson in her arms.

"Hazel, I am leaving," Emerson began, her throat tight with emotion, "I have to go!"

"Why? Talk with me first. Tell me what happened after you went off to find Marien, and what happened with His Grace?"

Hazel led Emerson over to the bench at the foot of her bed, and after moving a pile of clothes, they sat down. Emerson spoke through a fresh wave of tears.

"Marien told me Lathen was there with Kit when he died, and he has been lying to me all these years. Kit and Marien were supposed to be m-married!" A sob escaped as she spoke the last words, revealing her anguish.

At this, Hazel felt compelled to share what she had learned as well, especially since it seemed to directly contradict what Emerson was saying.

"Em," she began tentatively. She was worried about her friend's state. "I am not so sure you should believe anything Marien has told you. I do not believe you can trust her."

Again, she hesitated before taking a deep breath and finishing in a rush, "I found out from Lennox Marien was Kit's mistress. He dallied with her while he was at Oxford, but I do not believe he was going to marry her."

Emerson froze and several emotions crossed her face as she tried to process what Hazel said and place it within everything else she knew.

"Wait. Why would Lennox tell you that?" She sounded confused.

Hazel stared at the floor, reluctantly. It was now or never. She only hoped Emerson would understand why she had broken her confidence, even if she was not trying to reveal anything to Lennox, and despite what Leighton had already guessed.

"Oh, Em, I am sorry, but I had to say something," she finally answered, her face flushed with regret. "Not actually to him, but to Leighton, but only because I was trying to learn what she knew. He came in and overheard us. I would have left, but Leighton was able to get him to share what I just told you."

Emerson was quiet for a moment, while she processed what Hazel said, then she finally asked, "Did he say anything else?"

Hazel sighed in relief and recited every word she could remember. When she was done, Emerson was still thinking.

"Did he know anything else about how Kit died?"

"I am uncertain. He was quite open once Leighton forced him to talk, but I believe he knows more. He seemed to keep a bit to himself." Hazel thought for a moment, remembering the look on Lennox's face when he explained how Kit was trying to break off his relationship with Marien. "Yes, there is definitely more, something he did not wish to reveal."

"I see." That was it. Emerson was overwhelmed and had nothing else to say.

Hazel leaned over and put her arm around Emerson's shoulder, trying to comfort her. It occurred to her Emerson had said nothing about what happened with Lathen after she returned from Hyde, but she did not wish to push. Not right now.

The door to the sitting room flew open and shut just as quickly, making the two of them lift their heads curiously. They watched Leighton rush in without the usual formalities. She was out of breath and had obviously run up both flights of stairs to get there.

"Em...Hazel!" she panted and bent at the waist, her hand gripping her side, "I have just...overheard something!"

"What?" Emerson and Hazel asked in unison as they jumped off the bench.

"Lathen, and Grey, and Lennox," she said through excited breaths, "they have Marien kept up somewhere, and they are off to confront her right now!"

"Did they say where?" Hazel asked.

"Yes, but I do not know where it is. Nox House? I have heard it talked about before, but I know nothing of its location."

Emerson inhaled loudly. She knew what street it was on, and she was sure she could find it again, but she was also told, explicitly, to never go there again. It was not a lesson she wished to repeat.

Or perhaps I do? She dismissed the notion as fancy, almost as soon as it crossed her mind. Then she weighed the consequences of going versus the possibility of learning something vital, and she decided, *Lathen can punish me if he wishes, but I must learn the truth.*

"I know where it is," she finally offered. "But I know it is not a place either of you should go to. Being seen there could ruin your reputations."

Leighton and Hazel looked at one another and shared a nod, before turning back to Emerson with determined looks on their faces.

"I think I can speak for both of us when I say...bollocks!" Leighton said the last quite loudly, with a wide grin.

Hazel let out a nervous giggle and grabbed Emerson's hand.

"She is right, Em. You are not going anywhere without us," Hazel told her, her eyes steadfast, before lowering her voice and continuing, "plus, it will keep what happened last time from happening again."

As they were leaving, Leighton stopped suddenly and asked, "Wait, what happened last time?"

Emerson was not about to tell that story. Certainly not to Leighton. Instead, Hazel grabbed Leighton's elbow by putting her own arm through and pulled.

"Come on, Leighton. We must rush so they cannot get too far ahead of us."

chapter forty-seven

The de Clare carriage had barely arrived at the nondescript townhouse when Lathen, impatient to finally have Marien in his grasp, sprang out. Greyson and Lennox followed a few steps behind him.

Lathen walked through the unlocked black door, not bothering to knock.

"Master?" someone spoke from a small sitting room off the stark entry.

Lathen halted and glanced at Madam Irina who was coming toward him in a sedate, high-necked afternoon dress. She was an older woman, but the years had been kind to her, and she was still strikingly handsome. Her noble Rus heritage had given her high cheekbones and fair skin she obviously took great care of.

"Irina," he began, "where is she?" He did not bother to say who.

Lennox closed the front door after Lord Warwicke came in, and the three men overcrowded the narrow entry.

"I have her in the yellow room upstairs. She shouted a bit, but the room has no window, so it was safer there."

Lathen turned to go up the stairs and Madam Irina asked, "Master, what will you do with her?"

"Nothing she does not deserve," he gritted over his shoulder without stopping.

Irina sighed and turned to Lennox. "Do you think she will be alright, my lord?"

As Lennox had been worried about the same thing, he did not wonder at her question, but he still believed his brother was not one to hurt women, at least not one who had not asked him to. Lennox considered his response, but ultimately, he believed in his brother completely.

However, it was Greyson who finally answered.

"Listen, the chit deserves far worse than Lathen will ever do to 'er. I trust him. We should all trust him. He was the one who had tae deal with her all those years ago, and she was lucky Lathen did nae snap her neck. I am no' so sure I could have restrained myself."

Madam Irina grunted and shrugged her shoulders, the matter settled as far as she was concerned.

"Well then," she smiled, "can I get you boys some tea?"

"Nae," Greyson answered for them both, "but we can do wae a finger o' whiskey. Or two."

"Of course, my lords," Irina waved them into the sitting room and went to the drinks cart. The men sat down in a pair of overstuffed chairs by the low crackling fire. Greyson let his legs go wide, closed his eyes, and sighed with a grimace. It had already been a long day.

First, his mistress had cornered him for a ride in the park. It was an overwarm day, and being from the Highlands, he was used to cooler temperatures and had not been too keen to be out. Then, he was embarrassed when Leighton and the other ladies met them while they were out. If it had been just him, it would not have been a problem, but Greyson knew Lathen would be irritated with him for introducing Mrs. Nichols to Leighton and the others.

It was not that Genevieve was improper in any way. She was the daughter of a gentleman and the widow of another, and they had always been very careful to be discreet. As far as anyone from the *ton* was concerned, Greyson was simply courting her. Only their closest friends knew the truth.

Of course, it was not the only reason seeing Leighton riding towards them made him uneasy. Greyson did not want to delve too deeply into why, especially since their encounter at the masque, but simply seeing her that afternoon made his pulse race, and a flush come to his face. As a robust, healthy man, who prided himself on keeping his cool in impossible situations, his response was baffling. It was this awkwardness which led to him being so distracted he had not observed when Lady Haven slipped away.

He still felt guilty, even if, once he noticed, he found her quickly enough. He supposed it was good he was finally able to corner Marien, after feeling responsible for losing her over a month ago. Now Lathen could stop chasing after her.

Greyson had met no one else as self-possessed as Lathen was, and he had long been certain his friend was some sort of practicing monastic when it came to ladies in society. Greyson had worked very hard to emulate Lathen's calm, after growing up in a household that valued strength and winning a fight, far more than it cared for composure.

Madam Irina came over with his scotch and he took a deep swallow. The liquor burned a familiar trail to his stomach, and he relaxed a little. At least the Marien crisis would be over after today. He was grateful for that much.

A timid knock came from the front door. It was only loud enough because of the heavy metal knocker.

"I wonder who that could be," Irina muttered to herself as she handed the second drink to Lennox and left to answer the door. "I am not expecting anyone. Really, the only people who come to this door are already here."

She was right. Nox House was owned by Lathen. He, Greyson, and occasionally Lennox, were the only people who went there. Sometimes they might bring company with them, but they always used a different entrance when it was the case.

Madam Irina opened the door and gasped in surprise. She recognized Emerson immediately. She was the woman Irina had locked upstairs for Lathen weeks before, whom he had been angry to find there but then spent considerable time alone with once he joined her.

Two other ladies were with her. One she did not recognize, but did offhandedly note how voluptuous her body was, and how pretty her honey blonde hair was framing her delicate face. Next to her was a taller young woman she also had never met, but upon noticing her height and eye color, she realized must be the sister of His Grace.

Irina swore. Luckily, her expletive was soft and in her native Russian language. Then she tried to shut the door, but Leighton had the tenacity to walk in like she had every right to do so, making Irina back up to avoid being in her way.

"My l-lady," she stuttered and gave an awkward curtsy while still holding onto the door handle.

Leighton casually waved back to her while she was looking all around and taking in the small entry. Everything was painted black and dark grey. Even the floor was dark polished marble. It was not exactly a normal aesthetic. When she looked to her right, she saw Greyson and her brother sitting by the fire. Their astonished expressions at seeing the girls were almost amusing.

Leighton smiled brightly at them and walked into the sitting room while she removed her gloves.

"Well, fancy meeting you here Lennie, Lord Warwicke," she exclaimed cheerfully as she nodded to them both. She figured being bold was the best course.

Hazel and Emerson attempted to follow her lead, though both were less successful at keeping their nervousness hidden. Hazel could barely keep herself from wringing her hands, and Emerson kept looking around, as if she was searching for someone.

"What the bluidy hell are ye doing here? All of ye!" Greyson jumped up, spilling his drink. Then he swore under his breath, put down the glass, and wiped his hand on his leg while he glared at Leighton.

"Well," Leighton tsked at Greyson and shook her head. "If you must know, we are here to talk with Marien. I have it on good authority she is here and Lady Haven," she motioned to Emerson, "has ever so many questions to ask her."

Greyson sputtered at her nerve and went red in the face...again.

"Do yae ken how improper it is fer yae tae be here?" This was yelled down to Leighton. Meanwhile, she stepped closer to him and smiled serenely. She had never seen Greyson so rattled, yet she found she relished his heated outburst.

"Well, Lord Warwicke," she responded nonchalantly, "I am terribly sorry if we have offended your delicate sensibilities, but it would appear we *are* here, regardless of the propriety, and we absolutely refuse to leave without speaking to Marien. So be a dear, will you, and fetch her."

Emerson and Hazel were stunned. Leighton was often full of life and cheer, but not usually so bold. Still, they appreciated her courage. Neither one of them could envision standing up to Lord Warwicke. He was so tall and wide, and he seemed to tower over Leighton in his irritation.

Lennox was less shocked. He knew his sister well, probably better than anyone else, even Lathen and their aunt. He had been subject to this version of Leighton many times over the years. It made him chuckle to see how taken aback Greyson was to be experiencing it for the first time.

While this confrontation was happening, Madam Irina had slipped up the stairs and was now coming back down with Lathen in tow.

Silence met him when he walked in. He saw his sister nearly touching Greyson with her bosom as she glared up at him. His friend stared back, just as furious. Behind them was Lennox, sitting and covering a grin with his hand. To the left of the room stood Emerson, with Miss Atwood nearly hidden behind her. Both were wide eyed, watching Leighton confront Greyson. Emerson turned to him when she noticed he had entered and, as he watched, she put her shoulders back and a courageous look took over her features.

"All right," he said evenly, though he might have shouted it for how it affected most in the room.

Leighton jumped back from Greyson and tried to look demure. Hazel shook a bit, clearly alarmed, but she was still conscientious enough to grab Emerson and pull her friend closer to her. Lennox lost his grin and was doing his best to look solemn, while Greyson merely looked relieved to no longer need to deal with the situation.

"Does anyone want to explain to me what is going on?" It was hard for Lathen to keep from yelling. He could not believe everyone was there, especially his sister.

Silence greeted his question. Leighton seemed to flag under Lathen's distant look of disapproval, but Emerson's courage grew. She pulled off Hazel's grasping fingers and walked up to Lathen.

"Well," she started as confidently as she could and borrowed Leighton's words, "I am here to finish my conversation with Marien, and I absolutely refuse to be put off again. Kindly fetch her."

Surprise briefly flickered across Lathen's face before he quickly regained his composure. The only sounds in the room were the seconds ticking loudly from the carved clock on the wall. Lathen stared at Emerson and saw her determined chin waver before she squared her shoulders once more. No one else dared to even breathe.

Lathen weighed his options as he looked first at Emerson and then up the stairs where he had just been. As he saw it, he had two choices, both with their own consequences. He realized, after their earlier confrontation in his office, Emerson was feeling deeply hurt and distrustful. This bothered him more than he wanted to admit, and he felt the urge to do whatever it might take to help soothe Emerson's pain and rebuild her faith in him. His decision made, Lathen finally broke the silence as he turned to address Greyson and Lennox.

"Please take Leighton and Miss Atwood home."

Leighton made a noise of objection, but Lathen scowled, and she was immediately silent again. She put her head down and went with Greyson toward the door.

Hazel was also upset when Lennox came to her. She put up her hands to ward him off, but he took her elbow firmly and bent down to whisper something. Her eyes widened at whatever he said, then she also stopped fighting and just gave Emerson a look of apology as Lennox led her out.

"Was that really necessary, Your Grace?" Emerson asked with a deceptive softness after everyone was gone, deliberately using his title instead of his name. She found it incredibly frustrating when everyone always obeyed Lathen without question. She even noted offhandedly the older woman who answered the door left again as well.

Once more, she was alone with Lathen. Even as angry as she was, the very thought made her skin flush and her belly flutter, but it also frustrated her. She wished she could just stamp out all her feelings for him. It would make everything so much easier.

"Well, I suppose it was," Lathen answered her with an equally light tone as he stepped closer to her before bending down to her ear, "but perhaps you will forgive me in this case, as I am going to give you exactly what you have asked for, *Nyx.*"

chapter forty-eight

"Come," Lathen held out his hand, "if you wish to speak with Marien."

It was Emerson's choice whether she wanted to take his hand or not. But for her, there really was no choice, she had to know the truth. No matter how angry she was with Lathen, she had to go with him. She saw his gratitude when she did not spurn him. His hand reflexively tightened when she touched his, and her heart skipped a beat.

His palm was as she remembered. Warm and strong. It enveloped hers as he turned to lead her toward the stairs and up to the next floor. They went down the dark hallway with all the mirrors, but they did not go to the same black room as before. Instead, Lathen stopped at a door on the opposite side, facing the back of the house, in the middle of the hall. He reached into his pocket, pulled out a key, and unlocked it. When he pushed the door open, Emerson leaned forward to look inside, mostly to make certain Marien was inside before she entered herself.

"Did you really think I was lying to you?" Lathen asked with a slight frown.

Emerson shrugged noncommittally, but she felt a little guilty. After all, here she was, finally in the same place as Marien and Lathen, ready to learn the truth. He truly had given her exactly what she asked for.

She walked inside tentatively. Marien was sitting on a striped yellow and cream baroque chair. A single bed with a side table, and a tiny wardrobe in one corner, were the only other furnishings. It was small, more of a closet than a room. Emerson noted there was not even a window looking out.

Wearing a calculated expression, Marien watched them enter while keeping her hands folded in her lap. Her lips twisted into a sneer as they came closer, and her eyes flashed with spite. Emerson wondered how she could have ever thought the woman was beautiful.

"Well, Lady Haven, I see you have managed to come and visit me," she said primly, as though she were receiving guests in her own home. "I was just getting reacquainted with His Grace here. After all, we were once very, very close." Marien's voice dropped, and she looked slyly at Lathen and then back at Emerson.

What is she implying? Emerson wondered. *Did Lathen dally with her as well?* She looked at Lathen, however, and watched him stiffen as a brief look of disgust cross his face before he could school his features. *Well, if he once did, he obviously does not care for her now.*

"Yes, Marien, I came to finish our conversation." Emerson tried to sound unaffected. "I believe you were explaining how Kit was lost to you, before we were interrupted." She figured it was best to humor the woman for the moment and not ask about what Hazel had learned.

Marien turned away from them and stared into the flames of a low fire in the small hearth. As they watched her, the unpleasant look eased from her face, replaced by melancholy, as if she was thinking of something sad. Yet she did not answer Emerson and a long silence filled the room.

"Do you want me to tell her?" Lathen snapped as he finally lost his patience, making Marien flinch.

She turned back and glared.

"How can *you* tell her anything? It was all your fault. If you did not interfere, none of it would have happened. I would still have my Kit!" Marien's voice rose to a shriek.

Lathen remained stone-faced at her accusations, but his composure made Marien even angrier.

"You could not just let Kit be happy and make his own choices! You had to open your big mouth and break us apart!"

Emerson held her breath. She did not want Marien to stop talking because it felt like the truth was finally coming out.

"Marien, Kit was never going to marry you. You were only a simple comfort while he was far from home. Once he finished with you, he was more than ready to leave Oxford behind. To leave everyone behind." Lathen said this calmly, but Marien did not take it well. Her face grew mottled with red splotches, and she sputtered, nearly apoplectic in her anger.

"You liar!" She jumped from her chair, screaming so violently spittle went flying across the room. "He *was* going to marry me! He promised. It was only after you told him about us he tried to leave me behind."

"Us?" Lathen snorted in derision. "You snuck into my bedroom, dressed like a common strumpet, Marien. I wanted nothing to do with you. You were my best friend's mistress. I would never have touched you, even if I found you desirable. Of course, I told him about what kind of woman you are."

"No! You wanted me. I know it! I saw you watching me many times." Even to Emerson's ears, Marien's words rang untrue.

Lathen ignored her protest and continued. "Even if I had not told Kit, he already knew about all the other men, but he simply did not care. He thought it was amusing. It made it easier for him to not feel guilty for breaking your affair, and for letting you continue to believe you were more to him than you were."

Emerson gasped. She was learning so much. Her brother had a mistress, but Marien had only been that. She knew her brother would never have married someone like her, and it made sense why he never mentioned the woman in any of his letters.

But how did he die? I still need to know! The words ricocheted around her head, building to a scream.

Luckily, Emerson did not have to ask. It was as though Lathen understood there was no room for any more secrets, and it was time for her to know. Drawing closer to Marien, Lathen molded his features a gentle expression, and he softened his voice like he was talking to a child.

"I know it must have been hard to hear Kit say what he did. I know you never meant to hurt him, but you must finally accept responsibility for what happened."

As Emerson watched, Marien melted. Her face twisted and her body dropped to the floor in a heap. She lifted her hand, touching her temple with trembling fingers, the side with the small white scar curving into her hairline. A sound escaped from her, the moan of a wounded animal, but it was not sorrowful. She looked up, and it was pure hate on her face as she glared at Lathen.

"He deserved it!" She spewed at him, her eyes wild.

Emerson gasped in shock, and Lathen stepped back in a protective gesture.

"He told me he loved me! I gave myself to him, but he tried to say I was only a fancy piece. He had enjoyed our time together, but he was leaving to go home. Without me! He offered me money to go quietly. Fifty pounds!" She continued to scream as she used the chair to help her stand. "Like I was a common strumpet he could pay off. I deserved far more! I should have been his wife! I should have had Havenfield and been married to an earl! I should have been able to buy the same dresses as the ladies who always looked down on me!"

Emerson could not take it anymore. She finally snapped, raising her voice.

"What did you do to him?"

Marien turned her angry gaze to her.

"You bitch!" She howled. "You owe me! You have everything that was supposed to be mine!" The venom in her voice was palpable.

"What did you do to Kit?" Emerson ignored her and repeated herself firmly.

"You are so high and mighty. Like I do not know you and I are the same." Marien still evaded her question, and she began stepping toward Emerson, pointing a bony finger at her. "Oh yes, Lady Haven, I know all about you," she continued, laughing maniacally, "I have heard how you tease all the men of the *ton*. I have friends still. One particular friend has watched everything you have done and knows everywhere you have been!"

Lathen cut off her vitriol by stepping between them and putting his hand on one of her shoulders to keep her back.

"Answer her, Marien," he warned forcefully. "Or I will."

Marien's eyes were still overbright as she reflected on his words. She must have decided it was better for her to get the story out, or perhaps she just wanted to be the one to hurt Emerson with the information. Either way, her voice was grave when she finally continued.

"Kit came to meet me at the pub the night before he was going to leave. I had packed all my best dresses, not that I had many, and I was waiting for him to take me away, like he promised." Marien's voice dropped again, and she was staring at something far off.

"Instead of grabbing my trunk, he just laughed. He told me I was a silly bit of a girl. He said he knew I had been loose with my favors, and he was sorry, but our time was over. Then he tried to get me to take the money. He said it was for a fresh start, if I wanted one. 'So, I would no longer have to whore myself out!'" Angry tears filled her eyes.

"I told him I was no whore, and I was ready to be his wife, the mother of his children! He just laughed again and threw the money onto the table. I watched the shillings roll across it and fall to the ground."

Emerson could hardly hear her, so she leaned forward, holding onto Lathen as though she needed his strength to keep from falling.

"I was just so mad," Marien continued, barely above a whisper. "I still do not remember how, but one moment he was laughing and walking away from me, and the next he was at the bottom of the stairs below."

Emerson cried out, and Marien looked back at her.

"He must have just fallen. Do you not see?" Her tone was hopeful, as though she was trying to convince herself, not just Emerson. "Yes, that must be it," she continued softly, almost childlike, "he slipped and fell. I certainly did not push him."

The room began to spin, and Emerson struggled to breathe. She kept seeing flashes of her brother as Marien kept talking, explaining, coming up with different reasons for how Kit must have accidentally fallen. Emerson could no longer hear her. Instead, a howling emptiness filled her ears. She looked up and saw Lathen reaching for her. Her hands tried to grab his, but he seemed to get further and further away. Then the world, and the pain in her heart, went away.

chapter forty-nine

A cool breeze caressed Emerson's face. She realized there must be an open window because she could smell rain and flowers. Feeling relaxed and content, a smile spread across her face as she stretched her arms high above her head.

Then it all came crashing back.

Her eyes flew open, and she jerked up from the chaise she was lying on. She looked around at a room she did not recognize, noting offhandedly it was beautiful. Everything was in shades of white and cornflower blue. Vases of hydrangeas sat on the tables and a lovely woven rug covered the polished wood floor. There was a white bed frame along one wall, with a blue knit blanket thrown over it.

I think I would like a room like this. She knew it was silly, but her mind desperately tried to focus on something, anything, besides what she had learned today. It failed and a whimper escaped her.

Kit.

"Shh," Lathen was sitting on a chair beside her, and he reached over to brush a tendril of hair back from her face.

"She killed him." This time, it was not a question.

"Yes, she did."

"And you were there?"

"Yes. I was there. I saw him fall, but I could not get there in time to stop it." He sounded heartbroken, and Emerson saw tears shimmering in his amber eyes.

How could I have ever thought he was responsible? She wondered. *He looks just as devastated now, as he did when he brought Kit home to me.* Flashes of that day ran through her memory, but Lathen's sorrow did not ease Emerson's grief, nor did it lessen her outrage.

"How is she not in Newgate? Or better yet, swinging from a rope?"

"Emerson, I understand none of this makes sense, but I need you to think for a minute," Lathen began gently. "Kit died in a place little better than a brothel. He was a young lord, and he freely accepted the favors Marien offered. Can you imagine the scandal it would have been?"

Emerson's brow wrinkled as she picked a loose thread on her skirt. She deliberated over his words and, after several minutes, she realized he was right. She had seen firsthand how much everyone in London loved to gossip and how ruinous it could be. However, the unfairness of it all ripped at her heart.

"But did Kit not deserve justice?"

"Emerson, Kit was gone. He is still gone," he added gently. "I knew him well, better than anyone, except for you, of course. He only cared about one person more than anything. The only person who would have been hurt by the story getting out would have been the one who he wanted to protect."

"You mean me." Emerson bowed her head, and her hands twisted in her lap.

"Yes." Lathen once again brushed her hair that had fallen forward, his voice a husky whisper. "You." This time she leaned into his hand, accepting his comfort. Then something occurred to her.

"Alright, nothing happened to her then. What about now?" She raised her head and grasped at Lathen, digging her fingers into his arms in her eagerness. "I care not for the gossip. As you said, Kit is gone. I am no longer a child, and I can make the choice!"

Lathen shook his head. He was not sure she was going to accept everything he was going to tell her. She obviously wanted Marien to face some kind of justice. He did not blame her. One of the hardest things he ever had to do was let Marien get away with taking his best friend's life.

He offered an explanation, hoping his honesty would help her understand.

"That day, rage nearly consumed me. I have never come so close to hurting someone. I wanted to kill her, if I am being truthful, but when I climbed the stairs to get to her, she ran and tripped and fell into the corner of a table. When I grabbed her, she had a cut on her head and blood was pouring down her face."

"The scar. The faded one on her temple?" Emerson absentmindedly touched her own forehead.

"The same. Seeing her injured made me slow down enough to realize I could not hurt her, even if she deserved it. Kit would never want that. It would have made me just as bad as she was. Besides," he added as he touched his hand to her leg, "there would be no one to look after you, which I would have done no matter what, even if I was not made your guardian."

Emerson's eyes widened and she placed her hand in his, but she did not say anything.

"Instead, I made the tough decision to send her away," Lathen continued, "to Basque, in France, to a small mountain town where I had trusted friends. I wanted her away from anyone she could tell her tale to, so she could not hurt you anymore than she already had. Unfortunately, she disappeared about two years ago. It has been so chaotic in that part of the world with Napoleon's conflicts, and it took a long time for me to even receive word she was gone. It was only recently, in the last several months, I learned she was here in London."

In the back of her mind, Emerson could hear Lathen's placating words, and she knew he was only trying to help, but it did nothing to salve her own anger.

"Alright. That was then. But again, what about now?"

"Now? Well, I am going to send her somewhere she can never return from. It is not the same as prison, but it is as close as I can make it. She will never again have freedom. I will make certain of it." This was stated as a matter of fact. He would not change his mind.

"Emerson, I have said this to you many times, and I truly hope you hear me now. I have only ever wanted what is best for you. I will always do everything in my power to keep you safe. If I had my way, I would have spared you all of this. I never would have you exposed to such a woman as Marien or hear about what happened to Kit." He paused as he realized something. "How did you learn of her, anyway?"

The weight of their shared secrets was lifting and Emerson decided she wanted to be honest.

"Well, she first came to me the day after I arrived in London. She waited until I was alone at the dressmakers."

"She did?" Lathen exclaimed in shock. "How did she even know you would be there?"

"I am not sure, but she was also at the Royal Masquerade. It was her I was searching for in the maze."

"Hmm, you have been busy. And the park today? Were you supposed to meet her there? Or did she just appear again?"

"I met her there. She sent me a note this morning."

Lathen crossed his leg and leaned back in his chair, a thoughtful expression on his face.

"Did she also let you know she was here the first time you came to Nox House?"

Emerson blushed. How she had first come to Nox House still embarrassed her. After all, hiding under a gentleman's desk was not very becoming of a lady, even if the original intention was not to spy. However, their continued trust felt fragile, and she felt she had to answer him. It was only fair.

"I was in your office when Lord Warwicke came to tell you Marien was back in London. I was...hiding under your desk." She lowered her eyes and mumbled her answer. They shot back up when she heard him let out a bark of unfettered laughter.

"*Nyx*, I have to admit, I would have not guessed that in a million years. The very idea of you hiding under there amuses me to no end!" He was still chuckling.

Emerson felt her own laughter bubble up. After all the stress of the last months and all the revelations of today, it felt good. Yet as soon as their laughter waned, everything she had learned of Marien came pushing its way back to her mind.

Tears stung Emerson's eyes. The senseless loss of her wonderful, funny, and vibrant brother devastated her as if she had lost him just that day. The fact the woman who had caused his death was going to live her life with few consequences still burned in her mind, making her wish she could somehow do something about it.

I suppose none of this will ever make sense. She sighed at the thought, but she also realized Lathen was right. Even though her heart wanted revenge, she knew her brother would have never wanted her to be tainted by the circumstances of his death. In that way, Lathen had always done his best to honor Kit. She had to trust he would continue to do so.

She looked over at Lathen's face. He looked just as emotional as she felt. Just as broken. She raised her hand and let it skim lightly across his face. His cheek had a slightly rough shadow from not having shaved since morning, and his eyes darkened, looking like old whiskey, as he leaned into her hand. His hair was wild and burnished in the candlelight. It was strange in a way, seeing him there like this, so vulnerable he looked almost human to her. Since she was a child, she had always thought of him as a Greek god.

And he now calls me by a goddess' name. She wondered if they were always fated to be, but the idea drifted away as she searched his face, her eyes landing on his lips. She wanted him to kiss her. *No,* she corrected herself, *I need him to kiss me. I need him to take away this sorrow and replace it with something else.*

chapter fifty

Lathen read her mind, and he shifted forward. His lips met hers tentatively, as if he was not sure if she was ready for anything more. It was not long ago they both angrily vowed not to touch one another, and she just had an incredible shock.

Emerson was more than ready. She desperately needed his warmth and the pressure of his body on hers. With every bit of strength she had, she wrapped her arms around his shoulders and pulled him down with her as she lay back down on the chaise.

The kiss started as comfort for them both, a soothing balm after their collision with the past. Soon, it became more.

Emerson was the first to let her tongue slip into Lathen's mouth. She slid it gently against his, using everything Lathen taught her and feeling her way to her own revelations. She discovered Lathen enjoyed it when she circled his tongue like a slow waltz, eliciting a deep moan from his chest.

Lathen wrapped his powerful arms around her and lifted her, turning them both so she was lying atop him. Emerson never felt so safe and comfortable. It gave her the confidence she needed to explore.

Her fingers found his cravat and pulled at one end until it came loose. She stopped kissing him while she tugged it off his neck, letting it fall to the floor. With narrowed eyes, Lathen watched her every move, the intensity of his gaze making Emerson feel warm and wanted. It gave her confidence, and she moved to straddle him, finding the small buttons on his lawn shirt and methodically undoing them before pulling the tails from his breeches.

She was unsure how to get his shirt off, but he saw her dilemma and sat up, shrugging it off himself. It brought him close again, and she could not resist kissing him once more. But she wanted more than just his mouth. She placed her hands on his warm shoulders and gave him light kisses down his jawline, over the rough shadow, to his neck. There she stopped, inhaling his warm cedar, leather, and salted scent, before tasting him with her tongue and nipping gently with her teeth.

"Hey!" he chuckled at her and grabbed her hips, flexing his fingers to pull her closer. "Easy, *Nyx*."

Emerson murmured a low, sexy sound. She had no desire to be easy. Her hands drifted downward, on a path toward Lathen's chest. He had the sparse dusting of darkened umber hair across it, fascinating her. She let her fingers run through it, settling them over his nipples.

I wonder if he is as sensitive as I am. She bent slowly, letting her tongue swirl around the left, marveling how different he was from her, how firm compared to soft, before opening her mouth and sucking on it.

Lathen let out a low groan. With increasing assurance, Emerson leaned back and pushed him until he was lying flat again. She then looked down at the polished silver buttons on either side of his hips. Though her fingers trembled, Emerson was determined. The force of her desperate need was a physical thing, building and forcing her forward with the relentless power of a raging storm.

She made quick work of the three buttons on each side and pulled the front fold down. When released, Lathen's member stood proudly, hard and unyielding. Like a moth to a flame, Emerson reached forward and wrapped her fingers around him. Her hand slid over him, from root to tip, the way she remembered he liked.

"Oh! *Nyx*!" Lathen's head fell back, and his neck arched, showing his tendons and barely suppressed violence.

Her hand repeated the movement. Again, and again. Until a small, glistening drop of his essence slipped from the head. She scooted down even more, leaned forward, and curved her tongue around the wide crest, lapping up his salty taste. His back bowed and his moans grew louder.

Emerson felt powerful, but she felt this way before. In the black room across the hall. The memory of how that encounter ended was still fresh in the back of her mind. She was determined not to let this end in the same way.

With her free hand, she slowly reached down for the edge of her skirts, trying to pull them to the top of her thighs. She thought she was taking advantage of Lathen being distracted by her mouth, but when she glanced up through her lashes, he was watching her.

Her breath caught in her throat as she froze, waiting for him to stop her. After several heartbeats, it was clear he would not. Instead, he sat up and started on the line of tiny buttons running down her back. He did stop her by tugging her to stand by the side of the chaise, but it was only so he could pull her dress down her arms and untie her stays and underskirts. Those also fell to the floor and Emerson was left in only her thin undergarments and silk hose with their tied pink ribbons.

Lathen stared intently, his eyes slowly taking in every detail of her lithe, curved body. Emerson probably should have felt bashful, but the look on his face was of obvious approval and desire. It gave her the strength to look him in the eye while she pulled her light chemise over her head and undid the single pearl button on her lace underwear. They too drifted over her hips and fell.

"*Nyx*, you are stunningly beautiful." The awe made his voice hoarse.

Emerson felt she was. Perhaps, for the first time in her life, she felt wanted, and something nearly tangible shifted in her mind, giving her new confidence. Emboldened, she left her silk hose on, because Lathen always seemed to like them, and she stepped forward, intent on one purpose.

I want to make love to him. Now.

Lathen had another idea. He swung his legs to the side and grasped Emerson tightly by the hips. He pulled her core closer and lifted one of her legs so her foot rested on the chaise next to him. To keep herself from falling, Emerson gripped his wide shoulders as he bent to her exposed cleft, letting his tongue slide over the sensitive bundle of nerves he found there.

It was like he was kissing her deeply once again. Swirling his tongue around, delving inside, weakening her knees until they shook. Lathen could feel her trembling, and he seized her waist and turned her, so she was lying in the same position he was in earlier. His hands pushed on her knees, spread them wide, until her glistening womanhood was open for him. With one finger he traced the tiny pink shell nestled beautifully in her short dark curls, gathering her moisture. She was wet and ready for him, but he knew she needed to be stretched out more, so he took another finger and entered her slowly.

Panting, Emerson lifted her hips to meet his hand, while Lathen set up an achingly slow rhythm. He bent and teased her clit with the barest flick of his tongue.

Emerson wanted more. It was not enough for her to reach the climax her body had desperately needed for days. So, she reached down, tangled her hand in Lathen's hair, pulling him closer as she pressed her heels to the chaise.

Chuckling, Lathen shook his head and captured her hand.

"*Nyx*, you need to learn patience," he tsked, but with a smile as he withdrew his fingers.

A frustrated sob escaped Emerson's lips, as her need to come was a tightly wound coil deep inside her, but then Lathen shocked her. He grasped her chin with one hand and lifted his wet fingers to her mouth.

"Open." It was a command, and she obeyed without question.

He slipped them into her mouth, mimicking the movements he had used only moments before inside her body.

From down there!

"Can you taste yourself?" Lathen asked roughly. "It is like warm fresh peaches just picked off the tree at the end of summer. A picnic with the finest vintage of wine. Let it sit on your tongue and slide down your throat."

Emerson did as he told her. His forbidden words and actions made her belly clench hard, and her need rose to a fever pitch. Her lavender eyes boldly held his amber gaze while she firmly sucked on his fingers. Swirling her tongue around them, just as she had done to his manhood.

"That is a good girl," Lathen rasped as he moved his hand from Emerson's chin and ran his fingers through her hair, pulling out pins and letting the dark curls fall down her back.

He dragged his other fingers from her mouth, letting them trail down her neck and traced her collarbone. Emerson felt curiously empty, and she whimpered at the loss.

"Oh *Nyx*, I love to hear you," Lathen told her huskily. "You are so uninhibited and responsive, so true to yourself."

Emerson wondered at his words. *Is it wrong? Am I being too forward?*

Any doubts vanished as Lathen moved his hands to cup her firm breasts. His face turned nearly reverent as he ran his fingers in circles around them, watching as the tips pulled into tight buds in response. Emerson's mouth parted, the need for air only a reflex since she was too lost in his touch to care about such things. Then he used his thumbs and forefingers to pinch her taut nipples.

"Argh," a jumbled moan left Emerson. It was always a shock to her system when he did that. Somehow, she felt the sensation directly in her womanhood.

An echo, deep inside me.

Even though he was not even touching her there.

"Oh, yes, I know, *Nyx.* You like this." He pinched them even harder.

Emerson's answering moan came from a dark place. It was painful, yes, but it made her quiver, and moisture welled between her thighs. She was incredibly close to coming, simply from his rough touch and his words.

"Emerson. Look at me," he whispered, his voice trembling.

She moaned again, her head thrashing from side to side. The colors were there, just blurring the edges of her mind.

So, close...

"Emerson," he demanded, "look at me!"

She lifted her head and opened her eyes. She had not realized she had closed them. His gaze was smoldering.

"Are you ready?" He asked.

Ready? She was unsure what he meant. She nodded anyway, her eyes wide and expectant. She would have done anything he asked of her.

With her acceptance, he released her nipples. As the blood rushed back to them, he slipped down and pushed her legs wide and latched onto her clit. And sucked hard.

Emerson's orgasm hit her like a collision. It was like the crest of a huge tidal wave crashing upon her, coming up the shore, destroying everything in its path. Colors exploded as she screamed and grabbed the back of the chaise with both of her hands. Her back bowed off the surface so she could lift her hips even higher, twisting in her oblivion. It just kept going, intense and overwhelming.

After a while, she floated down. Lathen was staring closely at her, on his knees, and was continuing to grasp her firmly at her hips with shaking arms. The roped muscles on his abdomen were straining and his manhood was jutting straight out, as though it were reaching for her, begging for her. He was still in need.

Emerson was worried. Even though she just had an intense release, her need was still there, building again. She wanted him *inside* her. Deep inside, making love to her. Finding their completion together, instead of apart.

Is he going to refuse me again? Deny us even though we obviously both want this?

Lathen's struggle was unmistakable. The tendons in his neck were taut as his gaze was glued to her entrance.

"Lathen," she breathed his name. He brought his eyes to hers. "Please...fuck me."

chapter fifty-one

Her words hit Lathen hard, causing him to shut his eyes as his face twisted in torment. The intensity of his desire for Emerson was unlike anything he had ever experienced, nearly overwhelming his better judgement. He wanted to use the grasp he still had on her hips to lift her up and slam into her wet cunt. Behind his lids, he could still see her. She glistened, pink and swollen, flowering open for him.

He instinctively understood it would be the best sex he ever had. She would be tight and liquid fire. He could bury himself to the hilt and then pull her even closer, grinding into her until they were one. There was something else as well, something darker. There was a visceral need, inside himself, to possess her, to finally claim her as his.

Yet all the reasons he should not do so were still there. Nothing had changed.

I cannot marry her.

She deserves more.

There is still a secret she does not know.

These thoughts whispered in his mind like tangled ropes, trying to restrain him, to harden his resolve—until Emerson reached down and gripped his cock, destroying all reasoning and logic. Lathen's eyes snapped open, and his gaze bore into hers as he shook, sweat trickling down his back from his effort to keep still.

"Lathen, please," she begged, "I want you so badly."

His willpower was fading, and his fingers flexed into her soft skin. He made another attempt to stop himself before going too far.

"Emerson," he rasped, "I want you, too. You know I do."

Her hand stroked over his skin again, compelling him to silence. Up and down. Tightening with every caress, forcing his will to hers.

A mere facsimile of what her beautiful cunt will feel like, but I am wild for her.

"You are not playing fair, *Nyx*." He covered her hand to still her, her fingers splayed and entwined with his.

Emerson was not about to be stopped again. Not this time.

She scrambled to her knees and bent to take him in her mouth.

Lathen knew it was wrong, but he needed it. So, he let her. His hands pulled her unbound hair back, twisting it so he could watch her. She had learned her lessons well. She took him in deeply. So deep his cock felt the back of her throat and tears came to her lavender eyes staring up into his.

"Oh *Nyx*, you are so good at this."

The compliment emboldened Emerson, and she tried to take him even deeper, making her struggle for air. She timed her movements so she could pull back to breathe while stroking him with both hands and swirling her tongue on the sensitive underside of his wide crest. Lathen moaned at the sensation, and his head dropped back, his vision blurring.

He knew what she was doing. There was still part of him, the part used to being in absolute control, that thought he could still stop her, but those whispers in his head wondered if that was true.

It is like she is a siren, and I am helpless to her song. Then he corrected himself. *No, she is a night goddess with immense power over what happens in the darkness. To my darkness.*

Lathen's fingers tightened in Emerson's hair, pulling at her scalp and making her gasp as her mouth left him, her lips wet and deliciously red. He forced her back and looked down, trying once more to reason with her through gritted teeth.

"Emerson, if we continue, you will not have your innocence anymore. We must stop!"

As Lathen watched, Emerson's face flushed, and her lavender eyes shot sparks at him, deepening once again to a glorious violet. She was even more beautiful in her anger as she struggled against his grasp. Her hands rose to his chest to push against his hold.

"This is my choice! I want this! I am tired of being told what I may do and how I may act!" Emerson was shouting when she finished. Then she lowered her voice and continued, with a calculated look on her face, "If you do not want me, I am certain I can find someone else who will!"

Lathen froze, his heart pounding as anger sparked within him at her words, spreading like wildfire. Logically, he understood Emerson was trying to make him jealous.

The vixen thinks she can force my hand!

It was working. His rising fury at the idea of any man, besides him, touching Emerson was overcoming his guilt and good intentions. With his grip still in Emerson's hair, he forced her upright, to her knees, and he kissed her hard. With a groan, he poured his anger and pent-up passion into her. Emerson took it all and returned it with her own. Their kiss was deep and fast, a desperate twisting of tongues a near savage mating in its own right.

Lathen released her hair and grabbed her by the back of the thighs instead. He pulled them wide and upward, making Emerson fall to her back with a shriek. He followed her down, keeping their kiss going. From this position, his cock lay heavily across Emerson's lower belly. It would be the easiest thing in the world for him to draw back and enter her. It would be like coming home.

He restrained himself, however. This time it was because he knew he needed to calm down. He would not take her in anger.

Not for her first time. She deserves better.

With that thought, Lathen deliberately slowed down his kisses, sliding deep inside her mouth. He braced himself on his elbows and lifted his hands back to her hair. Tenderly, this time, he combed her silken black curls back from her forehead, attempting to soothe any pain he caused earlier.

Emerson felt the shift in his mood. She moaned softly and wrapped her arms around him, stroking his back with her fingers. It was a gesture of consent and a request for him to continue.

Lathen could not help but think of how nice it felt to have someone touch him solely because she wanted to, because she wanted him. *Not because I told her to.* He pulled back and stared down at her. He suddenly realized it was even more important to him it was Emerson who wanted him. After many years of her deliberately trying to frustrate him, to push away from him, she was now pulling him closer.

With a hopeful look, Emerson returned his gaze, waiting breathlessly for him to continue. There would be no more stopping from either of them.

Lathen still needed to make sure.

"*Nyx*," his voice was thick with need, "are you certain?"

Emerson let her hands drift down his back to his ass.

"Please." One word. A plea.

Lathen nodded and pulled his hips back. His cock was rigid and had several droplets at the end, and Emerson's entrance was soft and ready. He needed nothing more than a small shift to slide inside her.

Oh...my...God! She is so tight and wet!

Lathen gritted his teeth, his arms extended as he struggled to enter her slowly and deliberately, with as much gentleness as he could. His whole body trembled from the effort, until he met the resistance of her maidenhood. Sweat beaded on his forehead as he strained to not hurt her. He had never been with a virgin, and his mind went blank, completely unsure how to proceed.

He tried to pull back, but Emerson refused to let him. She lifted her legs to wrap them around his hips, using the leverage of her hands on his backside to pull him into her. Lathen felt a small pop, and he slid the rest of the way down.

A hiss of pain left Emerson, and her eyes squeezed shut before any tears could escape.

"Oh *Nyx*, I am sorry." His voice was heavy with remorse. "But I am afraid it was unavoidable."

He stilled, breathing heavy from the effort, and waited for her to adjust to him being inside her.

324

It was Emerson who moved first. At first, a tentative tilt of her hips. Then another, with more confidence. She gasped and her eyes flew open to meet his as she experienced the new sensation of having him all the way inside her. Fullness. A delicious burning.

Lathen let his own hips pull back and he entered her again. She moaned, her fingers instinctively tightening on his backside, pulling him even closer.

"You like that, *Nyx*?" Then he withdrew further and pressed back deeper.

She moaned louder.

"Well?" This time his voice was demanding.

"Yes, I like it!" she exclaimed as he withdrew and buried himself to the hilt. She lifted her hips to meet him.

Lathen shifted onto his knees, and he grasped her under her hips the way he imagined.

It was even better than he expected. He pulled her tightly against him and ground hard against her clit, looking down at where they joined. Every time he pulled back, he could see his own cock, glistening from her arousal, and her nether lips parted wide to accommodate his girth. Especially when he would pull out to where he almost left her, and his wide crest spread her even more.

Then he would crash back into her, making a wet slapping sound intermingled with his heavy breathing and Emerson's loud moans of pleasure mixed with a hint of pain.

It was obvious Lathen was slightly too big for Emerson. He could feel the end of his cock pressing up against her womb each time he went all the way in. He tried to not go so deep, but Emerson was lifting to meet every thrust. Digging her heels into his back to take him deeper. Each time, her moans grew sharper and more plaintive, and her eyes were glazing over.

In the back of his mind, Lathen wondered how far she could go, how far he could take her, but as it was her first time, he did not wish to scare her off. He wanted to keep to things she would understand. He glanced down and saw her nipples were tight and red from their earlier treatment, but he could not resist grabbing one of her breasts and pinching the tip again.

The sharp pain intensified Emerson's reaction. Her moans became garbled, and she pressed her feet into the chaise to give herself more leverage, lifting her hips higher. Lathen kept meeting her with his thrusts, but with his other hand, he reached down with his thumb and pressed against her clit.

Emerson went wild. Her hips lost their rhythm, and her fingers turned to claws, scratching his back. Her screams became words that should have shocked Lathen with their filthiness. Words about his enormous cock and how it felt in her pussy, how he was stretching her, touching her deep inside, how she wanted him to make her come again, and for him to come with her. It was language she should not even know enough to say.

Lathen was used to his lovers being quiet, yet he found he liked Emerson's uninhibited words. His cock swelled, and he fought to control his own response, so he would not embarrass himself and finish before her.

When Lathen knew she was about to come, he let go of her nipple, grasped both of her hips again and ground into her. Her spasms hit like an explosion, gripping around him like a fist. So tight, it was almost too much, but he kept pushing through, until, gritting his teeth, he let himself go.

"Fuck!" He growled while Emerson screamed incoherently.

He poured his seed as he pounded into her, over and over. Emerson was right there with him, and his orgasm triggered another for her.

When he was done, his breath was heavy, and his heartbeat was thudding loudly in his ears. He did not want to pull out of her yet. The connection felt too good, so he kept them joined and rolled over to his back, pulling her boneless body across his chest. Her head turned to the side as Lathen stroked her back, and he saw the barest smile of contentment crossed her lips while her eyes fluttered closed. Slowly, her breath deepened, and she drifted off to sleep.

Well, we did that. Now what? Lathen wondered, as he resisted the urge to pull her even closer.

He had thought the sex between them would be good, but he was not prepared for how good. It was phenomenal, like nothing else he had ever experienced, but there was something else. He felt a spark in his chest he had not expected, warming him, followed by a sudden unease. Emerson had reached him in a way no one ever had, or perhaps ever could.

Was Greyson right? Is it possible Emerson might be the one person I could have a future with?

Lathen was not sure, but for the first time he felt ready to consider it. However, before he could, there was something else he needed to show Emerson. One last secret he worried would be even more devastating than her learning how they lost Kit, and could make Emerson run from him.

Forever.

chapter fifty-two

Once again, Emerson awoke, but this time, as she floated to awareness, she was happy. With her eyes still closed, she stretched, feeling whole and deliciously sore, yet it felt like some part of her had been awakened from a long slumber. She opened her eyes, but it was to almost complete darkness. The fire had burned down to mere embers, and someone had blown out all the candles. She lifted her head and felt around with her hand. She was in a comfortable bed.

Someone must have moved me here after I was asleep, she realized, because she last remembered being on the chaise with Lathen.

Lathen!

Emerson sat up in a rush. She felt around with her hands, but she realized she was alone in the bed.

"Lathen?"

There was no answer. She was by herself in the room. It made her a little sad because she remembered falling asleep listening to Lathen's heart.

She lifted the coverlet and stood, carefully making her way around the bed until she got closer to the glowing embers. The hearth was the only landmark she could make out. Next to it, her trembling fingers found a small coal hod, and she added a couple of pieces to the firebox and used a stoker to stir up the hot ashes. It took a moment, but the coals finally caught, lighting the room a bit more.

She was in the same place. The blue and white room. The chaise on which she and Lathen made love was over to the right. She moved to it and trailed her fingers across the top. Images of the two of them flashed through her mind, making her flush.

But where is Lathen now?

Emerson saw her clothing, still strewn about the floor, but Lathen's were missing. She bent and picked up her things and slowly got dressed. She ached all over, especially between her thighs. Deep inside.

Still, I feel good. There are mysteries solved, and I have lost my innocence. After finally learning of Kit, I can close that chapter of my life, and move on to the next. I feel everything else happened as it should have. Emerson's mind was clear for a change. She felt light and full of possibility.

She got dressed, mostly, except for a few small buttons at her back she could not reach and her wild hair she used her fingers to bring under some semblance of control. She searched for her pins, but it was too hard to find them in the firelight, and she finally gave up, unconcerned as there was no one to see her disheveled state. She walked to the door, though there was a moment when she reached for the knob, she half expected it to be locked. However, it opened easily, and she stepped into the hall, quietly pulling the door shut behind her. No one was there, but candles were still burning, reflected in the mirrors. It gave off an eerie quality magnified by the deep silence in the house. She paused when she passed by the door of the yellow room and wondered if Marien was still inside.

I suppose she is. Yet Emerson found she no longer cared. She trusted Lathen and knew he would take care of Marien and, hopefully, she would never bother them again. *Good riddance to bad rubbish.*

With a deep breath of release, Emerson walked away from the door and tiptoed down the stairs, hoping to find Lathen. In the small sitting room, she only saw the same older woman from before. She was reading a small book by candlelight. Emerson tried to back away, unnoticed, but the woman looked up, catching her, so she continued inside.

"My lady," the woman put her book down and made to stand.

"Oh, please do not," Emerson motioned for her to stay. Obviously, she was in this woman's home. She was not just some servant, as Emerson had first assumed. It felt silly for her to have to get up and bow to a younger woman, just because Emerson happened to be born with a title.

"May I?" Emerson gestured to the other chair.

"Yes, of course," the woman replied in her heavy accent. Not for the first time, Emerson wondered where she came from. So, she asked.

"Oh, I am from the Great Russia. Moscovia," she explained proudly. "I come from an extensive family. Hundreds of us, related to the Romanoff himself. Not from a married branch, you see? We had to make our own way in the world. I have been here, in London, for many years. Since the Master was a young boy."

Master? Emerson again wondered why she called Lathen that. *Perhaps it is a Russian thing, what they call their dukes? Or maybe it means the master of the house in Russian?*

Emerson let it go. She was more curious about where Lathen was.

"Did His Grace go back to de Clare House? Am I to join him there?"

"Oh, no. He is nearby. He only went to get things ready, for you."

Get what ready? Emerson pondered, but as long as he had not left her, she was content to wait. She stared into the fire, still feeling at peace.

After some time, a loud mechanical click echoed from the back of the house. The Russian woman put down her book and rose expectantly.

Lathen walked by the opening, toward the stairs. When he noticed Emerson, he looked surprised, but he stopped and came back. He was carrying a small bundle in one hand as he came straight to Emerson, bending on one knee before her. With a gentle expression of concern, he tucked a lock of her unbound hair behind her ear. It was a gesture she had begun to cherish.

"Are you alright?" he whispered.

Emerson smiled shyly and her eyes drifted to the older woman, who was watching them with interest.

"Yes, Your Grace," she blushed as she answered. "But perhaps we should go home? I am certain everyone is wondering where I am."

Lathen's face changed in an instant. One moment, he was compassionate and caring. The next he was once again The Duke, shut off and distant.

Emerson shrank back in the chair, confused, but Lathen stood abruptly, seized her hand, and pulled her to her feet.

"No," he answered tersely, "we are not going home right now." He then left the room with her in tow.

"Master?" the woman called behind them.

Lathen slowed and glanced over his shoulder.

"What shall I do about the guest in the yellow room?"

Lathen looked down at Emerson before answering.

"I will have some armed men come tomorrow afternoon, to escort her somewhere safe. Keep the door locked until they come for her. Thank you, Madam Irina. I know this has put you out."

"Of course, Master. It is no trouble."

Emerson listened, wondering offhandedly if she ought to know more, but she shrugged it off. She was far more interested in where Lathen was taking her.

Lathen dismissed Madam Irina with a short nod and continued to a part of the house Emerson had not seen before. They went into a small library, lined from floor to ceiling with bookshelves, with a single leather-bound chair in one corner and a wooden table with an unlit lamp and a box of matches on top. Emerson wondered why they were there, but Lathen went straight to the back wall, grabbed for a specific book, and pulled it out. Emerson tried to read the title, but it was in Latin, and she did not have enough time to translate it in her head. Then there was a noise of shifting gears, and part of the bookcase swung open into the room.

Shocked, Emerson glanced inside the opening to see a dark, narrow passageway. Ageless, stacked stone walls rose to a low arched ceiling, and smooth stones, looking as if thousands of feet had walked over them, lined the path.

What the bloody hell? Emerson's mouth dropped open as she wondered if she was in some kind of dream. *Or perhaps a nightmare.*

Beeswax candles were placed in small niches within the damp walls, about every ten yards, letting off flickering pools of light, but doing little to illuminate anything else. Yet, with confidence, Lathen entered, sure of his path. He pulled Emerson with him. After they had gone about twenty steps, she heard the same click as before, but louder, and echoing. The light from the library was suddenly gone, and Emerson realized the noise was the secret door latching as it closed. Lathen kept going, and a sense of foreboding washed over Emerson as their footsteps bounced off the close stone walls.

Light from the candle. Darkness. Another light. More darkness. Other than their breathing and footsteps, it was eerily quiet. Every so often, they went down a few steps, showing a gradual descent underground. Unconcerned, Lathen continued, and after what seemed like an eternity, though in truth it was only several minutes, they arrived at another door. Lathen took out an old iron key and unlocked it. When they went through, Emerson saw they were in a simple, stone-walled room with four nearly identical wooden doors, one on each side. As Lathen relocked the door behind them, and slipped the key in his front pocket, Emerson looked closer and saw one of the doors had no handle or lock.

It is curious. How does one get inside?

Lathen turned and watched Emerson for a moment, as if gauging her reactions. He must have seen something he was looking for, because he grunted with approval and handed her the cloth bundle he was still holding.

"Here. Put these on," he told her brusquely.

333

Emerson's fingers trembled as she took it from him and shook it out. It was a dark hooded cloak and another object she flipped over in her hands a couple times before she realized it was a black, silk-covered mask. It was similar to the one she wore to the masquerade ball the night before, but plain, with no embellishments.

A question lingered unspoken as Emerson's eyes widened and met his, but the scalding heat in his gaze kept her from asking. Instead, she did as he asked. She had a feeling there was something Lathen desperately needed to show her, and whatever it was, it was through one of those wooden doors. So, she placed the mask over her face, shrugged the heavy cloak over her shoulders, and raised the hood. Then she took a deep breath and straightened her back.

She was ready to follow him.

chapter fifty-three

From his pocket, Lathen retrieved another mask, which he quickly slipped on. Emerson thought wryly it did little to hide who he was. After all, very few men had Lathen's imposing height and broad shoulders, much less his burnished hair, which always seemed barely under control. After their lovemaking, it was even wilder, like he had just stepped through a powerful storm. He did not have a cloak for himself but was still wearing his wrinkled lawn shirt open at his throat, and his black breeches which he had hastily half-tucked into his boots.

With calmness belying his disheveled state, Lathen crossed the stone room and rapped his knuckles on one of the other three doors, the one without a handle. Instead of opening, a hidden square near the top lifted, and a disembodied voice drifted out.

"Yes?"

"*Nox omnia secreta tenet*," Lathen responded firmly. From behind the door, they heard metal scraping across wood, and someone opened it to let them enter.

In her head, Emerson translated. *The night holds all secrets. What does that mean?*

The young man who opened the door bowed low to Lathen and, like Madam Irina, murmured in reverence, "Master," as they walked past.

Emerson tilted her head, wondering again about the unusual title, but as the door shut behind them and the man slid the old metal latch back in place, locking them in, her new surroundings distracted her. The smell of bergamot delicately enveloped her as soon as she walked inside. It stirred a faint memory in her mind, but it was too vague for her to grasp. Hundreds of massive golden beeswax candles, each the size of a man's forearm, cast soft, flickering light and added to the subtle aroma. The candles were hanging from enormous wrought-iron chandeliers and inside niches on standing pillars. They should have given off a generous amount of light. However, the walls were all the same dark stone as the passageway that led them there, and there was black velvet fabric draped along them. The effect swallowed nearly all the luminosity, giving a mysterious atmosphere to the large entrance. That was only the beginning.

Ahead of them, there was a set of iron hinged doors, thrown wide open, revealing an immense arched chamber beyond, nearly a hundred feet across. It was almost like the inside of a masonry gothic cathedral or a Roman amphitheater with a series of domed roofs above. Dozens of alcoves, each with heavy black curtains, lined the elongated oval room. Some were partially closed, and others were tied back. Inside the recesses she could see, there was furniture similar to the black room in the house above. It was all made with heavy beams of polished wood and had black leather upholstery. There were chairs, benches, small and large settees, and even several beds with high posts. The furnishings were in the alcoves and in the huge open area, and on nearly every one of them, there were people.

Perhaps a hundred men and women, each wearing masks to conceal their identity, and all in various stages of undress.

Emerson froze and her mind emptied. She did not know what to say or think. Or do. Nothing she had read about, or experienced with Lathen, could have prepared her for what she was witnessing.

Her gaze immediately went to a naked woman tied to angled crossed beams on the far side of the room. The restraints attached to each of the four ends resembled those used on her wrists by Lathen weeks earlier. *Leather, with soft sheepskin to protect her skin.* Emerson would never forget it. Seeing it happening to someone else affected her, triggering a visceral reaction deep in her belly, causing her to gasp for breath.

Unable to turn away, she kept watching as two men circled the woman, taking turns touching her. One was holding a thin wooden handle about a foot long, with several long leather straps hanging from one end. He used it to flick small bites to her body. The other man held a soft fur glove he was using to caress her skin, as if to soothe the stinging licks from the other man. All the while, the woman writhed in her bonds, her head thrown back with abandon, keening in ecstasy. The sensations the woman felt were clearly pleasurable to her, both the sharp pain from the leather and the soothing relief from the fur. A strange tingling sensation, like tiny answering flicks, began moving across Emerson's skin.

With a shake of her conscience, she finally forced herself to look away as she took a deep, cleansing breath.

A little further to the left, an enormous bed held four people. The sight of their naked limbs, entangled like vines and glistening in the candlelight, bewildered Emerson.

What the bloody hell? It is three women and one man!

The man was lying on his back, and while Emerson stared at him, a woman moved to sit astride his hips. She grasped his member with one hand, positioned it at her entrance, and lowered herself in one swift motion. She rode him like she would a horse. Her thighs and buttocks were clenching, and her arms levered on his lower legs as she leaned back, making her pendulous breasts push toward the ceiling. With her eyes closed and her mouth parted, a whimper of pleasure escaped her lips.

Another woman followed suit and mounted the man's head. He immediately grabbed her thighs and pulled her closer. She groaned so loudly Emerson could hear her from across the room. Then, to Emerson's shock, the two women leaned forward and kissed each other, their wet tongues intertwined. All the while, the third woman was watching them with lust on her face, eagerly stroking their breasts and bodies. Then she leaned forward and flicked her tongue across the man's chest.

Again, Emerson jerked away, blushing, but everywhere she turned, she saw people engaging in acts of passion.

An olive-skinned woman is bent over a bench as a hairy man stands behind, pushing himself inside her, slapping her backside as he might a horse!

Two men with their arms wrapped around each other, kissing passionately. Their muscles are straining like they are fighting one another, and they are wearing nothing but leather undergarments that do absolutely nothing to hide their bodies.

A woman with her head down between another woman's spread thighs while she looks down, watching her, grasping her long hair, pulling her closer.

Emerson did not want to call any of it lovemaking. She instinctively realized it was something entirely different. *Forbidden. Uninhibited. Wild and improper.* Those were the words floating in her mind. *I should be witnessing none of this!*

Emerson knew it was sinful, all of it, yet she had to admit it stirred something deep within her. Heat spread from her abdomen, her breath quickened, and she now knew from experience the rush of wetness at her core was her body's way of preparing her for her own passion.

For Lathen, so he can enter me.

Lathen, standing close behind, leaned down to whisper darkly in her ear.

"Do you see something you like, *Nyx*?"

The blush from her cheeks exploded at his words, burning its way down to her chest. Her nipples tightened and her insides clenched.

Surely, he does not mean for us to join with these people!

Once again, Lathen knew what she was thinking, and he laughed wickedly as he drew a single finger down her arm.

"No *Nyx*, I have found I have no wish to share you with anyone," he told her fiercely. "Something of a novelty, I can assure you." He murmured the last so softly that she was not sure if she heard him correctly.

Emerson did not understand his meaning or the reason he brought her to witness such

339

inappropriate behavior. In the past, he had always been particularly concerned with her innocence and keeping her safe from gossip. Yet here he was, showing her wicked things, people and places no unmarried lady should ever witness. Confused and overwhelmed, she struggled to discern reality from fantasy.

Perhaps I really have not woken, and I am still dreaming. Maybe if I shake myself, I will find myself back in the blue and white room. Or maybe the whole day was unreal, and I am still at de Clare House, safe after the masque!

"Come," Lathen grasped her hand again, his warm touch proving he was real and she was awake, "we need to talk." He led her past the moans, screams, and sighs, from the cavernous room, and into a long hallway, nearly hidden between two alcoves. Closed doors lined both sides and the only light source was a single candle at the end struggling to pierce the narrow stone corridor.

Coming up the passage, nearly blocking the meager light, was a woman with bright, almost unnaturally red, wildly curly hair. She was wearing nothing but a pair of black silk stockings and a lace mask doing little to hide her light leaf-colored eyes. Lathen stopped to talk with her, and Emerson formed an immediate and inexplicable dislike for her.

What a trollop! Emerson narrowed her eyes and glared, but the other woman did not seem to notice. Her green eyes were only for Lathen.

"Is the cantilever chamber ready, as I requested?"

"*Oui*, Master," she replied, her voice husky and low, with a heavy Parisian accent. She came up close to Lathen, so close the tips of her rouged nipples nearly brushed his chest. She reached up to smooth his wrinkled shirt with delicate fingers.

"May I join you, Master?" she practically begged, looking up through her lashes.

Emerson saw red. More than just the red of the other woman's hair. On impulse, she bared her teeth and lunged toward her, ready to pull every hair from her pretty head.

Lathen caught Emerson around the waist and easily stopped her before she got far.

"No, thank you, Ruby." he chuckled as Emerson struggled against his hold. "I do not believe my companion is inclined at the moment."

Ruby's mouth formed an exaggerated pout, but she did not argue. Instead, she brushed past them and continued to saunter away, toward the open room and the moans still echoing off the walls. Before she turned the corner, she glanced over her shoulder and sent a rude gesture with her hand to Emerson. Then she was gone and Emerson slowly relaxed.

"Apparently, you have no wish to share either. Fascinating." His tone was light and teasing. "However, you can sheath your claws for now, *Nyx*. This moment is just for the two of us."

With her mind overwhelmed, Emerson answered him with complete honesty.

"I am sorry, Lathen, but the thought of her touching you made me furious." It was a simple statement, but it visibly stirred Lathen. He inhaled deeply and his amber eyes flashed. Emerson felt as if something intangible had suddenly shifted between them, like they had found a missing piece to a puzzle and were nearly ready to complete the picture.

But not quite. Emerson realized there was something else.

chapter fifty-four

Lathen let go of Emerson's waist and righted her, waiting to make sure she was steady. Then he reached for her hand again, his grasp firm yet gentle, and kept going. Leading her to the last door on the left, he opened it and gestured politely for her to enter first.

The room was small, with a low ceiling, wider than it was deep, and nearly empty. A few candles revealed a small square table and two simple, carved chairs. Someone had deliberately positioned the chairs so they would face the back wall, where a thick wooden pillar stood. Above it, another beam hung outward, supported by nothing but the first beam. Attached to the cantilevered beam with thick ropes, swinging gently in the shadows, as though someone had recently pushed it, was a black leather contraption. There were multiple straps with buckles and what looked like a harness. As Emerson came closer, she grasped its purpose, to restrain someone as they were suspended in the air, and she tensed.

"Do not fret, *Nyx*." Lathen was standing close. So close she could feel his chest against her back, breathing against her. His voice was dark and enticing. "I know you. Nothing will happen in here you cannot handle, and I promise you can walk away anytime you wish. You have only to tell me you want to leave."

Emerson considered his words. She could honestly say she was aroused. Her thighs were wet, and her breasts felt heavy, aching at the tips. The soreness from losing her virginity had melted back into desire. The sight of the restraints brought memories of Lathen's punishment in the black room, with the riding crop.

She remembered her body being aroused then as well. As he stood behind her, finishing with the crop, and entered her with his fingers, she exploded around him. *Clearly, it did not make me stop wanting him. Not then and not now.* Yet she still wondered why he brought her to this room. *After what just happened, why does he feel like I need to be punished? And what is this place?*

There was so much Emerson wanted to understand, and it felt like there was a precipice before her. She could stay and learn more about Lathen's darkness and secrets, or she could leave and forever be curious.

I know I would always question what would have happened in this room. I do not think I could live with such uncertainty.

Her decision made, Emerson pulled the hood of her cloak down and untied the clasp at her throat. She let it fall to the ground. The mask went over her head and was also dropped unceremoniously. She was already imagining herself swinging before

Lathen, as she reached for the few buttons she had managed to close at her back, but Lathen grabbed her hands and stilled them. She lifted her face, frowning, doubt darkening her eyes.

"Lathen?"

Lathen shook his head as if to clear his mind, and he stepped back while he refocused his gaze on her face. Then, as she watched, his demeanor changed. He pressed his lips together, stood taller, and the shadows drifted across his body.

As if he actually darkened to match this place, she thought to herself, *he is not Prometheus, but rather Hades. A god of his own underworld.*

"First, like I said, we need to talk. And second," he lowered his voice, and his eyes bore into hers, "when we are here, *Nyx*, down here at *Noir*, you are only ever to address me as...Master."

Emerson recoiled in shock. At his words, yes, but mostly because of the stark gravity of his tone and the seriousness in his unwavering gaze. She obviously heard the others call him so tonight, and wondered why, but she had little doubt he meant what he was saying. She was not about to question him. Swallowing hard, she nodded in understanding.

"Say it. Now!" It was a command, made even darker because Lathen was still wearing his mask, and Emerson knew he expected her to do as he wanted. What surprised her was how strong her urge was to obey him.

"...M-master."

chapter fifty-five

She said it haltingly, barely above a whisper, but Emerson knew Lathen heard her when she saw a flash of victory light up his eyes. He reached for her hair and brushed the loose tendrils from her temples, tucking them behind both ears.

"You are incredible," Lathen told her. "You cannot imagine how hearing *you* say it makes me feel."

"But, why?"

"Because of this." He turned and gestured around the room. "This is who I am. Or at least a big part of who I am."

Emerson's mind was trying to sort through his answer, but her thoughts were muddled and filled with the vivid images and sounds she had witnessed.

Down the hall, naked people in masks are pleasuring each other in unnatural ways. How can this place, this place he calls Noir, *be a part of him?* She had to ask.

"I do not understand. You are a duke. The Duke of Windemere. What does this..." she glanced at the beams and the suspended contraption again, "...have to do with who you are?"

Lathen started pacing circles around the small room, his hands held together at his lower back.

"You are correct. I am a duke, but I am also the Master here, at *Noir*. Here I make sure everyone is safe. I control everything. I make the rules. I say who can come here, and when, and who they can bring."

"But what...is *Noir*?" Emerson's voice wavered. She asked him a question like this before, but it was about Nox House, back when she thought it was nothing more than a small row house in a respectable neighborhood.

With strange bedrooms and chains hanging from the ceiling. That was astonishing by itself. Now I know Nox House is much more. It is an entrance to get here. *A secret place below the normal world, accessible only by a path through the darkness. To* Noir.

She saw things in that gothic cathedral, not fitting with what society said was acceptable, and that was putting it mildly.

Surely, Lathen must know this! She told him so.

Lathen stopped pacing and stood right before Emerson, considering her words.

"You are correct." Lathen nodded and resumed his path around the room. "This is a society no one talks about, except in the most hushed of whispers. It is where princes, lords, and the very, very rich come to do all the salacious things they could never do with their wives or husbands. It has always been called *Noir,* after the darkest black of night. It is where all the most forbidden secrets are best kept.

"*Noir* is underground to keep the screams of passion quiet and the sights of writhing bodies from prying eyes. And I...well, as I have said, I am Master of it all." He paused for a moment to rest his hand on the large beam along the wall, staring up as if proud of the delicate balance it created with the one above it.

"You may wonder about the how and why, but that is a long story for another day. But believe me when I tell you I value being in control of *Noir*. It is who I am, and I cannot change that. Here, I dominate all and, if you choose to stay, you will submit to everything I ask. Beginning with...Asking. No. More. Questions." He finished slowly and forcefully, then turned back to make sure she understood, and to witness her reaction.

Without question? Surely, he does not mean I am to accept all this without knowing more.

Emerson opened her mouth to tell him so, but Lathen cut her off by covering her mouth with his hand. He gave a knowing nod.

"I always felt you would struggle with this," he said darkly. "Even now, I see it in your eyes. You are full of so much curiosity. It is why I tried to keep myself from you, why I tried to explain how hard it would be for us to be together...to warn you I was not for you. Yet here we are. Now, you need to accept this, to submit to me, in all ways. If you cannot, you can still walk away, and I will understand. There is still time."

Emerson's mind raced. *Can I do what he is asking? He is right. I have so many questions. But...perhaps...I can attempt to do as he asks. I could let go.*

She wanted to please him, and she really wanted to stay and find out more, to satisfy her curiosity. With a deep breath, she nodded her head in agreement, and kept her mouth closed.

Lathen's amber eyes gleamed with triumph once more. He lowered his hand and stepped back, motioning to one of the simple wooden chairs. Emerson went over to it, spread her skirts, though she noted offhandedly they were already wrinkled, and sat. It was sturdy, but not very comfortable, and it faced the leather bonds.

She trembled, a mixture of anxiety and anticipation coursing through her. In truth, she was also excited, and the familiar heat surged through her as her heart pounded.

"Good girl," Lathen nodded approvingly. "To reward you, I will elaborate. Then you can decide if you want to stay."

Lathen took a deep breath. Part of him was still afraid all of this was too much, and Emerson would not want to be a part of his world, and he could lose her forever. He also hoped he could trust her. He had, thus far, and, to her credit, she had not run. Certainly, he could see the fear in her eyes, but there was something else as well. He saw how she pressed her legs together for relief, and how her lips parted in anticipation.

Perhaps she really is my Goddess of Night, my Nyx. The hope was almost too much for him to bear, and he knew what he said next would be the actual test.

"First, I suppose I need to give you a brief history. What you saw tonight is not new. I did not create *Noir*. It was here before I was born. There have been people like me who have used places like this, for as long as civilization has been around. The Romans, the Greeks, the Pharaohs in Egypt. And the

Brahmins to the east. That was where I first found someone who showed me my path.

"My father sent me to India when I was sixteen, just after my grandfather died. I was supposed to learn about our family interests there, but I soon discovered so much more. It was the first time I felt a true release. I am speaking of more than just sex. More than fucking or coming. I had already done that. My grandfather made certain of it. He began sending me women when I was much, much younger, because he believed I could not be a man until I had experienced sex. Most were maids or servants, though I suppose some were actual whores." Lathen paused with his back to her, but he suddenly turned and continued, "No, what I am talking about is a pleasure far deeper. Somewhere inside my mind." He pointed to his head before letting his hand drop to his side and continued walking around the room.

"You see, my grandfather kept me separate for my whole life. From society, and even from my family. He taught me to always be in control of my emotions and to never let anyone get too close. He insisted it was the only path to leadership and shepherding others was my birthright. My destiny was *always* to be the Duke of Windemere. Grandfather believed my father would only be a visitor to the title, at best, perhaps because he could not control him the way he wanted. Unfortunately, the control and isolation he manifested for me meant I had to have those same things when I was with someone. It scared most women. I saw it time and time again. They only felt fear and subservience near me." He sighed as he recalled all the times he tried to be close with women in his youth, then shrugged as it was not particularly helpful, and he could do nothing to change the past.

"It was in India I discovered the depth of intimacy could extend beyond the physical. There is far more to it than fucking. It is still about pleasure, of course, but just as important, perhaps even more important," he paused, locking eyes with Emerson, "it is about pain. Giving and receiving it."

Emerson gasped and pressed herself back into her chair.

Pain? What the bloody hell! How can he be serious? She was speechless, which was probably a good thing because it left her unable to ask him any of the hundred questions screaming through her mind.

Lathen smiled knowingly at her, his eyes overbright. "You are wondering what I mean. It is only natural. I am talking about what gives me pleasure, *Nyx*. There are people who need to have control. To inflict pain on someone. To have someone trust you enough to receive it willingly. To have them embrace the pain, allowing it to elevate them to new heights, bringing them to an otherwise unreachable peak of existence.

"Take this apparatus, for instance." He moved to the other side of the leather straps and clutched the ropes tightly, his knuckles turning white, while he still stared intently at her. "This is for strapping you in and holding you in place. By itself, it is not painful. In fact, I am told it is exceedingly comfortable. But it requires your acceptance and absolute trust, an understanding you are going to take everything I want to give you, without being able to move or get away."

He released the ropes, and Emerson watched as the leather straps swung again, gently, back and forth, making a slight creaking noise. Unable to stop herself, she pictured herself as he told her. Naked, with the straps tightened about her wrist and ankles. Suspended, with the harness supporting her body. Swinging, with Lathen standing before her. It suddenly felt hard to breathe, and the cool stone walls did little to keep the heat from spreading through her veins.

"If you stay," he continued, bringing her thoughts and eyes back to him, "I will want to put you in there and whip every inch of your naked body until it looks like you are blushing everywhere. Then, as you are still hanging above the ground, dripping wet with your need, I will fuck you. Your thighs will be held wide open to me with the straps, and all I will need to do is swing you back before I pull you to me and bury myself so deeply, you will feel me touching the very end of your small, beautiful cunt. It will be hard, and there will be nothing to stop me, and it is going to hurt you, *Nyx*. Yet the pain will bring you to an orgasm so intense it will make you scream. Then, before you are done, while you are still throbbing deep inside, I am going to bring you to another. And another."

Emerson's eyes widened as his words washed over her. She had to admit to feeling two very distinct and disparate emotions. On one side, she realized Lathen's idea of lovemaking was more than she could have ever imagined. To his credit, he was trying to show her exactly what it was, so she could understand him better. It was not just about the sexual acts she had witnessed as he had walked with her through *Noir*. He was more than just a libertine. More than a hedonist. The possibilities of those things lent a sense of excitement. Her core clenched as he spoke, and her heart fluttered when she realized he trusted her enough to show her his world.

It was the other half scaring her. His attempt to convey the dark pleasures of pain was terrifying.

Control and trust. Pain and pleasure. Are not all these things in direct contrast to one another? Mutually exclusive? To be held somewhere and not be able to move. Having to trust the other person completely. Letting them hurt you. Wanting the pain. Who would want that? Why has he brought me here to tell me all of this? Is he mad? Plagued by the thoughts swarming her mind, each one coming before the other was finished, Emerson was unsure if she could stay to hear any more. Fear was taking over her curiosity. The heat was cooling, and gooseflesh rose over her skin. Yet there was one thing she had to understand, regardless of whether she chose to leave.

"M-master," she began tentatively, staring up at him, "can I ask you one thing?"

Lathen seemed to appreciate her calling him by his desired title. He nodded approvingly for her to continue.

"If you say you need control, to inflict pain to feel satisfied. Does it mean you have always wanted to hurt...me? Every time we have been together?"

Emerson's voice wavered. However, she noticed Lathen's face light up with pleasure in response to her question.

Lathen gently cupped Emerson's face, rubbing his thumb against her cheek. It gave her hope she had been mistaken.

Then he answered.

"Oh, yes, *Nyx*. Very much so." It was low and guttural.

It touched Emerson deep in her belly, making her clench her thighs once more, to stem the wetness dripping down them. She was also terrified. Her heart was hammering in her chest, and the low ceiling was closing in on her.

My God, what is wrong with me? With him? Emerson sprang up, pushing Lathen's hand away.

"No!" she shouted. "I want to leave!"

The finality overwhelmed the small chamber, echoing off the stone walls.

Lathen's shoulders dropped, and he closed his eyes. After a moment, he nodded and opened them again. There was a profound sadness in their amber depths. It almost made Emerson reach for him to soothe the sorrow, to hold him while she whispered for him to forgive her.

No!

Emerson stepped back instead and turned her back. To avoid being trapped in his dark world, she had to stop looking at him. It would be so easy to give in to her desire and ease his disappointment, to give him what he wanted, even though it felt so wrong.

She shook herself, stood straighter, and stepped to the door and opened it to leave, just as he promised she could.

"Wait!" The urgency in his tone was obvious.

Emerson did stop, but she stared out into the empty hallway and did not turn around. She tried to focus on the feeling of the cold stones beneath her slippers, and the damp stacked wall in front of her. Anything else but him.

Lathen sighed, then bent to pick up the cloak and mask from the floor and handed them to her, "You must wear these."

She still refused to turn to him, but she took them and put them back on, before walking out. Lathen remained a few steps behind, following her silently. Without his hand holding hers, the long hall felt ominous.

They walked back through the enormous open cathedral area. Emerson did her best not to look around her, but the noises of pleasure surrounded them, echoing off the buttresses and support columns. It was a twisted version of what she experienced before with Lathen, of what she had hoped for them to share again. The sounds chased her as she scrambled to escape.

chapter fifty-six

By the time they made it to the exit, which was opened quickly by the same young man who had let them in, Emerson was practically running. Once she got out, she rushed through the plain square room with four doors, to the one leading back to Nox House. She grabbed the handle, hurting her hand when she yanked it several times and it refused to open. A whimper of frustration escaped her when she realized Lathen would have to unlock it. She let go and stepped back to wait.

"Come," he mumbled as he brushed past her. After he unlocked it, he walked straight through, expecting her to follow. Then he relocked the door and continued up the narrow passageway. Again, he did not offer his hand.

Emerson trailed behind, with her gaze fixed on the dark shadows dancing across the well-worn stone path. As they ascended, the moist air felt cooler and smelled less of bergamot and beeswax. From the back of her mind, a memory finally came back to her. It was of a night, more than a month ago, when she had been desperate to see Lathen. She had waited for him to come home, silently staring over the stair railing at the landing below, where Lathen's rooms were. That night, the scent of bergamot and honey had drifted up to her, and now she understood why. It was because he had been down there, in *Noir*, and she could not escape the symbolism.

It is like I am emerging from the depths of Lathen's need. Even the smell is mocking me.

They finally stopped at what appeared to be a dead end. Lathen grabbed a candle sconce and pulled it forward. Like the book, it made a soft mechanical sound, and the hidden door opened.

This is unreal and macabre as well. After all, who the fuck has a secret door leading to an underground sex dungeon?

Stepping through, they were once again in the library, having left only about half an hour before. Emerson flinched at the loud click as the door shut behind them, and she felt like they had been gone for much longer. In fact, the entire day seemed to have taken place over weeks. *Or months.* Exhaustion overwhelmed her, and her body felt heavy, making each step a chore.

Lathen had a determined set to his jaw as he kept going, leaving her to follow him back to the sitting room, where Madam Irina was still reading by the fire. Emerson waited in the small entry hall, watching as Lathen bent to whisper something to the older woman.

When he walked back toward Emerson, he stared at her dispassionately. It was more than his usual shuttered expression. It was as if she were a stranger he barely knew. A hollow ache entered Emerson's heart at the mere thought.

"Madam Irina will see you get home safely." With those last words, he walked back towards the library without her.

Emerson knew, without asking, where he was going. *Back to* Noir. The pain in her chest spread as she understood he would find any number of women who would be willing to join him. Instead of her. *Like that naked red-headed whore! Or the girl who was tied up and begging those men to hit her, writhing in ecstasy when they did. Just like he wants!*

Tears sprang to her eyes, but she knew she could not go with him.

"Goodbye, Your Grace," she breathed as he was about to turn the corner.

Not Master.

Not Lathen.

She was not sure if he heard her or not. Then she watched him pause, glance back at her, and bow deeply. He straightened, gave her one last empty look, and disappeared into the library.

The last sound Emerson heard was the loud click of the secret door.

watching her

I am always watching her.

...watching her smile...
...watching her tears run down her cheeks...
...watching her every day for three years...

Someday, everyone will know she is mine, and
I will destroy anyone who dares touch her.

Emerson Haven is meant to be my wife.

The watcher followed Emerson. He was pretty sure she was returning to de Clare House, but he followed her anyway. He would not be the right man for her if he did not make sure she got home safely.

emerson and lathen's story will
continue in:

pursued at night

coming October 2025

p.s. To the readers! Awaken at Night was a long time coming and I cannot express how grateful I am if you have read this far and, hopefully, enjoyed my story. I wonder, if it is not too much trouble, if you could please take a few moments to leave a review wherever you purchased or read this. As an indie writer, our books live or die by how much word of mouth we can get, and it will help me continue the next books in the At Night Series!

special acknowledgements:

To S&M (I knew I'd find a way to use it!). Your insights were incredibly valued and appreciated. Perhaps more than you will ever know.

To G. I think you know, but just in case, thank you so much for all your support and for always understanding when and how I needed it the most. Thank you for everything you did for me today...

To all my Alpha, Beta, and ARC readers, and my amazing street team. What can I say? Not all heroes wear capes!